My HEAD SPUN.
This was the predator.
The animal.

The male who wanted to devour me.
And all I could do was accept him.

My arms circled his neck, my mouth opening even more for his sensual assault, my tongue not daring to defy his. He wanted me, so he would have me.

Obey or die.

He was right.

I didn't want to die.

But I also didn't mind living… for this.

"Fuck," he whispered. "I can't remember the last time I wanted someone like this."

His words startled me almost as much as his fangs sinking into my lower lip. I yelped, then moaned.

"Oh…" I liked that far too much—his tongue against the open wound. I trembled violently, the pleasure overwhelming all my senses. "What…?" I couldn't finish, my legs tightening around him. "Kylan," I breathed, unsure of what was happening.

His groin moved against the sensitive juncture between my thighs, heightening the sensation. I whimpered, my head falling to his shoulder.

What are you doing to me?

A knot formed inside me, twisting and pulling, shooting electricity to every nerve.

"Give in," he whispered, his hardness stroking my clit through the jeans.

How?

Why?

I'd been touched there before, but never like this. I usually squirmed, but he elicited a demand for more.

"Now, Raelyn." He captured my chin, pulling my mouth back up to his, and bit me again. I could hardly feel the sting through the euphoria that followed.

And then I was falling.

Blood Alliance Series
Chastely Bitten
Royally Bitten

Royally Bitten

Lexi C. Foss

This is a work of fiction. Names, characters, places, and incidents are either the product of the author's imagination or are used fictitiously, and any resemblance to actual persons, living or dead, business establishments, events, or locales, is entirely coincidental.

Royally Bitten

Copyright © 2019 Lexi C. Foss

All rights reserved.

No part of this book may be reproduced in any form or by any electronic or mechanical means, including information storage and retrieval systems, without written permission from the author, except for the use of brief quotations in a book review. This book may not be redistributed to others for commercial or noncommercial purposes.

Editing by: Outthink Editing, LLC

Proofreading by: Barb Jack, Delphine Noble-Fox & Love2ReadRomance

Cover Design: Covers by Julie
Cover Photography: Lindee Robinson
Cover Models: Sofiya Dmitrievna Vasilyeva & Nick Roberts

Published by: Ninja Newt Publishing, LLC

Print Edition

ISBN: 978-1-732535-68-8

To my readers, for embracing my dark side and allowing me the opportunity to play in this harsh world…

ROYALLY BITTEN

Book Two

A Note from the Author

Just a quick warning before we begin: Kylan's love is unconventional and sometimes cruel. He's an ancient vampire who takes what he wants when he wants it, and that may include Rae or others at times. Humans hold no rights in this world, and my lycans and vampires are not the kind you find in fairy tales.

There will be biting, sharing, and a lot of blood.

Enjoy,
Lexi

Once upon a time, humankind ruled the world while lycans and vampires lived in secret.

This is no longer that time.

Welcome to the future where the superior bloodlines make the rules.

PROCEED AT YOUR OWN RISK.

The Blood Alliance

International law supersedes all national governance and will be maintained by the Blood Alliance—a global council of equal parts lycan and vampire.

All resources are to be distributed evenly between lycan and vampire, including territory and blood slaves. Societal standing and wealth, however, will be at the discretion of the individual packs and houses.

To kill, harm, or provoke a superior being is punishable by immediate death. All disputes must be presented to the Blood Alliance for final judgment.

Sexual relationships between lycans and vampires are strictly prohibited. However, business partnerships, where fruitful and appropriate, are permitted.

Humans are hereby classified as property and do not carry any legal rights. Each will be tagged through a sorting system based on merit, intelligence, bloodline, ability, and beauty. Prioritization to be established at birth and finalized on Blood Day.

Twelve mortals per year will be selected to compete for immortal blood status at the discretion of the Blood Alliance. From this twelve, two will be bitten by immortality. The others will die. To create a lycan or vampire outside of this process is unlawful and punishable by immediate death.

All other laws are at the discretion of the packs and royals but must not defy the Blood Alliance.

KYLAN

Blood Day.

Humans lined up like cattle at the slaughter, all awaiting their fates at the hands of a vampire queen they considered to be a goddess.

A few would try to run, others would cry, and several would meekly accept their fate.

I sighed. These mortals were the lucky ones—the top five percent of their twenty-second year. All the other humans were on their way to the blood farms or were being held for the monthly moon chases.

Every ceremony, the same. A power play meant to keep the little lambs in line. As if they required it.

I skimmed the electronic records on my phone, eyeing the attributes of this year's harem selection. Nothing extraordinary. Of course, mortals couldn't necessarily flourish under these conditions.

"See any that intrigue you?" Robyn asked, her manicured fingers trailing up my suit-clad arm.

I glanced sideways at the blonde beauty in her little black gown. "Aside from you, darling?"

Her red lips curled, interest flashing in her blue eyes. "Shall we pick one together?"

Ah, this game. We played it so many times. Pleasurable, yes. Bloody, too. And mind-numbingly boring. Still, I had a reputation to uphold in this dance, one I couldn't afford to tarnish. Not with recent events blackening my good name.

"Did you have one in mind?" I asked, feigning intrigue.

"There's a brunette with promise. Prospect One Hundred and Eight."

I thumbed through the nude images on the screen, searching for her pick. A female with a slender waist, no curves, and dead eyes. Definitely Robyn's type. She loved torturing the broken ones.

"I'll consider her," I murmured, forcing a grin. "Anyone else?"

She shrugged. "Two thirty-eight isn't bad, but he's a bit scrawny."

As was to be expected when society forced the mortals to live on minimal sustenance. A glance at the profile showcased an emaciated boy who did not capture my fancy in the slightest.

"You always did have an eye for beauty," I praised, not meaning a word of it.

"Yes," she agreed, drawing her nails up my bicep. "I do."

"Flirting?" I teased, knowing her far too well.

She pinched my arm. "Flirting implies necessity. We both know I could have you on your knees with a glance, Kylan."

I leaned into her, my lips finding her ear. "The only one who will be kneeling is you, sweetheart." I nipped her neck hard enough to bleed. She knew better than to try to dominate me. "I'm not one of your toys, Robyn."

She licked her lips, her arousal darkening her eyes to a sapphire shade. "Then we'll pick one that submits to us both."

"An arrangement I accept," I murmured, relaxing as Lilith approached her throne. "You best find your seat, darling. It looks as though our queen is ready to shine." Or was she a goddess now? Hmm. Political affairs always did bore me.

"I'll see you after, lover." Robyn kissed me on the cheek and slid from her chair, leaving me blissfully alone.

Other royals glanced my way, none of them brave enough to approach.

Yes, consider me mad, I encouraged, not smiling. *I did kill my harem for sport, after all, right?*

That's what they all assumed, and yet, society intended to reward me with more humans to slaughter. Because that's how this world worked.

A total mindfuck. Boring and necessary and horribly old.

Chants rolled through the air, welcoming Lilith to her murderous stage.

Poor little lambs.

Let the Blood Day—or bloodbath—begin.

Chapter One

RAE

The white silk gown clung to my clammy skin despite the cool air. My legs shook, my muscles tense, as yet another sentence was delivered from the podium before us.

Willow stood frozen at the verdict, her fate assigned. *The breeding camp.*

My empty stomach clenched, my mouth going dry. *Please don't send me there, Goddess. Please.*

I'd spent my life preparing for this moment. My test scores were among some of the best in my graduating class, but so were Willow's.

Good stock, the Magistrate had murmured.

What if he said the same about me?

I swallowed. *Don't panic. They'll smell your fear.*

"Go on, then," the Magistrate urged, gesturing to the

area in the field where those destined to procreate the future human race were gathering.

Willow managed to hobble off the stage, her face ashen.

I'd never see her again.

Her bright eyes met mine, blinking once before she dutifully followed the Vigil guard down the row. We'd said our goodbyes on the bus a few hours before, but seeing her depart now made this more real.

I could be sent to the blood farms, caged for a moon chase, or sentenced to a short life of servitude.

My fingers threatened to curl into fists. There were no options. Nowhere to run. Nowhere to hide. Face my fate or die.

Several had already been punished for their inappropriate reactions. Colleen's remains littered the side of the stage, her head situated near the stairs like a morbid trophy for all to see. *Act like her and pay the price.*

Just breathe, I told myself. *This will all be over soon.*

Or begin.

"Prospect Seven Hundred and Two, Year One Hundred Seventeen," the Magistrate called. Silas brushed his knuckles against mine, wishing me farewell, before starting the walk to his fate.

I'm next.

The words reverberated in my head, clouding my vision. This was it. My final moments before everything changed. No more classes. No more training. Only my future position in society remained. Where would they send me?

"The Immortal Cup," the Magistrate announced.

My lips parted.

Holy shit.

Silas actually did it.

He got in.

We'd spent the better part of the last decade working toward that goal, hoping one of us—Willow, Silas, or me—would make it.

My eyes glazed. Goddess, this meant he may live a full

life. A happy one. An immortal one. But it also meant I stood no chance.

"Only two spots remain," the Magistrate murmured, sounding amused. But of course he would be entertained. The lycans and vampires adored the Immortal Cup. I grew up watching them annually, preparing, wishing for a chance.

Tension lined the ranks, everyone feeling their chances slipping from our grasps. Only twelve were gifted the opportunity to fight for immortality. My scores qualified me to be among them, but the same could have been said about Willow.

They're going to breed me...
Stop. You don't know that yet.

"Prospect Seven Hundred and Three, Year One Hundred Seventeen." The familiar designation sent a chill down my spine. It was my turn to face my fate. All the focus fell to me as I started up the path, my gaze averted in reverence. Blood splatters painted the fresh grass, the bodies of those who had disobeyed long gone. Except for Colleen's head, her dead eyes watching me as I ascended the stairs.

Breathe.

I inhaled slowly, exhaled, and repeated, my heels clacking over the stage. The silky gown swished against my legs, the front gaping just enough to reveal that I wore nothing beneath—a requirement for all graduates.

I kneeled before the Magistrate, head bowed in reverence. He ignored me in favor of his book, his clawed finger dragging loudly over the page with a patience I didn't feel.

"Interesting." He cleared his throat, the verdict hanging between us. "Prospect seven hundred and three is also destined for the Immortal Cup."

My heart stopped beating.
What?
Had I heard him right? The Immortal Cup?
Am I dreaming?

"That leaves only one available position," the Magistrate continued, his voice drawing me back to the present.

Not a dream.

Reality.

I stood, my limbs tense from shock. *I'm going to battle for immortality. With Silas.*

My legs gained strength with each step toward the waiting Vigil. He didn't bother with intimidating posturing, merely wandering along beside me with carefree strides. No one would run from this opportunity, even knowing only two would survive.

Silas stood on the sidelines, hands loose at his sides, but I sensed his elation at my joining him. Because I felt the same about him. Two of us had made it to the top.

Oh, but Willow. Fuck. This had to hurt her more than being sent to the breeding camp. Our test scores were the same, our appearances graded as well-above average, and our physiques acceptable.

Something about her genetics must have predetermined her aptitude toward breeding.

Silas's knuckles touched mine as I took the open position beside him. I didn't dare glance at him, nor did I acknowledge the affection in that simple graze. But I understood it.

I'm so glad you're here, he was saying. *And I'm sorry for Willow, too.*

The three of us were inseparable and known for our competitive standards. I used to hate Silas for always besting me. My lips threatened to curl at the memory of all the times Willow and I plotted on ways to bring him down. Then he caught us midsession and our lives changed forever.

Another brush of his fingers near mine, his subtle way of telling me to focus. Always coaching me, even now.

I swallowed my emotions. Willow's fate was out of our hands.

I'll remember you always, I vowed. *I'm sorry.*

The word wove a web into my heart, forever locked

away with the memories of our lives together.

Today, I was reborn.

No longer would I be known as Prospect Seven Hundred and Three of Class One Hundred Seventeen.

My name was now Immortal Cup Contestant Eleven, Year One Hundred Seventeen.

And if I won, I'd be known as Rae—my chosen name.

Electricity hummed over my arms, through my chest, down my limbs. The real competition would begin immediately following the ceremony. Only ten would move into the next phase. I would be among those ten.

The Magistrate continued his roll call, assigning fates.

"Royal harem."

"Vigils training."

"Breeding camp."

"Lycan mating."

"Lilith City service industry."

"Clan harem."

Each designation made me feel more and more relieved. The Vigils had been my second choice. None of the others had appealed, but were all better fates than the blood farms or the moon chase.

Being hunted for sport by lycans during a full moon... I shuddered. *No, thank you.*

"Prospect one thousand," the Magistrate finally called, designating the final human to be sorted. "Clemente Clan service industry."

My stomach tightened at the familiar name. The Clementes were renowned as the most powerful lycan clan. Their alpha was on the verge of retiring, his son—Edon—taking the reins. Whoever won this year's Immortal Cup would either join his clan or Jace's vampire ranks. The eligibility shifted annually, and our class was their pick.

Jace Region would be my preference, not that I'd be the one choosing.

"This concludes our annual Blood Day," the Goddess announced, taking over the stage. We knelt in respect, our heads bowed. "Vigils, if you would please escort your respective teams to their exits. The harem prospects and Immortal Cup participants shall remain."

It's beginning.

This was the part they never explained—the initial selection. While twelve were gifted the opportunity to compete, only ten contestants survived to see the first competition. No one knew how the numbers were reduced.

I'm about to find out.

"Rise, my children," the Goddess cooed, her voice as beautiful as it sounded on film. This was my first time in her regal presence. Her formfitting red gown was cut to her belly button, her long blonde hair flowing to her waist. Despite my high scores in physical appeal, my auburn hair and pale features fell flat in comparison. Another designation of her higher status and my lowly human one.

That is going to change when I win.

I stood with the others, my eyes lowered as I considered my opponents. Three-quarters of them were strangers from other schools. But I knew Silas, Clarence, and Daniella. Silas's weaknesses weren't ones I would use. The same could not be said about my other former classmates.

Silence fell as the last of the humans left with their Vigil escorts.

Goodbye, Willow, I thought, my eyes closing briefly. *Forever friends. Never forgotten.*

The rustle of clothing had my lids flashing open, my limbs tensing.

Vampires and lycans were surrounding us—the royals and pack alphas. Their elegant attires boasted wealth and status, their silence meant to intimidate. Years of studying helped me identify them by their emblems alone. Each wore a symbol of their territory or clan, usually in a ring, but some on a necklace or a bracelet.

Jace.
Robyn.
Clemente Clan Alpha.

Hazel.
Stella Clan Alpha.

I steadied my pulse by focusing on my breathing. They merely wanted a good look at the potential humans to join their ranks. That's all.

Claude.
Kylan.
Ernest Clan Alpha and his mate.
Naomi.

They kept moving, their steps soundless over the gravel. Some were behind me, some in front, all circling, admiring, but not touching. Silas remained absolutely still beside me. I focused on him, on our potential future, the destiny we desired. Immortality.

"Thoughts?" the Goddess asked, the crowd shifting to allow her entry. She stopped a few feet away from us, her delicate fingers clasped before her.

"These are the best?" a gruff male demanded, the snarl in his voice denoting him as lycan.

"Come now, Walter. You must see at least some potential?" She sounded hopeful, but a hint of chastisement underlined her tone. A miraculous combination that secured her position as head of the hierarchy.

The Clemente Alpha, Walter, snorted in reply. "Let's get on with it, Lilith. I'm tired of this game and it's my last round."

My breath caught in my throat at the use of the Goddess's given name, not her formal address. A human would be killed for such insolence. Would she punish a lycan, let alone an alpha, for the offense?

"In a hurry to claim your harem?" she teased, her voice filled with humor. "But of course you are. You all are. Vigils, please bring the prospects forward to join those selected for the Immortal Cup."

My brow threatened to furrow, but I quickly smoothed out the lines. Showing emotion was a weakness I couldn't afford. Not now. Not ever.

The lycans and vampires moved back, allowing the humans designated to the harems to join us on each side, forming a U-shaped crowd of white.

"Excellent," the Goddess murmured. "Now, we may begin the true selection process. All of you standing before us are the cream of the crop, receiving the highest aptitude scores in all the categories we value. That is why we offer you the gift of being in the presence of our most esteemed."

I forced myself to swallow. *This sounds ominous...*

"Those selected for the harems will enter a two month training course to learn how best to serve our physical needs. But a handful of chosen ones will be gifted with the opportunity to study under a royal or alpha exclusively. Or under their existing harem, if that's the preference." The smile in her voice did not match the implication of her words.

Was she implying that the royals and alphas were going to choose candidates to serve them—*now*—without any training? We received sexual instruction in school, but nothing at the level they would require.

This applies to the harems, not to—

"We have a history of selecting the best for our Immortal Cup, something that is a bit of a disappointment when only two of you survive to the end. As it's a waste of potential, all of you are to be considered during this round to help ensure our royals and alphas don't miss an otherwise desired opportunity. Well"—she clapped her hands—"Vigils? Please help the candidates disrobe."

My heart skipped a beat.

This was how they decreased the number to ten? Not through a battle or a death match, but by giving the royals and alphas the option to add one of us to their harems?

A Vigil stepped before me, his hands ripping the gown from my shoulders.

I didn't fight him. Didn't yelp or point out that I would have removed it on my own had he given me a moment to process. Instead I let the fabric fall and kicked it away with my heel before he had a chance to touch my legs.

Silas tossed his to the ground beside mine, his muscular form putting the others to shame. I'd seen him nude on countless occasions and had partnered with him in various class demonstrations. To say we knew each other well would be an understatement.

He remained close, his body heat a comfort I couldn't deny. With our gazes still downcast, the vampires and lycans moved closer, lining up in front of us.

"Kylan, the floor is yours," the Goddess said, deferring to the eldest of the living royals. His name sent a chill down my spine. The royals were essentially gods who led divided territories, and each of them was renowned for something.

For Kylan, it was cruelty.

He stepped forward in an all-black suit with matching tie. With my gaze lowered, I couldn't see his face, but I knew his features well—dark hair, matching eyes, sharp cheekbones, and a harsh jawline dusted in stubble. Gorgeous, as all vampires were, and brutal in nature.

"Hmm, and I'm only allowed one?" he mused, wandering slowly, perusing his choices.

"Killing your harem doesn't mean you're entitled to more of this year's crop," a female replied, her disdain clear. "Try not to harm them before we get a taste."

"I've always enjoyed your candor, Naomi." His tone held a touch of amusement that died as he continued. "But as your elder, I advise you to remember who it is you're addressing."

Even the royals had a hierarchy, and Kylan sat at the top. A chill frosted the air, the implication in his admonishment carrying its expected weight.

Fuck with me. I dare you, he seemed to be saying.

And from the shuffles backward, no one wanted to take him up on the offer.

"Apologies," Naomi gritted out.

"Accepted." Kylan moved closer to the vampire harem, his hand lifting and disappearing beyond my field of vision.

"She's pretty." The female yelped in response to whatever he did, causing him to tsk. "Well, that certainly won't do."

He repeated the action with several more, all of them reacting similarly. Kylan sighed dramatically, stepping our way. He muttered several words in an old language that had a few of his brethren chuckling.

His palm slid over a woman near me, causing her to flinch. I almost rolled my eyes. If she couldn't handle the touch of a royal vampire, then she stood no chance in these games.

When Kylan finally reached me, I forced my limbs to relax and kept my breathing even. *Move on, vampire. Nothing to see here.*

His gaze burned a trail over my exposed skin, scattering smatters of heat in his wake. I fought a resulting shiver, my body overriding my mind.

Don't attract him, I told myself. *Just feign indifference.*

He brushed my hip with his knuckles, almost as if he'd heard me and wanted to test my resolve. I didn't move. Didn't react.

Focus.

Just inhale, then exhale.

Repeat.

Kylan grabbed my chin and forced my attention upward, his dark brown eyes capturing mine. A spark shot through me, knocking me off-kilter. I grabbed his arm, needing something stable to ground me. Eye contact with a vampire was forbidden, a show of disobedience. Yet he'd just forced me to meet his gaze, and he held me there, scant inches from his face.

He tilted his head slightly to the side, his expression curious.

I swallowed, uncertain. Was he trying to force me into misbehaving? To give him a reason to punish me?

No. I wouldn't be tricked this easily.

My nails dug into his jacket, my forearm tensing, ready to react, push, *something*.

Wait… I'm touching him.
Oh, shit…

My hand locked in place and refused to loosen, reacting the absolute wrong way in this situation. I opened my mouth, an apology ready, when his lips covered mine.

I stood frozen, unable to process.

He's kissing me.

Why the fuck is he kissing me?

His tongue slid inside, exploring.

Oh, no. This wasn't good. I couldn't afford for Kylan to be interested, not with immortality dancing at my fingertips.

You can't want me, I thought.

But how did I convey that?

I… I…

Do something!

My jaw clenched in frustration, not knowing how to stop this—*him*. His grip on my chin tightened painfully, his growl vibrating my chest. It took me too long to realize why, to realize what I'd done.

His tongue was trapped between my teeth.

I'd just bitten him.

I'd just bitten a royal vampire.

And not just any royal vampire, but Kylan, the oldest royal in existence.

Chapter Two

KYLAN

She *bit* me.

From the alarm radiating from her ice-blue eyes, the reaction had shocked her almost as much as it had me. Yet her nails continued to dig into my suit jacket.

A fighter. Courageous. Just what I needed.

My penchant for picking from the lycan harem—just to piss off the wolves—disappeared in a flash.

I wrapped my palm around the back of the redhead's neck and squeezed. "That was a mistake, little lamb," I whispered darkly. Because now I wanted her. Badly.

Her lips parted, but no sound escaped. Not even an apology.

Oh, I'd enjoy this one.

I stepped backward, pulling her with me. "If I kill her

before the selection is through, can I select a replacement?" I asked Lilith without breaking eye contact from my chosen conquest.

"Considering her insolent display, I'll most certainly allow it." The irritation in Lilith's tone nearly had my lips curling. Of course she would wish to punish the girl for her reaction. That just made the auburn-haired beauty all the more perfect.

I nipped at her trembling lower lip and tightened my grip on her nape as I dragged her with me back into the circle of royals. They gave us room, no one wanting to risk any residual blood splatter.

The things they expected me to do.

Pity I wouldn't be obliging them in a show.

"I should force you to your knees, make you beg me for forgiveness," I growled. "But I'm not sure I trust that mouth of yours."

"Walter, if you please," Lilith said, signaling the Clemente Alpha for his turn. We would alternate for the next hour or so as everyone selected their initial prize. Then the Immortal Cup candidates would be reshuffled to meet the requisite ten.

What the lamb didn't know was that I'd just saved her life. Because had I not chosen her, one of the lycans would have. She was far too beautiful to be wasted on the Immortal Cup, with her fiery red hair, light blue eyes, and creamy skin. And her curves were mouthwateringly perfect as well.

She didn't look away, her defiance written in the lines of her flattened mouth. Because I'd threatened to force her to her knees? Or because I'd pulled her from the competition? Maybe both.

I brushed my lips over hers again and smiled when she clenched her jaw. "Oh, you do have a death wish, young one," I murmured. "I may just keep you for the fun of breaking you." The words were spoken for those around us more than for her.

She didn't reply, but the fire in her blue eyes told me everything I desired to know. This one had spirit. Such a rarity these days. Most of the humans were broken by the time I met them, their minds fractured from decades of harsh treatment or mental reform. But she possessed a fire I wanted to play with, not smother.

"What shall I call you, little lamb?" I asked against her lips.

Her gaze narrowed, delighting me more. She stood against me, clad in nothing but a pair of heels, her life very much in my hands, and she *glowered* at me.

A scream from the field confirmed Walter's choice. I ignored the howls of approval and focused on my prize. How had I missed her profile? Too busy skimming to care, I supposed.

"Jace," Lilith called, referring to the second oldest of the royals.

The name soured my mood considerably. Someone was fucking with me, and I strongly suspected the outwardly fun-loving, carefree royal to be the culprit. His recent appointing of Darius to sovereign only solidified my suspicion.

A shiver shook the woman in my arms, the midnight air chilling her bare skin. It seemed some of her bravado had worn off and the elements were touching her now.

I released her to shrug out of my suit jacket. Humans were so frail and easily susceptible to disease. I couldn't have her weakening on me too soon.

Her eyebrows rose as I wrapped the handcrafted material around her shoulders.

"What? Surprised I want to keep the sole member of my harem alive?" I asked softly, my lips twitching. I pulled the lapels of the coat over her breasts, tugging her to me. "I have plans for you, sweetheart. You'll need your strength."

She swallowed, her gaze finally leaving mine to drop to my lips before drifting upward again.

Jace made his selection while I watched my new pet, and

Lilith called on the next alpha. His choice resulted in an earsplitting scream that didn't faze my little lamb in the slightest. She continued to hold my gaze unflinchingly through the next several rounds, surprising the hell out of me. Any other human would have looked away in deference or subservience after mere seconds. But not her.

"Tell me your name," I demanded, my words for her alone.

Another shriek sounded as one of the lycans familiarized himself with his new toy in the most ancient of ways. I could do the same, bend this woman over on the ground and fuck her until she answered me, but that wasn't my style.

"Your name," I repeated, yanking on my jacket. "Or I will find another, more creative way to make you talk."

The grunts sounding to our left punctuated my threat. She swallowed, her icy gaze thawing the slightest bit with the first signs of discomfort. Fate was finally making her presence known. I almost pitied the woman, yet couldn't. Humans existed to serve their superiors, and she would serve me as required.

And she would enjoy it, too.

I slid my fingers into her hair to twine with her thick strands. "You're trying my patience, little lamb. I suggest you work with me before you see the results of my impatience."

"Why? So you can change my name before killing me?"

Fuck, the female oozed sex in every way. In her gaze, her full lips, those delectable curves hidden beneath my jacket, and in the sultry quality of her voice. I didn't even care that she'd still avoided my question. Just hearing her speak was enough to calm the most turbulent storm.

I tightened my grasp in her hair, pulling until she winced. "Keep pushing." Both a threat and a request tied up into two darkly whispered words.

Fight me.
Submit to me.
Give me everything.

My hand on the jacket slipped beneath the lapels to her bare hip. Her palms flattened on my abdomen as I forced her closer. My lips grazed her cheek before settling at her ear. "I want to know what name to growl later when I'm inside of you."

Her resulting shiver had nothing to do with the cold and everything to do with my lethal promise. And yet she remained tense, as if ready to hit me.

Fascinating.

"Prospect Seven Hundred and Three, Year One Hundred Seventeen," she gritted out. "Have fun with that."

A laugh escaped me—loud and enjoyable—causing several of the others to glance our way. I ignored them all in favor of the defiant female before me. "You're adorable."

Frost coated her blue irises as she remained infuriatingly silent again.

My already hard cock throbbed at the obvious display of resistance. This one would not break easily. No fear, no shame, no willingness to lie down and take it. I didn't realize humans like this still existed.

"We're going to have a lot of fun together, little lamb," I whispered, my lips brushing hers with each word. "And you will give me your name." Because I knew she had one. They all did, our records just didn't bother tracking them.

Challenge poured from her in waves, exciting me.

Fuck, I'd missed this. A woman who could actually hold her own, who refused to bow down to me because of my social status.

Even surrounded by predators, she didn't flinch. Because she would rather I kill her than take her home, perhaps? Hmm, a disappointing thought. One I wouldn't be obliging. My question to Lilith about selecting another had been all about maintaining my image. No, this feisty female I intended to keep, and her warrior tendencies may just keep her alive in this dangerous game called life.

The perfect bait.

I spun her in my arms, placing her back to my chest, and

caged her with my forearms. "Watch." I spoke the word against her ear. "See what your fate could become." Royals and alphas traded harem members all the time. Not that I ever participated, but she didn't need to know that.

The remaining humans still up for selection had huddled closer together. Most of my brethren had already made their choices. Robyn had gone with the scrawny male over the brunette. He knelt at her feet while she combed her fingers through his hair as one would a dog.

Jace's pick was the beautiful brunette I'd fondled first. She didn't appear as skittish now that he'd wrapped her up in his jacket. He met my gaze with a cocked brow, daring me to comment on his similar actions. I didn't bite and instead followed my pet's stare to the blond human male standing among those selected for the Immortal Cup.

I recognized him from the files. He was off-limits for this round, marked as a prospect both Jace and Walter had agreed would make a fitting immortal. The way he held his shoulders back, his strong legs spread, his expression bored, I had to agree with the designation. Six of the humans were favored, and of them, he clearly held the most promise.

But what had my lamb so entranced?

His focus never wavered, even as Naomi drew a nail down his sternum to his groin. She loved fucking with the recruits. If she weren't such a bitch, I might like her.

Then again, probably not.

My lamb tensed as Naomi pressed her lips to the male's ear to whisper a taunt. His lips curled in response, intriguing me, but not nearly as much as my pet's unsteady breath. She didn't relax until Naomi moved on to the next victim.

"Ah, a weakness," I whispered against her ear, low enough that no one else would hear except her. Not that anyone was paying us any attention. They were all too busy entertaining their new playthings or salivating over the remaining crop.

Her shoulders stiffened again, causing me to smile against her neck.

"Oh, yes, a definite weakness." I nibbled the tender skin covering her thundering pulse. "If I kill you, I could pick him instead. I've always found males to be more skilled at certain activities than females." I skimmed my nose along her jaw. "What do you think, little lamb? Should I dispose of you and request his company instead? Or perhaps you have something that might entice me otherwise?"

A cruel threat, one that left her quivering against me. I almost hated to do it, but I couldn't pass up the opportunity to reaffirm my dominion here. My brethren would have killed her the second she bit them. I didn't expect gratitude or groveling, but I did want her name. And I would push her until she gave it to me.

"Tick tock," I taunted, nuzzling her throat. "Your silence is boring me."

She grabbed my forearm, squeezing it as her body trembled. It was the second time tonight she'd used me for support without realizing it. The first time had intrigued me so much I hadn't been able to step away. Then she sealed her fate with that kiss.

"Rae." The word barely reached my ears over the animalistic groans coming from the sidelines. Jenkins, the Winter Clan Alpha, had given his new human pet to his son to play with, and the young lycan had wasted no time in becoming acquainted.

My female tried to turn, surprising me. I clasped her hips and allowed her to move, then met her infuriated gaze.

"My name," she said slowly, her voice a throaty purr that intrigued my male senses. "My name is Rae."

"Rae," I repeated, tasting the single syllable on my tongue. "Hmm." I liked it, but it seemed too weak for her. Too quick. *How about...* "Raelyn."

She shook her head. "No, it's Rae."

"I like Raelyn more."

Her gaze narrowed yet again. "If you were just going to rename me, then why ask for my name to begin with?"

"Because I wanted to hear you speak."

"Like a dog."

"Exactly."

She stared me down with such passion that I couldn't stop my lips from curling at the sides. I rather enjoyed her voice, but mmm, I would so enjoy evoking that look from her in bed.

"Your secret is safe with me, little lamb," I promised.

Her brow furrowed. "What secret?"

I pressed my lips to her ear, not wanting anyone to hear. "Whatever secret you share with that human male." I nibbled on her lobe, exhaling slowly and wrapping my arms around her. "But whatever it was, it's over. Because you're mine now, Raelyn."

Chapter Three

RAE

My tongue felt thick in my mouth, as if it had been Kylan who bit me and not the other way around. His hard body held mine, his lips at my ear breathing words I didn't want to hear.

Because you're mine now, Raelyn.

How had this become my fate?

One minute, I was destined for the Immortal Cup. Now, a royal owned me. All because I couldn't keep my body in check. After Kylan had suggested killing me to the Goddess, I'd stopped trying. Because what did it matter? If he was going to slaughter me anyway, I might as well go down with my dignity intact.

Except then he'd threatened Silas. My weakness. The one place Kylan could hit me to force me to behave.

Because I couldn't let my behavior lead to Silas's demise. Not after everything we'd been through together. He deserved a chance. I would do anything to see that through. Including playing nice with the royal I'd rather kill than fuck.

Kylan had ruined everything.

No, that wasn't true. I'd ruined it by biting him. By reacting to him.

He pressed an openmouthed kiss to my neck. "Has anyone ever bitten you, Raelyn?"

I clenched my teeth at his use of that ridiculous name. "Does it matter?" I countered, avoiding his question. "You're just going to bite me anyway." And use my body for his physical enjoyment.

Of all the royals to pick me, it had to be the one with a fondness for violence. The recent slaughtering of his harem had been a popular discussion amongst my vampire professors. No one had actually cared about the lives lost, just the wasted blood and the very real possibility that Kylan was going insane.

And now he owned me.

His incisors skated over my pulse in warning. "When I ask you a question, I expect an answer. Have you been bitten?"

My nails dug into his flat abdomen.

For Silas, I reminded myself. *Do it to save him. Then, when he's on his way to the next stage, you can push back.*

Because no way in hell was I going to willingly lie with this royal vampire. Gorgeous or not, I'd rather die. And I would go down fighting.

"No," I forced myself to say. "I have not."

He smiled against my neck. "Mmm, another point in your favor." He kissed my throat, then my jaw, and returned his dark eyes to mine. "Keep intriguing me, Raelyn, and I may just let you live." He tucked my hair behind my ear before palming my nape. "How were your test scores in sexual studies?"

He would ask that because that's all a man in his position

cared about. Yet, I felt compelled to correct him on that score. "My ratings in all subjects were at the top of my class."

"I imagine they would be to qualify you for the Immortal Cup," he murmured. "But I want your sexual arts scores in detail. What acts do you excel in, and what techniques require more"—his gaze dropped to the jacket covering my breasts—"training?"

"Kylan?" the Goddess called, causing him to shift his focus to where she stood. "Have you made a decision? The others are finished."

"Hmm." He glanced down at me, his cruel gaze unreadable. "Answer me, Raelyn." The *or else* remained unsaid.

I swallowed. *They're just test results like any other course.* "I'm rated as excelling in oral activities, and my pain tolerance is well above average. The only area I ever received a somewhat negative score in was submissive play, but I still ranked above average compared to my class." And the only reason I received that negative score was because I had a hard time giving up control when Silas led our exercises together. It just felt wrong to submit to him, regardless of how talented he was in the art of foreplay.

Kylan's lips curled. "Thank you, Raelyn." He whirled me in his arms, placing my back to his chest again, his hand at my throat while his opposite arm wrapped around my lower abdomen.

Silas's blue gaze flashed to mine, fear radiating from their depths.

I'll be fine, I tried to tell him. *Don't show them you care.*

The silence stretched, Kylan's grip tightening.

I will not cry.
I will not beg.
I will remain calm.

Black spots danced before my eyes, but not before I caught the pain in Silas's features.

Goddess, I hoped Kylan didn't pick him. But I knew he

would. This had all been a cruel game to force me to speak, to make an example of my behavior.

It had all gone so wrong. So horribly wrong.

I'm sorry, Silas. I'm so fucking sorry.

Kylan's thumb brushed my weakening pulse, his touch a brand against my skin. "It seems breath play may be something to explore later," he whispered against my ear. He lessened his hold just enough to allow air to flow back into my lungs. I sucked it in greedily, my gaze blurring from the humiliation of my body's necessary reaction.

A weakness.

I hated him in that moment more than any other.

He was fucking with me.

Pretending to kill me, just to drive home how easy it would be, and he'd made Silas watch.

"I think I'll enjoy breaking this one, Lilith," Kylan said, a smile in his voice. "Thank you for granting me the opportunity to keep her."

"If you're sure," she replied. "Seems more work than it's worth."

"Oh, I could use the amusement." He stroked the column of my neck while keeping his palm tight against my throat. I could breathe, but only barely, and the arm banded around my lower stomach wasn't helping.

"Well then, that concludes our selection process. Now there's just the matter of evening the ranks left of our Immortal Cup participants."

I counted the remaining members and found only six left. All the others had been selected. Two of them were on the ground, their chests unmoving and lower halves... I looked away, unable to process what had been done to them. One body was formerly Daniella.

That could have been me...

Kylan's grip loosened a bit more, his lips brushing my temple as if sensing the direction of my thoughts.

But no. That was impossible. If he could read minds, I'd be a dead woman because he'd see all the ways in which I'd love to kill him. Vampires couldn't die—or so they said—but I'd love to find a way to take him down. Make *him* beg *me* to breathe.

"Jace, Walter, please." The Goddess made a gesture as if to say, *Fix it.*

Jace handed his new harem member to the vampire beside him—a dark-haired male I didn't recognize as a royal. Beside him stood a woman with dark hair and matching eyes, wearing a formal gown made of translucent material. Her gaze was on the ground.

A human. But not from the selection. I'd missed her before, as well as her Sire, who was now looking directly at me with striking green eyes. I lowered my gaze with a flinch.

Have I completely lost my mind today?

No, just my life.

"She's a blood virgin," Kylan said softly against my ear. "And she's recently mated to Darius, Jace's new sovereign."

I blinked. Did he just explain something to me?

And what the hell was a blood virgin?

I glanced at the woman again. Gorgeous, well groomed, and no sign of fear. She appeared bored, like her master, who had refocused on the events unfolding before us. Jace had selected two humans, his palms on their shoulders. Walter had one and seemed to be struggling to find a second.

Silas hadn't moved, his posture confident while his gaze remained averted. *Good luck*, I wanted to tell him. *Not that you need it.*

Kylan's palm slid up to my chin, forcing my head back at an angle that met his gaze. "What did I say about it being over, Raelyn?" he asked softly, his pupils flaring in the moonlight.

My neck ached from the uncomfortable position coupled with the pain of having been nearly strangled. I tried to reply and couldn't, my throat raw. Tears gathered behind my eyes again, making me hate him more. I never cried. Never begged. Never complained. Yet, not even an hour in his presence and I wanted to weep.

I want to kill you, I told him with my eyes since my voice refused me.

He smiled before releasing me, his hands falling to my hips to keep me against him. His erection pressed into my backside, confirming the hatred between us was not mutual.

Fucking him would be my worst nightmare come to life. Because while my mind despised him, my body would react favorably.

His strength and power served as an aphrodisiac, and his face was crafted by the heavens. A gorgeous male encased in muscle and experience—I couldn't deny the physical appeal. And from what I understood, a vampire's bite possessed an ecstasy unlike anything a human could give to another.

He would take from me what he wanted, and a sick part of me would enjoy it while the rest of me loathed him.

His lips traced my neck again, his breath hot against my skin. "I'm going to destroy you, little lamb," he whispered darkly. "You'll never think of him again when we're done."

A chill swept down my spine. Because he was right. Once he fractured my soul, I'd no longer have cause to think about anyone, let alone Silas.

I lowered my gaze, a feeling of defeat settling inside of me.

So many I knew desired this destiny, to live in a life of luxury with the royals or alphas. But seeing the field around me, the already broken bodies, feeling the aroused male at my back threatening my fate, I realized it was all just a glamour. A false sense of hope instilled in us at birth to keep us in line. And for what? The minute chance at immortality?

Was it worth it?

Silas would say yes. I hoped.

"These are the prospects you wish to add?" the Goddess asked, her voice filled with surprise.

"They won't survive, nor are they lycan material. Send them for the chance." Walter sounded disgusted as he shoved the humans he selected toward the Immortal Cup selection.

I would have survived, I thought with a mental growl. The two he picked were meek and broken already. At least Jace's selections held merit, even if they stood no chance against Silas, or even me.

But I'm no longer competing.

To have the fate I desired for so long ripped from my fingers after only minutes of experiencing the potential glory was a cruel act indeed. Yet, so very fitting.

Vampires and lycans loved to play with their food and their pets.

This was no different.

Kylan's arms circled me again, his touch holding a hint of comfort I immediately rejected. He was no better than the rest of them. In fact, he was worse.

Words rolled through the air, the Goddess commending those chosen for the Immortal Cup, something about harem training, and a dismissal that all blurred together in my mind. I no longer cared. There wasn't any point.

Silas met my gaze, his holding a mixture of excitement and sorrow that broke my heart.

Kill them all, I told him with mine. *Rise, my friend.*

He gave me a subtle nod before turning to disappear, and Kylan sighed. "If you can't ignore a simple command to forget, then how will I ever train you to serve?"

I bit my tongue. *Don't react yet. Wait until Silas is safe.*

"Follow me, pet," he demanded, releasing me.

My feet threatened to do the opposite, to stand and stare at him in defiance. But my mind pushed me to obey.

He led us past the other royals, who all gave him a wide berth, their discomfort at his presence evident. The rumors claimed him to be going mad, an ancient who was losing his mind to immortality.

I considered that as we walked. His control over me and our situation suggested his mental state to be healthy and clear, strong even. He could just be toying with me, especially since he had suggested killing me a short while ago.

Does it matter? I wondered. *He's going to destroy you, remember?*

A shiver traversed my spine at the thought. He could mean so many things by that statement.

Kylan led me to a small black car with two doors. A beep sounded as he clicked a button, and the door rose. "In you go, little lamb."

Several humans stood near waiting cars, the other royals and alphas slowly making their way toward us. It appeared Kylan had led the pack.

He cocked a brow at my hesitation. "Disobeying me again?"

Always, I very nearly replied. Instead, I slid into the bucket seat and stared straight ahead. His chuckle was stilted by the closing of the door, but he still wore a grin as he climbed into the driver's seat beside me.

"Seat belt," he said, leaning over me to grab the item in question. "Safety first."

Alone in a car with a sadistic vampire. Yep. Very safe.

"Silence," he said, buckling himself in as well. "You're boring me again, Raelyn."

"Would you prefer I sing and dance?" I asked as Jace strolled by our car with his arm around the female Kylan had called a blood virgin. Darius moved behind them with the new harem member at his side. "You don't have any sovereigns," I said, recalling my studies about Kylan's territory. "I've always found that odd."

The engine purred to life, the throaty sound powerful like its master. "Sovereigns are trusted minions," Kylan replied as he pulled out of his spot. "And I trust no one."

A female appeared in front of our car, hands on her hips, causing Kylan to come to an abrupt stop before exiting the parking lot.

The royal female cocked her head to the side, causing him to sigh.

"Right." He put the car in park but didn't turn off the engine. "Don't touch anything or I'll be forced to punish you." He flashed me a look that said he meant the threat. "Now stay like a good little pet."

Chapter Four

RAE

My palms ached from how hard I dug my nails into my skin. Vampires and lycans had spoken down to me all my life, but never quite so condescendingly.

Kylan stepped out of the car without a backward glance before meeting the woman—Robyn—in front of me. He wrapped his hand around her neck and pulled her into a kiss that left me feeling sick to my stomach.

Vampires were always affectionate. These two were no different, but the way he handled her denoted a history I wanted to know nothing about.

Robyn's hands went to his sides before sliding up his black dress shirt to his shoulders, feeling him as if she owned him. He smiled against her mouth before catching her wrists in his free hand. Whatever he said to her in reprimand created a smile that was all female satisfaction.

I rolled my eyes and looked for her recent acquisition. He knelt on the ground—still naked—with his head bowed. She'd put a metal collar around his neck and connected it to a leash she'd dropped in favor of touching Kylan.

Whatever he said to her next had her lips flattening into a scowl. Then she looked directly at me in the passenger seat. Barbarity lurked in her eyes, making me reconsider Kylan's reputation as the cruel one. Because that look left nothing to the imagination as to what she wanted to do to me.

Kylan wanted to destroy me.

This woman wanted to shred me.

I should look away, but to what purpose? My fate was already sealed and in the hands of a monster.

Robyn started toward the car, but Kylan caught her by the elbow and yanked her back to him, his elegant expression morphing into the powerful predator lurking beneath the fancy clothes.

I couldn't hear them, but the conversation was clearly not in her favor. She scowled at him but lowered her gaze in submission. He kissed her on the head, as if praising a pet. Whatever platitudes he whispered seemed to calm her slightly, but her hands remained fisted as he walked away.

"I'll see you again soon, Robyn," he said as he opened the door.

"Yes," the woman replied as she retrieved the leash. She yanked the human toward her with so much force he skidded across the gravel.

I flinched at the display, my lips parting as she forced the male to crawl after her as she walked away at a clipped pace.

Kylan navigated us away from the scene, leaving me quite relieved despite not knowing our future destination. He'd given me his jacket and treated me somewhat humanely compared to the others. My neck still ached from his attentions, but I preferred that over a leash and collar.

And the sexual exploits in the field... I shivered. Kylan could have done much worse. So why didn't he?

Silence settled between us, both comforting and ominous, as he pulled onto a vacant road with the moonlight illuminating our path. Nothing existed out here apart from farmland. No buildings or other structures, no signs of the city, just the stars in a black sky. It was actually sort of peaceful, unlike the surroundings of my former university. Snipers, guards, cement walls lined with barbwire, and sky lights were the primary scenery.

Hmm, I wished there were trees here. I'd never seen one, but the grassy landscape, even in the night, was gorgeous.

"Robyn relishes in breaking her toys," Kylan said, his voice soft.

I glanced away from the serenity around us to eye the devil beside me. "And you?" I asked, unable to help myself. "What do you prefer?" *I'm going to destroy you,* his words from earlier whispered through my thoughts, taunting me.

"I adore submission," he murmured, his lips curling. "But I love a fighter."

Our surroundings whipped by us as he accelerated, my stomach churning both from the unfamiliar momentum and his reply. He wanted me to oppose him, to say no. That was why he chose me—because he knew I wouldn't submit easily.

He wants to force me to accept him physically. To hurt me in the harshest of ways, by taking my body whether I liked it or not.

A tremble I couldn't hide shook me to my core. I'd seen this done countless times, had heard the screams, had even witnessed it tonight on the field. But to know he craved it, that he was taking me home with every intention of injuring me, caused bile to rise in my throat.

He's going to kill me, but only after he fucks me.
And there's nothing I can do to stop him.

"Ah, there it is, the fear that's been missing all evening," he mused. "You were one of the few who didn't display an ounce of it during the selection. It's what drew me to you."

He turned without slowing, causing my insides to twist

violently. I pressed the back of my hand to my lips, refusing to be sick. Not here. Not yet. Not this easily.

Lights appeared in the distance, bright and white, with a few red dots spaced between. It grew as we approached, highlighting a wider road on the other side of a wired fence. Beyond it sat an item I'd only ever seen in my books.

A plane.

My lips parted in awe. It was so much bigger than I expected. Several bodies stood around, all dressed in black, a few of them guarding the gate Kylan navigated us toward at a much steadier pace.

"Your Highness," a human greeted, his gaze briefly looking me over in Kylan's jacket. "Everything is ready."

"Thank you, Jackson," Kylan replied, surprising me.

He knows the human's name?

Most vampires didn't acknowledge mortals, even Vigils.

Kylan drove around to the back of the aircraft to a ramp and maneuvered onto it with minimal direction from the humans standing guard. After pulling all the way inside, he shut off the engine and waited as the ramp lifted behind us, sealing us in the belly of the plane.

His dark eyes slid to mine, studying, saying nothing. I didn't dare look away, needing to know what he planned. He unfastened his seat belt and slowly leaned toward me.

My palms dampened. *This is it. He's going to hurt me now and expect me to struggle against him.*

Could I?

Would I?

It might be less painful if—

The click of my belt startled me from my thoughts. He smirked and exited the car, then walked around to open my door, his palm waiting to assist me.

I frowned at him and stood on my own.

"It's considered quite rude to ignore a formal gesture from a superior." He nudged the door closed with a finality that shook my spine. "I'm beginning to question your schooling and how you've survived this long."

So am I. Because I never acted like this in school. While rebellious thoughts often occurred, I never acted on them. I knew better. But with Kylan? I wanted nothing more than to punch him in the face.

And now that Silas was safe, I could.

Kylan caught my wrist before I lifted it and whirled me in his arms, placing my back to his front. He tsked against my ear. "I want a challenge in the bedroom, not in the garage, darling."

"Well, this looks fun," a male voice announced from behind us.

"You have no idea," Kylan replied, his thickening groin pressing into my backside. "Raelyn, this is Mikael, my blood virgin. Mikael, meet my new toy, Raelyn." He pushed me forward, causing me to stumble as I tried to regain my balance on my heels. I spun to face them both.

Mikael walked down a set of stairs to stand at Kylan's side, his blond hair long and brushing his broad shoulders. He wore a black suit that matched his master's, minus the tie, leaving his collar open at the neck.

"She's pretty," he murmured appraisingly, his light gaze running over me. "I like the added touch of dressing her in your clothes, Your Highness."

Kylan smirked. "Yes, she does wear my jacket rather well, doesn't she?"

"Mmm."

"Shall I ask her to remove it for you?"

Mikael scratched the stubble on his jaw, his gaze heating. "I would enjoy seeing the full package, yes."

"Raelyn?" Kylan asked, cocking a brow.

He wanted me to strip for his pet human? "No." If he wanted me to remove the jacket, he could do it himself.

Mikael's blond brows shot up as Kylan chuckled. "Isn't she fantastic?"

"Did she just deny you?"

"She did." Kylan cocked his head to the side, a smile playing over his lips. "Shall we try to entice her into stripping for us?"

"We could," Mikael replied, sounding perplexed. "But we've never had to in the past."

Kylan shrugged. "Perhaps I should explain how this is going to work."

"Can we do it upstairs in the lounge? The pilots are waiting to take off and won't while we're in the undercarriage." The human spoke with Kylan so casually, as if they were friends, that it shocked me into silence.

"Of course." Kylan held out a hand. "Come, Raelyn."

And my shock melted into irritation. "Woof. Woof."

Kylan chuckled again. "Do you require a collar, darling? Like the one Robyn gave her new pet? I do think I'd enjoy watching you crawl."

The image of the royal with that poor male was still fresh and flashed with precision behind my eyes. I shuddered at the memory.

"I didn't think so," Kylan murmured, his fingers waving impatiently. "Come here, Raelyn, or I'll drag you by your hair."

"I'd listen to him," Mikael added, turning toward the stairs. "The man doesn't bluff."

I gritted my teeth and strode forward, ignoring Kylan's hand. He grabbed me by the elbow and yanked me backward so hard I lost my balance and fell into him.

"That's two times you've ignored a polite gesture from me. Would you prefer me to be harsher with you?" he asked, his hands gripping my arms painfully as he kept me standing. "Because I can be, Raelyn."

I winced from his tightening grasp but refused to give him the satisfaction of an apology. "Silas is no longer here for you to use against me. I have nothing left."

His lips twitched. "Silas. An intriguing name for a prospect." He pulled me closer, his lightheartedness disappearing beneath a shadow of darkness. "Just because *Silas* isn't here doesn't mean I can't hurt him. He's in the tournament now. All it takes is a message to the organizers and your former lover will experience an accident he'll never recover from."

My heart skipped a beat. "You'd hurt him to tame me?"

"I'd do a lot more than hurt him, darling." The promise in his words pierced my chest, stirring up the nausea from the car again.

My stomach rolled, my throat working. *Don't throw up. Don't do it.* I swallowed, but the burn of acid brought tears to my eyes. Or maybe that was brought on by the heaviness settling over me.

Silas's life is in my hands.

One wrong move and Kylan would carry out his threat. How could I resist him, knowing the repercussions?

My shoulders sagged. There was no choice. "I'll do whatever you want."

Kylan's brows rose. "For a male you'll never see again?"

I didn't bother replying. My loyalty to Silas was none of his concern. "Do you still wish for me to remove the jacket?" Because I would. And I'd crawl, if he so desired it.

His grip loosened, his eyes narrowing. "He's a human you'll never see again, Raelyn. And if he wins, he'll forget all about you. Why give up your fire for him?"

I met his gaze with a sigh, my body more exhausted than it had been in a long time. "Because he at least has a chance at a future. I wouldn't jeopardize that for anything in the world, even my own dignity." I moved out of his grip and let the jacket fall from my shoulders. "I'll do whatever you want, Your Highness," I repeated more formally.

Defeated, I turned toward the stairs, ready to face my fate.

Kylan wanted a fighter in the bedroom.

Well, he'd just extinguished my flames.

Hopefully, he'd settle for a submissive instead.

Chapter Five

KYLAN

I watched Raelyn ascend the stairs to where Mikael stood waiting at the top platform. He raised a brow in question and I nodded, knowing what he intended to do.

The girl needed a shower, clothes, and food. Mikael, being human, would be able to handle all of that better than me. He always took care of my harem, and in return, most of them usually cared for him. We established the relationship after I purchased him from an auction a decade ago. Sometimes we shared the females, but only when they preferred it.

Raelyn assumed a great many things that I should have clarified in the car but chose not to. Sometimes actions spoke louder than words. And in time, she would realize I had no intention of forcing her to do anything with me. I preferred my partners willing, and when I mentioned loving a woman with courage, I meant a female who could challenge me in the bedroom, not lie there and take it.

Rape was for the weak.

I was not weak.

If Raelyn preferred isolation, I'd allow it. Her relationship with the human—Silas—went deeper than I had originally realized. When I used him against her, it was merely a tool to keep her in line so the others wouldn't kill her. And my words just now were only meant to taunt her but had the completely wrong effect.

Killing her spirit was never my intention. I needed her strong to face the trials to come. Because someone was framing me by painting me as an immortal gone mad with age. They destroyed my harem, leaving me with the choice of claiming the massacre or admitting that someone had breached my territory. Neither was acceptable, both suggesting a weakness. But I'd rather be known as a mad immortal than an inadequate one.

With a sigh, I retrieved my jacket and trailed after Mikael and Raelyn.

Mikael was one of very few who knew the truth. He'd been with me long enough to know I'd never harm my harem, even out of boredom. And we'd mourned their loss together.

I'd chosen Raelyn for her resilience, knowing I needed a replacement who could stand up for herself. Yet, now, I wasn't as certain in my choice. She loved another male, something I could tolerate even if it did have me considering ways to destroy him, and she was willing to sacrifice herself for him.

Mikael met me in the hallway near the jet's only bedroom, a glass of champagne laced with blood in his hand. I traded him my coat for the flute. "You always bring me the best gifts."

He grinned as he hung my jacket in the closet beside us. "You looked like you could use it after that display downstairs."

I snorted and sipped the bubbly liquid with a sigh. "Yeah, I think I messed that up."

"Just a bit," he agreed, his dimples flashing. "But we'll fix it. She's lying down, though, and refusing to shower or eat. To use her words, she just wants to get it over with."

My lips twitched. "Poor darling expects a quick performance."

"Apparently."

"I'll prove her wrong, but not tonight." She was nowhere near ready for me. I'd rather have her begging me to fuck her than taking her in a dull state. "Can you let the pilots know we're ready for takeoff? I'm more than ready to go home."

"Only if you go talk to her in the interim." He pointed at the door. "Explain the rules, at a minimum."

I set the glass aside. "You're always such a spoilsport."

"And you're an ass," he returned, not at all afraid to voice his opinion. "Go show her who you really are so she stops pouting. It's unbecoming."

"Unbecoming," I repeated, shaking my head. "You would use that term."

"Stop stalling or I'll withhold blood."

I raised a brow. "Now you're attempting to be in charge? What the fuck is happening to the world today?"

He chuckled and tried to move past me, but I grabbed his hip, pulling him to me. I brushed my lips over his pulse, his essence singing to my instincts. Blood virgins were rare and delectable and addictive, but I always paced myself with Mikael. I'd chosen a male because, while I had no problem drinking from him, he wasn't my preference sexually. Which meant I never lost control with him, even when he encouraged me to.

"You can't deny me anything," I whispered, my tongue teasing his vein.

He shuddered against me, his hands going to my sides. "I would never want to."

I pierced his neck, just enough for a taste and to tease him with my endorphins. His cock hardened against mine, his body always receptive to whatever I wanted to give him and more. Sharing women with him was easy as a result. We both enjoyed it, and each other, but never engaged in acts alone with just the two of us. It wasn't my preference, nor his.

He groaned as I pulled away, and I smiled. "What was that about withholding blood?"

"Fuck you," he growled, his light eyes aroused. "Go talk to her."

I shrugged. "Only because I want to."

"I bet." He ran his fingers through his long hair and wandered off down the hall toward the main seating area. "I'm borrowing Zelda for a bit. Don't come looking for us."

I smirked. "Is that why you brought my favorite chef along for the journey?"

"No, I knew the girl would need food, but now I'm going to use Zelda to feed something else." He glanced over his shoulder with a smolder. "So I hope you're not hungry, because we'll be busy for a while."

I chuckled. "We'll fend for ourselves." As I assumed he or Zelda had already left food in the bedroom. I hadn't eaten much with tonight's festivities, and they would know that.

"You always do," Mikael replied with another flash of those dimples and disappeared toward the front of the jet.

With a shake of my head, I knocked on the bedroom door. Raelyn didn't respond. I took her silence as permission to enter and found her curled up on the edge of the bed, staring at the wall. Her high heels were on the floor, tucked against the wall, leaving her completely nude.

I loosened my tie and removed my cuff links to roll my sleeves to the elbows. Raelyn shifted her toned legs but remained infuriatingly silent. My taunts regarding the boy had clearly pushed her too far. Such a pity. I had hoped it would take a lot more than that to subdue the courageous spirit inside of her.

Humans were fragile beings, most of them shattering with a mere glance. But this one held promise. I'd just have to coax her defiant side back out to play.

I placed my shoes beside hers and stood before her, hand on my belt. "Shall we test your oral skills first?" Just the idea of it had me hardening, but I had no intention of following through. I merely wanted a reaction.

Her lips flattening was all she gave me.

I sighed and moved to the opposite side of the bed to lie down beside her. "You're boring me again, Raelyn."

Nothing. Not even a flinch.

"Do I need to bring up Silas to make you cooperate?" I asked, curious. "Is that how I provoke the reaction I desire?"

"What do you want from me?" she demanded, rolling to face me. "You want me to suck your cock? To prove my high marks?" Her hand went to my belt. "Because I can do that if it's what you want. Just tell me so I can get it over with."

I let her get as far as unfastening the buckle before I grabbed her wrist to still her movements. "Your skills in foreplay and pillow talk clearly require development."

I pressed her hand into the pillow beside her head and nudged her onto her back, my thigh sliding between her legs as I settled over her.

She grabbed my shoulder with her free hand, pushing. I tsked and captured both of her wrists beneath one of my palms over her head while my opposite hand went to her throat. The bruise blossoming over her skin confirmed I'd been too rough with her earlier. I'd meant it as a demonstration to my brethren, to show I had her well under control, but seeing the mark now left me uneasy.

"Are you sore?"

"Because you care?" she growled, causing me to smile.

"You know nothing about me, little lamb," I whispered. "Only what society has shown you."

"I think the last few hours, or however long it's been, in

your presence have shown me what I need to know."

"Is that so?" I tilted my head, holding her gaze. "And what do you know, Raelyn?"

Those gorgeous baby blues narrowed at me, thrilling me. *There you are, darling. Come play with me. Intrigue me.*

"I offered you my jacket when you were cold," I murmured, recounting the evening. "I didn't just bend you over and fuck you the way several of the others did to their new toys, and I didn't let Robyn punish you after you boldly stared her down from the car. I also allowed you to live when few others would never have tolerated your disobedience. So, tell me, darling, what all does that say about me?"

The bed rumbled beneath us as the jet picked up speed, causing her gaze to fly to the nearby window. I allowed her the moment and released her hands, expecting she may want to grab on to the headboard or bed. She latched onto my shoulders instead, her expression filled with a mixture of wonder and concern as we accelerated into the air.

Most humans had never flown, at least not consciously. It was far easier to drug them and stow them away on a massive cargo plane, like one would cattle. Her lips parted, her eyes widening.

"Would you like to look out the window?" I asked, amused.

Her gaze flew to mine. "I, no, I…" She swallowed, her brow furrowing. "I've never, I mean—"

"I know." I tucked a strand of hair behind her ear while balancing on my elbows on either side of her head. "If you want to look out the window, you can, but be careful." I started to roll off her, but her grip tightened, fear tinging the air.

Flying scared her, but my lips near her neck did not.

I almost laughed. Society had deadened her to the obvious threat who happened to be lying on top of her. No wonder most of the humans came to me broken.

She started to relax as the plane stabilized, her brow

smoothing out on a sigh. It wasn't until she met my gaze again that she realized she'd basically clung to me the entire time, but rather than let go, she froze.

"Tell me again what you know about me?" I taunted, unable to help myself. I pressed my lips to her throat—gently—and nuzzled her jaw. "Mikael wants me to tell you the rules. Sometimes he fancies himself in charge, but he's not."

It had taken a year to unleash the personality he kept hidden beneath the Coventus's indoctrinated training. He barely resembled the male I purchased from that dreadful auction. Mikael was much stronger now and not afraid to call me on my shit, making him a good friend and an even better partner.

"That's my first rule," I continued. "This is my territory, Raelyn. You are now mine and you will do as I say, which includes allowing Mikael to care for you." I considered that the second rule. "So if he tells you to shower and put on clothes, you shower and put on clothes."

Her gaze narrowed. "You're the one who told me to remove the jacket."

My lips twitched. "No, I asked if you wanted to remove it. You were the one who chose to drop the jacket."

"No, that's not—"

I pressed my mouth to hers, silencing the argument.

She'd inferred my comment as a demand, which I may have done on purpose, but the fact remained that I'd never actually commanded she drop my coat. Her lips remained flat beneath mine, not yielding or receptive, which brought us to my next rule.

Forcing a woman in the bedroom held little appeal.

However, seducing an unwilling woman, I very much enjoyed. Especially one who didn't want to be attracted to me.

This was my unspoken rule, one that Mikael understood, that I would never voice out loud. What would be the fun in putting Raelyn at ease? I much preferred her defiant and hating me. Her submission would taste so much sweeter as a result.

I rolled us so I lay beneath her, her legs straddling my hips, and tucked my hands beneath my head. She sat up, her palms on my abdomen for balance, her chest heaving from the shock of our rapid movement.

"You have gorgeous breasts," I praised, admiring the rosy peaks and the firmness of her tits. The subtle curve of her waist led to the shaved apex between her thighs. Whoever forced her to remove those beautiful red curls needed a good beating because I bet she was gorgeous when properly groomed.

I slowly returned my gaze to hers and found her cheeks flushed to a delectable pink shade. Mmm, yes, I enjoyed that almost as much as the glowering.

"I don't... What do you want from me, Kylan?"

My name in her throaty purr of a voice went straight to my groin. Humans rarely addressed superior beings by their given names, and the way her hand covered her mouth now said she'd just realized her error. Her blue eyes widened. "I... I... I didn't—"

"You may call me Kylan when we're alone. In fact, I prefer it." Mikael always used my formal title of *Your Highness*. It could be kinky, but it grew old when everyone referred to me as such.

Her shoulders relaxed, her palm falling to my abdomen. She didn't seem fazed at all by her nudity—a conditioning my brethren had ingrained in her. I should feel bad about that, but I really couldn't.

"What do you want from me?" she asked—again—her voice barely a whisper.

"What don't I want from you, darling?" I reached for her, wrapped my palm around the back of her neck, and dragged her over me, placing her mouth a scant inch from mine. "What do you think I want from you?"

"T-to challenge you."

I nipped her bottom lip. "Good girl." I kissed her

again—because I could and I wanted to—and smiled when she growled.

"I'm not a dog."

"No, you're definitely not," I murmured, licking the seam of her mouth. "Open for me, princess."

"I don't—"

My tongue interrupted her, my yearning to really kiss her taking over. The exploration on the field was just the beginning. I craved more, needed to properly taste her, to *know* her.

She grabbed my biceps, her arms tensing to push away. I tightened my hold on her nape and grabbed her hip to rotate us again, placing her back against the mattress and settling myself between her splayed thighs. Her nails dug into my shirt, causing me to smile. "That's it, Raelyn," I whispered. "Keep protesting. We both know you don't mean it."

"I hate you," she panted, her hips arching into mine in direct contrast to her words.

"I know." I would hate me, too. This world. This life. What current society had demeaned her to. There wasn't a damn thing I could do to stop it, but that didn't mean I accepted it. Mikael was proof of that. My treatment of her, even now, also a testament to my core beliefs. I recognized my position of power over her—a right my kind earned by being the superior species. But did that make it right? A question I often pondered.

She groaned into my mouth, her palm sliding up my arm to my neck, her fingers digging into my hair as her tongue finally responded to mine.

Because she wanted this? Or because she wanted to trick me into stopping?

Clever girl knew I wanted a challenge and giving in was the opposite of that request. Although, the arousal dampening my trousers suggested it might be a mixture of both defiance and lust. An intoxicating invitation that I accepted by deepening our kiss, taking command of our mouths and teaching her what I preferred. She reciprocated in kind, her nipples hardening into alluring little points against my chest.

Oh, she approved, even though I knew she didn't want to.

I pressed my erection against her welcoming heat, coating my pants in the evidence of her mutual appreciation. My lips brushed her cheek, sliding to her ear. "You're making quite a mess for someone who supposedly hates me." Her breath hitched at my words, causing me to smile. "I should make you lick my trousers clean in punishment for lying, darling. Teach you a lesson in humility and truth."

"My body might approve," she said on a sharp exhale. "But my mind never will."

Yes, there was the challenge I coveted. I nuzzled her neck, luxuriating in her escalating pulse. "Just give me time, little lamb. I'll conquer your mind just as easily as your body."

"Never."

"Maybe I'll go for your heart too," I whispered darkly. "Steal it from Silas." Just saying the human's name cooled my ardor. Having a pet who fancied another certainly did not appeal. At all. "How did you two manage to hide your relationship?" It was unlawful for humans to engage in affairs. Bonding could lead to uprisings, and Lilith certainly didn't want anything to impact her queendom.

Raelyn stilled beneath me, her breathing all but stopping.

I pulled back to meet her gaze. "Worried I'll tell someone? Ruin his chances at immortality?" Because it would. One breathed word about their forbidden connection would have him killed. A human with a weakness was not worthy of immortality by most standards.

Her lower lip trembled as tears marred her beautiful gaze. "What do you need me to do?" she asked, her voice broken. "I don't... Please don't..."

Ah, there was that sacrifice again, her willingness to do whatever I wanted just to protect a mortal boy she'd never see again. Such a human reaction. Impractical and contrary to a warrior's mentality. Silas truly meant a lot to her, but from experience, I knew the male wouldn't reciprocate her loyalty. Survivors did whatever they needed to remain alive, something she would do well to remember.

I pushed away from her before I did something truly catastrophic. Like make a phone call while she listened and request the male be strangled and killed on live video. I had more than enough cause to convict him, Immortal Cup status or not.

"Kylan," she pleaded, her voice breaking.

Definitely not the kind of begging I preferred in the bedroom.

I'd give her this moment, this night, to get over it. Blood Day was intimidating and emotional, and having her recruited to my bed likely hadn't been at the top of her selection list.

But she needed to realize there were a lot of worse places she could have gone.

My reputation paled in comparison to some of the others, a fact she would soon learn. Especially if Robyn followed up on her request to visit.

"Get some sleep, Raelyn. You're going to need your strength if you intend to remain alive in this world." I wove compulsion into my words, knowing she'd ignore me otherwise. We had a long flight ahead of us. She may as well use it to rest.

I paused at the door, my hand on the knob.

Fuck.

I couldn't help the glance over my shoulder. Raelyn had succumbed to slumber as I willed her to, but not before allowing those tears to fall. They streaked over her delicate features, destroying her warrior mask.

"Such wasted promise," I said, sighing.

I almost left her but couldn't. If she slept in that position, her neck would be worse in the morning, and I'd already done enough damage.

She felt frail in my arms as I shifted her in the bed, sliding her legs and torso beneath the covers. Her red hair spilled across the pillows, reminding me of fresh blood. My thumb drifted over her steadying pulse as I wondered if the colors would match.

"We'll try again tomorrow, Raelyn." She couldn't hear me, but the words were for me more than her.

Normally, I would hand her over to Mikael and leave him to groom her. But as my sole harem member, I felt obligated to keep her safe. There was a target on her back, not because of anything she did, but because someone wanted to portray me as insane. Until I resolved that issue, her life, quite literally, rested at my feet.

I always fiercely protected my territory, and Raelyn would be no different. It meant we'd be spending more time together than I usually did with my humans. We'd have to make it fun, which would be difficult if she only lived to protect another.

There had to be more to her existence than a boy. I just had to find what made her tick. Good thing I enjoyed challenges.

I tucked the blankets around her shoulders and brushed a kiss against her temple. "Sweet dreams, little lamb."

Chapter Six

RAE

Light surrounded me. Dull, white, and foreign.

I blinked, my gaze on the floor-to-ceiling windows and the whiteness beyond it.

Mountains, my mind supplied. *Real mountains.*

"No fucking way," I breathed, rolling out of the flannel blankets and bounding toward the closed doors of a balcony. A twist of the handle allowed a cold burst of air into the room, but I didn't care.

There. Were. Mountains. Outside.

And trees.

Real. Trees.

I stepped through the threshold and flinched as my bare feet touched the cold texture below.

Snow.

My mouth fell open as I dropped to my knees, my hands going into the fluffy whiteness and coming away frigid. "Oh!" That was so cold, but so beautiful. I repeated the action, thrilled by the phenomenon I'd only read about in books.

The moon vibrantly displayed the grounds, illuminating every silvery detail. That was the cause of the foreign brightness—the clear night sky and nearly full moon bouncing off the wintry landscape.

My lips parted in awe even as my limbs began to shiver. "It's so beautiful," I marveled to myself, shocked.

"Yes," a deep male voice replied.

I jolted backward into something—someone—hard. Warm arms came around me, immediately dispelling the coolness from outside. Only then did I realize someone had clothed me in pajama pants and a shirt.

Kylan.

"Welcome to my home, Raelyn."

I blinked. This was his home. His room. Because he owned me. Because I'd been selected for his harem, to be fucked however he pleased until I died.

This was now my life.

My excitement died on an exhale. There would be no exploring or enjoying the scenery. Only submitting to the royal behind me.

"You need to eat," he murmured, his lips against my neck.

My stomach grumbled in agreement, reminding me that it'd been hours, maybe even days, since I'd last eaten. Mikael had tried on the plane, gesturing to a plate of food on the nightstand. I hadn't bothered, not wanting to be sick when Kylan touched me afterward.

But now, I had no choice. Not eating would only weaken me, and I couldn't afford that in Kylan's presence. That I'd slept as long as I had said a lot about my debilitating state already.

"More silence," he said on a sigh. "How repetitive." He

spun me, my feet slipping over the cool ground. His hands caught my face, his dark eyes smoldering. "You will eat."

"I never said I wouldn't," I retorted, irritated that he was already manhandling me. "And if you'd given me more than two seconds to acclimate, I would have replied."

His eyebrows lifted as though impressed. "Much better."

I almost rolled my eyes. Almost. "You must lead a very boring existence if this is entertaining to you." I couldn't believe I was saying these words out loud. It had to be this location overwhelming my senses, because I knew better than to speak to a vampire, let alone a royal, in this manner. But damn, the man was infuriating.

His mouth curled into a feral grin. "You have no idea, sweetheart."

And I had no desire to know. "I thought you wanted me to eat."

"I do."

"Then why are you holding me like this?"

"Because I want to." He tightened his grip. "And I can."

"Fine," I snapped.

"Fine," he snapped back.

We stared each other down, his dark eyes on my light ones, my feet freezing in the snow. I desperately wanted to turn back around to gawk at the mountains once more, but his thumbs held my chin in place. The ice spread from my toes to my limbs, sending a shiver up my spine. While the snow was very pretty, it was also extremely cold. My teeth started to chatter, causing me to clench my jaw in protest.

Kylan dropped his hands to my hips and lifted me before nudging the door closed with his boot. He sported jeans and a black turtleneck sweater that I begrudgingly had to admit looked good on him.

He set me down inside a walk-in closet filled with clothes. "Let's get you properly dressed, and I'll take you outside after you eat."

"For a walk?" I asked, a hint of sarcasm in my voice.

His grin was wolfish. "Yes, little pet. For a nice, long

walk. Would you like me to grab a collar and leash as well?"

I gave him my best curtsy. "If that's what you want, *Your Highness*."

He laughed out loud and shook his head. "If sleeping makes you this feisty, I'll be forcing you to dream often."

"Forcing me..." My jaw clenched as the realization of why I'd slept so well became abundantly clear. "You compelled me to sleep."

He gave me a sardonic look. "I did a lot more than that." He grabbed my shoulders and spun me toward a rack of feminine outfits. "Pick something."

"Why? You seem to dress me just fine."

"Then you'll go naked."

I shrugged, not caring at all. "If that's your choice."

"You'll freeze outside."

I shrugged again. "That'll hurt you more than me."

"Oh?" He wrapped his arms around my waist, his chin falling to my shoulder. "Do explain your logic."

"A frozen toy is a dead toy." *What the hell is wrong with me?* I was essentially taunting a monster with the idea of making me freeze to death outdoors.

His resulting chuckle vibrated my back. "Oh, Raelyn, you truly are a treat."

Well, while on a roll, I might as well say, "Rae." I spun in his arms, my gaze narrowed. "Raelyn is a ridiculous name."

"The same could be said about Rae."

"Well, that's what I respond to. Either deal with it or expect me to ignore you."

His eyebrows rose. "Where has this bout of confidence come from, my darling lamb?"

"I don't know. Maybe I realized I have nothing to lose, and before you even say it, no. You won't use Silas to taunt me anymore." The words spilled from my mouth as my mind pieced together a crucial piece of our fated puzzle. It just clicked, as things often did, and I couldn't help the smile that followed. "You can't."

Kylan looked far too amused. "Oh, I can't? And why is that?"

"Because you can't," I repeated, feeling elated by my self-discovery.

He wrapped a hand around my neck to walk me backward into the wall beside the clothes. "That is not a satisfactory explanation, Raelyn. Try again."

I refused to let him intimidate me. "If you get rid of Silas, you'll have no more leverage over me, Kylan. I'll be a shell, a broken toy, and then what?" He'd no longer have any interest in me, and the way he stared down at me now proved it.

A shadow of respect lurked in his shrewd gaze. "How have you survived so long in this world?"

"By being the best in my class." And understanding my opponents better than they understood themselves.

"Because you desired immortality."

"Or to become a Vigil."

He cocked his head to the side, his expression almost evil. "Yet, you ended up in my lair instead."

I tried not to let that last point hurt, but it did. "Only because you picked me."

"If I hadn't, another would have."

"You don't know that."

"Oh, but I do know that. You were marked as fair game. One of the lycans would have selected you in a heartbeat, and that valiant spirit of yours would have been smothered and killed on that field for all to witness." He released me so suddenly that I nearly fell. "It's a cruel play, Raelyn, but you were never meant to fight for immortality. The ceremony was just crafted to make you believe it for a second, to give you that false sense of hope and rip it away for our regal enjoyment. That's how our society works."

He turned and started going through the clothing rack while I gaped at him.

To give you that false sense of hope and rip it away for our regal enjoyment. Was he implying that everything had been staged?

That I'd never actually been selected to compete? Just a human pet to be led on and mentally tortured for the cruel entertainment of others?

It matched what I knew of vampires and lycans. And Kylan telling me now only added to the torment.

"Here." He held out a crimson V-neck sweater and a pair of jeans. "These should fit."

I didn't accept them. "I was never meant for the Immortal Cup."

His sinful gaze grabbed mine. "No, you were destined for my bed, which is precisely where I'll put you if you don't start changing clothes."

"And Silas?"

His pupils flared. "The damn human again. How many times have I told you to forget him now? Three, four maybe?"

"Tell me what will happen to him," I demanded, ignoring the annoyance in Kylan's tone. "Is it all just a mind game for him too?"

Kylan dropped the clothes and pushed me up against the wall again, his hands on either side of my head. "You are trying my patience, which, I should warn you, has been extended only for your benefit. Do not push me."

"Then tell me what will happen to him." I grabbed his waist, his silky sweater soft against my palms. "I need to know he has a chance."

"None of you have a chance."

"No." I shook my head, refusing to believe that. "He has one. Tell me he has one."

His brown eyes simmered with violence. He'd kept the predator veiled, but now he peeked at me with unconcealed fury. I would have taken a step back if I weren't already pushed up against the wall.

This is the real Kylan.
The oldest royal in existence.
And I'd just infuriated him.

I swallowed, my mouth trying to form an apology while

my heart refused. I had a right to know, didn't I? If this was all just a ruse meant to torment my oldest friend, me, all of us, then I wanted him to admit it. I *needed* him to tell me.

His cheekbones tensed into brutal lines as he growled, "I am not your friend, nor am I someone you have a right to question or command, Raelyn."

He would never tell me. Because he saw me as a pet. A human without rights.

None of us were worthy.

I bowed my head in deference.

For too long a moment I'd forgotten who stood before me. Not a man, not a person, but a royal vampire with a very long history of slaughtering those beneath him.

And right now, it seemed he wanted to kill me.

I'd well and truly lost myself. Standing up to a superior... *Who am I?* I'd been verbally sparring with him the way I would Silas or Willow. I knew better. This was not a human but a supernatural being who could kill me with a flick of his wrist and no one would care.

Because I have no one.

No friends.

No allies.

No choices.

Kylan *owned* me, and I'd dared to stand up to him. No, I'd demanded something from him, had refused from him the comfort of clothes, had rejected his every common courtesy. Why? Because I blamed him for stealing my chances at immortality.

I never had a chance.

What had he called me? Fair game? It had all been a mental device meant to entertain. *Look at the mortal who thinks she's worthy; how adorable is she?*

All my courses, all my scores, none of it mattered. It just groomed me to be his glorified pet for as long as he wanted to play with me.

"He's one of the preferred candidates," Kylan said, his voice laced with annoyance. "If your former lover wins, he'll become an immortal and he will forget you, Raelyn. But it seems you'll die remembering him."

He pushed away, his steps silent.

"He's not my lover," I whispered, unsure of why I bothered clarifying. "Just my best friend, like Willow."

I closed my eyes, suppressing the tears that threatened to fall. We always knew our fates would divide, that upon our twenty-second year, we'd never see each other again. But the reality of it *hurt*.

My knees shook, my body exhausted all over again. I really did need food. But what did it matter? I thought I wanted to be strong before Kylan, but I'd more than proven that to be impossible. A few quarrelsome words were nothing compared to his brute strength and power.

I would spend my remaining days serving him and die when he grew tired of me, or be relegated to a member of his staff so he could take on younger, newer lovers.

A passing amusement.

What a legacy.

His palm cradled my face, his thumb brushing away a tear I hadn't realized had fallen. I hadn't even heard him come back to stand before me. "It's a savage time," he whispered, his lips against my forehead. "Take a moment for yourself, Raelyn. Have a shower, get dressed, and meet me in the hallway. We'll eat and I'll give you a tour of the estate."

Chapter Seven
KYLAN

Just my best friend.

Her words had doused my ire in an instant, leaving me more than a little perplexed. Why had I been so infuriated to begin with? Because she had a human lover? Who the fuck cared? Yes, she belonged to me now, but why should I be bothered by her past or current feelings?

I ran my hand over my face.

"You need to shave," Mikael said by way of greeting, his gaze pointedly on my three-day-old stubble. "Or I really will withhold my blood."

"Why do all the humans in my home think they are in charge?" First Raelyn, now my blood virgin. "I'm starting to think I just need to fuck some sense into all of you."

Mikael's gaze brightened. "Please do."

I snorted. He would immediately accept the offer. The man preferred women but wouldn't turn me down if I desired a change. Unfortunately for him, it rarely appealed. His mouth, however, I rather enjoyed.

Except I was craving something a little more feminine and feisty at the moment.

Shutting Raelyn up by shoving my cock down her throat... Mmm, yes, now that did sound divine.

Mikael leaned against the wall beside me, his blue-green eyes alight with curiosity. He'd tied his hair back into a low ponytail today, leaving his neck exposed, just the way I liked it. "You let her sleep in your room."

"Yes."

"That's new."

"Yes," I repeated. The harem had their own wing. That was where I fucked them, never in my private quarters. "Current circumstances warranted the change."

"You're worried someone will get to her."

"Can you blame me?" I glanced at him sideways. "You know she's a target."

He nodded. "Killing her would further harm your image."

"They won't just kill her, Mikael. They'll make a scene of it." After her defiance during Blood Day, no one would truly blame me for administering a death sentence. Which meant, to imply my insanity, the murder would have to be spectacular and public.

"Have you gotten any closer to identifying the culprit?"

I shook my head. "No, but I have a list of suspects I intend to invite for a visit now that I've acquired a new consort to dangle before them as bait."

Jace was at the top of my list.

His recent appointment of a new sovereign provided the perfect opportunity. I knew Darius already, but arranging a formal introduction to a royal's new regional leader was perfectly in line with vampire politics.

And, as Jace Region bordered mine, it seemed obvious

that he or one of his minions might be the culprit for my harem's demise. Because, if I were proven incapable of leading, Darius—as the heir of a former royal—could feasibly inherit my entire territory.

That put Jace at the top of my list of suspects. The conniving royal was up to something. I sensed it every time I saw him.

"Sounds draining," Mikael said, his lips curling at the pun.

I leaned into him, my hand going to his hip. "You're mine to share or not to share."

Yearning deepened his irises to a harsher shade of turquoise. Such a beautiful man, with those sharpened cheekbones and delicate jaw. As if I'd let anyone touch him without my permission.

"I know," he murmured, his palm lifting to my cheek. "You always take care of me."

"And that's never going to change," I vowed softly just as the door opened.

Rather than acknowledge Raelyn, I pulled Mikael closer to brush my lips over his. He returned the kiss, his body molding to mine in a familiar way that left me feeling like a king. I slid my tongue into his mouth and relished in his resulting groan.

Dominating a male—especially one as strong as Mikael—was a rush unlike any other. I loved the feeling of establishing my dominion, stamping my claim, and bending him to my will.

This was what I wanted from Raelyn, the complete faith Mikael laid at my feet as I devoured him. His fingers slid into my hair, holding me to him as my grip tightened against his hip in warning. He loved to push my boundaries, to try to take what wasn't his, to challenge me in every way.

I shoved him against the wall, my lips leaving his in favor of his neck and piercing his vein without warning. Raelyn had put me in a mood with all her talk of that human. Fortunately, Mikael could handle the consequences on her behalf. He loved my brand of pain, even when I pushed him too far.

"More," he moaned, his body quivering from the pleasure I unleashed with my bite.

Making him come would be cruel, especially in front of Raelyn. It would be so easy—just increase the endorphins and send them straight to his groin. The curse leaving his lips said it was working, that I was taking him to a point of no return without so much as stroking him. Oh, he'd loathe that more—my forcing him to explode without offering the kindness of my touch.

But the worst torture of all would be to leave him high and dry, to make him seek out one of the maids, or Zelda again, for relief.

His sweet essence burned in my throat, reminding me why I'd paid so much for him. Blood virgins were bred for their rare blood, hence their significant cost. Most were fucked once and discarded, but I chose to keep mine for companionship, and frankly, because I liked him.

"You're killing me," he hissed, referring not to my drinking but to the ecstasy flooding his veins.

I chuckled but continued to swallow as he rubbed his hard cock against my hip.

"Fuck, Kylan," he growled.

His use of my name told me how far gone he was to my bite, causing me to smile against his neck. "And you wanted to withhold your blood." I licked the wound closed and met his smoldering gaze. "You can't even last a day."

"Asshole," he said, his voice low and pissed off, and tinged with arousal.

I palmed his erection. "I was trying to save you the embarrassment in front of Raelyn."

"Still an asshole."

I smiled, rubbing him in the way I knew he preferred—the way I enjoyed as well. "Shall I finish it, or would you prefer Zelda?"

He grabbed my wrist, his orgasm clearly close. "I hate

when you do this."

"I know."

"Yet you do it anyway."

"Yes." I nipped his bottom lip hard enough to bleed and licked the wound, causing him to spasm once more.

"Kylan," he growled.

"Tell me you want more."

"You know I do."

I glanced at a very flushed Raelyn, her lips parted as she fought to steady her breathing. "Would you like to see him come? It's really quite glorious." I applied more pressure, causing him to groan louder and grab my arms for support. "Well, Raelyn? Shall I let him come? For you?"

Her eyes rounded, her face deepening to a darker crimson.

"I'm not sure she's ready, Mikael," I murmured, my eyes still on her as I massaged him torturously through his jeans.

His head fell to my shoulder, a curse slipping from his lips. "Fuck…"

"I'm not sure she's ready for that either." I tilted my head to the side. "Raelyn?"

She licked her lips, her pupils darting from me to Mikael and back. She must have seen the agony in Mikael's expression or posture because, slowly, she nodded.

"Say it," I encouraged.

"Yes," she whispered.

Mikael shuddered against me, his relief palpable. He knew if she had refused, I'd have refused him too.

I unfastened his jeans and drew down the zipper to relieve his engorged shaft. He jerked as it landed against my palm, his breathing heavy as I stroked him from base to tip with harsh, swift movements. He always preferred me to be rough instead of soft, his desire to be mastered only evident in moments like this.

Rather than force him to wait—as I usually preferred—I gave him what he craved and pierced his neck once more.

He came on a guttural yell, his body exploding from my

bite and my touch. I wrapped my arm around him, holding him through his violent spasms. The sensations would both hurt and please, the force of his orgasm doubled by my fangs in his neck. He whispered my name as a curse and a plea, his muscles bunching and twitching against me.

So much strength for a human.

So much beauty.

I drank my fill, satisfying my thirst, and gently closed the marks on his neck. Raelyn stood to the side, her breathing loud in the hallway, her sexual interest more than evident. Gone was the broken female in the closet, and in her place a woman realizing the potential of her situation.

Because this could be her in my arms, and I let her see that with my eyes.

Mikael's head rested against my shoulder as he fought to regain his control, his pants from exertion heady and intoxicating.

I held her gaze, letting her feel the passion of the moment. From the way she clenched her thighs, I knew she enjoyed the show, maybe even wanted to join us.

But she wasn't ready for any of that yet.

I brushed my lips against Mikael's temple as I eased him away, his spent cock still hard in my palm. He'd made a mess of my sweater, as well as his own, but his satisfied expression said he harbored no regrets.

"Thank you," he whispered.

"I think you needed that." Especially considering he'd spent just last night with Zelda.

"You know I did," he replied, gazing up at me from beneath hooded eyes. "I'd return the favor, but that's not what you really want."

Sometimes he knew me too well. Rather than acknowledge it, I pulled my sweater over my head and handed it to him. "Have that cleaned."

He pressed it to his groin and used it to wipe himself off. "Sure."

Raelyn's deepening arousal tinged the air, causing my

eyes to find hers. They were firmly affixed to my bare abdomen. "I think she approves, Mikael."

"She'd have to be blind not to," he returned, glancing over his shoulder with a smirk. "Be a good pet and maybe he'll let you touch him."

I would be allowing her to do far more than that. "Don't go anywhere, Raelyn. I need another sweater."

She nodded mutely, her focus having fallen to my groin. Her silence now didn't bother me nearly as much as earlier. She wet her lips, causing my cock to pulse behind my zipper.

We'd definitely be testing those oral skills—soon.

I ran my fingers through my hair and entered my suite. Several black sweaters lined my racks, making my choice easy. I pulled another turtleneck over my head and grabbed a scarf for Raelyn to wear when we ventured outside.

"It's a unique bloodline," Mikael was explaining. "Blood virgins don't attend universities like you did. We are raised in the Coventus and auctioned during our twenty-second year."

"Auctioned?" she repeated, sounding intrigued. "Similar to a Blood Day?"

"No, not really. The Magistrate reads your fate. Wealthy vampires buy mine, and fortunately, Kylan found me worthy enough for the highest bid."

Fortunately, I thought, nearly rolling my eyes. He wasn't wrong, but he wasn't right either.

"So he bought you."

"Yes."

"And how long have you lived with him?"

"Over a decade."

I chose that moment to rejoin them, mostly because I wanted to see her expression, and she didn't disappoint. Her jaw was on the floor. "And don't you look surprised, darling," I teased, closing the door. "Mikael is an example of what happens when I like a human. I let him live. Fancy that?"

Mikael narrowed his gaze. "Stop being an ass."

"As you've pointed out several times tonight, that's my specialty."

He just shook his head. "I give up trying to help you."

"One might think you owe me."

"I paid my debt in blood," he retorted, turning away with a pointed look. "Have a good outing. I'm going to take a nap."

I smiled at his backside. "Something exhaust you, Mikael?"

He held up a one-finger salute in response, making me laugh. Heavens, he was so much more fun now than when we first met. All those old movies and television shows had taught him how to be a proper human, equipped with a filthy vocabulary and all.

Raelyn stared after him with a perplexed expression. "I don't understand what that means."

Of course she wouldn't. Most of my kind despised crude behavior and language. "He's telling me to fuck off."

Her gaze widened. "And you allow it?"

"You cursed in my presence earlier without any reprimand. Why would he be any different?" Which inspired a good question. "Who taught you that language?"

She frowned. "What language?"

"Fuck."

"Are you kidding? The lycans use that word all the time."

Ah, yes, they would. "That makes sense."

"Would you prefer me not to use it?"

"On the contrary, I hope you do." I stepped closer, crowding her against the wall. "Especially in the bedroom. The phrase 'Fuck me' is a personal favorite. Feel free to use it anytime." I wrapped the scarf around her reddening neck and slowly draped the long end between her breasts. "Mmm, that is a gorgeous color on you."

She swallowed, her blue irises heating. "Th-thank you."

I nearly kissed her again when her stomach rumbled just loud enough to remind me of her mortal needs.

Food.

Yes.

Then a walk outside to entertain my pet. My lips curled at the reminder of her reaction earlier. While I hadn't appreciated her comments about Silas, I had enjoyed her banter.

I brushed my knuckles against her cheek, down the column of her neck, and over her breast, then linked my fingers with hers. I brought her wrist up to my lips. "Time for mortal sustenance."

Chapter Eight

RAE

I'd witnessed vampires take humans several times over the years, but nothing compared to Kylan and Mikael. Normally, the screams were of pain, not pleasure. But Mikael had clearly enjoyed Kylan's attentions.

My thighs tensed just thinking about it.

"You all right, pet?" Kylan asked, a devious twinkle in his gaze. He could probably smell my arousal.

"I'm fine." I forced myself to take another bite of the food he'd given me. Some sort of creamy pasta with far too much flavor. When I'd asked for protein and greens, he'd laughed and handed me this instead, calling it a treat. All I sensed was that I would be very ill later.

I pushed the half-eaten bowl away. Kylan smirked and plucked the spoon from my hand to take his own bite. "The richness, right?" he asked after swallowing. "The universities, as you call them, only provide you with basic nutrition. But don't worry, I'll retrain your taste buds in time, and you'll thank me for it later."

"Why?" I asked. "Food is meant to give you energy. Nothing else."

"Oh, darling." He gave me a look. "Food provides pleasure. Trust me."

"How?"

"Remind me to introduce you to chocolate later." He finished my bowl and placed it in the sink. "We'll eat more after our walk."

I touched my stomach and shook my head. "I don't think I can handle that."

"Believe me. You will." He grabbed my hand and pulled me from my perch on the counter. "Come, little lamb. Time to go outside and play."

"You really want me to punch you," I muttered.

"I'd love for you to try, yes." His attention fell to my feet as he frowned. "You need shoes."

I hadn't known what he wanted me to wear with the pants, so I'd not chosen any footwear. Most of my wardrobe at school had been heels and dresses—the proper wardrobe of females. I only deviated from the norm during physical training, where I typically wore nothing.

"Right," he muttered, releasing my hand and disappearing in a blink.

A literal blink.

Like he phased before my eyes.

I'd seen vampires do that at the university, but nothing quite that impressive.

He really is ancient. Over five thousand years old, if the textbooks were right. But he didn't act the way I expected. He was almost... playful.

"Here," Kylan said, appearing before me again, boots and socks in hand. "Put these on. Now."

He said it as if he expected me to argue. I accepted them

with a sweet smile and donned them without a word, just to prove him wrong.

I stood and batted my eyes at him. "I'm ready to play outside, Your Highness."

Amusement lightened his near-black eyes to a luscious brown shade. "So you can behave like a good little pet. I'll remember that later."

He pulled a knitted hat over my head and ears before I could mutter a retort and led me through the oversized dining area toward a set of glass doors.

All my irritation fled at the gorgeous sight ahead of us. *Mountains. Snow. Trees.*

My heart skipped a beat, my lips parting in awe. Not even the blast of cool air could dispel my fascination. I stepped through the open threshold, my attention on the mountains in the distance.

Gorgeous.

I wanted to get closer, to explore. I started to run, eager to—

My feet tripped over one another, sending me forward into a bank of snow. I pushed upward, confused, and slipped onto my side with an "Omph" before rolling onto my back to stare up at the stars.

Or perhaps those were just the lights flickering behind my eyes.

Ow.

"Well, that was graceful." Kylan appeared, his expression amused as he held out a hand. "How about we try that again, but instead of trying to jog on top of the snow, you learn how to walk through it."

I blinked, my teeth beginning to chatter from the cold seeping through my clothes to my bare skin beneath. He waggled his fingers and I grabbed them, not knowing how else to move. With a tug, he had me standing again, his palms brushing the fluffy white flakes from my arms.

"Take a step," he urged.

I did and nearly fell again, his arm around my waist the

only thing keeping me upright. I grabbed his sweater, pulling him closer for balance.

This was not nearly as fun as I expected.

He chuckled, his hands falling to my hips. "I suddenly have the urge to take you skiing, just to see how you handle it."

My brow furrowed. "What?"

"It's a sport and one of my favorites. I'll show you sometime."

A sport? "Like a game?"

He shook his head, his expression saddening. "While I understand the shifting of balance and power, I will never agree with the destruction of your culture."

I stared at him. "What do you mean?"

"You believe the world to have always been led in this way, but it's a lie, little lamb. Humans ruled once while the rest of us hid." He palmed my cheek. "It all changed after a lycan took the wrong female. Your kind tried to weaponize his pack, and we retaliated."

My breath quickened. *Humans ruled once?* What? How was that even possible?

"You outnumbered us," he added as he wrapped his arm around my waist and gave me a nudge. I took a step only because he forced me to, and another after he nudged me again. "There you go," he praised, coaxing me alongside him. "It's about nine inches deep here. If you keep a steady pace, you'll be fine."

Somehow I doubted that. While the snow gave way with each of my movements, it also threatened to trap my limbs by clinging to my boots.

"Anyway, back to what I was saying. You outnumbered us quite significantly, but a flock of sheep pales in comparison to a pissed-off wolf. And exterminating ninety percent of your race, give or take, made controlling you all the easier."

My legs moved—slowly—with his while my mind fought to process his words. Humans were fragile with shortened life spans. How could we have ever led these superior beings? Why would they bother to hide?

Kylan picked up our pace, his arm a band around my lower back.

"It's the one hundred and seventeenth year of this new world, Raelyn." His sigh mingled with the night air, denoting the cooler weather. I marveled at it and his words. All my years were shrouded in humid nights or the occasional cool evening, never this crisp air littered in wintry delight.

This is my new life.

It wasn't perfect, far from it.

But it could be worse.

"I miss the old world," he continued, his voice soft. "More often than I should."

I gazed up at him, curious. "What do you miss about it?"

His eyes were on the stars as we walked, his expression distant. "I've always preferred my peace and quiet, but I could always count on humans to provide some form of entertainment. It evolved over the centuries, changing from generation to generation, always a new shift in cultural evolution. Until we destroyed those with determined souls and left only the meek alive to be retrained and bred for our personal diversions."

A shiver traversed my spine at the harsh statement.

"There's no hunt anymore," he murmured. "No excitement. An hour drive to Kylan City will place me in the center of a metropolis where I can have whatever I want, whenever I want, without so much as batting an eye. How is that enjoyable?" He finally looked away from the sky, his gaze returning to mine. "Humans don't argue or fight anymore. You just bend over and take it. I miss the challenge, Raelyn."

We stopped walking, the tree line of the forest before us and the estate at our back. His pupils pulsed, the predator inside him lurking in wait. I should submit, glance down, anywhere other than directly at him, but I found myself hypnotized by his beauty.

Seeing him in his true form with Mikael had awoken something inside of me, something hungry. Which had, of course, been the point. I was smart enough to realize that. But I couldn't deny his enigmatic appeal.

"How have you survived?" he marveled, repeating his question from earlier. "You should be a shell of a woman, just like the others, but there isn't an ounce of fear in you. How did your professors not notice your potential?"

"Do you want me to fear you?" Because a logical part of me did. Yet something about him inspired me to bite back instead of yield.

He wrapped his palm around the back of my neck, beneath my hair, and pulled me against him. "I want to know why you don't when everyone else does, how you've managed to go undetected in a society where even the slightest hint of rebellion gets you sent to the blood farms."

I trembled at the mention of the infamous factories where humans were sent to be bled to death. So many of my classmates had been sent there throughout the years, and several more just this week instead of attending the Blood Day ceremonies.

Only a thousand were chosen across the world.

Out of how many, I didn't know.

"Even now, you don't jump to reply as you should," he whispered. "I could kill you without blinking, Raelyn, yet you trust me not to."

"Maybe I'm not afraid to die," I whispered back at him.

His grip tightened. "Don't lie to me. You want to live. Why else would you have desired immortality?"

He had me there. "I should be afraid of you."

"You should," he agreed.

"But I'm not."

"I know. Now tell me why."

"I can't." *Because I don't know why.*

He cocked a brow. "Perhaps I need to inspire a better reply."

"That—"

His lips silenced mine as he walked me backward. Something hard hit my back—a tree, maybe?—causing the air to whoosh from my lungs. I clung to his sweater, needing his strength to ground me. His palm moved to my throat, holding me where he wanted me as his tongue slid into my mouth, taunting me to retaliate.

But I couldn't.

Not after what I'd seen.

Not after how my body responded to his.

I practically melted against him instead, my resolve tarnished and destroyed in less than twenty-four hours in his presence. I didn't want to be attracted to him, to desire him, to *need* him. Yet, I did, more than anyone I could recall ever yearning for before. Was it his age? His experience? Being the head of a bloodline?

Warmth caressed my veins despite our frigid surroundings, his tongue unleashing endorphins I'd never knew existed.

Goddess, I'd never felt anything like this, as if he'd lit my soul on fire from within. Why him? Why now? Why here?

It couldn't last. It wouldn't. I'd die in a blink of his lifetime, gone and forgotten.

But at least my life would have purpose and fulfillment.

Would it, though?

His hips rocked into mine, derailing my thoughts. So demanding, so *big*. I shuddered against him, both terrified of his potential and excited. The palm around my throat slid downward to my breast. A jolt hit me dead center at the contact.

Oh, I like that...

Silas had touched me there previously, but only in a classroom setting. I'd been his subject for an exam. He was being measured by how fast he could bring me to orgasm, of which I helped him by faking it. He had returned the favor an hour later for my own test.

But Kylan's touch was different, rawer, more real and

intense. He tweaked my nipple through the fabric, causing me to moan.

I couldn't remember the point of this demonstration anymore, or why he'd started, but I didn't want it to end.

He lifted me up, causing my legs to wrap around his waist as he balanced me against the hard surface behind me. Then he began kissing me in earnest. Before was just a taste of what he could do, an introduction, a test. And I must have passed because he unleashed everything now, dominating me down to my very core.

My head spun.

This was the predator.

The animal.

The male who wanted to devour me.

And all I could do was accept him.

My arms circled his neck, my mouth opening even more for his sensual assault, my tongue not daring to defy his. He wanted me, so he would have me.

Obey or die.

He was right.

I didn't want to die.

But I also didn't mind living... for this.

"Fuck," he whispered. "I can't remember the last time I wanted someone like this."

His words startled me almost as much as his fangs sinking into my lower lip. I yelped, then moaned.

"Oh..." I liked that far too much—his tongue against the open wound. I trembled violently, the pleasure overwhelming all my senses. "What...?" I couldn't finish, my legs tightening around him. "Kylan," I breathed, unsure of what was happening.

His groin moved against the sensitive juncture between my thighs, heightening the sensation. I whimpered, my head falling to his shoulder.

What are you doing to me?

A knot formed inside me, twisting and pulling, shooting electricity to every nerve.

"Give in," he whispered, his hardness stroking my clit through the jeans.

How?

Why?

I'd been touched there before, but never like this. I usually squirmed, but he elicited a demand for more.

"Now, Raelyn." He captured my chin, pulling my mouth back up to his, and bit me again. I could hardly feel the sting through the euphoria that followed.

And then I was falling.

Tumbling.

Darkness consuming my vision, followed by bright lights.

A scream I hardly recognized as my own.

And a satisfied chuckle that was all Kylan.

The explosion went on and on, my limbs shaking uncontrollably as pleasure overwhelmed every sensor.

An orgasm. A real one.

I thought I'd experienced them before, but no. Nothing compared to this, to Kylan, to the way he so masterfully owned mine.

No wonder Mikael had been so exhausted. I could barely continue kissing Kylan, let alone pull away. If his arms weren't holding me upright, I would have fallen.

"I stand corrected," he murmured against my lips. "*That was glorious.*" He took my mouth again, harsher now, his body rock hard against mine.

It took me a moment to follow his reference, to remember his words about Mikael coming earlier.

"Would you like to see him come? It's really quite glorious."

I wondered how that worked, the relationship between them. It was clearly sexual in nature, but Kylan hadn't taken any pleasure. Did he expect me to reciprocate now on both our behalves? An image of taking him in my mouth flashed behind my eyes. I knew the mechanics, could perform them well. Was I to offer now? To kneel in the snow? Unzip his pants and swallow his cock?

"Still not afraid," he said, smiling against my mouth. "It's amazing."

His pupils engulfed his irises, a startling sight in the night, especially with me being the focus of his unveiled lust. "Why would I fear you after that?" I asked.

He chuckled darkly and drew his nose across my cheek. "Why indeed." The words were low, seductive, and eerily controlled. "I could destroy you, Raelyn."

"You already said you would."

"Yes," he whispered, his lips sliding to my neck. "I did. And yet, you cling to me as if I'm your source of life."

"Because you are," I replied, arching into him. "You own me."

He stilled, his mouth hovering over my pulse. "Do I?"

"Yes." I felt exhausted despite barely doing anything today, my body replete in the strangest of ways.

"And you don't fear me." Not a question, but a statement.

"I should, but no, I don't." Not really, anyway. Not the way I should. "If I'm going to die, I'll die with my dignity intact." He only derailed that resolve for a second with his threats against Silas, but now that no longer applied.

I would die when Kylan deemed it time.

I wouldn't beg for a different fate, nor would I just lie on my back and accept it.

But to fear the inevitable no longer seemed rational. What would happen, would happen, with or without my compliance.

"Why obey when the end result will never change?" I asked, drawing back to meet his sheltered gaze. No sign of emotion dwelled in his expression. No anger. No curiosity. Just Kylan inscrutably observing me.

"The end result being?"

"My death."

"I see." He tilted his head, his hands falling to my hips. "You assume so quickly that death is all I have planned for you."

"Don't you? That's your method, isn't it? Fuck the harem, then kill them?"

I regretted the words as soon as I said them. They were abrasive and challenging, and they simmered in his gaze as he stared back at me. I'd struck a nerve, one that shrouded us in ominous silence for far too long.

Was he reliving the moments in his mind? Relishing in what he'd done? Envisioning how he would eventually slaughter me? Because his darkening expression suggested he wanted to now, as did the way his grip tightened almost painfully.

"You should be careful, Raelyn," he said, his voice low. "I'm understanding to a point, but speaking of actions you know nothing about is liable to earn you a punishment you won't appreciate."

He lifted me off him, forcing me to stand, then released me so suddenly that I nearly fell.

The loss of his body heat coupled with the frost coating his features sent a chill down my spine. "This has been enlight—" He spun with a growl as a dark-skinned female ran across the grounds at incredible speed.

A vampire.

No, not just any vampire.

Angelica.

The human who won the Immortal Cup when I was fifteen. She'd been an inspiration to me, proof that females could win immortality just as well as males.

I gaped as she fell to her knees in the snow at Kylan's feet, her brown hair splaying around her. "Y-your Highness. I came as s-soon as I could."

"What is it?" Kylan knelt beside her, his hand going to her sweater.

Blood, I realized. She was covered in it.

"What's happened?" he demanded when she didn't immediately respond.

"T-Tremayne," she whispered, her shoulders shaking.

"What about Tremayne?" he asked, clearly recognizing

the name whereas I didn't. My studies focused on the royals, not their constituents. "What did he do?"

Angelica trembled, her fear palpable as he forced her to lift her head and meet his gaze.

She's terrified—not of the situation, but of him, I realized.

Kylan palmed her cheek, his voice softening. "I won't discipline you for his actions, Angelica. Now tell me what he's done."

She swallowed, doubt radiating from her expression. Kylan was renowned for his wicked punishments, his reign not a kind one. Yet he'd been mostly gentle with me, even when I'd clearly pushed him over the edge.

Which version is the real Kylan?

"He killed them all, Your Highness," Angelica whispered.

"All of them," he repeated. "All of whom?"

"Every single human under his employment at Tremayne Tower." Her pupils widened. "It was a bloodbath. I came here to tell you, to warn you, that he's in Kylan City now and I think he's going to do the same at K Hotel. He's saying..." She shuddered, her expression falling. "He's telling everyone that you executed the order."

Chapter Nine

RAE

Kylan went eerily still.

Angelica whimpered, returning her head to the ground while I stood frozen behind them.

He's telling everyone that you executed the order.

To slaughter humans as he did his harem?

It seemed something he would do, based on his reputation, but the rigidness in his spine suggested otherwise.

He rose slowly, his hands fisted at his sides. When he turned toward me, I saw the royal in full display—regal brow, tightened jaw, cold eyes.

His expression required submission.

I tried to bow, to yield to his dominance, but my knees refused to bend. Even my neck protested the notion.

You don't fear me. His words from earlier taunted my mind, trying and failing to inspire reason.

I should. I know I should. But you're right; I don't and I have no idea why.

He took in my disobedient form with a sweep of his gaze before refocusing on the other woman.

"Rise, Angelica," he demanded. "We have work to do." He glanced at me again. "I need you upstairs in my suite. Now."

I didn't argue, not with the barely contained anger simmering in his dark eyes. He looked ready to kill, and I didn't want to be the target of that rage.

I pulled my jacket closed and scurried into the house, up the stairs, and directly to his room.

Now what? I wondered, chewing my lip. Did he want me naked again? Was he planning to join me at all? Had I just been dismissed for the rest of the evening?

I toed off my boots, setting them on the mat inside the closet. Then I removed my jacket and hung it on a nearby hook to dry. What next? My clothes?

The door opened before I had a chance to disrobe, Kylan's sudden presence behind me ominous. I turned slowly, terrified of what I would find in his expression, but needing to know all the same.

He merely stared at me, his dark eyes hiding every detail.

Does he not care?

Is he just bored?

But as I studied him, a glimmer of something flashed in the depths of his gaze. It was there and gone so quickly that I almost missed it, could have easily just made it up. But no. It was definitely there.

Devastation.

"We need to take a trip to Kylan City," he said flatly, stepping closer. He pinched my chin between his thumb and his forefinger, his gaze intensifying. "I need you on your best behavior, Raelyn, which means bowing and engaging in all the formalities." His chest met mine as he backed me into the wall. "If you disobey, I will be forced to punish you publicly, and you do not want me to have to do that."

The promise in his words sent a chill down my spine. No, I definitely didn't want that. "I understand," I whispered, swallowing.

"This is not how I wanted to spend our first week together, but Tremayne has left me no choice. If I could leave you here, I would." He almost sounded apologetic, which made no sense. Royals took their favored harem members with them everywhere. Being his only consort at the moment left him little choice. "I mean it, Raelyn. I need you to behave."

"I said I understood," I replied, then quickly added, "Your Highness," to lessen the tone of my words.

He shook his head disapprovingly. "Not off to a good start, Raelyn."

"We're not in the city yet," I muttered.

He raised both brows, his patience clearly nonexistent. "I love your courage, but now is not the time unless you want me to beat your ass red and then fuck it in front of a room full of my constituents. And if you're really disobedient, I'll be forced to let them enjoy you as well. Is that what you want?"

My lips parted, shocked by his brash description and the furious way he said it, as if even the notion of it all infuriated him. I cleared my throat, searching for the nerve to respond. "I… No. Of course I don't want that." Who the hell would?

His grip on my chin tightened, his gaze narrowing. "My reputation is what keeps this territory alive. You may not fear me, but others do, and I need it to stay that way. Do you understand?"

I blinked.

Had he just… confided in me? Explained why he needed me to behave? Essentially admitted that the mask he wore was for the public alone? Because that fit what I'd seen so far, that the Kylan of my textbooks did not match the Kylan standing before me now.

The royal I'd read about would have no issue with fucking me in public—including during Blood Day—and would do so again now without caring at all about the report Angelica had just delivered.

But he did care.

Enough to necessitate a trip to Kylan City.

Which meant he never gave the order for those human deaths.

I studied him, his darkening gaze, the tight line of his lips, the tension in his cheekbones, and his strained posture as he continued to hold my chin firmly between his thumb and forefinger.

He wanted me to understand not only his request but also the importance behind it. He needed me to comply. "You don't want to punish me." The words weren't the ones he was waiting for me to say, but they were the first my mouth allowed me to voice.

"Not in the way our society requires, no," he agreed. "But I will if you do something that necessitates it."

"Like argue with you in public." Something I never thought I'd consider saying out loud, let alone do, but my reactions to Kylan hadn't been sane since the moment he stood in front of me on that field.

"Yes, or anyone else," he replied. "I need your fear, Raelyn."

"And if I can't give you that?"

"Then I'll be forced to make you fear me."

The words alone caused me to tremble. "I don't want that."

"I don't either."

"Why maintain an image of torment when you don't enjoy it?" I asked, genuinely curious.

"Because it keeps the peace. Someone has to be the bad guy, Raelyn. It's a burden I've carried for centuries, and my people thrive beneath it—or they have, anyway—until recently."

"Until recently?" I repeated.

He shook his head. "I've already said more than I intended to say." He stepped back, releasing my jaw to rub his own and allowing me a brief glimpse at the exhausted male behind the charade. The male who led under a cloud of brutality because he believed it to be the best governing method, and maybe he was right. This society thrived on violence, and he was the notorious king—the eldest of them all, save the Goddess herself.

"Tell me you'll behave, Raelyn."

I essentially already did, I wanted to say, but he clearly needed to hear the words to believe them. So I did the only thing I could to pacify him. I kneeled, my head bowing to the floor as I gave him the highest form of respect a human could give a superior by leaving myself exposed and completely at his mercy.

"Yes, My Prince," I said, refusing to move or look up until he released me.

He said nothing for so long I thought he might be testing me, but then he crouched before me and used his finger to lift my chin. "I like you in this position, Raelyn," he murmured. "It could only be improved by you being naked."

Good luck with that, I wanted to say. Instead I whispered, "Whatever you wish, Your Highness."

His lips quirked. "I almost believe that, Raelyn. But your eyes imply otherwise." He brushed his thumb over my mouth and stood again. "You're going to need a new outfit. I'll ask Mikael to arrange it." He glanced at me. "I'd be lying if I apologized, so I won't, because I'll definitely be enjoying every minute of it."

My brow furrowed.

What kind of outfit will I be wearing?

* * *

Lace.

That's what Kylan meant when he mentioned my need

for new apparel. The deep-red translucent dress—if it could be called that—left everything exposed beneath and ended at the tops of my thighs. Kylan had wrapped his suit jacket around my shoulders for the journey, but I knew it would disappear as soon as we arrived.

He sat beside me in the back of the limousine, his palm on my thigh while he gazed out the window at the growing city lights. Mikael was across from us in a black dress shirt and pants, sipping a glass of red wine, his face hidden ominously in the shadows.

The moon illuminated the snowy landscape, which ended against a harsh blockade coated in floodlights. A chill crept down my spine at the familiar structures dotting the perimeters—watchtowers. Vigils maintained those huts, all serving the sole purpose of keeping humans in line. I'd wanted to join their ranks because they were afforded certain privileges where others were not. Such as decent sleeping quarters and food.

Most would say ending up in a royal harem or clan harem was an even better fate because of the luxuries provided to those who served their masters sexually. After hearing the way some of the mortal consorts were treated on Blood Day, I strongly begged to differ.

But Kylan had been good to me. So far.

His palm tightened on my thigh as the limousine slowed, approaching the city's primary gates. "Remove the jacket and straddle me, Raelyn." Not a request, but a command.

Arguing wasn't an option, not with the perimeter of military-clad men and women waiting for a reason to hurt a defiant slave. They were trained to capture, not to kill, for a reason.

Vampires and lycans loved to punish errant humans.

I had no desire to join their list of insubordinates.

The wool slipped from my shoulders as I slid onto Kylan's lap, my too-short dress bunching at my hips. Mikael gave an appreciative noise, my ass clearly on display.

"She's beautiful, isn't she?" Kylan murmured, his palm

wrapping around the back of my neck.

"Gorgeous," Mikael agreed.

"She tastes amazing, too." Kylan spoke the words against my mouth. "Open, Raelyn."

I parted my lips for his tongue and shivered as he dipped inside to mark his territory in the hottest of ways.

Damn, I didn't want to like him, but the man knew how to kiss. He wasn't my first, but he was certainly my best. So much passion, experience, and heat wrapped up into a technique that made my toes curl.

He pulled me closer to rest the rigid length of his erection right against my sensitive flesh. One upward stroke had me damp and ready despite his pants between us. I almost hated his ability to convince my body to take him even when my mind resisted, but I couldn't muster enough anger to care when he pressed into me again.

To be desired by such a powerful man, to be handled with such confidence, was an intoxicatingly addictive sensation.

I shouldn't love this.

Shouldn't enjoy it.

But fuck if I could stop myself from moaning in approval.

His incisors pierced my lower lip sharply, whether in reprimand or excitement, I didn't know. It stung, bringing tears to my eyes as he pulled away to examine his inflicted wound.

The window whirred down beside us, but his focus never left my mouth. "Yes?" he asked, his voice holding an edge I never wanted to hear directed at me.

"Forgive me, Your Highness. We were not expecting your arrival and—"

"Do I require an invitation to my own city?" he demanded.

"N-no, My—"

The window closed before the human could finish. Kylan traced the blood oozing down my chin with his tongue and followed it up to my mouth. His murmur of approval went straight to my heart, sending it into a chaotic rhythm against my rib cage. He'd lightly bitten me earlier, but this was different, more intimate, more purposeful.

A marking.

He kissed me with purpose, his lips dominating mine and leaving no room for questions or arguments. I belonged to him, to kiss, to fuck, to do whatever he wished with, and he wanted everyone—including me—to know it.

My head spun from the onslaught of sensations and emotions pummeling me at once. I didn't understand what he'd just done, or how he'd done it, but it forced me to bow to his will.

His gaze glittered as he released my mouth, his pupils dilated with unrestrained hunger. "You may just survive this yet, little lamb."

Chapter Ten

KYLAN

I hated the city, especially at midnight. Vampires littered the sidewalks and roads, running errands or grabbing a bite to eat on their work breaks. Several wore managerial robes designating their roles in overseeing the city's various human employees. No one wanted to do the necessary grunt work to keep our society alive, hence the mortal purpose.

A cruel world, but a practical one.

Money flowed as it always had, just in different currencies now and to purchase more useful items—like blood.

And I sat at the top of the food chain in this territory, which necessitated certain protocols. Such as keeping Mikael's presence a secret.

I kept Raelyn on my lap in case we were stopped again

and also because I enjoyed her there. She held on to my shoulders, her red hair falling around us as I kissed her again, softly this time.

Whether she realized it or not, she was already learning my tastes and preferences. Her lips parted for my tongue, accepting what I desired and granting me unhindered access.

My fingers knotted in her silky strands, holding her where I wanted her as my driver gave an indication of our arrival by flipping the locks. Raelyn didn't notice, too lost to our embrace, her sweet arousal singing to my cock and begging me to do more than just kiss her.

In time, I would.

But not now.

I eased her away with a gentle tug on her hair. She blinked at me as if lost in a daze, causing my lips to curl. "I barely fed from you and you're already passion-drunk."

That little bite of my fangs against her bottom lip had been enough to mark her as my possession, but not nearly enough for a proper taste. Yet, she clearly enjoyed the introduction.

I rapped my knuckles against the window, indicating it was safe to disturb me now.

Judith wasted no time, greeting me with a formal bow before she finished opening the door. "My Prince."

Gavin and Karl joined her on their knees, waiting for me to allow them to rise.

The three of them were among the most trusted on my security team, Judith being their superior.

I lifted Raelyn off my lap to place her on the seat beside me as I slid out of the car. "Come, little lamb." I held out a hand for her to join me and brushed my lips against her temple as she obeyed without argument.

She shivered, the heated garage around us doing little to protect her exposed skin from the wintry elements outside. I fixed her dress, pulling it down to her upper thighs again, and sighed at seeing my three security members still kneeling. "Stand," I said. "Status, Judith?"

My favorite lieutenant straightened her spine, meeting my gaze. "We're safe here, Your Highness. I've already turned the security feeds on a loop all the way up to the suite."

I smiled. "Excellent. Mikael, would you like to join us?"

"Of course, Your Highness," he murmured, exiting the back seat with a grin for my security detail. "Judith."

A faint blush tinged her cheeks as she replied, "Mikael."

My blood virgin charmed everyone in his path, proving him more than worth my time and investment. Hence my reason for hiding him. The target on his back was almost as wide as mine, everyone knowing what he meant to me. I never announced his whereabouts. This trip was no different.

I retrieved my suit jacket from the limousine and wrapped it around Raelyn's trembling shoulders. "Lead the way, Judith."

She inclined her blonde head and turned with Mikael beside her. I followed, my palm against Raelyn's back to keep her with me, while Gavin and Karl trailed behind us. The elevator ride up went by in a flash and deposited us in one of my favorite homes—a lavish penthouse boasting seven bedrooms with en-suite bathrooms, two kitchens, several lounges, and floor-to-ceiling windows overlooking the city.

Perfection, opulence, home.

Zelda appeared in the hallway, blue eyes downcast, and a smile tilting her lips. Some of my human staff had arrived before us to prepare the space. It seemed wasteful to employ different help at all my homes, so I required them to travel with me.

"Midnight lunch is ready," she announced while curtsying.

Mikael wasted no time in following my blonde chef, while Raelyn remained dutifully beside me. She could be herself here without fear of punishment, but I refrained from telling her that. This was our practice round. If she passed, I would take her with me to visit Tremayne. If she failed, I'd keep her here with Mikael under Judith's protection.

There were very few I trusted with my valuable possessions, and Judith was among them.

I removed my jacket from Raelyn's shoulders and handed it off to Gavin. "Are you hungry, little lamb?" I asked her. She hadn't eaten anything since the pasta from the house, and that was hours ago.

"Yes, Your Highness," she replied, her voice low and sultry.

So far, so good. "Then let's follow Mikael, hmm?" I nudged her lower back with my palm, sending her in the direction Zelda had come from.

Raelyn's steps were steady, but her heart rate raced in my ears. It seemed far longer than twenty-four hours since I selected her for my harem, which was odd. Life spans usually passed quickly, not slowly, but I seemed to be savoring my time with her as if a year passed with each minute.

Mikael glanced up as I entered, his expression not contrite in the slightest for being caught standing between Zelda's open legs. She was hoisted up on the counter, her cheeks red, her lips parted.

"I see you had another meal in mind," I murmured, Raelyn freezing at my side.

My blood virgin shrugged. "After that show in the limousine, can you blame me?"

I arched a brow. "Are you implying I didn't handle you thoroughly enough earlier?"

His dimples peeked at me. "That was before my nap."

"Insatiable," I said, returning his smile before focusing on the tense woman beside me. "Raelyn, eat something and wear whatever Mikael gives you. We leave in an hour." I turned, then glanced back at my blood virgin with a pointed look. "Mikael, don't make a mess in my kitchen."

His responding snort trailed after me as I went straight to my office to make the requisite calls.

By now, my presence in the city would be known, as word traveled quickly. No one enjoyed my surprise visits, which was precisely why I chose to make them.

Judith joined me, phone in hand. "Where are you headed, Your Highness?"

I smiled at my always prepared lieutenant. She would help dismantle the security feeds. "You may want to sit down, Judith. I have a list of arrangements for this visit." We would be staying for a few weeks to clean up this mess, and while here, I might as well invite a few royals.

What better way to narrow down the list of suspects than by throwing a party? Alcohol loosened tongues and provided a breeding ground for suspicious behavior. It would also afford me the opportunity to reassert my place as the eldest living being of the royal lines.

Yes, vampire politics was a devious dance I'd mastered through the ages.

Raelyn would be my bait.

And the culprit would attempt to bite.

Welcome to Kylan City. I dare you to come out and play.

* * *

"Mmm, you look positively edible, little lamb."

Raelyn stood in the foyer wearing a black gown, her auburn hair pulled back to expose her neck. Lace bled into silk, leaving her seductively covered in all the right places. I traced the plunging neckline with my finger. Her nipples beaded in response, the rosy color concealed, but the shape outlined perfectly.

The slits up both her legs made removing the dress unnecessary, but I very likely would indulge in the pleasantness of it later.

I kissed her thundering pulse and skimmed my nose up her throat to her ear. "Mikael tells me you've been the picture of obedience." I'd stopped by his room on my way to meeting her in the foyer. "Unfortunately, rather than reward you, I need you to accompany me on what is likely going to be an unpleasant visit."

I tilted her chin, forcing her gaze to mine.

"I realize your university training has equipped you with the proper protocols, but this meeting pales in comparison to your meager preparation. As such, I'm inclined to gift you with a safe word. If, at any time, you feel you're about to break decorum, refer to me as 'Your Highness' and I will do what I can to improve the situation. Otherwise, continue to address me as 'My Prince' to let me know you're all right. Do you understand?"

It was the only leniency I could grant her, and even then, it didn't guarantee I could help her. Vampire society maintained certain requirements for humans, and while I may not admire them all, I understood them.

Humans were inferior beings, their place at the bottom of the food chain well established. But unlike many of my kind, I chose to remember how we started—as mortal.

Raelyn swallowed, her pupils flaring. "I understand, My Prince."

"Kylan," I corrected. "When in private, you call me Kylan."

"Kylan," she repeated. "I'm trying to obey," she added, a slight edge to her tone that forced my lips to twitch.

"There's my spirited female," I murmured, drawing my thumb over the mark I'd left on her lip. "Don't lose her tonight, Raelyn. I'm hoping to play more with her later."

"You want me to obey one moment, then rebel the next." Her gaze narrowed. "Would I be punished for calling you mercurial, Kylan?"

I laughed.

I'd certainly been called far worse.

"Oh, little lamb, we're just getting started." She hadn't seen my cruel mask yet, but she was about to. "Let's go."

Chapter Eleven

RAE

Kylan's palm burned against my lower back as he handed his car keys to a human. He'd insisted on driving himself, taking a sleek black two-seater from the garage that resembled the vehicle we rode in after the Blood Day selection.

Was that just last night?

It felt like a decade ago.

A female dressed in a tailored suit opened the door for us with a low bow, her shudder evident.

Kylan guided us through the threshold, ignoring the woman, his steps sure.

Several vampires milled inside, some sitting on leather couches, others in the lounge near a bar boasting oversized televisions, and a handful standing in line before a long wooden welcoming desk.

I followed Kylan's movements as he led me to an elevator bank near the back, his thumbprint calling the car down as a human appeared.

"May I help you, Sire?"

The palm against my lower back tensed as Kylan addressed the man. "Do you have any idea whom you are speaking to?"

A shiver traversed my spine at the lethality lurking in Kylan's tone. Referring to a royal as anything other than *My Prince* or *Your Highness* was a grave offense, especially for a human.

"I-I... no... Y-your—"

Heels clacked loudly over the marble floors, approaching us from the left and silencing the poor human boy who had fallen to his knees. "Your Highness, I apologize. I hadn't expected your presence, or I would have properly informed my employees. Please forgive me." A woman knelt beside the male, her dark head bowed.

The elevator chose that moment to arrive.

Silence fell around us, everyone waiting for a response. Kylan had finally been noticed and recognized.

Rather than grant them a show, he guided me through the threshold, punched a button, and allowed the doors to close. I didn't dare speak or ask for an explanation. The boy had insulted his position; that had to burn. All humans were taught to recognize royals at a young age. How that human failed to realize the one in charge of his own region was beyond me.

Kylan pressed his thumb into my back, massaging gentle circles.

Is he trying to reassure me? Calm me?

A ding announced our arrival, and the motion against my back stopped.

The doors whirred open to reveal two suited men with guns, both aimed our way. I forced my gaze to the floor, not wanting to encourage retaliation, but it wasn't needed. They dropped to their knees with murmurs of apology upon recognizing Kylan.

He ignored them and escorted me into an ornate suite with windows overlooking the city—much like his own home. It took effort to keep from studying my surroundings with the elegant furnishings glittering beneath the lights.

Gold, I realized.

It lined the floor as well, weaving its way between the marble stones, exuding squandered wealth.

Kylan didn't seem fazed or impressed, his palm steady at my back as he led us down a few steps into a living area filled with plush couches circled around an oversized metal—*gold*—table.

Two human females lay atop it, naked, pleasuring each other.

Kylan released me to circle them, leaving me alone and cold.

"Your Highness," a male greeted as he entered the room while buttoning his dress shirt.

The lack of shoes and socks suggested he'd dressed in a hurry. He bowed his blond head but didn't kneel like the others, indicating his higher ranking in society. I averted my gaze, knowing better than to make eye contact.

"To what do I owe the honor?"

"I hear you had quite the eventful evening, Tremayne." Kylan drew his finger down the spine of the female who lay on top of the other, his voice intrigued. "I stopped by to learn more and brought my new pet along for a potential lesson."

That's why he gave me a safe word.

My stomach clenched with the realization, my palms suddenly clammy.

If he asked me to join those women on the table... Oh Goddess, I couldn't even process the notion. That sort of training had been an optional course in school that I ignored in favor of a fencing class. My oral sex qualifications were for males alone.

"She's beautiful," Tremayne said, the sensation of his gaze crawling over my skin. "A rare redhead. Blood type?"

"B positive." Kylan returned to my side and stepped behind me, his hands on my shoulders. "Would you care for a closer look?"

"Always."

Kylan hooked his thumbs beneath the straps of my dress and slid them from my shoulders, down my biceps and lower, exposing my breasts. My nipples pebbled in the cool air, an army of goose bumps stampeding down my arms to where his hand stilled just below my elbow.

"Responsive," Tremayne praised, his voice lowering to an octave that churned my insides. He stepped close enough for me to smell his alcohol-laced breath. "Rosy, too. Remarkable choice, as always, My Prince."

Kylan kissed my nape and drew up my sleeves, re-covering my chest. "I agree," he murmured, his hands falling to my hips. "Now, tell me what happened earlier." He pulled me backward and sat on the couch, his hands guiding me onto the cushion beside him.

Tremayne took a seat across from us, leaving the women on the table between us. "I assume you are referring to my purging of useless staff members?"

"I am." Kylan teased the slit of my dress while he spoke, his palm sliding inside to rest against my bare thigh. "Did they wrong you in some way?"

"They bored me." His tone suggested that alone justified the extermination. Kylan must have given him a look that said he required additional details because Tremayne sighed dramatically. "I desired a change of pace, new flesh to play with. These two are auditioning for a replacement role in my household, as are the three I left in my bedroom."

"The winner gains employment," Kylan translated, his hand branding my skin. "And the loser?"

"Doesn't deserve to live." Tremayne slapped the ass of the female on top. "This one's currently winning, having made the bitch below her orgasm twice so far. But honestly,

I'm not all that impressed with either of them, which is why I'd left them out here to practice with each other. The universities clearly require better instructors, Your Highness."

Kylan didn't reply immediately, his touch sliding farther up my leg to reach the apex between my thighs. "Is that true, Raelyn? Do you feel inadequately prepared to service me orally?"

His fingers brushed my intimate flesh, sending a jolt through my system.

I didn't want to like that.

Not here.

Not now.

But my body seemed hell-bent on denying reason, the memory of his touch earlier rekindling a flame meant only for him.

I swallowed, subduing the sensations and focusing on his question. "My studies"—I started slowly, considering each word before I uttered them—"groomed me to sexually satisfy males, My Prince. As a result, I feel confident in my oral abilities." Something he already knew after asking me about my highest marks.

He lightly traced the seam of my sex. "Having only owned Raelyn a day, I've not yet experienced the pleasure of her mouth, but her marks were quite high. Shall we put your theory to the test, Tremayne? See if Raelyn lives up to my standards? Because I assure you, they are quite high."

Here?

In front of Tremayne?

My palms dampened despite the ice grazing my spine. *What if I failed?*

"If I'm proven right?" Tremayne asked.

"Then I'll look into the matter personally with Raelyn as my star pupil for demonstration purposes." He slid a finger inside me, punctuating his point and sending my heart into a chaotic rhythm. I hadn't known what to expect from this visit, didn't have a clue where he intended to take me, and that was all entirely the point.

He owned me.

To do whatever he wanted, including finger-fucking me in front of a vampire subordinate.

I had no choice.

No argument.

No will.

No rights.

I'm Kylan's property.

The realization slammed into me so fast my breathing hitched. I'd been lying to myself for the last twenty-four hours, pretending to have a chance against a royal when none existed. I'd literally lost my mind, failed to remember my position in this world, and Kylan was effortlessly putting me back in my place.

His kiss during the selection ceremony had jarred my mind.

No, my unintentionally biting him had sent me down this path. That accidental clench of my jaw had flipped a defiant gene hidden deep inside me—the unmistakable urge to fight. I had wanted to die with my dignity intact.

My greatest error was believing Kylan would kill me immediately in response.

But of course he wouldn't. That'd be too easy.

No, he wanted to snuff out the light inside me before granting me death.

There would be no dignity left when he finished with me.

Another mental trick, just like the Immortal Cup selection.

Another way to break the human spirit.

That explained his mercurial behavior. He wanted me to oppose him because it prolonged his entertainment, but he also needed me to follow his orders to prove his power over me. Except no one would ever question his superiority, not even me.

"But if she proves you wrong," he continued, his voice

lowering. "Then we will have a very serious conversation on human potential and how to properly dispose of undesired employees."

"Properly dispose?" Tremayne repeated, snorting. "I burned them, just as you did your harem."

The reminder had my legs tensing, which resulted in Kylan sliding a second finger inside me—deep. A punishment for reacting? I clenched around him, my muscles unused to the intrusion. My training included superficial penetration, a way of keeping my innocence intact, something he was dangerously close to discovering.

Some humans chose to go through more in-depth erotic training, including intercourse, mostly because they desired to be in a harem.

I had never wanted to be in a harem or to be used for sexual gratification.

Becoming a Vigil or competing in the Immortal Cup had been my chosen path.

"Did I?" Kylan asked, his voice holding an edge. "I don't recall—"

A moan from the table cut him off as the female on the bottom began to convulse. Both men admired the show, making bile inch its way up my throat.

Tremayne smacked the ass of the human on top again, reddening her skin. "That's three, babe. Keep going."

The woman on the bottom squirmed, her moans turning to noises of protest, her body clearly not ready for more.

"Do you see my issue?" Tremayne asked, standing. "Switch positions. Now."

A pair of panicked green eyes met mine as the humans jumped to obey. It took considerable effort not to react. Not wanting to join them was a good motivator to remain still.

Kylan continued fondling me as if nothing had happened, as if the woman now lying on top didn't have red lines marring her skin from lying on the hard surface.

Tremayne pushed her bottom half down onto the other woman, causing her to whine in protest. His hand cracked across her ass so hard even I flinched.

"Do your job, slut," he growled, punctuating it with another slap.

Kylan chuckled.

Fucking laughed.

But of course he would. This was his playground, only a scaled-down version of it. He favored pain. Punishment. Hurt.

"Raelyn comes beautifully, something I learned earlier this evening." The motion between my legs shifted, his thumb sliding upward to stroke my clit. "Perhaps she should give a demonstration of how to properly display pleasure. Then she can return the favor by proving her oral worth. Assuming you're interested in the offer to test your previous theory, of course."

"I want to join you in investigating the universities."

"A bold request."

"It was my finding," he pressed.

Kylan's touch stilled, his thumb resting over my sensitive nub. "All right. If Raelyn proves unsatisfactory, then we'll approach the universities together. But I have a requirement of my own, Tremayne."

"Go on."

"If she proves herself valiant, then we will not only discuss the disposal of employees, but you will tell me why everyone in this city is under the impression that I issued an extermination edict."

Chapter Twelve

RAE

The air in the room chilled considerably.

Disapproval emanated from Kylan, the hand between my legs unflinching.

"You... you didn't issue an edict?" Tremayne asked, the first hint of unease entering his tone.

"No, I did not." He removed his touch, lifting his hand to my mouth. "Open, Raelyn."

I parted my lips, allowing his fingers to dip inside and coat my tongue in my own arousal. A new flavor I'd never experienced, one that sent a fresh rush of heat between my thighs despite the tension building around us.

"Don't play the fool, Tremayne," Kylan said, sounding bored. "I don't issue edicts indirectly, something you are more than aware of, so you know what I think?" He withdrew from my mouth to glide his damp fingers across my cheek and down my neck. "I think you've been spreading rumors based on assumption. Prove me wrong." He folded his leg over the other and dropped his arm over my shoulders.

Tremayne stood. "If you'll allow me a moment, I need my phone."

Kylan gave him a dismissive gesture with his hand. "I'm waiting."

"Your Highness." He bowed before scurrying out of the room, leaving us alone with the still-performing females. They had to be exhausted, and from the lack of moans, they were clearly not enjoying themselves.

"On your knees, Raelyn," Kylan murmured. "Between my legs."

My heart skipped a beat.

He didn't mean...

He couldn't really want me to...

Not after...

His arm shifted, his palm going to my nape and squeezing. "Now, Raelyn."

"Yes, My Prince," I managed, my throat dry.

I shifted to the floor, my knees immediately disapproving of the marble tile. With my head bowed, I placed my palms on his thighs, waiting for his next command.

"Prove your worth, little lamb. Show me how you earned those test scores." Challenge underlined his words.

Did he not believe my academic records?

Or was this because of Tremayne's comments regarding the universities?

A combination of both?

I drew my nails up his strong thighs to his belt and unfastened it without hesitation. If he wanted me to demonstrate my skills, to validate my education, then so be it.

Tests were something I excelled at.

This would be no different.

Unbutton.

Done.

Now, the zipper.

I swallowed as my ministrations revealed his more-than-impressive cock. Silas was my only comparison, and I didn't remember him being quite so... pronounced.

Kylan relaxed, his arms spreading across the back of the couch. "I'm already bored, Raelyn. Perhaps Tremayne is right, hmm? Do I need to leave you here to learn with his other toys since I don't have a harem of my own to properly teach you?"

My eyes narrowed. No. I absolutely did not want to be left here. Nor would that be necessary.

Unless I mess this up.

Which I'm not going to.

I hope.

Just do it, Rae. Pretend it's Silas.

Except this was most definitely *not* Silas. Not in size, stature, or power.

No, Kylan was bigger, longer, and far more intimidating.

I wrapped my hand around his shaft. *This is not going to fit inside me.*

It will. It has to.

My thighs clenched at the notion of him penetrating my innocence, a foreign ache burning in my lower belly that made me feel a little dizzy.

He would be harsh. Demanding. Maybe even cruel.

As if sensing my thoughts, he threaded his fingers through my hair and harshly tugged my head back to meet his smoldering gaze.

"Am I not being clear?" he asked, his grip tightening. "Suck my cock, Raelyn."

"Yes, My Prince." The hoarse quality of my voice betrayed my nerves, and the arch of his brow confirmed he'd heard it as well. Or, more likely, that was his way of expressing irritation.

What is wrong with you? You know how to do this.
But it's Kylan...
Just fucking do it!

I stroked his shaft, learning the silky feel of him. So long, soft, *hard*. I bent and traced the path of my palm with my tongue—from base to head. His fingers knotted even tighter in my hair, his impatience clear. My lips parted over the tip of him, sliding down as far as my throat allowed and sucking as I went.

"Your Highness, my phone," Tremayne said, appearing beside me.

I started to pull away, but Kylan pushed me right back down, causing his cock to go even deeper than before. My training kept my gag reflex at bay, allowing me to take the harsh thrust, but my breathing faltered.

He extended his opposite hand. "What am I looking for?" he asked, sounding completely unfazed.

My throat worked as I tried to inhale and failed. His palm held me in place, refusing my attempt to move.

Does he realize I can't breathe?

I couldn't use the safe word to tell him, not that I expected him to listen anyway.

"The second item," Tremayne said. "It shows you as the sender."

My eyes flicked up to Kylan's face, but he was too busy studying the device to notice. Tears clouded my vision, my lungs burning with the need for air. I swallowed—or tried—causing my throat to constrict around him. His grasp shifted just enough to grant me an inhale that instantly cooled my insides.

"Hmm, I see," he murmured, his hold loosening even more. "Continue, Raelyn," he said softly, his focus still on the item in his other hand.

I sucked him deep again—to the point of near pain—and hollowed my cheeks around him. His lack of an outward reaction almost irked me. He seemed too consumed by whatever he was doing with Tremayne's device to even notice my efforts below. I tried again, grasping his base with my palm and swallowing him all the way down to my hand.

The slight pressure on my head, the twitch of his fingers, confirmed it was working, despite his steady expression.

Again, I decided, perfecting the move and adding a swirl of my tongue to the tip. A hint of his salty essence leaked from the crown, fueling me onward.

His grip in my hair tightened again, his thighs tensing.

"I'll be keeping this." He tucked Tremayne's phone into his pocket and slid that palm to the back of my neck. "My technician needs to trace that message, as it was not sent by me."

"I didn't know, Your Highness. I thought—"

"No, Tremayne," he growled, his palm squeezing my nape as he took control of my rhythm. "You want to know why I won't name you sovereign? It's because you don't fucking think. You never fucking think." Kylan's head fell back on the couch. "Good God, she's proving you wrong right now."

I almost smiled, but he shoved himself down my throat again.

"That message came from you," Tremayne snapped. "How the fuck should I have known it wasn't real?"

"Because a good subordinate knows his royal," Kylan replied on a sharp exhale, his legs straining around me. "*Fuck*, Raelyn."

Heat blossomed inside me at hearing him lose control because of *me*. This powerful male was lost to my mouth, the subtle sweeps of my tongue against his sensitive head, the way I sucked him deep when he reached the right point in my throat.

"Your assessment of the university…" He trailed off on a low growl, the predatory sound searing my being. "Is inaccurate." My scalp ached with how hard he held me while my heart thudded loudly in my ears.

I'd always seen this as an act meant solely for the man,

but it was just as much for me. Seeing his jaw go rigid, feeling his hands clutch me tighter, and sensing the orgasm coiling within him—it was a heady intoxication I could easily become addicted to.

He may own my body, but in this moment, I owned his.

"Your Highness—"

"Enough." Kylan's cock pulsed inside my mouth, his fingers clenching in my hair. "Swallow, Raelyn. All of it." He shoved me down, forcing me to take his seed directly into my throat as his pleasure erupted on a groan.

I consumed his salty essence without flinching. My eyes were on his face, memorizing every inch of his ecstasy.

Such a beautiful male.

I'd noticed before, but it was even more evident now. His full lips were parted, his aristocratic features somehow less severe, and his dark eyes had turned a molten brown with desire and approval swimming in their depths. He stared down at me, a smirk playing over the edge of his mouth.

It took me a moment to realize why.

I was staring at him without permission

And I'd completely forgotten my need to breathe.

His grip loosened as I pulled back, sucking as I went to ensure I had every last drop of him, and I dropped my gaze to his still-erect cock.

Even that part of him was beautiful.

Of course. Because all vampires were gorgeous.

"Oh, darling, you certainly earned your high marks." Kylan stroked his thumb against my pulse, his palm still against my nape while the other had fallen to his abdomen. "Your theory could not be more incorrect, Tremayne. Which means, we now get to discuss your inappropriate disposal of human property."

Tremayne snorted. "Why do you think I believed that edict, Kylan?" His familiar use of the name had Kylan freezing beneath me. "You slaughtered your harem. Why can't we do the same? They're just humans."

A squeal from the table ended in a scream as something warm and slick landed against my back. Gurgling filled the air, the sound of someone struggling to breathe, followed by violent slurping.

Kylan didn't move or react, his posture relaxing as he lifted his palm from my neck to my head to begin gently stroking my hair.

Another shriek sounded, causing me to flinch.

He's ripping them apart.

I couldn't see, but I could *feel* it.

That's blood oozing down my back.

Blood from the women.

And Kylan's doing nothing to stop it.

"Are you done throwing your tantrum, Tremayne?" he asked after a beat, his tone bored.

"Isn't that how you killed your humans?" he retorted. "Why don't you demonstrate with the new one? Show me how you prefer it to be done since clearly you feel I'm doing it wrong."

My shoulders tensed, my heart stuttering.

He won't.

He might.

Kylan kept petting me, his fingers running through my strands. Then he sighed. "Stand up, Raelyn."

Rocks settled firmly in my throat, making swallowing impossible. *What's he going to do? Slaughter me? Give me to Tremayne?*

I closed my eyes, refusing to let him see the tears threatening my vision, and slowly climbed to my feet. Not even the ache in my knees could distract me from the pounding in my ears.

Kylan stood as well, his body heat doing little to dispel the chill engulfing my being.

The sound of him zipping up his pants and fixing his belt had me chewing on my lower lip, my eyelids refusing to open. Then he palmed my cheek and placed a kiss against my forehead.

"Why would I kill a female with such fantastic oral skills, Tremayne?" he asked against my skin. "I've not nearly enjoyed her to the fullest extent."

I almost sagged in his arms, relieved, but he was already setting me off to the side.

"That's what you fail to grasp," he continued, stepping away from me and toward the other male. I peeked at the ground.

Blood splattered against gold.

Human blood.

From the two women.

Their corpses were both lying on the table, their throats ripped wide open, their expressions frozen forever in terror.

My stomach rebelled, threatening to expel my earlier meal. I clamped down my jaw, refusing, causing my body to shake from the effort.

"You just don't understand," Kylan continued, tucking his hands into his pockets. "A human may no longer have a use to you, but that doesn't render the mortal useless to others. You can buy and sell property, Tremayne. I have explained this to you several times."

"Who would want to buy used goods?" he retorted, his posture bordering on aggressive. "Isn't that why you killed your harem? Because they lacked profit?"

Kylan slipped out of his jacket and set it on the couch.

"Another thing you fail to understand, Tremayne, is that all property within this region belongs to me. That includes all the possessions—material or otherwise—of the vampires under my care. Which means, those humans you just slaughtered—the ones who were auditioning and not even your property yet—were mine. As were all the others you murdered earlier today."

He scoffed. "You're seriously going to chastise me over a few mortal lives after the example you've set? That's rich."

"And lastly." Kylan paused to begin slowly rolling up the sleeves of his dress shirt. "You seem completely unapologetic about your actions."

"You want me to apologize for committing the same acts as you." Tremayne actually laughed, sounding genuinely amused. "So, what, only royal Kylan is allowed to kill slaves when he tires of them? The rest of us have to ask for permission?"

"Humans may be property, but their lives are what keep us thriving. To kill them without purpose is unacceptable and will not be tolerated in my territory."

"So your harem was killed with purpose?"

"Indeed." Kylan's forearms were exposed as his hands returned to his sides. "But you're mistaken on a key element to all of this, Tremayne."

"Yeah? And what's that, *Your Highness*?" he asked, mocking the formal name.

"I didn't kill my harem."

Kylan's arm moved with impeccable speed as he punched Tremayne in the face, following up with another hit to the male's abdomen and a third to his chest, all in the blink of an eye. Meanwhile, his words rattled around in my head.

I didn't kill my harem.

Tremayne lunged at Kylan with a furious roar, but the royal was too fast for him. Security rushed into the room, but a look from Kylan kept them all at bay.

My hand flew to my mouth as Tremayne used the distraction to his advantage, his fist connecting with Kylan's jaw.

The royal chuckled and shook his head.

"You might be one of the eldest in my region, Tremayne, but I still have nearly two thousand years on you."

A flash of a blade followed his words, glinting in the light as it sailed into Tremayne's skull. He fell to the ground with a thud, only to be picked up by Kylan and carried to the windows.

"You're hereby excommunicated until such a time that I allow you back into my territory. Enjoy the fall."

Crash.

My jaw dropped.
He'd just thrown Tremayne through the window.
From the top floor of the hotel tower.

Chapter Thirteen

KYLAN

Raelyn's gasp disappeared beneath the wind roaring in through the broken glass. I brushed the debris from my shirt, unrolling the fabric from my elbows as well, and retrieved my jacket from the couch.

She stood gaping at the destruction, her shoulders locked and coated in blood thanks to Tremayne's ridiculous show of aggression. This outcome had been a long time coming. He frequently tested my boundaries, always looking for a way to outdo me.

Whoever impersonated me sent that edict to him with purpose, knowing he would jump at the opportunity. Which meant it was someone with knowledge of my territory. That still suggested Jace, considering our close proximity, unless the culprit was working with someone from within.

I'd give the phone to Judith and have her team do some digging and also determine if anyone else received a similar note.

From what Angelica had said, it sounded like Tremayne had started the rumor of my supposed declaration. Well, that would be fixed. Right now.

"Come, Raelyn," I called over the wind, extending my hand. She carefully maneuvered around the blood on the floor, her arms covered in goose bumps.

We turned, facing half a dozen armed guards all kneeling with their heads bowed, waiting for my directive.

Right.

Tremayne's former staff.

"Clean up this mess," I demanded. "You'll have a new supervisor soon. Make sure the girls in the bedroom are alive and get them some food and clothes. Harm them in any way and I'll kill you myself."

There'd been enough meaningless death in this building tonight. I would not be adding those females to the list, even if they preferred to die after whatever Tremayne had done to them.

Sick fuck.

"Yes, My Prince," the leader of them said, head still bowed.

Having nothing left to say, I pulled Raelyn along with me to the elevators and pushed her inside as soon as it arrived. Her back hit the wall, her lips trembling as she kept her head bowed.

Please don't be broken.

I selected the Hold button with my fingerprint, forcing the car to stay in place after the doors hissed closed.

Raelyn didn't move as I approached, didn't flinch as I aligned my body with hers—thigh to thigh, pelvis to pelvis—and gripped her chin between my thumb and forefinger. I tilted her head back to properly search her eyes.

Bright blue irises focused on me right back, her pupils flaring.

I smiled. The trembling had been from the cold.

Good.

"There's a camera over my shoulder, but it doesn't have sound. You may speak freely, Raelyn."

"And say what?" she asked, her voice hoarse from the way I'd fucked her throat raw. Mmm, I needed to fix that.

"Whatever you want," I breathed, brushing my lips against hers. "But first…" I sliced my tongue against my incisor and slipped it inside her mouth. She jolted, her palms clasping my biceps as I deepened the kiss, sending my blood down her pretty, talented throat.

After the tentative way she'd stroked my dick, my expectations of her oral skills had decreased drastically. But the female had surprised me. No, she'd floored me. It'd been a long time since someone had learned my preferences that quickly and applied them, and under pressure as well.

Fucking perfection.

I thanked her with my mouth, worshiped her with my tongue, and vowed to return the favor later—thoroughly.

She moaned, losing herself to the endorphins of my essence.

Blood exchange with mortals was a rare activity, typically reserved for those with promise whom a vampire desired to protect. It granted increased healing and strength and enhanced their senses. Temporary powers, so to speak, that could easily become addictive. But if this was how Raelyn reacted—by rubbing her body against mine—then she could drink from me whenever she pleased.

I licked her bottom lip, the mark I'd left earlier healing now, thanks to my blood. Mmm, it didn't matter. Any vampires who scented her would smell my essence all over her.

Mine.

And I was not sharing.

I admired her lust-fused gaze, nuzzling my nose against hers. "Feeling better?"

"What did you just do to me?" she asked, awed.

"Rekindled your spirit with a little immortal flare." I kissed her again, loving the taste of her mingled with my essence—both blood and sex. A hint of fear trickled through the air, a sign that my brethren were beginning to react to the message I'd delivered to the sidewalk down below.

They would want to know why.

And I would explain in my own way.

"We're not finished yet," I warned, pulling my mouth from hers. "I have more work to do here."

She blinked up at me. "Okay."

I studied her expression for signs of terror. The initial stirrings of it had escalated her pulse several times, particularly when Tremayne crudely suggested I kill her. But she merely gazed back at me now, her heartbeat steady and strong, her cheeks tinted with pink. "You're still not afraid of me," I marveled.

"You'll have to do better than throwing an asshole through a window to frighten me," she whispered. Then her eyes rounded upon realizing what she'd just admitted out loud. "I mean—"

I chuckled, pressing a finger to her lips. "You're always free to speak openly in private with me, Raelyn, especially if it includes calling Tremayne an asshole, which he is."

"Is?" she repeated, frowning. "Meaning, he's not...?"

"Dead?" I finished for her. "No, he'll live. It takes a lot more than a fall to kill a vampire, but it's going to take him a while to heal. Primarily because I'm going to forbid anyone from helping him. He's earned his agony and excommunication. Let him pick up his own pieces without bringing anyone else down."

Cruel, maybe, but necessary to make a statement. I would not tolerate mindless killing in this territory, even if they believed my behavior to be an example.

I pressed my forehead to hers. "Which brings us to the next task of the evening. Ready?"

"Do you really need my permission?"

"No."

"Then why ask?"

"I'm allowed to care at least a little bit, Raelyn," I said, turning to select the bottom floor. The car began to move while I kept her crowded against the wall. "I didn't kill them."

She swallowed, her gaze holding mine. "Then who did?"

"That's what I'm trying to find out, and until I do, you're accompanying me everywhere. Because I suspect whoever did this will want to make a violent example out of you."

Her pulse finally faltered. "W-what?"

The elevator dinged, announcing our swift arrival. Raelyn remained frozen, her face paling.

Well, at least her reactions would be appropriate now.

Even if it was a bit cruel to give her the truth so bluntly.

I held her chin as the doors opened. "Don't leave my side, and remember decorum." I brushed my lips against hers and released her. "Come."

My ire weaved an ominous cloud through the air with every step. The vampires under my protection would be able to feel my fury, even as I observed them all with a carefully blank expression. Several stopped speaking and fell to their knees. Others—the oldest in the room—bowed their heads in respect while the humans whimpered and fell to the stone floor in supplication, passively begging for their lives.

I moved slowly, hands in my pockets, surveying them all. Raelyn followed at my side, her gaze downcast, her skin still pale.

Good. That's the way a harem member should act after seeing what transpired upstairs.

Myers burst in through the lobby doors. "He's a fucking..." The long-haired vampire trailed off upon seeing me in the center of the room, his knees immediately bending and taking him to the floor.

"Finish your statement, Myers," I prompted, curious. "He's a fucking what?"

The male's tan skin whitened, his terror palpable. "Mess, Your Highness."

"Who?"

His throat bobbed as he managed to reply, "Lord Tremayne."

"Lord?" I repeated, chuckling. "No, surely not. He is, however, exiled until I say otherwise. Any vampire found assisting him in any manner will answer to me. Do you understand?"

A chorus of "Yes, My Prince" and "Yes, Your Highness" sounded throughout the room, no one daring to argue or look me in the eye.

"For those wondering, the crime that earned him this sentence was the spreading of false information. I have not and will not condone killing mortals indiscriminately in this territory. If you're craving a bloodbath, order a human from the food service or entertainment industry."

I waved my hand toward the dining area of the hotel designated for that explicit reason. Several humans adorned in chains were on the tables, some dead, others barely breathing. That was their purpose. To feed a vampire's hunger. Whether or not I agreed with it was a moot point. We were vampires. Humans were food.

No one dared comment or raise a question, so I continued.

"Tremayne required the reminder that everything in this region belongs to me, including your humans. Do not meaninglessly harm my property just because you're bored. It is unacceptable and prohibited."

More silence, but a hint of discontent underlined their inclined acceptance.

"Tremayne argued that killing my harem served as an indication that you all can do the same. I will only address two points. First, harem members are sexual servants who provide entertainment. Enjoying them to their fullest extent is acceptable, just as you are allowed to indulge in your entertainment purchases. Second, as my property, it is my prerogative to do whatever the fuck I please. If anyone disagrees with these points, speak now."

Of course no one did. And that hint of discontent disappeared as well.

No, I am not losing my mind to immortal age.

Yes, I am still your royal.

And this is my fucking territory. If you don't like how I run things, leave.

"Well, hearing no questions, I have an announcement to make. Rise."

The vampires in the room quickly abided my command while the humans remained on the floor, leaving Raelyn as the only standing mortal. I wondered if she realized the symbolism in that, that there were perks to being in a royal's harem. This was one of them.

"The K Hotel Enterprise CEO position is officially open. I will be accepting applications throughout the week and will make a decision in a month." Whomever I selected would inherit not only this hotel but also several like it across the territory, including one in the heart of Lilith City. The competition for the position would be an entertaining one, as several vampires in this region were old enough to take over Tremayne's former empire.

"Spread the word," I demanded, referring to my warnings in addition to the employment opportunity.

Chatter spread as my constituents did as requested, sending messages to their contacts and murmuring expectations amongst each other. Some of the names mentioned were ones I would be contacting directly.

"Your Highness." Cherise curtsied with the greeting, her head low and her interruption insufferable. Had she not learned her lesson when I closed the elevator in her face? "About earlier, I wanted—"

I silenced her with a slice of my hand through the air. "What did you do with the human who failed to recognize me?"

The voices around us quieted, waiting.

She swallowed. "I-I gave him to the kitchen staff to add to the menu."

Well, I supposed that was better than killing him herself. "That punishment implies you blame him for his failure, yes?"

"He should know his prince, Your Highness." She lifted her chin, her position on the matter clearly resolute.

"I agree. And who do you believe is responsible for teaching them, Cherise?"

Her nostrils flared. "The universities, My Prince."

"Initially, yes. But who is responsible for maintaining that knowledge and preparing the humans for face-to-face interactions with their royals?"

A tendril of fear sweetened the air, her cheeks losing color.

Too little, too late, Cherise. You brought it up again.

"Their s-superiors, Your Highness."

"Meaning *you* as the reception manager in this case," I translated. I would have let this go, having more important matters requiring my attention. Alas, Cherise had to say something to remind me of the earlier altercation. In front of the room, no less. "You sent the human to the kitchens for slaughter. That's Maeve's department." I searched for the blonde vampire and found her leaning against a wall, expression impassive. "Join us."

She didn't hesitate, her leather boots clacking against the stone with each step. The jeans and sweater were very last century, denoting her younger vampire age. Most from that generation chose comfort over style.

"My Prince," she greeted, bowing instead of curtsying.

"Is the human still alive?"

She pointed a red nail to the brown-haired male on a table in the dining area, his nude form in a fetal position and shaking.

So yes, still breathing and untouched, from the looks of it.

Excellent.

"How do you feel about reception management, Maeve?"

Her hazel eyes glittered. "It would be a desired change from overseeing the kitchen, My Prince."

"I just so happen to have a new opening, if you're interested. But I have a requirement."

Cherise sputtered. "Your High—"

"Was I talking to you?" I demanded, sending her my best glower. "Kneel, Cherise, and do not dare stand or speak again until I say otherwise."

Raelyn's pulse jumped at my tone, reminding me of her presence beside me. I palmed her lower back and pressed a kiss to her neck out of habit more than necessity, earning me a few raised eyebrows from the room. Apparently, showing affection to my harem was unexpected. Good.

"As I was saying, I have a requirement and it involves the male. I want you to take him off that table and retrain him. Consider it an audition for the role. I'll return later in the week to assess his improvement. If he passes, you can keep the job. If he doesn't, you'll go back to the kitchen with the boy."

Her lips curled. "Thank you for this opportunity, My Prince. I won't let you down."

No, I suspected she wouldn't. "Excellent. Please retrieve the human and start tonight."

"Your Highness." She bowed and moved with purpose toward the dining hall.

Now to handle the vampire at my feet. I sighed, my thumb drawing little circles against Raelyn's back. "Cherise, I'm disappointed not only in your lack of leadership but also in your lack of candor and respect. Perhaps a new role in kitchen management will help refresh your outlook on life, hmm? Make the arrangements to switch roles with Maeve, and when I check in with her in a week, I better not hear of any issues."

She said nothing, her head still bowed.

Very good. She'd taken my instructions regarding standing

and speaking seriously. There was hope for her yet.

"Go on, then." I gestured for her to leave. "I'm tired of your presence."

I wrapped my arms around Raelyn and kissed her softly. The move effectively told the room I considered my consort more important than Cherise because I dismissed her in favor of a human. It also showed everyone that I could be tender with my property when I desired it.

Raelyn's mouth opened for mine, allowing me to take her as I craved. I ignored Cherise's movements and words as she left, ignored everyone watching us, and reveled in her addictive taste.

My cock hardened against her lower belly, needing more.

I could force her to give everyone a show, to demonstrate just how skilled she was with her tongue, but that seemed more of a punishment than a reward. And my darling, obedient little lamb had earned my praise, not my wrath.

"The valet better have my keys ready," I murmured against her lips. I kissed her soundly once before addressing the room. "Enjoy the dawning hours and expect an invitation shortly for a gathering at Kylan Tower later this month."

A few grins flashed, the idea of a party exciting the audience. There were enough vampires here to initiate the rumor mill, but Judith would assist in sending formal memos to my constituents in the early evening. There were close to five thousand in my region, one of the largest in the world. Only fifty or so appeared to be here tonight, which didn't shock me. This was a hotel, not a residence, nor had anyone expected my arrival.

I guided Raelyn toward the waiting valet and plucked my keys from his hand without acknowledging him. The passenger door opened, and as I helped Raelyn inside, I noticed Tremayne's splatter all over the paved sidewalk and hotel furnishings.

"Myers," I called.

The lanky male immediately joined me outside, his hazel eyes downcast. "My Prince."

"See that this mess is cleaned up, and ship Tremayne's remains east toward the border with the Calgary Clan. Do not help him in any way."

Myers bowed his head, his lips curling at having been given a task. "Yes, Your Highness. Thank you."

I left him with a nod and joined Raelyn in the warm interior of my two-seater. Not the best for snowy roads, but the engineered tires helped with handling the slick concrete. And the humans did a reasonable job plowing and shoveling.

Reaching over, I buckled Raelyn in before pulling away from the hotel. "You may be yourself again, darling lamb."

She remained quiet for a beat. "I'm not sure I know what that means."

I chuckled. "We're alone, which means punishment is far less likely."

"But still a possibility."

"Always, yes." I had standards. If she broke them, she'd know. I shifted into a higher gear to pick up speed, wanting to make it difficult for anyone to follow us. Owning half the city made guessing my whereabouts difficult. I preferred it that way. The underground tunnels would help. My engineers had crafted them into mazelike patterns while transforming the destroyed city formerly known as Vancouver into Kylan City.

I navigated onto a ramp leading us downward into the stone-crafted caverns and placed my palm on Raelyn's thigh. "You were remarkable this evening, little lamb. Proof that somewhere inside you is a properly trained human."

"I know the rules, have followed them all my life. Until you kissed me." She sounded frustrated by that.

My lips curled. "Do you think it was the stress of the moment?"

"Maybe. I just didn't want you to pick me, and, well, I bit you."

"Most humans want to be selected for a harem, thinking they'll be granted access to the finer luxuries in life." What they failed to consider was the cost. Several of the royals and alphas preferred pain to pleasure. I preferred a mix of both.

"I wanted to go into the tournament."

"Yes, I know, my immortality-craving lamb." I squeezed her thigh as I turned off the car lights to hide our trail.

She tensed, her mortal eyes not granting her the same sight as my night vision. I accelerated for fun, enjoying the way it escalated her heartbeat.

"Lilith dangles immortality before you all as a controlling measure. Rather than work together, you squabble with each other over the minute possibility of a better future. Although, it does seem you bonded a bit with Silas." Something I suspected contributed to her spirited responses to me. "Did you ever banter with him?"

She snorted. "We started as academic rivals and fought all the time, but Willow brought us together. She pointed out that we were essentially the same person, just in female and male form." A hint of nostalgia entered her voice, her fondness of her old life clear.

"Where was Willow sent?" I didn't know any of her class by name, apart from Raelyn and Silas. My kind preferred numbers. Easier to manage and remember.

"The breeding farms," she whispered.

Ah, yes, that was a sad fate. Forced human procreation. It was necessary to keep the numbers high, and we only wanted those with quality bloodlines to continue. "She must have had significant test scores."

"The same as mine."

I nodded. "Likely, yes." Because Raelyn would also make good breeding stock, but luck of the draw had sent her to the final selection rounds instead. The Magistrate pretended to have everything down to a science. Realistically, he put a bunch of scores into his computer and randomized the results for those in a certain breed and class.

Silas had been meant for the Immortal Cup, selected years ago for his potential by Jace and Walter, just as I had selected a handful a decade prior. The top of the class were followed and reviewed frequently, their skills and attributes setting them apart from others.

I turned into another tunnel, winding our way beneath the city and using the technology built into my car to disrupt the video feeds.

Judith was magical.

"What will happen to her?" Raelyn asked softly.

"Do you really want me to answer that?"

She was quiet for a long moment, her pulse slowing as she breathed deep and exhaled. "How many children will she bear?"

"It depends on her biology. She can only safely have one pregnancy a year, sometimes even fewer. Our scientists have learned how to move the process along, but Mother Nature refuses to fully cooperate. And as human life is actually sacred to our kind, as your lives are necessary to our survival, we do what we can to keep the breeding stock healthy until they are no longer of use."

"And then?"

"They go to the blood farms or into the service industry." Zelda was an example of someone previously used for breeding who now worked in a household. She'd been sent to Vilheim's property in the city to help in the kitchen, and I'd quickly learned about her skills through her superior and Vilheim. "Some of them end up in reasonable accommodations."

"But not all."

Not most. I squeezed her leg once more before returning my hand to the shifter. An apology threatened my tongue, something that rarely happened. *A wolf does not apologize to a lamb; he simply eats it.*

I cleared my throat and changed the subject to something safer. "We'll be staying in the city for several weeks, perhaps months. Also, the party I mentioned will have other royals in attendance, which means I need to escalate your sexual training. They'll expect you to be on a level similar to their own consorts, and should I have to share you with one, I'll need you properly prepared."

Her pulse stuttered at the mention of sharing. Not surprising. She probably assumed I'd give her to Robyn. Not a chance in hell I'd allow that to happen without supervising. I wasn't even sure I intended to share Raelyn at all—given the potential threat to her life—but I had to instruct her on the rules regardless.

"We'll begin immediately." Why waste any time when the sun wouldn't rise for another two hours?

God, I loved winter.

Long nights, short days, and endless hours to play in bed.

Which we would.

Starting tonight.

Chapter Fourteen

RAE

"Undress." Kylan wasted no time after guiding me through the threshold of his bedroom suite, his single-worded demand a warm caress against my ear.

Sexual training.

For the purpose of sharing me with other royals.

Royals like Robyn.

My stomach twisted in protest. I didn't want a collar or a leash, or to be hauled across the concrete.

Were there others like her? Were they worse?

Does it matter? I have to survive Kylan first.

I shivered, recalling the way he handled Tremayne and then the others downstairs. That had been the Kylan everyone feared, the one who exuded power and authority and did not take disobedience lightly.

Yet, he'd treated me—

"Raelyn." The slight hint of admonishment in his tone said he didn't appreciate my hesitation.

Right, I needed to focus.

And undress.

I pushed the thin strap off my shoulders and let the gown fall to my feet, leaving me naked except for my heels. I bent to remove them, but his palm on my nape pulled me back up.

"Those can stay." He nipped my ear, pressing his suit-clad chest to my bare back. "Get on the bed and spread your legs. I want to see you, Raelyn, and explore every inch of your sexy little cunt."

Heat pooled between my thighs at his vulgar words.

Goddess, what is he going to do to me?

Was it really only earlier this evening that he'd pushed me up against that tree? And just last night that he selected me?

No wonder my limbs shook as I climbed up onto the oversized bed. This had been the longest twenty-four hours of my life, even with the rest on the plane.

Or maybe it was his blood coursing through my body. I'd felt more alive, more alert, since he kissed me in the elevator. As if my very being had been lit on fire from within. My senses were more acute, my body more aware. I could almost *feel* Kylan's desire from his predatory gaze alone as I lay back on the bed.

Pure, unadulterated hunger.

I swallowed.

That was the look of a male who either craved sex or violence, or perhaps a mixture of both.

My legs trembled as I slid them apart, revealing my intimate flesh for his perusal. His focus shifted downward—slowly—searing a path along the way before centering between my thighs.

That heated look stirred something inside of me. Something hot and intense and foreign.

I shuddered, the desire to close my legs almost overriding my mind. *He wants them open. But oh, I need... I need...*

Kylan slipped out of his jacket, laying it over a chair beside the bed. His tie was next. He stepped closer, his nimble fingers plucking at the buttons of his shirt one by one to slowly reveal the muscle beneath.

I'd seen him shirtless earlier, knew what to expect, but him undressing with the intent of touching me intensified the experience.

Vampires were all perfect. It seemed to be a requirement of their immortality.

But Kylan? He redefined the meaning of perfection.

All hard, clean lines wrapped up in smooth skin.

My mouth watered just looking at him.

His lips curled as he dropped his shirt on top of his jacket. "Your arousal is intoxicating, Raelyn," he murmured, prowling toward me. My limbs tensed as he crawled onto the bed between my legs, his intent clear.

He gave me less than a second to react—not even that—before licking a path up my sex. I gasped, my fingers curling into the covers on either side of my hips.

Fuck...

Silas had done this more than once, but it never felt anything like *this*.

Kylan repeated the action, this time applying more pressure, causing my body to convulse uncontrollably. He smiled against my clit, his teeth touching the sensitive nub and shooting even more spasms up and down my spine.

"You swallowed me so beautifully earlier, little lamb. Allow me to return the favor."

Wha—

Oh Goddess...

I arched off the bed on a groan, only to be pushed back down by his palm on my abdomen. His opposite hand went to my hip to hold me in place while he devoured me with his tongue.

Fierce waves of energy rippled over me—through me—consuming me completely. I couldn't breathe, couldn't think, couldn't move; I could only feel.

I had no idea this type of pleasure was even possible. It almost hurt in its severity, burning through my veins to singe each nerve ending.

"Kylan," I whimpered, unsure of whether to push him away or grab his hair. "It… it…"

His incisor skimmed my sensitive flesh.

He wouldn't—

I screamed, the pleasure too much. My body shook, my lips trembling incoherently while Kylan obliterated my senses.

He'd bitten me.

Down there.

Or maybe he'd only nicked me. It didn't matter. He'd set my essence on fire.

But, Goddess, that shouldn't be allowed. Ecstasy mingled with pain as he laved the wound with his tongue. Sucking, nipping, pulling me under a cloud of insanity that lacked reason and focused primarily on feeling.

My limbs tingled.

My heart raced.

My lungs fought for air.

"You're denying it," he murmured, approval in his voice. "But you won't win, sweetheart." Another lick that sizzled through my veins. "Give in, Raelyn. Submit to the sensation. Submit to me, love."

He scraped me again, and I grabbed his shoulders, my nails digging into his skin.

"Kylan." It was both a plea and a curse, a desire for more and a need for him to stop. I couldn't stop shaking, the flames burning inside me close to ripping me apart.

This was nothing like what he did to me against that tree. That had barely qualified as an introduction.

"Raelyn." His growl vibrated my core, shooting sparks up my spine. "I want to feel you come on my tongue." I quivered, my entire being lost to his will and the movements of his mouth. "Now."

His command hummed through me, reaching the depths of my soul and forcing my compliance. The world shattered around me, painting my vision in shades of black and white. Kylan's name rolled off my tongue with disjointed words chasing after it.

I felt destroyed.

Misplaced.

Liquid.

My chest burned as euphoria vibrated my limbs.

"Your pleasure is addictive, Raelyn," Kylan murmured against my wet flesh. "I need more." His tongue speared me deep and sent me over another cliff of oblivion.

How was that even possible?

Was it because I'd imbibed his blood?

Oh, it didn't matter. Not with his ability to do *that*.

I squirmed against his mouth, his nips and licks sending me into a fog of disoriented bliss. My mind fractured, thought no longer possible.

Just sensation.

Heat.

Sex.

Fuck.

I barely registered Kylan removing his pants, too consumed by the starry abyss swimming before my eyes. My shoes had disappeared too.

How?

When?

What had he just done to me?

His cock pressed against me—there. My clit throbbed and protested as his thick head rubbed against it, his heat obliterating my senses.

"Kylan," I whispered.

I've never—

His lips captured mine, silencing what I needed to say, his shaft sliding purposely through my arousal. I quivered beneath him, terrified and excited, all at the same time. But rather than push into me, he merely slipped through my slick folds, coating his hardness in my damp heat.

"Open," he murmured, his tongue tracing my lips.

I complied, granting him access to every part of me. He continued to saturate himself in my essence while coating my mouth in the aftermath of my orgasm.

"Do you taste yourself?" he asked softly. "Your sweet pussy wept all over my tongue, sweetheart." He punctuated the point by kissing me again, deeper this time, his ownership abundantly clear. "Some of my kind no longer enjoy giving pleasure, but I find that, when done right, it's very gratifying." His cock slid lower, the head finding my entrance.

I tensed, waiting.

It would hurt.

A lot.

But I had to take it.

That was his right as my owner.

"Mmm, a virgin." He smiled. "That inspires several intriguing possibilities, little lamb."

I shivered as he sat back on his heels between my knees, his hand wrapping around his shaft.

"Fuck, your arousal feels divine against my cock, Raelyn." He ran his palm up and down, his grip harsh and hypnotic. His abdominal muscles flexed with the movements, pulling taut as his tempo increased.

I licked my lips, going up onto my elbows to see more, fascinated.

Wasn't that my job?

And what did he mean by "intriguing possibilities"?

Better yet, how did he know I was a virgin?

"Stay just like that for me," he said, his voice low and deep.

He slid forward, straddling my hips with his knees, providing an even better view of his ministrations. The stirrings of that addictive sensation began again, pulsing and tensing in my lower belly.

I wasn't anywhere near ready for another wave of pleasure, but watching him stroke himself was undeniably stimulating. His forearm flexed.

"Open your mouth, Raelyn." The command was underlined with a growl that went straight to the ache between my thighs.

I parted my lips, holding his gaze.

"Fuck." He grabbed a fistful of my hair with his free hand, tugging me forward. His orgasm erupted onto my tongue in hot, thick spurts that slid into the back of my throat, forcing me to swallow.

His face contorted in such beautiful agony that I couldn't help memorizing every detail—his tightened jaw, the fan of his long lashes against his cheekbone, the way my name fell from his beautiful lips.

"Suck me clean," he demanded, his grip in my hair yanking me forward.

I took him as deep as my throat allowed, the remainder of his ecstasy mingling with mine against my tongue. His grasp only tightened, holding me in place as I hollowed my cheeks around him.

"Every last drop, Raelyn. I want you full of my cum, my essence, so everyone knows you're mine."

I shuddered at the possession in his tone. Vampires and lycans were notoriously proprietorial.

Yet, he plans to share me with other royals.

I ignored that thought, refocusing myself on the task. Kylan's hold eventually loosened, his fingers combing through my hair as he stared down at me with a look of almost wonder.

"You look gorgeous like this," he murmured, his other hand going to my jaw. "Your mouth wrapped around my cock." He pushed himself farther, a devious twinkle in his gaze. "Your lack of a gag reflex confirms your throat training—an advanced course—yet you've never been fucked. That's fascinating."

I swallowed around him, my eyes beginning to water from the harsh intrusion. He slid back, the head slipping from my mouth with a satisfying pop.

He glanced down, a smirk playing over his lips. "Spotless. Beautiful, Raelyn."

His mouth captured mine before I could reply, his body flattening mine against the bed. He placed his elbows on either side of my head and settled his groin against the soft spot between my thighs.

"I could kiss you for hours," he whispered. "Fuck you for even longer. Dine between your thighs for a century." He nuzzled my nose. "But I can sense your exhaustion. It's been a very long evening, and you'll need rest for your next set of trials."

"Trials?" I repeated.

"Sexual training." He kissed my jaw, his lips trailing a path to my ear. "We'll need to be inventive now that I know you're a virgin. That's a playing card I intend to use during the right situation."

I swallowed, uncertain of what he meant by that.

Did he intend to gift my innocence to another? In exchange for something of higher value to him?

While proprietorial, vampires were also practical and notorious for trading property. It kept them from becoming too attached. By swapping items frequently, their possessive instincts remained only on the surface.

Very few kept a human long-term.

But he's held on to Mikael for a decade...

"We'll discuss this more later." He kissed me softly, his tongue coaxing me into responding. "I'm very pleased with you, darling lamb. You'll make a fine consort."

An ache formed in my chest at the reminder of who I was to him.

For a moment, I'd almost forgotten, too lost in the sensations he'd evoked.

But this was all temporary.

A pleasure he would enjoy and forget in the blink of an

eye.

While for me, it would be my entire existence. Born only to serve in the bedroom of a royal vampire. And soon there would be others as he expanded his harem, forgetting me, moving on to the others…

That shouldn't hurt.

It *couldn't* hurt.

Emotions were for the weak, and I wasn't weak.

My name is Rae and I will survive this.

There was no other choice, no other option, no other way.

Live or die.

My choice will always be life.

Chapter Fifteen

KYLAN

I combed my fingers through Raelyn's red strands. The color was such a beautiful contrast to her creamy skin.

Such a gorgeous human.

Skilled, too.

And definitely a virgin.

The way she'd tensed had suggested her innocence, and her file confirmed it.

She never took an intercourse class. Fascinating. Most humans did, but she'd opted for physical sports instead. Likely because of her Vigil inclinations. Hmm, that path would have suited her. But so did the path to my bed.

I stroked her neck while skimming through her university notes with my free hand, reading about her curriculum choices.

The beginning years were the same for all humans—indoctrination courses meant to provide a stern introduction to society's requirements. Those who passed moved on to the next level, which included basic academics. The elite scores of that round, of which Raelyn's were impressive, were given certain liberties to advance their studies.

That's where the choices came into play.

Humans were allowed to pick their paths, but it was all a clever test—a way of observing their natural inclinations. Raelyn's record indicated varied interests, her coursework not identifiably specialized.

Fencing.

French.

A political science course surveying clan leadership throughout the last century.

Religion.

That last one made me snort. Lilith certainly did enjoy forcing the humans to worship her. If they only knew she was just a vampire like the rest of us and actually younger than me.

Cam was the eldest of our kind.

I sighed up at the ceiling, wondering for the thousandth time what actually happened to him. Lilith claimed him to be dead, but I knew her better than that. She had the old vampire locked up somewhere. The same place I would end up if anyone managed to prove me insane with immortal age.

Which wasn't going to happen.

I'd left Tremayne's phone with Judith and expected to hear from her any minute now. But I couldn't bring myself to leave Raelyn just yet. She intrigued me—her innocence, her defiance, her submission.

She's a virgin.

My lips curled in triumph. It provided me with the perfect angle and opportunity to manipulate the royals. They would desire her even more, and with a little training, she'd become the perfect bait for whoever had dared to make me an immortal enemy.

Typically, I would expect my other consorts to explain the formal procedures to Raelyn, to provide her with warnings and properly initiate her into the royal harem world. But they no longer existed.

That left Mikael as the only available teacher.

His experiences were similar, and he'd been with me long enough to understand my usual protocols when it came to sharing.

Yes. He would do well.

That task I would assign to him while I handled festivity arrangements. Personal invitations would be required, and I needed to ensure certain accommodations.

I sighed. Entertaining others was one of my least favorite activities, but it was the best play. Put them all under the same roof, set up Raelyn as bait, and see who pounced.

My phone buzzed, Judith summoning me from the bed.

I'm in the living area, she wrote.

I'll be there in five.

I wasn't quite ready to leave Raelyn yet. She'd snuggled into me to use my chest as a pillow, thus my arm being around her shoulders and my fingers in her hair. The female fit so perfectly, her legs scissored with mine.

Amazing what sleep revealed—her body already trusted mine. A dangerous proclamation considering what I could do to her, but the woman lacked fear. It had to be a result of her illegal friendships with Willow and Silas, a fact her files neither proved nor disputed.

There were, however, several videos of her oral exams with the male where she'd clearly faked her orgasm. That alone confirmed her lack of sexual feelings for the male, something that pleased me far more than it should.

I liked her. And her file only endeared her to me more. My feisty little lamb would make an excellent consort and may very well prove to be a favorite.

She stirred against me as I set my phone on the

nightstand.

I kissed her forehead as I gently rearranged her on the pillows. "Sleep, darling. I'll have Mikael bring you evening breakfast in bed." He'd enjoy finding her naked. My gift to him.

Dressed in a pair of sweatpants and nothing else, I met him and Judith in the living area. Mikael handed me a cup of coffee—black and laced with his blood.

"You do love me," I murmured before taking a sip. "I left you something in the bedroom as well. She needs training on royal seduction and general expectations. I assume you're up to the task?"

His blond brows lifted. "Is that your way of saying she didn't live up to your expectations last night? Because her screams suggested otherwise."

My lips twitched. "On the contrary, she's quite gifted. But I need her properly informed on certain society requirements, which may necessitate a few hands-on tutorials."

His light gaze glimmered. "You're giving me permission to play."

"I'm giving you permission to teach," I replied, grinning around the rim of my coffee mug. "Enjoy."

"She'll need food first." He started toward the kitchen. "Then we'll get to work, Your Highness."

"I expect results," I called after him, settling onto the sofa beside a straight-faced Judith. Her severe blonde bun and white pantsuit deeply contrasted with my casual attire. I placed my ankle on my knee and relaxed into the leather cushion. "Tell me you found something, Judith."

"I did." Her gray eyes met mine. "You're not going to like it."

I took another sip of the coffee and set it off to the side. "I'm listening."

She handed me a tablet, the screen showcasing a series of lines and numbers. "The message went through a series of coordinates, but after an hour, I finally pinpointed the origin and original send time." Her index finger swiped along the screen. "It originated from your plane, Your Highness. During the Blood Day ceremony."

The proof glared at me from the device. "How is that possible?"

"I have a few theories, the strongest being that someone hacked into your systems while sharing airport space. There were other jets close enough to do so, and once hacked, it would be easy to send an email from one of the many devices you had on board."

"You've just suggested your team isn't handling my security properly," I noted dryly.

"Which is why I've already begun an investigation into the apparent breach."

The woman was constantly proving her worth and loyalty. "Good."

"I also put together a list of the royals and alphas who used the same airport and had planes in the same vicinity as yours." She pushed something on the screen that populated a series of names. "They're in order of closest to farthest, although that detail isn't important. Any of them could have accessed the plane's systems given their proximity."

Naomi.

Walter from the Clemente Clan.

Niklas from the Stella Clan.

Robyn.

Claude.

"Jace isn't on the list," I noted.

"No, they didn't have a plane. He stayed in Hazel City for a few days with Darius and Darius's new *Erosita* before driving in for the ceremony. All the surveillance confirms he returned to Hazel City after the Blood Day selections and is still there now."

"Meaning he didn't fly home."

"Not yet."

"But he could be working with someone." Of course, that would imply more than one royal was out to destroy my name. Or, perhaps, a clan leader. "Where were Brandt and Luka?" I shared borders with the Calgary Clan and the Majestic Clan. They would be ideal partners in this game, sharing equal desires to possess my land.

She took her tablet and began skimming through notes, her lips twisted to the side. Mikael chose that moment to appear with two plates—one of which he handed to me.

"Eat," he demanded.

My brow arched. "You humans seem to have a penchant for commanding me."

"I wouldn't dream of it, Your Highness." He gave a mock bow before heading toward the master suite with a skip in his step.

Raelyn would be either thrilled or mortified.

"They both landed on the other side of the ceremony site," Judith said, tapping the screen. "Unless they sent some lycans in stealth mode, it's highly unlikely they infiltrated your systems."

I plucked a piece of bacon from the plate and enjoyed the savory flavor while considering this new information. "Paints Jace in an innocent light."

"Which could be precisely what he wants," she murmured, still playing with her tablet. "Although, if that's the case, he's doing a great job of it. There's absolutely nothing to suggest he's the culprit."

I nodded. "True." He was in Naomi City when someone massacred my harem. "Of course, he could be hiring others to carry out his missions." I ate another slice of bacon while pondering. "Have there been any suspicious breaches on my property?"

Judith had installed several additional security measures after the incident. I'd grown comfortable in my leadership, assuming no one would be foolish enough to attack me on my own turf.

It was a mistake I would not be making again anytime soon.

She shook her head. "Nothing, and while impossible, all

signs still point to there not being a break-in to begin with."

"Yes, because whoever killed my consorts wanted to make it look like it was me."

"And they did an excellent job," she muttered.

I couldn't agree more. "Well, what fun would this game be if the culprit was obvious?"

"Game," she repeated with a snort.

"What else would you have me call it?"

"A suicide mission?" she suggested.

"Well, there is that," I agreed. Because whoever challenged me to this duel would die. Of that I was certain. "Invite them all to the party, including Jace, Brandt, and Luka."

Their schedules and behavior may indicate innocence, but my gut still told me Jace was hiding something. I'd known the royal a very long time. He played the political arena almost as well as I did. Which meant, if it wasn't him, he might be able to aid me in my search.

"Actually, I'll call Jace personally."

Her eyebrows rose. "You will?"

"I will." I'd invite him to visit early with his new sovereign and give them both an opportunity to interact with Raelyn. Their reactions would either prove them innocent or increase my suspicion. I took another bite from my plate and set it on the table. "Anything else, Judith?"

"Yes." She hit a few buttons on her screen before showing me two identical messages. "Zion and Vilheim also received copies of your supposed edict."

I arched my eyebrows. "And you didn't think to lead with that?"

"They're both being monitored. Neither has acted on the message."

"Yet," I added flatly. Well, it seemed visiting two of the oldest vampires in my region had just been escalated to my top tasks of the day. I'd have to call Jace from the car. Priorities and all that. "Is there anything more you need to tell me?"

"Only a final logistical clarification, My Prince. I assume we're hosting the party at K Hotel?"

I nodded. "Seems appropriate. I'd like Tremayne's former quarters completely renovated as well."

"That project has already been assigned to Bethany."

"Brilliant." The woman possessed an eye for detail and had decorated several of my properties. I stood, then remembered a final item. "I need you to promote Angelica."

The young vampire had risked her life and position by visiting my compound uninvited, and she'd somehow managed to circumvent my security to reach me. All impressive, if a little suicidal. However, she'd shown great loyalty by not only informing me of Tremayne's affairs but also knowing I'd never send that message.

Very few would question the edict. That Angelica did made her valuable.

Judith's gray eyes flashed up to mine. "The freshling?"

"That freshling, as you call her, is the one who warned me about Tremayne's behavior. She might be the youngest vampire in my region, but she has potential, Judith. I want to see that potential cultivated and rewarded."

She held my gaze for a long moment and nodded. "I'll add her to your detail."

"Good." I didn't trust her implicitly yet, but it would give me an opportunity to properly judge her value. "Thank you, as always, for your due diligence, Judith."

"My Prince." She bowed her head as I stood.

Zion and Vilheim would make for a tiring evening. Both wanted to be promoted to senior leadership positions due to their age and power. Zion was the only one I'd even consider, yet he hadn't bothered calling me after receiving my supposed edict. That alone disqualified him.

I sighed, heading back to my bedroom to change.

Raelyn's pleasant tones greeted my ears, causing my lips to curl.

The fun had begun.

Too bad I couldn't stay to play.

Chapter Sixteen

RAE

"Raelyn." The male voice drifted over me—somewhat familiar. "I brought you evening breakfast."

I rolled in the cloud of blankets, my red hair covering my face. A warm hand helped brush the strands from my eyes, allowing me to see Mikael smiling down at me. I sat up and nearly knocked the plate from his hand.

His gaze fell to my breasts, causing me to frown.

I'm naked.

Right.

I yanked the blanket up and moved backward until I hit the headboard. My knees bent to my chest, acting as a shield.

His lips twitched. "You'll challenge Kylan but run from me. That's fascinating, Raelyn."

"It's Rae, and I barely know you."

"You don't really know Kylan either," he pointed out. "I brought you unsalted eggs, steamed broccoli, and a donut."

I eyed the items, my brow furrowing. "A donut?"

"Hmm, one of my favorite breakfast foods. I thought you might want to share one." He sat on the bed, the plate in his lap. "It's plain since your taste buds aren't ready for more, but it'll provide a good introduction nonetheless." He picked up a round, bready-looking food and held it out for my inspection. "Try it."

"I'd rather not."

"Suit yourself." He took a bite and set the plate beside me with a fork. "Go ahead and eat."

The broccoli was familiar, but the eggs were unlike any I'd ever seen.

"They're over medium instead of that scrambled packaged crap. Trust me, you'll appreciate the difference." He nudged the food closer. "Now, eat, *Rae*."

He'd actually used *my* name. The shock must have crossed my expression because he chuckled.

"I may have been trained through the Coventus, but I'm just as human as you are, Rae. I provide blood and you provide sex. Both items meant to satisfy His Royal Highness and no one else." He shrugged and savored another piece of his donut. "My fate was just slightly more defined than yours; that's all."

He had a good point.

Another human—only, male. Like Silas.

I lifted the plate and balanced it on my knees. Eggs and broccoli. Normal items. I could eat these. Besides, I needed the energy after last night. Kylan's blood had waned and left me feeling off somehow. Not exhausted so much as down. Or maybe that was waking up to find another man in the room, not him.

The broccoli provided nutrients my body required, whereas the eggs were a bit rich. I ate them slowly while Mikael watched, his donut long gone.

"Zelda comes from the universities as well," he

murmured. "She knows what humans are used to and how to slowly introduce you to new flavors. You'll see. She's fantastic in the kitchen."

I'd met the blonde briefly last night, her cheeks bright red after being caught with Mikael. She'd seemed pleasant enough.

"How did last night go?" Mikael asked. "At the hotel?"

I swallowed the bite of egg in my mouth. "What part?"

"In general, I mean. Were there any issues? Anything you didn't know how to handle?" He cocked his head to the side. "Kylan says you need training, and I want to know where I'm starting."

I set the fork down. "Y-you're training me?" I hated that it came out unsteady, but Kylan hadn't mentioned Mikael being the one to train me. I thought he meant to continue my sexual instruction exclusively. Not invite his human pet to play, too.

"That's Kylan's directive, yes." His light gaze held mine. "It can be hands-on or hands-off, Rae. I'm here to coach you, not force you."

I frowned. "How can you properly instruct me without touching me?"

"Not all education requires physical contact, Raelyn." Kylan entered the bedroom wearing nothing but a pair of sweatpants sitting low on his hips. His muscles flexed as he moved, drawing my eyes downward to the impressive bulge below. My mouth watered with the memory of his orgasm. I shouldn't be craving him. Not like this. But I couldn't help it. Just being near him had my legs clenching with a need for *more*.

What has he done to me?

It had to be his blood. I thought it was out of my system, but clearly, it wasn't.

His lips curled. "She's just as insatiable as you, Mikael. Perhaps you two can work out an arrangement." He brushed a kiss against my temple that shot ice through my veins.

Such a casual statement about sharing. Would it really mean nothing to him for another male to touch me?

But of course it wouldn't. Kylan would have a harem in a few months, or sooner, and I'd just be one of a few. A toy to pass around to his royal friends, like Robyn.

This is my life.

How had it taken me this long to realize it?

Shock?

Hope for something more?

A wish to trade places with Silas?

I could be Willow. The thought had me shuddering. *It could be worse.*

Kylan pinched my chin and lifted my eyes to his. Whatever he saw made him frown. "Start with the formalities, Mikael. Detail your experiences as well so she knows what to expect."

"Yes, Your Highness."

"I have two items that require my immediate attention." He threaded his fingers through my hair and yanked me upward to my knees, causing the plate to fall as well as the blankets. "When I return, I'll provide the hands-on part of your training."

He brushed his lips over mine, rekindling the flames inside me with an ease that almost frightened me. Almost.

His bare chest seared mine, causing my nipples to pebble to painful points.

I knew my body would betray me, would adore worshiping his, but I never expected to *enjoy* it.

Kylan had warned me that he intended to destroy me. I had accepted that fate, assuming he meant physically.

No.

This being would *shatter* me before he was finished.

He's going to demolish my very soul.

"I want you wet and ready for me the moment I walk through that door, Raelyn." Kylan ran his nose over my cheek, his inhale heady and intoxicating. "Don't disappoint me." He pressed a kiss to my thundering pulse. "Most evenings, I'll expect you to join me in the shower on your knees. Alas, pressing matters supersede the pleasures of life. You'll make it up to me later."

The bulge in his pants was noticeably more pronounced as he stepped away, leaving me cold and naked and kneeling.

"She's exquisite, isn't she?" he asked.

"Indeed," Mikael replied, his voice deeper.

He's staring at me—at my breasts.

I swallowed.

I've been naked in front of men before.

This isn't any different.

Yeah, no, it's extremely different because I actually want *one of them.*

Kylan's mouth curved. "Yes, little lamb. Wet and waiting, just like you are now. I'll be back to taste you soon." He winked and left for the bathroom, leaving me staring after him with a hint of discomfort between my thighs. I slowly sat on my heels, my breathing somewhat erratic.

"He's addictive, isn't he?" Mikael sounded almost sad, his voice soft. "Try not to fall in love with him, Rae. Remembering who and what he is helps. At least a little."

I met his light gaze and caught a glimpse of the male lurking behind his confident mask.

Pain.

He blinked it away, his lips curling again. "Well, shall we begin by going through the invite list? I can ask Judith for a copy, and we can review each of their kinks."

"You've been with them all?"

He lifted a shoulder. "Several, but not all."

"Because Kylan shared you."

A glimmer of sadness filled his expression again. "I do whatever pleases him, just as you will too."

I stared at him, finally *seeing* him.

He's like me.

He'd said as much earlier about his body being used for blood and mine for sex, but now I *saw* it.

An ally.

"Does it hurt?" I whispered.

"Depends on the task," he answered quietly. Then his gaze lit up, his eyes crinkling at the side. "I know. How about you throw on a robe, and we'll take a walk around the penthouse. It's big with a lot of rooms filled with surprises you won't believe until I show you."

"Like what?"

Mikael shook his head, sliding off the bed and taking my plate with him. "Follow me to find out." A pair of adorable dimples followed that pronouncement. "But get dressed first. I'll meet you in the hallway. Going to get rid of the dish and let the maids know to change the bedding after Kylan departs." He waved over his shoulder. "There are robes in the bathroom or clothes in the closet."

Both of which required me to go near Kylan in the shower.

Great.

Mikael left without another word, leaving me with a decision. Either I waited for Kylan to come out or I braved his presence in the bathroom.

Neither option appealed.

Both provided the same results—seeing Kylan again.

At least one option left me with clothes.

Decision made, I rolled off the bed. If I hurried, maybe Kylan would still be—

His hard, wet chest met my face as I turned the corner directly into him.

He caught my hips, holding me in place when I would have bounced backward.

"Couldn't wait until I returned, hmm?" he teased, his dark eyes capturing mine.

"I, uh, no. I, well, I need clothes." Why did I sound like an ineloquent dolt all of a sudden?

His lips quirked up. "I beg to differ, Raelyn. I very much prefer you without clothes." He slid his palm to my lower back, holding me against him. Only a towel separated us, his impressive arousal hot through the fabric. "I expect you naked and in my bed every night until I say otherwise." His mouth hovered over mine. "Understood?"

"Yes," I whispered.

"Good." He kissed me softly. "The shower is all yours if you need it."

Mikael just told me to find something to wear, but washing off sounded better. I'd be quick. Then he could show me whatever had excited him enough to bring out his dimples.

Chapter Seventeen

RAE

A television.

But not just any television, one that showed *humans*.

I'd only ever used these to watch clips from the Immortal Cup or a televised broadcast from the Goddess.

Never anything like this.

Every day this week, Mikael took me into the theater and showed me a new film. Today's was some crazy film about a human traveling through portals into other realms.

Mikael handed me a bucket of popcorn, a new food I could only stomach in moderation. I took the requisite three bites and gave it back to him. We'd spent the early evening reviewing the royals and alphas again. He picked two each day to go over, telling me about his personal experiences with each, their preferences in the bedroom, and their potential requests.

Today had been Robyn and Luka. The latter was happily mated and therefore not a threat. Robyn, however, enjoyed females and males and would very likely request a night with me. Mikael explained her proclivities in detail, confirming his intimate familiarity with the sadistic female.

I shivered.

Kylan had been demanding each evening, his passions in bed seeming to escalate each time he touched me, but he'd not done anything like what Mikael described.

Robyn favored pain, something I had initially expected from Kylan given his cruel reputation. Yet, he seemed more intent to please me than to hurt me.

I'd never felt so replete and exhausted in my life, and there were courses in school meant to kill my kind— literally. But nothing compared to the way the royal mastered my body.

I orgasmed five times last night.

Five.

That shouldn't even be possible, but Kylan forced them from me, refusing to stop tonguing my clit until tears streaked down my cheeks.

Then he'd healed me with his blood again, something that was expressly forbidden between humans and vampires. Yet, Kylan continued to force me to drink from him in small amounts.

He was clearly a rule breaker.

And a fierce lover.

A crash on the screen returned my focus to the movie. Mikael chuckled and said the words out loud with the human on the screen.

Actors, he'd explained.

From a previous world.

One where humans ruled.

Apparently, these films were outlawed, but Kylan had kept them anyway. *Yeah, definitely not one to adhere to or follow rules.*

I sipped my water and selected another kernel from the bucket. Mikael had added more butter to this one, his goal to gradually warm me up to more savory foods. I finally gave in and tried a donut today. The sweetness limited me to two bites, but I begrudgingly approved. Tomorrow we were supposed to try chocolate.

The door opened, Kylan appearing in a suit, his gaze searching.

My lips parted. *He's early.*

We'd fallen into a routine: Kylan disappearing before evening breakfast to handle work-related items, leaving Mikael in charge of my royal and alpha tutorials. After midnight lunch we watched a movie, and Kylan always returned during dinner, or rather, *for* dinner.

Mikael glanced at Kylan. "I'm introducing her to pop culture."

"I see that." He shut the door behind him and removed his black jacket, his gaze going to the screen. "This is a favorite of mine."

"I know."

Kylan folded his suit coat over the back of the couch and settled onto the cushion beside me. "Come here." He pulled me into his lap, his arm wrapping around my back for support. "I'm disappointed to find you clothed."

"I wasn't expecting you yet," I admitted.

He tsked. "You should be waiting for me," he whispered against my ear. His palm slid up my thigh, pushing between my legs to force them apart. "And you could have at least worn a skirt for me."

"She prefers jeans." Mikael held out the popcorn. "Want any?"

"Why do you think I'm here?" He nuzzled my neck.

"I meant the popcorn."

"I meant Raelyn."

"And you call me insatiable." Mikael held a kernel up to my lips, and I accepted it with my teeth. "She likes it."

"She likes a lot of things," Kylan replied, his lips against my pulse. His thumb traced up my center to unfasten the button of my pants. "I want these off, Raelyn." He drew the zipper down with the words, exposing my intimate flesh.

There were no undergarments in the wardrobe he'd assigned to me, not that I wore them to begin with. Vampires and lycans had a preference for mortal nudity.

"Off," he repeated, tugging harshly.

Mikael snorted and shook his head. "So impatient."

Kylan grabbed Mikael by the collar of his dress shirt, yanking him closer. "No, Mikael. *This* is impatient." He struck so fast I yelped, his fangs sinking deep into Mikael's neck, causing popcorn to scatter over the floor.

Mikael groaned, his eyes rolling into the back of his head. Kylan had left one hand on my jeans and gave them another sharp jerk. I scrambled to pull them off, his hot palm against my freshly exposed skin not making it any easier.

My feet helped, kicking the fabric from my legs.

Kylan's fingers trailed over my mound and lower, piercing me two at once.

Shit. I stole a deep breath through my nose, out through my mouth. He normally eased me into this, but something restless lurked beneath his skin tonight. I could feel it in the tense lines of his body, the way his forearm aligned with my lower body, holding me in place.

Was he angry about finding us in the theater instead of studying?

We had two weeks left before the party, and I'd reviewed almost all the portfolios, as well as endured the nightly sexual training.

What else did he want?

"Kylan," Mikael breathed, his nails digging into the cushion. "Fuck!"

"You're in need of a long-overdue reminder, Mikael," Kylan growled against his neck. "You serve me."

"Yes, My Prince." His face contorted into agonizing lines, his eyes falling closed. "Always."

"And in return, I take care of you," Kylan continued, his

tongue tracing the column of Mikael's throat. "Don't I?"

"Yes," he agreed, voice soft. "You do."

"I do." Kylan released me. "Stand, Raelyn. Now."

My legs shook as I complied. The movie still played behind me, casting shadows oddly throughout the room. It gave Kylan a darker, more sinister glow that revealed his true nature.

Predator.
Vampire.
Old.

I swallowed. He was unreadable and highly unpredictable. What did he want from me now? Was this another lesson? A punishment? Playtime?

Kylan settled his ankle over his knee, his arm going over the back of the couch behind a lust-drunk Mikael. "Remove your sweater for us, Raelyn."

A shiver worked its way down my spine. I licked my lips, his ominous gaze tracking the movements while he waited.

He cocked a brow. "Is there a problem, Raelyn?"

With both of them seeing me naked? No, not really, except I hadn't really done anything like this in front of Mikael yet. He'd more or less become a friend over the week. But we were never meant to be platonic with each other, not when we both existed in Kylan's sexual playground.

It's just a sweater, I told myself. *Nudity is the easy part.*

I pulled the fabric over my head, my nipples hardening from the cooler air.

Mikael seemed to relax, his light eyes slowly tracing my form while Kylan toyed with a lock of his blond hair. "Isn't that better?" Kylan asked conversationally as he used the remote to pause the movie.

"Than the jeans?" Mikael smirked. "Yes."

"I should have them removed from her wardrobe, just give her short dresses from now on to showcase her legs." His focus shifted to the apex between my thighs. "Maybe some lingerie, too."

"Red," Mikael added.

"Absolutely. I'll discuss it with Taylor. Raelyn requires additional outfits for future dinners anyway." He continued stroking Mikael's blond hair while speaking, his expression inscrutable. "Or maybe she should attend naked."

I'd seen worse, such as mortals dressed in metal piercings and chains. *Collars, spikes, covered in blood.* I shuddered. *No, thank you.*

"Nervous, little lamb?" His dark eyes glimmered. "Because this is exactly what I'll do to you with my fellow royals. Let them see you, pet you, maybe even fuck you."

My stomach churned with those last two words. *Fuck you.* He hadn't done anything other than take my mouth all week. Would he truly allow someone else to take my innocence?

A playing card, he'd called it.

I still didn't know what that meant.

"Isn't this more entertaining than an old movie?" Kylan asked.

Mikael glanced sideways at him. "Is that why you're doing this? You're dissatisfied with my training methods and felt the need to make a scene?" His tone earned him a sharp tug on his hair that didn't even make him flinch.

"On the contrary, I'm quite pleased. I merely feel it's time to introduce Raelyn to the next level. She pleases me amazingly well, but I wonder, how does she do with others?" He bent to lick the wound on Mikael's neck, slowly, purposely. "Would you like her to touch your cock, Mikael?" he asked softly, his tongue drawing a wet path up his skin. "To get down on her knees and suck you off with that pretty mouth of hers?"

My lips parted, my throat going dry.

Kylan wanted me to pleasure Mikael.

While he watched.

Was this what he would do with his royal friends? Tell me to get on my knees and orally please them while he observed?

Mikael had explained that the harem members went through training for two months, and would be fully experienced in the sexual arts before joining Kylan's harem.

It was Kylan's job to provide me that same training.

And Mikael's, too.

His light eyes lifted to mine, his pupils eerily glowing in the dull light behind me. Knowledge and understanding colored his expression. He knew this wouldn't be easy for me but also understood that I had no choice.

This was life with Kylan. Life with a royal. Life with a vampire.

We both existed to serve, and this was what our superior required.

He gave me a small nod, a shared moment of compassion before saying, "I want her mouth."

Kylan smiled. "An excellent choice. Raelyn, I believe you're familiar with this requirement?" He cocked a brow.

"I am, My Prince." Not *Your Highness* just in case our safe word remained. Because I could do this. It was just Mikael.

Something akin to approval passed through his features. Because I didn't argue? Could I even try to debate him in this mood? "Good, little lamb. On your knees, then." He continued combing through Mikael's hair, his dark gaze on me while I knelt between his blood virgin's sprawled legs. "You know what to do."

I gingerly placed my palms on Mikael's thighs, gliding them upward to the bulge growing beneath his zipper. My fingers threatened to tremble at the wrongness of touching a male that wasn't Kylan.

It's okay. He wants me to.

But I don't want to.

What you want doesn't matter. This is for him*, not you.*

As if sensing my hesitation, he brushed his knuckles down my cheek, reminding me of his presence. His desire. His command.

Pausing like this with another royal would earn me a

death sentence.

They would expect confidence and seductive skill, not a trembling mess after barely touching another man's thighs.

I am not the right woman for this.

Yes, you are. You're a survivor.

"I think she needs proper motivation," Kylan murmured, his lips against Mikael's neck again and trailing to his mouth. Their resulting kiss had my heart skipping a beat.

Primal heat singed the air.

So virile.

So erotic.

So intoxicating.

My own lips parted, my tongue darting out to dampen them as if I were the one being kissed.

I'd seen them embrace before, but not quite like this—all hunger and raw energy and *need*. Kylan reached for my palm and placed it over Mikael's arousal, forcing me to stroke him through his black pants. I could barely focus, my attention on their devouring of each other, the dueling of their tongues.

I want that...

The devotion.

The intensity.

The trust.

Mikael gave in to Kylan completely, his body a puppet for his master to play.

What did Kylan and I look like together? As fitting? As sexual? As savage?

The pressure against my hand intensified, the order clear. I unfastened the pants, allowing Mikael's arousal to spring free. Kylan guided my fingers, wrapping them around the base and guiding my stroke upward and back, his instruction thorough and unmistakable.

I followed his lead, letting him direct the pace. Mikael groaned, his arousal pulsing as Kylan nipped his lip hard enough to bleed.

"Asshole," he growled.

Kylan tightened his grasp around my hand, causing me to squeeze Mikael's shaft. "Careful. She might be the one touching you, but I'm very much in control."

"You're always in control."

"Yes, I am." Kylan took his mouth again with an intensity that stole my breath. He didn't stop guiding my hand, his movements sure and experienced, his lips even more practiced.

I pressed my thighs together, the ache building between them almost unbearable.

I wanted Kylan to kiss me like that while Mikael knelt between my thighs.

To be between them.

To share them.

To let them share me.

The foreign thoughts roused a flame in my center, spreading warmth through my veins, touching my nerves, and bringing my core to life.

I moved my hand in earnest now, no longer requiring Kylan's expert touch. His hand brushed my cheek, sliding upward into my hair, and urged me downward toward Mikael's cock.

He wasn't as long as Kylan, his head slightly rounder, but equally as proportioned and beautiful. I traced his throbbing vein with my tongue, smiling as he jolted, and slipped his crown between my lips.

"Fuck," Mikael growled, his muscles tensing as I swallowed him down to my fist and sucked upward.

"I told you she's skilled," Kylan murmured, his fingers knotting with my hair and pushing me to take Mikael deeper. "I hope you're ready to swallow, Raelyn. I expect you to take everything he gives you and more."

My eyes began to water from his grip in my hair and the cock hitting the back of my throat. Mikael may not have been as well endowed, but he was certainly long enough.

I met his heavy-lidded gaze. All signs of apology and

understanding were gone and replaced by a male deep in the throes of passion. Kylan moved to his neck, his bite eliciting a soft curse from his blood virgin. The violent pulls into Kylan's mouth sent shock waves of energy through Mikael, his body tensing and spasming beneath my touch and his cock surging in my mouth.

He'd grown impossibly larger.

My throat constricted, my lungs protesting.

Air...

Kylan didn't relent, his grasp in my hair not allowing me to move.

"Fuck!" Mikael groaned, his orgasm ripping through him and spilling into my throat with a force that would have sent me backward if Kylan hadn't been holding me in place. I swallowed because there was no other option, his seed hot and plentiful as it slid down my tongue.

It didn't stop.

A second round of ecstasy tore a yell from him as he came again. My nails bit into his thighs as my vision began to blur behind black dots. I couldn't... I needed... But fuck, I consumed him anyway, his essence, forcing it down as my lungs ached.

Kylan pulled me back a fraction, opening my airway, and I breathed in greedily. I craved more, a break, but as soon as I filled my lungs, he'd shoved me down again in time for another explosion.

"Kylan..." The name left Mikael on an exhale, drawing my blurry vision upward again. He'd gone pale, his lips turning a shade of blue that didn't look right.

Because of my eyes?

The force of his rapture lacked the heat and power from earlier, his body notably less tense, almost relaxed.

"Please," he whispered, his palm going to Kylan's leg. "I..." He cut off on a whimper, his eyes flashing open. "Kylan..."

No.

He wouldn't...?

His hand remained in my hair, but the rapture had fled, replaced by a cooling skin that had my heart dropping to my stomach.

I froze on my knees, unable to speak, to move, to react.

Mikael grew colder, his skin paling to a deathly shade I knew all too well.

His light eyes flicked to mine, real pain staring back at me.

And then his lids closed.

A tear escaped the corner of my eye.

I barely knew him, but he'd been so kind to me. How could I just sit here and watch this happen? Why would Kylan do this to him? To me? To us?

I pushed away, Mikael's erection long gone, but Kylan held my hair, forcing me to remain between the dying man's legs as he continued to feed.

"Try not to fall in love with him, Rae. Remembering who and what he is helps. At least a little."

Mikael's words rattled in my thoughts as an ominous reminder.

I'd not heeded his warning nearly enough.

Because, for a minute, I had started to trust Kylan. To maybe even like him a little.

This was the royal I had feared.

The one I'd read about.

The cruel master who killed meaninglessly.

The one who claimed to have not massacred his harem.

A liar.

A vampire.

A monster.

Chapter Eighteen

KYLAN

Mikael's heartbeat faltered, the final draws of his mortality calling to me in warning.

I released him, sealing the wound with my tongue, but not immediately pulling back.

Raelyn's mounting fear called to the predator inside me, begging me to pounce. If I looked at her now, I'd take her—harshly. And she wasn't ready for that yet.

"You're evil," she whispered, hatred pouring off her in waves.

My eyebrows rose. "Excuse me?"

"You heard me." The raspy quality of her voice intrigued me. I'd love to hear her yell my name in that voice, especially as I made her come. "He trusted you."

"I know." It was one of Mikael's biggest flaws, and a trait

I adored. He loved pushing my boundaries as a result, never afraid of what I could do to him. Fortunately for him, he'd never pushed me too far. I finally met Raelyn's blue eyes, then dropped my focus to admire her swollen lips. "You did such a good job, little lamb. I owe you a reward."

I tried to pull her up onto the couch, but she protested, her head yanking from my grasp at the expense of a few red hairs. She stood and scrambled backward until her back hit the theater wall. "I don't want anything from you, *Your Highness.*"

My heart faltered at the use of her safe word. I held my palms up and relaxed into the couch, confused as hell. "Talk to me, Raelyn. Tell me what pushed you too far."

"Are you fucking kidding me?" She sounded furious, her tone unlike anything I'd heard from her to date, and incredibly disrespectful.

"Have you forgotten who I am?" I wondered, shocked.

She laughed without humor. "Oh, apparently I did, but thank you for the bloody reminder. I'll never forget again. That's for damn sure."

I blinked. What the hell was she going on about?

"Is that how you killed your harem?" she demanded, pointing at Mikael. "Or did you just rip their throats out like the monster you are?"

"I didn't kill my harem, Raelyn." Something she already knew. "Why are you acting like this? What did I do?"

She gaped at me. "What did you do?" The shrill quality of her tone prickled my ears. "That!" She pointed at Mikael again. "You killed him while making me... Goddess, he trusted you and you killed him. Bled him to death, as if he meant nothing to you, which, of course, he didn't. None of us do. You're all a bunch of fucking monsters who prey on the weak and force us, force us..." She trailed off, her legs giving out and sending her to the ground on a sob.

Something fractured inside me, a sensation I hadn't felt in a very long time.

Regret.

I'd unintentionally hurt this beautiful, warrior soul.

"Raelyn," I whispered, moving to her side on the floor. She pulled her knees in close, trying to squirm away, but I lifted her with ease into my lap. "Raelyn."

"I hate you." Her fist connected with my jaw with more strength than I expected, sending a shock wave down my spine. She scrambled off me and threw another punch that I caught before it could connect with my nose.

"Raelyn," I repeated with more force, pushing her hand away. "*Stop.*"

"No!" She started to struggle in earnest, tears pouring from her eyes as she attempted to hit me again. Her fist met my palm, but her other one managed a jab at my side. It fucking hurt.

"That's enough!" I snapped, done with this foolishness. I flattened her on the ground, trapping her wrists in one of my hands over her head as she bucked her hips futilely beneath mine. I'd have enjoyed it a lot more if she wasn't spitting angrily in my face.

"Kill me!" she shouted, still trying to fight despite my impenetrable hold. "I'd rather die than be here with you another moment. I'll bite you, scream at you, I'll—"

"Fuck, Raelyn, he's not dead," I growled. As if I would ever kill Mikael. I adored the male. "He's just drained." Rather literally. But the blood I'd slipped into his mouth would heal him back to normal.

She finally stilled, her breathing erratic. "W-what?"

"He'll wake up in a few days with a hangover and have a few choice words for me but will otherwise be fine." I wiped the spittle away from my jaw with my free hand. Not appealing. "I needed him incapacitated to protect him."

Her watery eyes locked on mine. "I don't... I don't understand."

"Jace will be arriving tomorrow with Darius and Darius's new *Erosita*. Mikael being indisposed reaffirms my reputation and marks his blood as off-limits." While I'd kept Mikael's whereabouts a secret originally, everyone would expect him to be with me now. That meant the visiting royals could request a bite, something I refused to allow.

Territorial behavior was seen as a weakness among my kind. And I couldn't afford to be seen as weak. Not with the rumors of immortal insanity hanging over my head.

"You don't want to share him," she said softly.

No point in lying to her. "No, I do not."

"But you'll share me."

I shrugged. "Well, it's customary to swap consorts." Although, I didn't really want to share her. I'd almost enjoyed incapacitating Mikael, something that had never been the case before. I usually gave him a warning and drained him slowly, but watching him benefit from Raelyn's attentions had set my blood on fire. Which was strange considering I always shared my harem with him and others.

But Raelyn, well, I hadn't enjoyed watching her service him. At all.

Our circumstances were different, a result of the madness of these last few months. She slept with me every night, a pleasure I'd never preferred. I typically met my consorts in their own rooms and varied my visits between them, never really having a favorite. Sometimes I even went a month without seeing any of them.

And I never used a consort multiple nights in a row.

Until Raelyn.

She'd kept me entertained all week, and I still desired more from her. Her virginity was only part of the draw. I looked forward to seeing her, to finding that flame in her gaze that seemed to ignite in my presence.

My fearless little vixen.

She'd landed not one but two hits. An impossible feat for a human, even with shock on her side. Her daily regimen of imbibing my blood may have helped her too, but I was still impressed by her nimble movements.

"You do realize punching a vampire, let alone a royal, is grounds for death, yes?" I asked, amused.

Her gaze narrowed even as pain radiated from her blue

depths. "I'm not sorry."

"No, you're not." I cocked my head to the side. "And you're still angry with me."

She bit her lip, saying nothing.

"The silent treatment again?" My brow lifted. "Surely you can be more inventive than that."

"I'd hit you again, but you have my hands secured."

"Tell me why you're angry."

"Because I hate you."

"More words, Raelyn. I want an explanation."

"Why?" she retorted. "It's not like you care."

I laughed. "If I didn't care, I wouldn't ask." I learned long ago not to bother voicing an opinion or wasting words over useless drivel.

She still said nothing.

"I've told you Mikael will be fine." A slight ache formed in my gut with the words. Did she truly adore him this much already? They weren't romantically involved from what I'd witnessed, just friends. But clearly, the thought of his death bothered her immensely. Or was it that I'd so carelessly disposed of him? "Talk to me, Raelyn."

"Fine. What will you have me do with Jace?"

Of all the things I expected her to say, *that* was not even a consideration in my mind. "You'll follow decorum, as always."

"I mean, as your consort." She spoke the words with such disdain I nearly cringed. None of my consorts had ever acted like this, even the ones I'd selected and groomed myself. They were always eager to please me or others.

"Be blunt, Raelyn. What is it you want to know?"

"Blunt," she repeated, a flash of fury igniting her gaze to a gorgeous azure color. "Are you going to make me fuck Jace?"

The question slapped me across the face.

Would I allow her to fuck Jace? No, *make* her, was her phrasing.

I nearly laughed.

Like hell would I grant him—or anyone else—such a valuable opportunity.

"You're mine, Raelyn."

She had the audacity to roll her eyes. "Yes, I'm aware. I'm yours to share and all that. The least you could do is give me an idea of what to expect when Jace arrives—or any of the others, for that matter. But no, you can't even afford to give me, the lowly human, the courtesy of knowing how you plan to... What was the phrase you used? Oh, right, use my virginity as a playing card." She tried to maneuver out from beneath me again and huffed when I didn't move. "*Fine.*"

I hadn't heard a human female mutter that word—in *that* tone—in ages. Clearly, allowing Mikael to introduce her to the cinema had rubbed off on her, and in only a week's time, no less.

"You want to know how I plan to take your innocence?" I asked, bemused. "And you're angry that I haven't told you?"

She merely glared at me in response.

"Has it occurred to you that I haven't decided yet?"

More silence.

"Would you like me to take it now?" I settled more firmly between her thighs, allowing her to feel my thickening arousal. "Because I'll gladly fuck you, Raelyn, if that's what you desire from me."

Her nostrils flared. "Fuck you."

"That is the topic at hand, yes." I ran my nose over her flushing cheeks. *Delectable.* I was well fed, but her blood tempted me to bite. "Would you hate me less if I fucked you, Raelyn? Because I suspect you'd hate me more. Especially since it would mark you as a consort with every option available."

I nibbled her thundering pulse, reveling in her heady scent. Fear mingled with desire and anger, creating an aroma I could hardly turn down. My incisors begged me to truly taste her. She wouldn't satisfy my cravings in the same way Mikael's blood did, but oh, how I longed to devour her entirely.

"Every option available?" she repeated, her voice pitched low in a whisper.

"Mmm, yes." I skimmed my incisors across her sensitive skin. So easy. So tempting. "Once I've fucked you, everyone else can request you. Is that what you want, Raelyn?"

Because I didn't. I wanted to savor her and keep her as my own for as long as I could. No royal or alpha would be interested in just her mouth. They'd want the entire package, which was off-limits until I sampled her for myself.

"They can't... until...?" She swallowed, falling quiet.

I pulled back to meet her conflicted gaze. "You thought I meant to share you before I've had you?" I tsked. "Darling lamb, that's never going to happen."

She searched my face. "But you called it a playing card."

"Because it is." I released her wrists and went to my elbows on either side of her head. "One I can play against my opponents. Not by offering your innocence, but by protecting it. Unless you'd prefer I take it now?" The offer was still on the table, and I'd happily oblige.

It would put her in danger.

Or not.

Only a fool would kill a royal's property while on loan.

No, my adversary was smarter than that. She or he would strike when I least expected it.

Still, I didn't want to risk Raelyn being accidentally harmed.

You don't want to share her, my darker side whispered. *She's ours.*

It was that same side who took over at the end, adding a hint of pain to my bite as I pushed Mikael over the edge into unconsciousness. A subtle punishment for indulging in *my* female.

Spending all week with her was fucking with my head.

I needed a fresh perspective, a break.

Or maybe I just need to fuck her to get her out of my system.

My cock hardened at the prospect, nudging against her tender flesh. It would be so easy with her already naked and wet beneath me.

"N-no," she said, shaking her head. "I... I don't want to be shared."

Her words slid over me on an icy wave, cooling my ardor. "You don't want to be shared?"

She shook her head again. "I... no. I really don't."

I just told her I wouldn't share her yet. Did she require a reminder already? Or was I not clear? "I won't be sharing you until I've had you myself, Raelyn."

She bit her lip. "B-but I don't..." She seemed to be reconsidering what she wanted to say, causing my brow to furrow.

"Are you saying you never want to be shared, Raelyn?"

She was silent for a long moment, a war battling behind her eyes, as if she couldn't decide how to properly respond. "Y-yes."

I nearly laughed. "But you're my consort and that's your purpose—to fuck whomever I tell you to fuck." Did she not understand the design of a harem? "Surely the university explained this to you."

She trembled, some of the fire dying in her eyes. So fragile and broken and hurt.

That was the look Robyn's pets wore, not mine.

The fuck just happened?

"Yes, My Prince," Raelyn whispered, her gaze falling from mine.

Her submission sliced my heart and stirred a maelstrom of emotions inside me. At the forefront was extreme disappointment.

"Is it that easy to break you?" I demanded. "How very unfortunate." I expected at least a flare of disapproval or a frustrated snort, not outright acceptance. I pushed off of her, standing. "Get dressed, Raelyn."

She didn't move.

I shook my head, not able to handle this foolishness any

longer. If she wanted to shatter beneath the truth of her station, so be it.

"If you want to fuck me, then do it." The unadulterated rage in her voice caused me to pause with my hand on the doorknob. "If you want to give me to one of your royal friends, then do it. But don't ask me what I want and put me down after I give you the truth."

I turned, curious, and found Raelyn standing with her hands on her hips, her cheeks red from her exertion.

"You can do whatever you want to my body, but my mind is my own, Kylan. So fuck off."

My eyebrows rose. Did she learn that phrasing from a movie or from a foulmouthed lycan? Maybe Mikael had mentioned it to her.

Either way, she should not be using those words on a royal, least of all me.

And worse, I absolutely should not have enjoyed hearing it nearly as much as I did.

I stalked forward, backing her up into the wall, my palm circling her throat as she stared me down. "And what if I desire your mind, little lamb?" I asked softly, my thumb stroking her escalating pulse. "What if I demand it?"

"You'll never have it."

I squeezed, just enough to threaten. "Oh, but I own all of you, darling. Or did you forget that detail?"

"No." Her voice shook with a mixture of fear and anger. "I own my mind, my heart, and my spirit. All you have is my body, and I refuse to give you anything else. It's my right to choose."

"You have no rights."

"Not anymore." Her gaze narrowed. "But I used to."

I smiled and it was almost sad. "No, love. You never did."

"Humans did."

"In the past," I agreed, pressing my hips to hers. "We live in the present, where your liberties are forfeit and belong to me. You're mine, Raelyn."

"To fuck, to touch, to command." Her pupils contracted, allowing more of that pretty blue flame to shine through. "You can try to manipulate my mind all you want, Kylan, but I will never give in to you. I refuse."

"Whom are you trying to convince here, sweetheart? Me or you?" Because it sounded as if it was she who needed the pep talk, not me. "Because I've not even begun to manipulate your mind."

She scoffed at that, her courage bright and palpable despite being trapped naked against the wall. "I tell you I don't want to be shared, and you hastily remind me that it's my purpose. You want me meek one moment and strong the next. You told me I was never destined for the Immortal Cup, saying it was all just a cruel play, but the only one playing here is you, Kylan. And I'm done participating."

My grip loosened, startled by her far too accurate assessment. I'd been toying with her as one would an intriguing pet. It was never my intention, but when summarized so bluntly, I couldn't deny the validity of her words.

I desired a warrior and required a submissive. Two very different objectives, both correct.

For the first time in centuries, I lacked a retort. The woman had outwitted me, leaving me only one thing to say. "You're right." I released her and took a step back. An apology threatened my tongue, shocking me more.

I never apologized.

Ever.

"I... What?"

"You're right," I repeated. "Do not make me say it a third time." I couldn't even believe I'd admitted it twice. But I supposed it was the least I could do.

"You've been playing with me."

"That's what you said, isn't it?"

"And you admitted it."

I folded my arms. "This has just become boring again."

She laughed, the sound near hysterical in nature. "How

is this my life? Why is it my life?" She ran her fingers through her hair and laughed again, but it lacked joy. "Was everything you said about my virginity a lie too? A way to give me confidence just to shatter it when you hand me over to someone else?"

A growl built in my chest. "Absolutely not." My hands fisted at my sides. "No one touches you except me."

She gave me a disbelieving look. "Okay, Kylan." The dismissive way she said it set my blood on fire.

"I've never lied to you, Raelyn, and I do not take lightly to the accusation."

Her hands went to her hips again. "No, you've just been fucking with my head."

"I prefer to call it 'providing conflicting priorities,' which does not equate to dishonesty." I stepped toward her again and she held her ground. "I have been more honest with you than with any other consort."

"Easy to do since you killed them all."

I didn't bother correcting her. She knew the truth. "Are you trying to provoke me into hurting you, Raelyn? Because I would not advise continuing down this path."

"What more could you do?" she countered with another of those humorless laughs. She threw her arms out to the sides. "Do your worst, Kylan. I dare you."

"You dare me?" I raised a brow. "That's a dangerous proposition for someone who believes me capable of mass murder."

"You're a vampire, Kylan." She pointed at Mikael's prone form on the couch. "And you're clearly capable of hurting people."

"I've taken care of him for a decade. Try again."

"You just drained him while forcing me to suck him off and didn't bother to tell either of us your intention. That's harmful."

Back to that again, then. "Mikael knew my intentions the second he tasted my blood. He didn't protest, so we proceeded."

She arched a brow. "Then why did he beg at the end?"

I sighed, running my fingers through my hair. Why was I even indulging this tomfoolery? I had far more important tasks to complete today.

Two more minutes, I told myself. *That's all she gets.*

What had she asked?

Right, she wanted to know why Mikael had sounded so betrayed before losing consciousness. "I withdrew the pleasure at the end, causing him to feel a hint of pain."

"And why did you do that if you didn't mean to hurt him?" she demanded.

"Because I didn't like seeing you between his legs, Raelyn. And I hated how much he enjoyed it." The words were out before I could stop them, surprising us both.

Why did this woman constantly force the truth from me?

Her lips parted, her cheeks reddening. "But... but you made me..."

All right, two minutes were up. "Meaning I only have myself to blame, yes?" I'd thought it would be a good introduction to expectations, but it'd backfired in my face. My territorial drive to take her for myself was far too strong for sharing, something I needed to get over, and quickly.

Once I fucked her, it would be fine.

But I couldn't yet. Not until after the party.

Unless I wanted to risk another royal or alpha taking her.

"I have work to do," I said, turning away from her. "I'll find someone to carry Mikael back to his room. Go to bed early, Raelyn. You'll need your rest before Jace arrives tomorrow."

I didn't wait for her reply, just slammed the door behind me and headed to my office. The damn woman accused me of playing mind games with her? Well, it seemed she was doing the same to me.

But I would win.

I always did.

Chapter Nineteen

RAE

I woke up alone, Kylan's side of the bed as pristine as it was when I went to sleep.

He never joined me last night.

That should have pleased me, but my lips curled downward instead of upward.

Because I didn't like seeing you between his legs.

His words had stayed with me throughout the night, carrying over into my dreams. What did they mean? He kept harping on my purpose to serve yet said he disliked it when I did. Another mind game? Kylan seemed to favor them, but he'd sounded so earnest when he had spoken those words.

He claimed to be honest with me.

Truth or a lie?

I couldn't tell, and I hated him for that. He lived in riddles, constantly requesting one thing while demanding the opposite. I'd lost it last night and given him a piece of my mind.

And he never retaliated.

My behavior would have earned a severe punishment at the university. I'd witnessed death sentences handed out to those who behaved far better than I had last night. Yet, Kylan merely walked away.

Did he have something worse planned today? To make an example of me?

I sat up, my head foggy with too much sleep. Worrying over Kylan and his intentions would drive me insane. Nothing was predictable with that man. Nothing.

A soft knock on the door had me pulling the covers up to conceal my bare chest. I'd slept naked, expecting Kylan to join me. Which, of course, he hadn't.

My frown curled downward more as Angelica's head appeared. Her dark eyes met mine, and surprise at seeing her again held me captive in the bed. "K-Kylan isn't here," I said, unsure of what she needed. I hadn't seen her since the incident at his home.

Her lips twitched. "I know. He's on a business call but asked me to tend to you."

Uh, and that means...? "Oh, uh, okay," I mumbled.

She entered with a plate in one hand and shut the door behind her.

"Spinach eggs," she said as she moved closer. "I ate a lot of these growing up, figured you probably did the same." She set the food on the nightstand and pinched her lips to the side. "Kylan has requested I assist you with your wardrobe. Jace and Darius are expected to arrive within the hour."

My lips parted. "Oh." I didn't know what else to say. Mikael had been the one to guide me around all week, but of course, he couldn't do that today. Not after what Kylan did to him.

"Yeah, so, uh, you eat that"—she pointed to the plate—"and I'll go find you a suitable outfit." She walked away muttering, "Because apparently feeding and dressing up humans is my job now."

"I can do that on my own," I offered. "If, I mean, you don't..." I trailed off, biting my lip as she faced me with a surprised expression. Right. Decorum completely broken. It was bad enough that I constantly challenged Kylan. To speak out of turn to others, to even look them in the eye, broke so many protocols.

I clearly have a death wish.

And worse, I'd acted this way in front of Angelica, a freshly turned vampire who *knew* the rules just as well as I did, if not better than me.

"F-forgive me," I whispered, lowering my gaze.

She laughed, the sound churning my stomach.

Angelica couldn't kill me—not without Kylan's consent—but she could reprimand me. Maybe.

I frowned. *No one touches you except me.* Did he mean that? Did it apply to discipline as well?

A shiver shook my spine at the thought of Kylan's version of a punishment. He'd yet to chastise me in any way aside from a few verbal threats. And I'd more than earned it by constantly challenging him.

Except that's what he wanted—a challenge in the bedroom and an obedient dog in public.

Technically, I was still in the bedroom.

"Do you have any idea how long it's been since I've been around an unbroken human?" Angelica asked, collapsing on the bed beside me. "Fuck, it's been ages." She fell backward on a huff. "Everyone bows and refuses to look at me, as if I'm some scary monster. But I was human less than a decade ago."

I waited for her to say more, but silence fell between us, oddly peaceful.

"What's it like?" I asked softly. "Transitioning from, well, human state to a vampire?"

She rolled to her side, her brown eyes meeting mine. "Not nearly as glorious as one might expect. They start you at the very bottom, with minimal income and bare essentials, and force you to work your way up. I'm only here because Kylan requested it, something Judith made very clear when promoting me to his security team. His decision is going to cost me, I think. Everyone wants to be closer to him, to his power, and I'm the youngest and most worthless of them all."

"If Kylan promoted you, then he sees potential in you." The words left my mouth without thought. They just sounded right.

Angelica remained quiet for a long moment, her lips pinched to the side. "I hope you're right."

"She is," Kylan murmured from the shadows, his body seeming to materialize before our eyes as he stepped into the light cast by the windows. "Why are you not eating, Raelyn?"

My jaw had dropped at his unexpected appearance, my voice forgotten.

Angelica leapt off the bed with a strangled sound, falling to her knees. "Forgive me, My Prince. It's my fault for—"

"I highly doubt it's your fault at all," he replied. "Raelyn?"

Rather than reply, I picked up the plate and shoveled a giant bite into my mouth. He cocked a brow, his lips twitching at the sides, and shook his head.

"Angelica, please find Raelyn a suitable dress. Jace's plane just landed, making him early."

"Of course, My Prince." She rose and went straight to the bathroom suite, her head bowed the entire way.

I consumed a forkful as he approached, my heart thundering in my chest. "Shall I punish her?" he asked quietly. "For chitchatting with you instead of following through on my demands to feed and dress you?"

I narrowed my gaze, swallowing the half-chewed food in my mouth. "I'm perfectly capable of feeding and dressing myself without a supervisor."

He tilted his head. "Is that what you told her?"

"No, I asked her what it's like to be a vampire." Which went against protocol, but was the truth.

"Because you want to become one?"

"What's the point in desiring an impossibility?" I countered, setting the plate down despite eating only half the contents. My appetite was nonexistent.

"Everyone has dreams, Raelyn." He tucked a strand of hair behind my ear and leaned in to brush his lips over mine. "Even gorgeous pets."

"Dreaming is for the weak."

"It used to be for the spirited."

"Well, as you pointed out just last night, we live in a very different time, don't we?"

"Indeed we do." He kissed me again, lingering. "But you remind me of a time I preferred, Raelyn." He straightened and turned as Angelica returned.

"Does this suit, My Prince?" She held up a deep-red silk gown that would barely cover my breasts. At least the skirt fell to the ground.

"It does," he replied, holding out his hand for the dress. "I can take it from here. Please inform Judith that I've changed my mind and will be entertaining Jace here instead of at K Hotel."

Angelica noticeably paled. "O-of course, Your Highness." She bowed and retreated quickly, leaving me alone with Kylan.

He laid the dress over the bed and began unbuttoning his shirt. "We have time for a quick rinse. Go turn on the water and wait for me there."

Part of me wanted to refuse just to irritate him, but the dangerous glint in his gaze forced me from the bed and into the bathroom.

The shower had just started to warm when Kylan appeared—naked—behind me.

Tracing, I realized. Only the oldest of vampires possessed that ability. They couldn't teleport long distances, only a few miles or so, but it was as if he disappeared and reappeared before my eyes.

He kissed my shoulder, his hands on my hips and guiding me forward beneath the spray. This was the first time he'd followed through on his comment about wanting me in the shower with him every evening.

I waited for the demand to kneel, to satisfy the prominent erection resting against my ass, but the words never came. He combed my dampening strands, spreading the moisture evenly.

His lips met my temple as he reached around me for the shampoo. He continued his ministrations, creating suds on top of my head before rinsing me clean, and repeated the action with the conditioner.

"Turn," he said softly, picking up the soap.

I swallowed and did as directed, facing his immortal beauty.

This was a far cry from a punishment.

Unless he meant to tease me to death.

Each stroke of his warm palm over my skin excited my hormones, stirring an inferno in my lower belly that spread through my veins. His touch slid over my abdomen, lower to the tops of my thighs, and up my side, missing all the areas I desired him most.

A groan fought its way up my throat, but I caught it with my teeth, clamping down so tightly something cracked.

Kylan chuckled, his hand moving to my shoulder and down my arm. "Your determination is admirable, Raelyn. But I'll win."

"Win what?" I managed to say through my teeth.

"You," he replied simply, the soap returning to my sternum to slide between my breasts.

My breath hitched as he continued down to my belly button and lower, brushing the top of my mound. "Y-you already own me."

"I do," he agreed. "But according to you, it's your body

I own and nothing else." He dipped between my legs, causing my heart to stop completely. "But I want more, Raelyn."

It took serious effort to concentrate on his words and not his hypnotic touch. Because, Goddess, that felt amazing. A single night without him had ignited an overwhelming need, one only Kylan could satisfy.

"I want to possess all of you," he added, his silky voice a deep caress against my ear.

A tremble licked across my skin, trailing goose bumps along the way despite the hot water. "That's never going to happen," I managed on an exhale.

"I disagree," he whispered, his lips flitting across my cheek to hover over my mouth as he pulled me against him. "I'm going to start with your mind, not by playing a game but by telling you the truth."

Another shiver shook my being, teasing my nipples into sharp points against his too-hot chest. "The truth," I repeated, trying with all my might to focus on the conversation and not on his hand between my legs. The soap had switched to his other palm, gliding up my side.

So much sensation.

So much *heat*.

"Yes." He tugged on my lip, sucking it into his mouth. "Turn around, Raelyn."

My feet moved before my mind could even process the demand.

"Put your hands on the wall."

I did.

He trailed the soap down my spine. "Spread your legs."

That was the opposite of what I wanted. My core ached for friction, something he'd taken away when he forced me to rotate. But I followed his order, sliding my thighs apart and widening my stance.

"Beautiful." He pulled my hair over my shoulder, exposing all of my back to him, and began massaging me in slow circles, the floral scent tickling my nostrils.

No one had ever done this to me before. I felt almost cherished, worshiped, which couldn't be his intention.

"Now, as for the truth." He kissed my nape and nipped the tender skin, shooting sparks to all of my nerve endings. "Jace is arriving early because I asked him to. Despite evidence to the contrary, I think he's behind the attack on my character."

I blinked. *What?* "Jace?" *Why?*

"His territory borders mine, and his new sovereign would be next in line to inherit my region, providing them both a motive and an opportunity." Kylan's palm slid downward, slipping between my cheeks and shooting a shock up across my skin.

He couldn't mean to—

His incisors pierced my neck, sending euphoria through my bloodstream. I quivered against him, my legs threatening to collapse.

"Kylan," I breathed, arching back into him. The soap disappeared, his arm circling my waist to hold me in place while his opposite hand remained against my ass—considering, prodding, testing my boundaries.

I'd never been touched *there*.

Until now.

Flames ignited across my flesh at the forbidden nature of his exploration. The university had offered courses on this. I'd avoided them, not knowing why anyone would favor such an act. But oh, maybe, just maybe, I'd been wrong.

Ecstasy pooled between my legs, Kylan's bite exciting all my senses. And his finger—no, fingers—were doing wicked things to my insides.

My nails scraped the tiles, my arms shaking from holding my position.

Too much sensation.

The hot water trickling over us only added to my misery, overriding my being with a foreign elation that rattled me to my core.

Only my body, I vowed. *Only this.*

But, *fuck!*

My head fell forward on a harsh exhale. He'd intensified the pleasure, ripping me in two, his intrusion below overwhelming my being. The hold around my waist was all that kept me standing, my legs no longer functioning.

"I, oh..." I trailed off on a hiss, his resulting chuckle sliding over my senses.

"Too much?" he asked softly, my neck throbbing with desire.

So that's what it feels like to be bitten.

No wonder Mikael enjoyed it.

My limbs vibrated, my palms barely balanced against the wall. He was destroying me. Slowly. Fully. Completely.

But not my mind.

His hold shifted, his palm sliding down to cup my sex while he continued to penetrate me from behind with his opposite hand.

"K-Kylan..." I didn't know whether to beg him to stop or demand more.

He kissed my pulse, his tongue lapping at the wound he'd left open on my skin. Each swipe sent another tremor through my body, centering in my core. His finger circled my clit, deepening the moment, shooting off stars behind my eyes.

So close.

But not enough.

I *needed*... Oh, I didn't even know.

His name fell from my lips once more, his teeth moving to my earlobe to nibble instead. "I can't wait to fuck you, Raelyn. In all ways. Your pussy, your ass." His fingers plunged into me with the words, stoking my inner flames. "I will own all of you. Including your mind."

I shook my head, swallowing. "No."

"Yes." Another thrust, this time from the front and the back. I moaned in reply, my heart thudding in my ears. My muscles had pulled tight, my abdomen curling with that familiar ache only Kylan could relieve. "Your heart, too, princess. Your spirit. I want it all."

"No," I repeated, my nails threatening to break against the wall from how hard I dug into the hard surface. "Never."

He nuzzled the sensitive spot below my ear. "Are you on fire, little lamb? Feeling as if you might explode?"

I groaned as he increased the pace, stimulating my orgasm without giving me that extra push my body required. "Y-yes," I whispered. "I don't... I can't..." It was right there. So close. So fierce. And refusing my embrace. A frustrated scream built up in my throat, my body begging for the edge that eluded me.

"That's your mind, Raelyn," he whispered. "Waiting for my command, refusing to let you come without my permission." He licked my throat again, showering wildfire across my being, piercing my very soul.

"Kylan," I whimpered, no longer able to process anything other than the passionate spell weaving a binding pattern beneath my skin, forever labeling me as *his*.

"Your mind longs for my approval. Beg me, sweetheart, and I'll let you shatter." The words were a dark promise against my ear.

I quivered, unable to deny his power. "Please." My body clenched around him, urging him to finish it, to grant me the release I so desperately craved. "Please, Kylan."

His amusement trickled over me, his fingers fucking me in earnest. "More."

"What do you want?" I asked, water prickling my eyes from the insanity throbbing within me. "I can't give you all of me. Anything else, but not that."

"Don't you see?" His lips were against my ear. "I already *own* you, Raelyn."

"No." I shook my head, tears falling freely. "No."

"Oh, yes," he murmured, pushing deep. "Come for me, princess." He punctuated the demand by sinking his incisors into my skin.

I screamed as my world came undone.

Everything shook.

The ground.

The air.

My very being.

Devastated.

Broken beyond repair.

He owns me.

The words reverberated in my thoughts as his name left my mouth as a curse and a prayer.

It hurt. It overwhelmed. It destroyed.

And I wanted him to do it all over again, to take me to this place of oblivion that only existed with Kylan. Only existed in his arms, beneath his touch, with his *permission*.

Fuck, I hated him.

I adored him.

I wanted to kill him.

To fuck him.

To hit him.

My knees gave out from the onslaught of emotions and feelings, my body incapable of such a divine experience. Kylan caught me, lifting me into his arms with the ease of a much stronger being. His lips whispered over my cheek, his tongue tasting my tears.

He'd obliterated me.

I couldn't even open my eyes.

"I'm becoming addicted to the way you say my name in the throes of passion, Raelyn." He held me beneath the water to wash away the soap. The warmth prickled my too-sensitive skin, eliciting tremors from my lower body.

He kissed a path to my mouth, his tongue dipping inside with ease to fill my mouth with his blood. I choked, not ready, but he was relentless, forcing me to swallow or risk inhaling his essence.

My insides tingled, welcoming the energetic boost and healing properties of his being into mine. The heady fluid wrapped me in a euphoric cocoon, one I craved far more than I should.

Kylan was creating an addiction, one only he alone could satisfy. I longed to fight it but couldn't, not when it left me feeling so blissfully complete.

Mine, a foreign voice whispered through my thoughts. *My world. My place. My purpose.*

I blocked the seductive chant from my mind, refusing to let it guide me. I would not—could not—fall into Kylan's web.

Too late...

No.

The water shut off, and Kylan stepped out with me still in his arms. When had we stopped kissing? Was he even clean?

He enveloped me in a towel, my feet somehow sturdy on the ground despite the fog clouding my mind.

What had he done to me?

Who am I?

"Jace will be here soon," Kylan said, his palms rubbing my arms with the cotton fabric. His erection stood proud between us, a firm reminder of my lack of reciprocation.

Would he push me to my knees now?

My legs started to bend, anticipating his demand, but his grip on my biceps kept me upright.

"Later, Raelyn. Jace is our priority right now. I need you to listen to me."

I blinked at the water droplets dancing along the planes of his chest. *Male perfection.* I bent to trace the line with my tongue, loving the taste of him. One of his hands went to my hair, his fingers knotting in my strands.

Now he would force—

"Raelyn." He yanked me back to meet his gaze. "I need you to focus."

I just smiled. "Then you shouldn't have showered with me."

He chuckled and shook his head. "You're blood-drunk."

I shrugged. Or I tried to. My shoulders just seemed to

flop. "Okay."

With a smirk, he wrapped a towel around his waist and picked me up to carry me into the bedroom. "You need more food." He dropped me unceremoniously onto the bed and handed me the half-eaten plate of eggs. "I want those gone by the time I'm finished talking."

My nose crinkled, but I forced a forkful of cold eggs into my mouth and chewed.

"Good, little lamb." He patted me on the head.

I narrowed my gaze, which only caused his lips to curl in response. "Jackass," I grumbled, recalling the term from a movie earlier this week. It seemed to be an appropriate nickname for Kylan.

His laugh startled me. It was full of life and humor and nothing like his usual low chuckles. His face crinkled into lines I'd never seen, his enjoyment almost palpable.

He grabbed me and kissed me so hard I almost forgot how to breathe. Kylan released me just as suddenly, his smile still firmly in place. "Careful, darling, or I'll keep you forever."

I snorted. "Not likely."

His eyebrows rose. "Excuse me?"

Oh, had I said that out loud? Hmm. I ate another bite of egg and just stared at him. We both knew he couldn't keep me forever, so why even discuss it?

He sat beside me on the bed, his palm going to my cheek.

"Truth," he murmured. "I don't trust Jace, and I'm concerned he may try to hurt you. Not directly, but indirectly, to cause a scene. Assuming he's the one framing me for insanity, I mean. So I need you to stay by my side all night, and I need you to behave for me."

I swallowed the last bit from the plate and set it on the nightstand beside me.

"You really think he's the one who killed your harem?" Because it didn't match the Jace I'd studied in school, the Jace who was a political mastermind and nearly as brilliant as Kylan.

"I think he has the best motive."

"Which makes him too obvious."

He tilted his head to the side. "Meaning?"

"Meaning he's too obvious," I repeated. "Would you do something so conspicuous?"

He snorted. "No, for several reasons, the primary one being I'm more strategic than that."

"And Jace isn't strategic?"

"He is, which explains the lack of evidence and his perfect alibis. It's exactly as I would play it."

"Minus the obvious part," I pointed out.

He opened his mouth, then closed it, his dark eyes glimmering with appreciation. "Fascinating," he murmured. "You're the first person brave enough to counter my opinion."

My brow furrowed. "There's nothing brave about logic." And it seemed too easy for Jace to be the culprit.

"There is when it's contrary to a royal's thoughts on the matter. You'd be surprised how many of my constituents are afraid to debate with me."

"I'm not debating." Or that hadn't been my intention, anyway.

"No, you're forcing me to see beyond a millennia-old rivalry and acknowledge reason." He drew his thumb over my bottom lip. "This meeting with Jace may just prove even more enlightening than I originally anticipated. Thank you."

"I didn't really do anything."

"On the contrary, little lamb." He kissed me softly, his tongue playing over my lips. "You did more than you realize." He nudged me onto my back and settled his hips between my legs, the towels the only fabric separating us. "Jace will be here in twenty minutes. I'm going to spend ten of those minutes kissing you. Then you're going to ready yourself to help me greet him."

"O-okay," I whispered, swallowing.

"I won't be sharing you, Raelyn," he vowed against my

mouth. "As a royal and his elder, it's my birthright. Besides, as you may have learned, I'm not particularly fond of rules."

I nodded. "Yes."

"Good. Now open your mouth."

Chapter Twenty

KYLAN

My lips tingled. Actually *tingled*.

I resisted the urge to touch them.

Raelyn made me feel... young. Alive. Oddly at peace.

I hadn't meant to go to her, but after hearing the comments about Angelica's promotion, I couldn't stop myself from appearing. That was my consequence for eavesdropping.

Raelyn had asked about the transition to becoming a vampire, a clear breaking of the rules, and Angelica had replied. Both of them should be punished, but how could I discipline them when my lips had lifted in response? Sending Angelica to Judith with news that I'd changed meeting locations was penalty enough.

My phone buzzed with a message from my most trusted

lieutenant. *Jace has arrived.*

Send him upstairs, I replied, knowing full well she hated this plan. Of course, she said nothing. No one ever questioned me.

Except Raelyn.

She wore the red silk gown perfectly, her breasts barely contained by the low-cut fabric. Her luscious red locks were pulled up on top of her head in a messy array I'd assembled myself. The only problem was my blood had healed her mark.

Something I should fix.

I grabbed her hip and yanked her against me. She wobbled on her heels, her hands going to my biceps for balance.

"I love this dress." The slits went up both sides to the tops of her thighs, and her back was completely exposed. "Removing it later will be a great joy."

She shivered, her blue eyes lifting to mine. "You wear a suit nicely."

My eyebrows lifted. "Did you just give me a compliment?"

Her lips twitched. "Maybe."

She'd surprised me. Again.

"Who are you?" I marveled softly. The woman constantly shocked me, from the very first bite on my tongue. I wrapped my palm around her neck and debated where to mark her. The pulse point was too easy. I wanted something more intimate, more scandalous.

"Rae," she replied, a defiant flash in her gaze that went straight to my chest. It had not escaped my notice that Mikael had called her that name all week.

"Raelyn," I corrected.

I didn't give her time for a reply, my need to bite her too strong.

My incisors met the flesh of her breast, right next to her silky dress, striking deep and fast and eliciting a yelp from her. Her nails bit into my jacket, her breath hitching as I sucked hard, ensuring my claim remained even with my blood thriving inside her. It would partly heal, enough to stop her bleeding, but the blemish would be fresh for introductions. Especially with the elevator announcing Jace's impending arrival.

Ignoring the sound of steps over the marble, I continued feeding, Raelyn's moans music to my ears. She'd lost herself to me, unaware of our audience, and I adored it too much to stop. Not right away.

I gave it a long moment, easing her out of the oblivion before righting her again and smiling down at her. "Say your name," I whispered.

"Rae," she replied, her gaze drowsy.

I shook my head and smiled. "Defiant until the end, hmm?" I turned to face Jace and his new sovereign. "What do you do when a pet misbehaves, Jace?"

Raelyn froze beside me, finally realizing our company had arrived.

"It depends on the infraction," he replied coolly.

"Failing to remember her given name." I cocked a brow. "What would you do?"

"Make her repeat the name while I fucked her mouth. And I wouldn't stop until I was convinced she remembered it."

I smiled and wrapped my arm around Raelyn's lower back. "A sound idea. Raelyn?"

She bit her lip, her gaze on the floor. "As you wish, My Prince." It came out soft but sure. I kept her upright when she started to bend her legs and pulled her tight to my side.

"A punishment for later," I whispered against her ear. One I may or may not indulge in. It would depend on the rest of the evening. "Ah, well, welcome, Jace. Darius." I held out a hand to them both, shaking firmly while holding Raelyn at my side. They both noted the fresh marks on her breast, but neither remarked on it.

"We appreciate the invitation," Jace murmured, following formalities. "Darius, introduce Juliet."

"With pleasure." He guided the striking brunette forward with a palm against her lower back. "This is my blood virgin and *Erosita*, Juliet." She curtsied low, her translucent gown displaying all her assets and two sets of fresh bite marks. Had Jace and Darius shared her on the way here?

Whatever they had going between them should have fascinated me a hell of a lot more than it actually did. Having Raelyn at my side, her aroused screams still fresh in my ears, dulled me to Juliet's charm.

"She's beautiful," I murmured. "I can see why you kept her, Darius." She remained in a low bow, waiting to be released, her training abundantly clear. "She's welcome to stand."

Darius returned his hand to her back as she obeyed, her focus on the floor, just like Raelyn's.

"Did you leave your consorts at home?" I asked Jace, noticing his lack of an entourage.

"They weren't needed." A smooth reply. "Not when I have access to Juliet's finer attributes. You should hear her scream. It's a lovely sound."

I considered that with a smile. It seemed a clever excuse for keeping his harem from me, which suggested he feared what I might do to them. Because he believed me insane, or because he expected retribution? Time would tell.

"Well, this is my Raelyn." I nuzzled her throat. "She, too, screams beautifully. Care for a demonstration?" Her pulse escalated at the suggestion, a hint of excitement underlying the alluring rhythm.

"I may enjoy that later," Jace murmured. "Juliet would be happy to reciprocate, right, Darius?"

"Of course." He seemed almost cold, his posture stiff, aloof. The rumors stated he had only taken an *Erosita* to prove his wealth and power and kept her because Jace enjoyed the benefits. His bored expression and light touch against the female's back confirmed the speculation. No outward signs of possession apart from the mark on her neck and she certainly didn't seem all that inclined to him.

But it's too perfect, my instincts whispered. It was exactly how I would act should I ever take a mate. Which would never happen. Not even with…

Raelyn.

I glanced at her, realization slamming me in the gut.

She was an untouched virgin.

Never bitten.

Until me.

I'd unknowingly initiated the ceremony between us by exchanging blood.

Fascinating. No wonder I felt so connected to her.

Well, I certainly needed to fix that problem, and quickly.

But first, our guests. I returned my gaze to Jace and grinned. "Can I interest you in a drink before dinner?" Zelda probably needed another hour to prepare considering I'd switched the meeting location at the last minute.

"Wine?" my fellow royal suggested, his lips kicking up at the sides.

I tightened my grip on Raelyn. "With a splash of blood to top it off?"

"It's as if you read my mind, Kylan." He glanced at Juliet, the indication clear. "Speaking of decadent items, where's your favorite pet?"

"Ah, Mikael is feeling a bit drained at the moment." I led the way to the seating area while adding, "He had a little too much fun playing with Raelyn yesterday."

Jace chuckled and settled into an oversized chair. "I bet." He held out a hand that Juliet accepted and assisted her into his lap. Darius took a seat beside them on the sofa.

An intriguing dynamic, one that came off as natural but struck me as intentional.

Protective, even.

Because they feared I might ask for a bite? Or something else?

"Raelyn, would you mind asking Zelda to help us with the wine? Tell her a French red will do nicely; she'll understand." I had a cabinet of favorites that she kept well stocked.

"Of course, My Prince." She curtsied beautifully and strolled off with a confidence I admired. Her dress revealed her curves without putting them on display like Juliet's gown.

"I'm glad you didn't kill her," Jace remarked, his silver-blue eyes on Raelyn's ass. "Would be a shame to waste such gorgeous talent."

I welcomed the jibe and reference to my former harem. "Yes, she's rather disobedient. Very different from my previous consorts."

He smirked, giving nothing away. "Then hopefully you'll keep her around for a while."

My lips curled. "You mean, as opposed to what was done to my deceased harem?"

"Yes, some may refer to that as a misuse of resources." Jace pulled Juliet's hair over one shoulder while speaking and kissed her neck. Her pulse remained admirably steady, her familiarity with Jace evident. "I prefer to reallocate my pets when I grow bored of them," he added, his focus on Juliet. "But to each his own."

Perfectly played, as always.

He didn't admonish my behavior yet managed to offer his opinion—disapproval. Was it all a ploy because he orchestrated the deaths himself? Or did he truly feel that way?

Obvious, Raelyn had said. *All right, little lamb. Let's see if you're right.*

I took up the opposite end of the sofa from Darius and folded my ankle over my knee. "Congratulations on your new position."

"Thank you," he replied, confidence and age radiating from him. "It's an intriguing change."

"I bet." I considered him carefully. Darius was old enough to be a royal, had the bloodline in him as well. And his maker, Cam, had been one of the best chess players I'd ever known. Which labeled Darius as a fierce competitor even without Jace seated beside him.

"So what sparked your interest in joining the political arena after all this time?" I asked, genuinely curious.

Raelyn and Zelda returned with the wine, but Darius's focus remained on me. "Mainly, I didn't feel there was anyone else better qualified in Jace Region to run. And secondly, I'm tired of being governed by vampires half my age."

A fair statement, one I could respect.

I accepted the glass Raelyn handed me and pulled her into my lap, leaving Zelda to pass out wine to the others. She finished and left without a word, her focus on dinner.

"But why now?" I asked Darius. "Because of Adrian Loughton's untimely demise?" Mauled by a pack of rogue lycans, if my sources were correct. But I suspected the lycans were actually hired. That's how I would have played it, anyway.

"His passing afforded me a new opportunity." He snapped his fingers, and Juliet raised her wrist. No tremble. No fear. Merely a soft scent of arousal.

Well, now *that* was fascinating.

She liked him.

And the slight twitch in her lips proved it.

An *Erosita* could communicate telepathically with her master. Were they speaking to one another right now? Darius kissed her wrist before sinking his fangs into her delicate skin. She didn't flinch, not even as he squeezed to force droplets of her addictive essence into his glass. Jace shook his head in polite—yet odd—refusal.

What kind of vampire turned down the offering of a blood virgin? Especially after suggesting it in the foyer.

One with a secret up his sleeve.

I didn't follow suit with Raelyn, having enjoyed my fill earlier.

Darius sealed Juliet's wound and her lips twitched again, her arousal piquing.

Oh, they were most definitely communicating.

I met Jace's penetrating gaze, noting the protective quality lurking in those silver depths. Of Darius, Juliet, or both?

"I wonder," I said slowly, determining my phrasing. "How far will your new political aspirations take you, Darius?"

He relaxed into the sofa, leaving Juliet on Jace's lap, where she relaxed far more than a human should. Even Raelyn's shoulders were lined with tension, her pulse beating seductively in my ears.

"I'm quite content with my new title," he replied smoothly.

"Of course." I slid my palm up and down Raelyn's arm in an attempt to smooth the goose bumps pebbling her creamy skin. "But what of the future? You're of royal blood—Cam's line—and could qualify for a region of your own should one become available. Surely that's a consideration?"

He chuckled, sharing a glance with Jace. "No. I've never had—nor will I ever have—a desire for my own territory."

Truth or a lie.

I sipped my wine while continuing to stroke Raelyn with my opposite hand, her body slowly easing into mine. She must have expected me to bleed her into my glass. Poor little lamb, always guessing. I kissed her shoulder softly. "Would you like a sip, little lamb?" I asked, holding the wine before her.

She glanced back at me with wide blue eyes, then dropped them. "No, thank you, My Prince."

Her breach in decorum had me grinning. "What color are Juliet's eyes?" I wondered out loud, refocusing on Jace and Darius. "I mean, does it bother you at all that they are constantly lowered?"

"You would prefer her to be more direct?" Darius asked, his eyebrow lifting.

I shrugged. "I would prefer to admire her beautiful face,

not have her hide beneath a veneer of dark hair." My grip shifted to Raelyn's neck and up into her messy array of red strands, gently pulling her upward. "My consort has gorgeous blue eyes that she constantly hides. Wouldn't you rather see them?" I glanced between our guests, waiting.

"Are you offering a closer look?" Jace asked, his heated gaze traveling over Raelyn suggestively.

An irrational urge to growl tempted my throat. *Never.*

"Not tonight," was my response instead. It came out slightly deeper than intended, my instincts rioting against even the possibility of sharing her.

That's new.

It's the bond...

I studied Darius, Juliet, and Jace, an idea forming and solidifying, an answer to a question I hadn't even realized I'd asked.

But I had to be sure.

I took a long sip, debating my next play. Yes. The rules. I released Raelyn to stroke my thumb over her cheek, appreciating the delightful blush blossoming beneath the skin. "I'm just wondering why we force such beautiful women to hide their best features," I murmured, feigning curiosity in the trivial statement.

"Decorum," Darius replied simply.

"Yes," I agreed. "Lilith's version of it, anyway."

I waited and caught the surprise I expected in Jace's features. Darius did a better job controlling himself, but the flare in his pupils confirmed my suspicions.

"What? Don't tell me you prefer all her ridiculous rules too?" *Because I can tell you don't.* I sighed and waved it off as a flippant comment. "Well, if you prefer they hide, they can hide. But I am curious about something."

Jace affixed a bored expression, his part in this play almost perfect. Almost. "Regarding?"

I finished my glass and set it aside, taking my time and drawing out the moment. Darius's responses were too perfect, and Jace's body language was too practiced.

The perfect facade.

And if anyone could see through such a charade, it was me.

I'd suspected for months that Jace was up to something and had assumed it revolved around plots to obtain my territory. But Raelyn's commentary earlier forced me to see beyond the rivalry I'd quietly enjoyed with Jace for millennia.

Oh, he possessed a secret all right, but it had nothing to do with me and everything to do with the female on his lap.

She was too calm.

Because his touch remained mostly neutral. She wore a practically nonexistent dress, and his hand remained on her upper thigh.

He didn't kiss her.

He denied her blood.

And Darius remained completely at ease while having his *Erosita*—his mate—on the lap of another male.

I'd barely engaged in the ceremony with Raelyn, and I already felt the stirrings of possession, hence my cruelty with Mikael just last night. Just the mere thought of sharing her now with either of these men had my blood boiling.

No.

There was absolutely no way Darius would approve of Juliet being manhandled by another male, even his royal and superior, unless they had an arrangement.

I wrapped my arms around Raelyn, pulling her close, but also having a hold on her in case I needed to remove her quickly.

"You might be wondering why I invited you both here this evening," I said.

"You're not one to engage in political platitudes," Jace replied, his shrewd gaze narrowing. "So yes, I am. Are we finally going to arrive at the point?"

Ah, there was the royal who reminded me too much of myself—my rival for good reason. "I thought, perhaps, you were responsible for killing my harem, but I see now that's not the case at all."

His gaze widened a fraction, the only indication of shock he displayed. Darius, however, had gone eerily still, his green eyes focused with the predatory senses of a male detecting a threat—not to himself, but to his female.

I smiled. "Yes, that's what I thought," I continued. "But that's not the case at all, is it?"

"If I wanted your territory, Kylan, I wouldn't frame you for mental insanity," Jace said flatly. "Which I assume is what you suspected of me."

Yes, my rival indeed. And also a potential ally.

"It was, until about an hour ago when Raelyn mentioned it was too obvious." I kissed her temple, proud of her instincts.

His dark brows shot upward. "You're taking advice from your consort?"

"You're surprised?" I tilted my head, my lips threatening to twitch. "That's intriguing considering you're playing some sort of game with Darius. I mean, you are in fact only pretending to enjoy his *Erosita,* yes?"

Chapter Twenty-One

KYLAN

Silence.

Tension thickened the air as Juliet's breath finally faltered.

Yes. I'd definitely read the situation accurately. "You don't want anyone to know because having a mate is perceived as a weakness and you refuse to share."

Darius neither confirmed nor denied it, merely waited.

"Prove me wrong," I encouraged. "Put on a show for me, Jace, with Juliet." I waved at the table. "It's not like I haven't seen you fuck a woman before." We'd shared plenty of females together once upon a time.

Jace's jaw tightened. "What do you really want, Kylan?"

"Oh, I already achieved my goal for the evening by confirming you're not the one framing me for immortal insanity. This is merely fun."

"So you didn't kill your harem." He removed Juliet from his lap and handed her over to Darius, who gladly accepted her into his arms. "But someone managed to get through your defenses and frame you."

"Indeed."

"Which explains why you're hosting a party in two weeks. You intend to draw out the guilty party by using your new consort as bait. They'll want to make it a grand show, after all." He set his barely touched wine aside. "Clever."

"Yes, well, you are—or were—at the top of my suspect list."

"I'm both flattered and insulted."

Yes, I'd feel the same if the roles were reversed. "Could it be Brandt or Luka?"

Jace snorted. "No. Luka has no desire to be near water, and Brandt is abrasive, not strategic. If he wanted your land, you'd know."

That'd been my assessment as well. "Any suggestions?"

"Off the top of my head?" Jace rubbed the back of his neck, his gaze traveling upward. "Naomi's hatred of you is no secret, and she has the resources to pull it off."

"Yes, I suppose she would be quite satisfied by my removal." But she wouldn't gain anything else. My land was nowhere near her region in what was formerly known as South Africa. "If I consider all those with personal vendettas, essentially everyone would be a suspect."

Jace smirked. "You do have a penchant for pissing off the lycans."

"Vampires, too," I pointed out. "But it has to go beyond mere revenge for something petty. Whoever it is sent someone into my house to kill my property. That takes a level of skill and planning that not many possess."

"Unless it's someone who's bored and craving a diversion," Darius said while combing his fingers through Juliet's hair. She'd relaxed against him, her head on his shoulder and her dark eyes on Raelyn. It seemed decorum had gone out the window, fucking finally.

I shifted Raelyn to my side in an attempt to make her more comfortable and wrapped my arm around her shoulders. "That begs the question: who would be both brave and foolish enough to challenge me?"

"Another royal," Darius suggested. "Someone who wants to knock you off the top of the ladder."

"That would place Jace at the top." I arched a brow at him. "And we just decided it's not you."

"Which implies that I would be the next target," he inferred. "Hazel would be next, but it's not her."

"No, it's not," I agreed. It wasn't her style. When Hazel wanted something, she was blunt and direct. She'd never been the game-playing type.

"Which brings us back to the diversion potential," Darius murmured.

It was an angle I hadn't considered. "Any ideas?"

"Robyn," Jace said, chuckling. "That bitch always wants to play."

I laughed. "She knows better than to fuck with me."

Jace shrugged. "True. But I wouldn't rule anyone out."

"Except you," I replied dryly.

"If I wanted your territory, Kylan, I wouldn't try to discredit you; I would kill you." A blunt statement, not a threat. "I know better than to leave you alive after engaging in such a game."

Because he knew I would come after him and return the favor tenfold. "Touché." I felt the same way about him. "Well, how would you like to move forward? I've expressed a weakness by admitting I didn't kill my harem, and you're clearly hiding a weakness of your own." I looked pointedly at Juliet.

Jace considered, his silver eyes blazing with intelligence. "We've spent a thousand years or so working against each other when we used to work quite well together."

It was true. Our rivalry had begun over a conflict of interest in properties. We always enjoyed similar luxuries, and it became almost a game of chess as to who could acquire the most the fastest. None of it really mattered now, not in this new world.

"Do you miss it? The way things used to be?" I drew my thumb up and down Raelyn's shoulder, considering my own questions. "Because I do. I miss the challenge and the lack of responsibility for anyone other than myself."

Running a territory of vampires was a necessity more than a choice. They required justice and order. It was the only way to control the population, to maintain proper blood supplies, and to ensure the survival of the human race.

"Cam always thought we could coexist with humans differently," Darius admitted.

"Yes, Lilith clearly didn't agree." Since she'd put the eldest of our kind on a public trial that ended in his death sentence, except I never actually saw her carry it out. "Do you suppose Cam is alive somewhere?" It was considered treason to speculate or discuss the past, but Lilith and her army of enthusiasts didn't scare me.

Jace's pupils flared. "Why would you suspect that?"

"It's something I've wondered and thought you might know. If anyone was invited to his execution, it would be his only living relatives, yes?" Darius as his only progeny and Jace as his cousin.

"You think he might be alive?" Darius asked.

"Did you see him die?" I countered.

He remained silent for a long beat before saying, "No."

"Then." I waved my hand, signifying my point as made. "So where is he and who has him?"

"I thought we were here to discuss the issue of you being framed," Jace said slowly. "How did we switch to Cam?"

"Darius brought him up after I asked about former times." I narrowed my gaze. "But it's interesting that you want to avoid the topic."

More silence fell, the tension of earlier returning.

Ah, so there was more to his secrets, something to do

with Cam. "Do you know where he is?" I wondered, fascinated.

His nostrils flared, but still he remained quiet.

"Then you don't, but you want to know." I glanced between him and Darius and noted the way Juliet had avoided his gaze. Even she was in on the ploy. "Oh, now I'm fascinated. You've been holding out on me, Jace."

"We're not friends, Kylan. We're not even allies."

"But we used to be," I reminded him.

"A long time ago."

I gestured around us, to Juliet, to Raelyn, to the floor-to-ceiling windows overlooking Kylan City. "It's a new world, Jace, filled with fresh beginnings."

"You invited me over tonight because you thought I was trying to steal your territory," he growled.

"Which you've proven isn't the case and have instead brought me a wealth of intriguing information." I eyed the blood virgin again before meeting Jace's gaze directly. "If I can see through your charade, how many others will?"

"How many will believe you've gone mad?" he countered.

I snorted. "Several, and I welcome the accusation. I'm more than capable of holding my own."

"As am I."

"But together we would be formidable, and no one would ever expect an alliance between us."

That gave Jace pause, his jaw tightening. He knew I was right. Our notorious rivalry painted us on opposite sides of the playing field. Working together would be the last thing anyone would anticipate, something I could use to help solve my current problem and something he could use to his advantage in whatever scheme he had going.

"What are your terms?" he asked slowly.

"For starters, I would appreciate your assistance at my social engagement in two weeks. Someone may say something to you, or near you, assuming you would never pass the information on to me. In return, I can offer assistance in hiding Darius's, shall we call them, affections?"

Darius arched a brow. "And how do you propose to do that?"

"The same way Jace is helping you now. You'll be staying in my city for the weeks prior to the party. We'll let assumptions be made about *how* you spent your time here."

"Wouldn't that imply a partnership of some kind?"

I smiled. "Not if we spin the gossip appropriately." Something Judith excelled at greatly. "Perhaps I took a liking to your *Erosita* and proposed a temporary trade. Being your elder, you can hardly refuse."

"And what will actually be occurring?" he pressed, his grip around Juliet tightening possessively.

"You and Juliet can remain here, and I'll take Raelyn to my estate north of here." That would give me plenty of time to fix this accidental bond I'd created while also offering Darius and Juliet a moment of solitude disguised as something far darker. Two birds, one stone. "Everyone will believe we made an arrangement, one you could negatively discuss during the festivities."

"The part of a disgruntled houseguest," Jace translated. "Sharing is fine, but the least Kylan could have done was respect Darius's property. Some of the marks were a little too deep, almost as if he'd lost himself to the moment."

"All signs of immortal insanity," Darius added. "Coupled with how he slaughtered his harem, I'll admit that I'm concerned."

"Rightly so." Jace picked up his wine again, his gaze meeting mine. "He's certainly lost the plot."

I chuckled and shook my head. "You're nearly as old as I am."

"Yes, but I wear my age far better than you do."

I snorted. "The key is being realistic, not going off on fantasy tangents."

"We'll handle it just fine," he murmured, swirling the contents of his glass. "Am I to stay here as well? Because that would be less believable."

"You had business to attend to and left me behind to keep an eye on Kylan, worried that his recent behavior may impact the borders to your territory. I agreed and used Juliet as my bargaining chip to procure an invitation." Darius kissed her neck, causing her lips to curl. "The party is the first time we've had a chance to connect, hence our resulting conversation over Kylan's antics."

"Brilliant," Jace replied. "I knew I promoted you for a reason."

Darius smirked. "More than one."

Their easy camaraderie revealed a true friendship, one I knew existed but hadn't seen in over a century. All the formalities Lilith insisted upon in society had removed all semblance of humanity, even among ourselves. Everything was about law and order, running a smooth region, following protocols, and respecting the elders of the species.

Being at the top afforded me opportunities very few would ever see. That's what Angelica had mentioned to Raelyn—being a vampire wasn't nearly as glamorous as humans were led to believe. The youngest immortals started with nothing unless their royal or alpha decreed otherwise.

"We'll do this for you," Jace said, drawing me back to the conversation at hand. "If all goes according to plan, then we should discuss the notion of an alliance more in depth."

A test.

He meant to see how this all played out before deciding to trust me.

"That's fair." Because I, too, wanted to see how he and Darius handled themselves. I had no doubt they weren't the culprits, but we'd shared surface-level secrets this evening that could easily be used against one another.

"Then we have an agreement." He stood.

I joined him, extending my hand. "We do."

Zelda entered with her blonde head bowed as we shook on the tentative partnership. "Dinner is ready, My Prince," she informed me, curtsying again and leaving us as quickly as she'd appeared.

"Dinner," I repeated. "Shall we, then?"

"One thought before we do," Jace murmured, releasing my hand. "I imagine you've already looked into this, but as the attack happened at your estate, you should be searching for accomplices, perhaps within your own staff."

"You're right. I've already vetted them all." I trusted my team implicitly and kept them happy in order to secure their loyalty. "That said, I'm always listening and watching."

"I would expect no less, as I would do the same." He nodded. "Well, I'm famished and I believe Juliet is as well, aren't you, darling?" His gaze sparkled as he grinned down at her. "You can speak freely."

"I am hungry, yes," she admitted softly.

Darius chuckled and nuzzled her neck affectionately. "She's learning the joys of real food."

I glanced at a stunned Raelyn and held my hand out to her. "Raelyn still desires spinach and broccoli with her eggs for evening breakfast. Come, little lamb. Perhaps Juliet can demonstrate how to properly enjoy food."

Raelyn's nose crinkled as she joined me.

I lifted her chin with my index finger. "You can stop hiding now. Jace and Darius won't bite." Not Raelyn, anyway. "Come out and play. I miss you."

Her icy blue eyes glittered up at me. "I've been sitting beside you for the last thirty minutes."

My lips quirked up. "As my obedient slave, yes, and I'm quite proud of you for it. But I want my defiant princess."

"Another mind game?"

"Just the truth." I tapped her head softly. "You know what I want."

"It's never going to happen."

"It's already started." I kissed her nose. "And now we have a week at home to deepen my hold."

The party preparations were well underway and didn't require my involvement. All the vampires interested in Tremayne's former role had submitted their candidacies, and my meeting with Jace was complete.

"I'm looking forward to spending time with you, Raelyn." *And fixing this bond between us.* That was more important than keeping her virginity intact. I couldn't afford to have an emotional connection. Not now, not ever.

She scowled at me. "A week isn't going to change anything."

"On the contrary, darling, a week alone together will change everything."

Chapter Twenty-Two

RAE

Dinner was not what I expected. It turned into a reminiscence between the vampires, filled with laughter and references I didn't understand. Juliet had appeared just as lost as I had, her dark eyes finding mine several times throughout the meal and her eyebrows lifting.

I wished we could have spoken so I could have asked about her unique relationship with Darius, but Kylan had been eager to leave once we finished eating.

He drove, using the tunnels and evading the city's security on the perimeter. Judith followed with Mikael and some of the staff, her displeasure at us moving locations evident by the look she'd given Kylan before we left. If it fazed him, he didn't show it.

The snowy landscape enveloped the world outside of the

city, causing my heart to race at the picturesque views. They'd been hidden behind the buildings, the streets freshly cleared, leaving little traces of the gorgeous wintry mix.

Kylan squeezed my thigh, his touch hot through the thin silk of my dress. "You want to explore again, don't you?"

"It's just so beautiful," I whispered, awed by the moonlight illuminating the snow-dusted trees.

"You prefer this to the city." Not a question, but a statement.

Still, I felt compelled to say, "Yes."

"Me too." He drove in silence a few minutes longer, the hum of his engine the only sound in the still night. "There's still plenty of time before dawn. How would you feel about a hike when we get back?"

I blinked. "With you?" The question left before I could swallow it, my shock at his request evident in the way my voice squeaked at the end.

He chuckled. "Yes, with me, Raelyn."

A hike. With Kylan. I'd never been on one before, let alone through the snow. I glanced at my dress, my lips pinching to the side. "Can I change first?"

His chuckle turned into a laugh and he shook his head. "You're adorable."

"That's not an answer."

"You're right. It's not. As much as I'd enjoy watching you try, you can't hike in heels, little lamb. Last I saw, you could hardly walk through the snow in boots."

My brow furrowed. "I figured it out."

"Yes, you did." His palm disappeared from my leg as he turned off the main road. "We'll venture into the trees where the snow is less thick. The trees more or less protect the ground."

His estate came into view, framed by the mountains behind it, taking my breath away. I definitely preferred this to the city.

The outer gate opened as we approached, granting us entry. Kylan maneuvered down the path with expert ease, pulling us up to the front of the manor where two of his staff members waited to open our doors. He greeted them by name, handing the tallest human the keys.

Most of Kylan's staff were mortals of varying ages, something I noticed more and more throughout the week. Judith was one of the few on his staff of vampire origin.

She parked behind him, exiting without assistance, Angelica in the passenger side wearing an ashen expression.

That must have been an uncomfortable car ride.

"Raelyn and I are going hiking," Kylan informed her, taking my hand. "Get settled and enjoy the rest of your evening, Judith."

"Do you think that's wise, Your Highness?" she asked, glancing around pointedly.

His lips twitched. "I am more than capable of handling myself and protecting Raelyn, unless you meant to suggest otherwise?"

She stilled, her jaw tightening. "Of course not, My Prince."

"Then what are you trying to imply, Judith?" His thumb brushed my pulse, his expression expectant.

"That it may not be safe," she admitted. "But I know you can handle yourself."

"Yes, I can." He turned, pulling me with him. "Good night, Judith."

Her response—if she made one—was lost to the winter elements as Kylan guided me into the foyer, past more staff, toward the grand staircase. "All right, little lamb. Time to bundle you up for the weather."

* *.*

I couldn't feel anything.
    Not the ground beneath my boots.
    Not the air separating my red strands.
    Not the snow in my gloved hand.
    And I hated it.

I glowered at Kylan dressed only in jeans and a sweater, his dark hair windswept and gorgeous. "This is ridiculous," I mumbled from behind the scarf he'd wrapped around my face.

His dark eyes glittered with mirth as he looked me over. "I think you look adorable."

I patted the puffy jacket with my oversized gloves and snorted. Or attempted to, anyway. It was barely heard over the thick layer of wool swathing my head.

He caught my hand and pulled me forward with a chuckle. "It was this or risk frostbite."

"I'm going to melt to death instead," I grumbled. At least my legs were mobile in the jeans and boots.

"I'll strip you before that happens," he promised, a dark note underlining his words. "Come along, little lamb. Time to explore."

"Yes, master," I deadpanned, causing him to laugh. I'd learned that little quip from Mikael after watching a movie featuring a sarcastic female. She was my kind of human.

"Fuck, I adore you." He yanked me to him and kissed my scarf-covered nose. "Now try to keep up."

He led us to a nearby forest path shrouded in tree cover, the snow more scattered and shallower inside. I followed, my jacket snagging on the branches as we went, our path darkening with each step.

The distance between us grew as we moved, his long strides far more efficient than my short, careful ones. Another tree caught my arm, jerking me back. I shifted, trying to untangle myself, only to find myself worse off.

"Dress warm," I grumbled, repeating Kylan's words from earlier to myself. "It'll protect you from the elements." It seemed nature disagreed.

I yanked my arm away from the sticky needles with so much force my feet slid over the ground, sending me tumbling to the forest floor.

"Protect indeed," I wheezed, my head and back aching from the collision.

Kylan appeared above me, his face shadowed in the night. "Not very graceful, Raelyn."

I just stared at him, unable to reply. Because what could I say? He was right. The tree definitely won.

He held out his hand. It took me a moment to focus enough to grab it, my mind protesting from the jarring fall. I finally managed to accept his help up, my mittened hands grabbing his biceps for balance.

"Can I please take these off?" I asked, irritated by my forced clumsiness.

He flicked the top of my zipper with a smirk. "Not used to wearing so many clothes, hmm?"

"I keep getting stuck on the branches."

"Is that your excuse?" He slowly drew down the metal clasp, exposing my sweater beneath. "Because I think you just want me to undress you." He reached my lower abdomen, the coat falling open. "I think you prefer to be naked in my presence."

A shiver slipped up my spine, not from the weather but from his words. "It's just the jacket," I whispered.

"Uh-huh." He pushed the puffy material from my shoulders, causing it to fall to the ground behind me. Cool air weaved through my wool sweater, taunting the heated skin beneath.

I sighed in relief, my forehead falling to his shoulder. "So much better." I'd felt suffocated by it, my upper body protesting the additional weight and layers. My arms felt freer, lighter now. "I'm ready."

"Oh, I know, but not yet." He tugged on my scarf and stepped away, his grasp on the wool around my neck forcing me to follow. "No more excuses, little lamb." He gave the fabric another pull, causing my eyes to go round.

He'd fashioned my scarf into a leash.

A fucking leash.

Like a dog.

And he was now walking us through the forest as one would a pet.

I tried to unravel myself, but another yank compelled me forward. "Kylan," I growled.

"Yes, pet?"

"This isn't funny."

"On the contrary, I find myself very amused." Another tug. "Pick up the pace, darling lamb." He leapt over a log that I nearly tripped on, but by some miracle, I managed to mimic his action.

He moved slower, but not by much, his long legs far more accustomed to this activity than mine. I tried futilely to loosen the suffocating item from my neck, except each way I went only seemed to tighten the knot.

Why had I let him dress me?

I ignored the scenery—not that I could see it in the dark anyway—and focused on not falling while trying to keep up with him.

A glimmer of light caught my eye a few yards before us, the temporary whiteness blinding me and causing me to stumble into his back. He chuckled. "Eager, hmm?"

"To kill you?" I asked. "Yes." Not that I ever could.

"Oh, love, that would be a fun game indeed. Perhaps we can try fencing sometime. Your marks in the sport were quite high." He started moving again, leaving me only two options: follow or strangle myself.

Damn vampire.

He could see in the dark, allowing him to move freely while I had to watch every step, which was exceedingly difficult when leashed. Not that he seemed to care.

I threw one of my gloves at him because I had nothing else to throw. He laughed, earning him a second glove to the head.

"You'll regret that later, little lamb."

Yeah, yeah. I had pockets. I'd be fine.

The light grew before us, replacing some of my fury with curiosity. It seemed brighter than the courtyard by his house, as if the moon was reflecting off a stronger source.

Kylan stepped through the last of the trees and turned,

blocking my view of what lay beyond him. I thought he meant to tease when he pressed a finger to my lips, his body tense with warning.

What? I wondered. *What is it?*

Be very still, he replied in my head, nearly sending me backward.

His hand found my hip, holding me upright while my eyebrows reached my hairline. *How are you in my head?* Vampires weren't telepaths. Unless my books and professors failed to mention that part.

It's temporary, he said. *Just don't move.*

Why?

Shh. He released me slowly and turned, his broad shoulders hiding the scene beyond him. "You know me," he said out loud, his voice low and growly.

My brows furrowed. Did he expect me to reply to that?

"Come," he added, extending his arm. "You know who I am."

I frowned at his back, baffled. *What—*

Shh.

I almost growled at him but froze when something *did* growl.

"Oh, that's how it's going to be tonight?" He tsked. "Gone a few weeks and you forget your alpha."

The creature responded with a snarl, raising goose bumps along my arm. I gripped Kylan's sweater. He no longer held my scarf, giving me freedom, and I found I wanted to be attached to him even more now.

"She's harmless and mine," he snapped. "Stop snarling."

A grumble was the reply.

Silence fell over the forest, the sound of rushing water overwhelming my ears. What was happening? Had a rogue lycan found its way onto Kylan's land? Was this the threat? The monster lying in wait?

Something nudged Kylan, his leg bumping into mine. I glanced down to see a white tail wrapping around his thigh. My nails curled into his wool sweater, my heart thudding wildly.

The wolf grumbled again, causing Kylan to chuckle. "Yeah, her fear is intoxicating; I agree." He squatted, leaving me awkwardly hanging on to his sweater while almost falling over him. Bright yellow eyes met mine, causing me to scramble backward into a tree. The wolf rubbed his giant white muzzle against Kylan's face and licked his cheek.

"A lycan," I whispered.

Kylan snorted. "No, this is a proper wolf. The alpha of his pack." He gestured with his chin to the scene beyond— a frozen lake spreading into the distance and framed by mountains. At the water's edge were several wolves, all standing, alert, their eyes on us.

"W-we should go."

"Nonsense." He stood, patting the alpha's head. "They're old friends. Just irritated with me for disappearing for a few weeks." He scratched the wolf's ear, earning him another kiss on the hand before he trotted back to his pack, who noticeably relaxed. His lips twitched at finding me glued to the tree behind me. "Showing fear makes you smell like dinner to them and to me. I suggest lowering it a notch."

"They're wolves."

"Yes."

"Real wolves."

"Yes." He cocked his head to the side. "You fear them and not me? Because I assure you, I'm the bigger predator here." He prowled forward, wrapping his hand around my scarf again. "And I have every intention of eating you, little lamb."

"You have pet wolves," I whispered, swallowing.

"I wouldn't call them pets," he replied, brushing his knuckles over my cheek. "That term implies a certain level of obedience and submission that they lack. Consider them wild friends who understand my animalistic side."

He stepped closer, his hips pinning mine.

"This is one of my favorite places, Raelyn," he murmured, his mouth scant inches from mine. "I come here when I need to be alone and think."

My brow furrowed. Why bring me here if he wanted to be by himself? "But you're not alone."

"Indeed I'm not." He kissed me softly, his grip on my scarf tightening. "I wanted to share this with you as a thank-you for being honest with me earlier and pointing out the obvious nature of my accusation."

I started. "You're thanking me?"

His lips curled. "I am, by sharing a special place with you. It's magical out here. Let me show you."

"I..." Words failed me. He was rewarding me for pointing out the obvious? No, for being brave enough to poke a hole in his assessment. For being defiant. For having a brain and using it. For being *me*.

I blinked.

He likes me.

I do, he whispered back at me, his dark eyes glimmering. *Come play with me, little lamb. I'll make it worth your while.*

"How are you doing that?"

Amusement teased his features. "It wasn't intentional, I promise, and I'll fix it, but let's enjoy the moment while it lasts. Please?"

Okay, now I'd seen everything. "You're begging."

"I prefer the term *urging*. And besides, this so much more pleasant than forcing."

"You own me."

"I do," he agreed.

"So you don't need my permission to do anything with me."

He tilted his head. "True, but perhaps I desire it."

"Why?"

"Because having you at my mercy willingly is far sexier than demanding your compliance." He nipped my lower lip. "You're already out here. Let me show you the beauty of it, and maybe the wolves will let you return."

I glanced around him at the pile of white fur by the shoreline, all lazing about without a care in the world. Much better than the growling from earlier.

Kylan kissed me again, his tongue dipping inside for a taste that was all too brief.

"Let me reward you, Raelyn," he murmured. "I promise you'll enjoy it."

My blood heated at the underlining prospect of his words. He meant to do more than hike and sightsee.

I have every intention of eating you, little lamb, he'd said.

Oh...

"Yes," he mouthed, still listening to my thoughts. "I'm going to devour you until you implore me to stop." *And I'll continue even then,* he added, the words a caress against my thoughts.

I quivered, my thighs clenching.

Having him *inside* me, whispering to me, increased the intimacy, heightening the sensations.

He desired my mind.

He'd won.

I waited for bleakness to fall, to take me under a shadow of depression, but curiosity consumed me. If Kylan had entered my thoughts, then maybe I possessed the ability to reach his as well. I could turn this around and beat him at his own game.

"Okay," I said, wanting to explore this more. To be inside Kylan's reasoning, to learn his true musings and his goals? That was a priceless opportunity.

I could understand him—the man behind the regal mask, beyond the fondness for games.

I would finally know the real Kylan.

Chapter Twenty-Three

RAE

"Welcome to my version of paradise." Kylan led me down the path to the edge of the glistening lake surrounded by snow-covered trees with mountains in the distance.

My breath caught, the winter wonderland something I never thought to experience. "It's gorgeous," I whispered, spinning to take it all in.

The echoes of moonlight lent a hypnotic glow to the air while the stars painted a picturesque sky. I'd never seen anything like it, not even in my textbooks.

Something prodded my thigh, causing me to freeze midstep. I glanced downward to find a pair of yellow eyes gazing up at me.

"Kylan," I mouthed. *Kylan!*

His chuckle infiltrated my thoughts. "Well, I wouldn't

suggest running, or you'll excite his prey drive." Kylan relaxed on a log near the water's edge, his dark eyes sparkling in the night.

Another poke.

What does he want?

"Give him your hand," he replied. "He'll smell my essence on you and back off."

I swallowed. *My hand. All right.* I slowly extended it toward the muzzle filled with very sharp teeth and waited. The wolf gave it a sniff and nuzzled it forcefully until my palm landed on his head.

Kylan chuckled. "Well, now he wants you to give him a good scratch."

"H-he wants me to pet him?" I slowly stroked his fur, surprised by the soft texture. It felt... nice. "Oh." I drew my nails over his head, down to his nape, and back up again, repeating the action over and over, awed. "He's beautiful."

"Yeah, just don't let his mate hear you talk like that." Kylan gestured to a lean wolf watching me with keen eyes. "She's possessive."

The wolf beside me sat, leaning against my legs and almost toppling me into the snow. I shifted for balance while supporting him, my hand still on his head.

"Ah, he likes you," Kylan murmured, approval in his voice. "He's validating you to the others and showing trust."

"He barely knows me."

"Wolves, like most predators, rely on their instincts." His gaze intensified. "And sometimes you just know."

"Is that how you judge most people? By your initial impression?"

"Always, but I also constantly evaluate." He looked me over slowly, thoroughly, his irises deepening to a molten shade along the way.

I shivered, feeling naked despite my abundance of clothes. "And what do you see when you evaluate me?" I asked, my voice dropping to a husky whisper by the end, my fingers curling into the wolf's fur.

"Mmm." Kylan relaxed, his palms resting on the log beneath him, his legs stretched out and crossed at the ankles. "A warrior spirit I long to tame for my own use, a body I desire in my bed more than I probably should, and a mind filled with an intelligence I feared was lost among the human race centuries ago."

"You see all that?" I managed, my throat suddenly tight.

"I do." He leaned forward. "And while you claim you're not afraid of me, deep down, I know you fear what I might do to you. Even more, you're terrified that you might enjoy it." His eyes locked and held mine. "I guarantee you won't just enjoy it, Raelyn, you'll love it."

I swallowed, my hand stilling against the wolf.

"You were made for my brand of ownership, little lamb." The dark words slithered over my senses, heating my blood. "I will possess you, mind, body, and soul." His lethal promise lanced my being, marking me as his even while I protested.

I'll own you, too. The thought rose unbidden, coming from a secret place deep within me. If he made me his, he'd be mine too.

He smiled. *You can try, princess.*

I followed his taunt to the source, piercing his psyche—such a natural reaction, a defense to being teased. And found the truth lurking behind the fog, the realization that he'd never initiated a link of this nature with anyone prior to me.

Mine, the predator before me whispered. *Finish it*.

What happened then?

I took a step toward him, craving more.

The connection.

The binding.

The proper insight into his mind.

He wasn't good for me, would destroy me, but it seemed I could do the same to him. I sensed a note of panic within him, an unease his expression and words didn't otherwise show. He didn't want to let me in, to show me more, but a part of him demanded it.

I straddled him on the log, my body moving as if controlled by an energy I couldn't contain.

More.

He cocked his head, his dark eyes radiating an intoxicating mix of need and confidence. But I felt the concern resting within him, the worry that we might connect completely, providing me the deepest insights to his soul.

And in return, he would have mine.

A mutual binding.

A promise.

My lips brushed his, my yearning to learn more overruling all logic and thought. I wanted to be inside him, to *know* him on the most basic level. This was the way to that goal.

I wrapped my arms around his neck, holding him to me as I kissed him in earnest, my tongue parting his lips to explore the cavern of his mouth. He always led, always dictated our pace, but he gave me this, allowed me the moment of learning I so craved.

He remained utterly still, his muscles clenched.

My seconds were numbered before he took control. I refused to waste it by thinking and gave in to feeling him, memorizing every detail, reveling in his masculinity and power, the way his tongue felt against mine.

Kylan, I breathed into his mind. *Give me more.*

I didn't want to play. I wanted *him*. All of him.

He growled, low and deep, his fingers knotting in my hair while his other hand caught the end of my scarf and gave it a sharp tug. My nails bit into his biceps, reacting to the sudden tightness around my neck.

"Careful, little lamb." The fabric tightened even more, restricting my airway. He drew his tongue over my bottom lip, his dark eyes holding mine. "I give the commands here, not the other way around."

"Yes, My Prince," I mouthed, unable to draw in oxygen.

His pupils flared. "Mmm, I like that, Raelyn. You at my mercy and still obeying." He kissed me softly. "It's arousing." Another kiss. "Addictive." Harder this time. "Invigorating." The scarf loosened but his grip in my hair strengthened, forcing me to remain against him while he devoured my mouth. I melted on top of him, my body his for the taking.

I want you, I whispered.

I know. The cloth around my neck pulled tight again, cutting off my ability to inhale. "Are you wet for me, Raelyn?"

A whimper caught in my throat, unable to pass. I nodded, my thighs clenching around his.

"Even in the woods, surrounded by wolves," he whispered against my lips. "Fuck, you're perfect." He released my scarf, his palm falling to my hip. "And so fucking mine."

Kylan took possession of my mouth, stealing my breath and forcing me to survive on him alone. I clutched his arms, holding on while he devoured me. Bound me. Owned me. Worshiped me.

He unraveled the wool from my neck, his other hand sliding up my abdomen beneath the sweater to palm my bare breast. I arched into him, moaning against his tongue.

More, I begged.

He tweaked my hard nipple, his touch rough and all Kylan, and exactly what I needed.

So demanding tonight. His mental voice caressed my thoughts, stirring a quiver deep within. I liked him there far too much. Something to consider later. Right now I could only care about his hand, his mouth, his hard arousal pressing into the apex between my thighs.

"Kylan." I yanked my sweater over my head, feeling brazen and alive, and much too hot despite the cold air.

"Fuck, Raelyn," he hissed, his mouth going to my neck and lower. He palmed my ass, forcing me to my knees to provide him easier access to my breasts.

I loved having his mouth on me, his tongue lashing my skin, his breath warming my being. Each caress was a brand, each scrape of his teeth a reminder of his possession, his right, his claim.

His touch slid to the front of my jeans, his clever thumb unfastening them with dexterous skill. I dug my fingers into his hair, holding on, requiring more, yearning for his bite.

He skimmed my peak with his incisors, taunting, playing, cascading goose bumps across my flesh before pulling away. "Stand up."

I swallowed, my limbs trembling as I complied.

My boots disappeared.

My pants.

Leaving me naked in the snow and not the least bit cold. I only burned for him more, his gaze blazing hot paths down my body. He removed his sweater, laying it on the ground near mine, and stood. "Take off my jeans."

I licked my lips, my fingers trembling as I worked his button and zipper. He grabbed my wrists, my palms on his hips.

"Kneel, Raelyn." The command shivered down my spine, coiling between my legs.

"Yes, My Prince." I lowered to the ground, his sweater protecting my bare shins and knees from the snow.

He released me. "Finish the job."

I tugged on his jeans, freeing his engorged cock and revealing his strong thighs. His gaze glittered with intent, his arousal seeping from the thick head and enticing my instincts. I leaned forward, desire fueling my movements, and took him into my mouth, sucking the precum from his tip.

His fingers threaded through my hair, holding me there, his growl echoing around us. I pulled his pants down to his ankles, and he kicked them off with his shoes.

"Look at me," he demanded, his voice low and menacing.

I met his gaze as he forced me to take more of him, his

head hitting the back of my throat.

"Did I ask you to suck my cock?"

I tried to shake my head but couldn't. *No.*

That's cheating, Raelyn. Use your voice.

"No," I mumbled, his shaft preventing me from being coherent.

"Try again."

I did, but it came out just as garbled.

He tsked. "Now I have to discipline you."

I narrowed my eyes and swallowed more of him in response. *You can't punish me for doing something you enjoy, Kylan.*

His lips twitched. "Defiant even on your knees."

I sucked hard in response, my nails biting into his thighs.

"Fuck," he muttered, his fingers clenching in my hair.

I repeated the action.

He hissed and tugged me off of him and onto the makeshift bed of clothing and snow.

My thighs fell wide as he settled between them, his mouth hovering over my clit. "You need a firm reminder of who is in charge here, darling." His tongue teased my already aching bud, causing my hips to buck against him. "Mmm, I'm going to enjoy this far too much."

"Ky…" I trailed off on a scream, his bite shocking me senseless.

I couldn't move. Couldn't think. Could only feel and endure.

And, oh my Goddess, was it something to endure.

Sensation unlike anything I'd ever felt rocked my core, slicing my being in two, splintering my ability to breathe. It hurt so good. My vision blackened, whitened, the stars overhead spinning in a cloud of ecstasy I could taste on my tongue. He lit my veins on fire, my blood rushing to meet his mouth while he replaced my essence with pure euphoria.

My throat ached from chanting—yelling—his name.

Time froze.

Unfroze.

Froze again.

Mine. His voice echoed through my mind, lancing my soul.

Yours, I agreed, unable to process, to remember why I didn't want to agree. But anything to end this sweet, blissful agony destroying my body. *It's too much.*

You'll take it, Raelyn. His growl vibrated every part of me, his dominance taking hold of me in every way. I couldn't fight him, didn't even want to.

Yes, I whispered. *Anything.*

Everything, he replied, his dark mind blossoming to mine. So many secrets wrapped up in complicated webs of reasoning established over thousands of years.

Ancient, powerful, sophisticated.

I pushed my way inside, only to be stopped by a wall.

"Kylan," I breathed, begged, craved. I writhed beneath him, my orgasm endless and capitulating. "Please."

His fingers were *there*, his throat still swallowing, my body drifting into an odd, cooler state.

Was he drinking me dry?

Numbing me?

Snow started to fall around us, or were those the stars? I couldn't distinguish.

Another wave crashed over me, shaking my limbs and causing my back to bow. Kylan's palm against my belly held me down, his touch literally grounding me when my soul threatened to fly.

I can't take anymore...

You can, he replied. *You will.*

A sob escaped me, equal parts needy and devastated. *You're destroying me.*

I'm owning you, he clarified.

I want to own you, too. And I did. In every way. He couldn't take all of this from me without giving some of himself in return. *Please, Kylan. I'm begging you.*

He growled, releasing me from his bite. "This bond is going to kill me."

Bond?

"Yes." He laved my clit once more, sending a shock wave of pleasure through me. Was he healing me? Oh, fuck, I didn't care. I just wanted him. To know him as he did me. To be with him.

"I need you," I whispered, my veins cooling without his bite, or maybe from his bite.

"I know," he whispered, crawling over me. "I'm here, Raelyn."

His mouth captured mine, my arousal tinged with his blood gracing my senses. I quivered beneath him, overwhelmed and exhausted and titillated all over again.

Kylan threatened to destroy me.

I understood what he meant now.

Because I was completely bewitched, ready to do whatever he desired for just another taste.

His cock nudged my weeping heat. *Yes...* Not that he needed my consent. It was already given, acquired, owned.

"Tell me you're mine." His lips whispered over mine. "Tell me you want this."

"I want *you*," I replied, wrapping my legs around his waist. They shook from the cold, but I didn't care. "I'm yours, Kylan." *And you're mine.*

He sighed, his tongue dipping into my mouth, providing me more of his essence. Each swallow burned in the most delicious of ways.

His hands grabbed my hips, holding me in place. "You're so fucking wet." He sounded almost distraught, his voice breaking at the end. "Fuck, Raelyn. I can't. I shouldn't, but I can't stop."

"What—"

Unexpected pain cut off my words, silencing my voice. I grabbed his arms, my body freezing beneath his.

He's inside me, I realized. And fuck, it *hurt*.

"I can't remember the last time I wanted someone like this," he whispered, his mouth brushing mine. "It has to stop."

My brow furrowed, his words not making sense. "I

don't…"

"Shh…" He kissed me again, his tongue tender and coaxing, his body still over mine. "Focus on the sensations, Raelyn. Focus on me. My cock deep inside you, stretching you, filling you, owning you."

His words warmed me in a foreign way, igniting a flame in my lower belly. He shifted, causing me to flinch, anticipating pain. But nothing followed, only a tiny shudder that tingled through my legs. He repeated the action, this time with more force, and my body jolted in response.

I moaned, the fire increasing, heating me inside and out.

A thrust—harsher and sharper—had my nails scoring his back, my jaw threatening to clench around his tongue.

"Mmm, that's it," he praised. "Hang on to me, princess. Enjoy, feel, scream. I want everyone to hear you, to know who is fucking you, to know whom you belong to."

I opened my mouth to protest, to demand the same, but my words cut off on a harsh exhale as he truly started to move. He'd been kind before, easing me into the movements.

Now the predator had come out to claim his prize. To dominate me. To destroy me for every other man.

"Kylan," I groaned, an inferno coursing through me, consuming me from head to toe. He'd already taken me to unspeakable levels of bliss. There couldn't be more. I wouldn't survive another dose, let alone a headier one.

But fuck, he wasn't stopping.

His cock hit me deep, pressing a euphoric part of me that paralyzed my being.

I was a slave to his ministrations, lost to his will.

"So fucking good," he growled, his mouth against my neck. "You're hugging my cock, owning me with your little cunt." His teeth slid into my skin, forcing rapture into my bloodstream and sending me spiraling over the edge of oblivion.

Again.

No warning.

No buildup.

Just shattering.

And my body succumbed to him without preamble.

It almost hurt.

"Fuck, Raelyn." The guttural curse against my throat sounded almost pained.

Energy hummed between us, his shoulders and arms tightening. My name fell from his lips once more, the invocation in his tone so agonizingly beautiful it brought tears to my eyes.

His orgasm poured into me, sending me to the stars with him, my mind departing my body and gracing the heavens above. I'd never felt anything like it, this electricity zipping between us, binding us, forcing me to a plane of existence I never knew was possible, with Kylan at my side.

Such beauty.

Such intensity.

Such torment.

...not the way...

...break it...

I can't be bonded to her!

Not like this.

Too much.

I need to end it.

There's only one way...

A vision slammed into my heart of Kylan giving me away, to be taken by another. Fucked. Fed on. *Used.*

No choice, his voice drifted through my thoughts.

I clawed deeper, trying to understand. More words, ceremonial chants, *Erosita*, the binding between a virgin human and a vampire, the connection of our minds, bodies, and souls.

Kylan had bound me to him in an ancient ceremony meant for mates.

And he wanted to break it.

More visions, his plans, his obligations, all striking my chest, lashing at my heart and soul.

A mistake. Those two words burned. *I never meant to do this.*

More thoughts—his thoughts—filled my head. Some old. Some new. All wrapped up in the same truth.

I have to kill the obsession.
Once I do, it'll be fine.
Back to normal.
Good.
Yes.
Just have to share...

I tore my mouth away from his, not even aware that we'd been kissing, my eyes blazing with tears. "You're going to give me to another royal?" I demanded, my voice hoarse from all the screams, the pain, the pleasure, the rapture we'd just shared that meant nothing to him other than to be a means to an end.

He stared down at me, a mixture of agony and dismay in his gaze. "Raelyn..."

"This was all... all..." I couldn't think of the right word, my heart breaking.

I wasn't supposed to fall for him.

I wasn't even supposed to like him.

My mind. My heart. My soul.

When had he slipped through? How?

My hands curled into fists, my nails biting into my palms.

Fuck, how ridiculous was I? Letting hope possess me. For just a moment, I thought there might be something special between us. A unique bond. A relationship. A connection. Something.

He called it a mistake.

An obsession he had to dismantle.

My heart.

That's what he would destroy.

Oh, how wrong I'd been. It was never my body he wished to shatter, but the fundamental part of me. My spirit.

To link us in such a passionate way, to give me insight into his mind, to take full control of my own, all to just sever it with a demand. To fuck another.

"But you're my consort and that's your purpose—to fuck whomever I tell you to fuck."

A sob caught in my throat, my soul withering up inside of me. "It was all just a game," I whispered. "A mental ploy to lower my guard."

He never cared.

Just a vampire playing with his new toy.

And it only took him a little over a week to break me.

"Raelyn." He cupped my cheek, but I looked away.

"Stop, Kylan," I begged. "Just stop." There wasn't a point. Not anymore. "You won." The words were barely a whisper, my fight deflated.

He said he would own me.

I'd naively thought—hoped—I could own him too.

What a fool I'd been.

There were no happy endings in my world.

Only pain and suffering.

And Kylan had just delivered the worst punishment of them all.

A soulless life, forever serving at his side.

I closed my eyes. "Just leave me here to die."

Chapter Twenty-Four

KYLAN

Speechless.

Raelyn had rendered me frozen, immobile, unable to comprehend how such a beautiful moment could shatter so catastrophically.

I hadn't expected her to enter my mind so easily, to see the truth of my intent. But it'd been at the forefront of my thoughts, my frustration over our situation.

I had to share her to break the bond.

But I didn't want to share her.

I possessed a newfound respect for Darius and his allowances with Jace because even the notion of letting someone touch Raelyn had me wanting to commit murder. It was a weakness I couldn't allow, one I knew would be removed by letting another fuck her.

A growl caught in my throat, the agony of the plan searing me inside.

I can't let this consume me.

I was stronger than this.

Raelyn lay utterly still, her eyes taking on a lifeless quality that nearly broke my resolve. She'd be okay. She had to be. My fighter would return. She just needed some space to see that this was the best solution. Her emotions were just as tied up as mine, the bond to blame. We'd work through it.

I pulled away from her, noting the discoloration in her limbs. Sex in the snow was not the best idea for a mortal, but now that my immortality ran fresh through her veins, she'd heal quickly.

Immortality I plan to take away from her.
Because it's the only solution.

I ran my fingers through my hair, irritated with my own uncertainty. Decisions were easy. I made them daily, quickly, and efficiently. This woman—Raelyn—had changed everything.

No, the bond had.

Fucking ceremony.

Why hadn't I realized that was happening? I never gave consorts my blood. Only Mikael and only because he required substantial healing.

I rubbed my jaw while Raelyn lay motionless on the ground, a tear streaking across her cheek.

I sighed, hating that I'd hurt her. "This wasn't my intention. It just sort of happened." Probably the lamest excuse in the history of time. And why was I explaining myself to her? She wasn't my equal. Just a human—a *consort* I'd indulged in a little too heavily.

A few days apart would fix this.

I'd let her heal, then find a proper candidate—my jaw clenched—to break this bond. There was no other choice.

"We need to get inside," I told her, noting the horizon. We'd been out here far longer than I originally anticipated.

This female was toxic for my routine and common

sense.

"Raelyn."

No response. Not even a flinch.

So that's how this was going to go.

I palmed the back of my neck. "Do you want me to compel you to follow me inside?"

Do whatever you want, she replied, her mental voice solemn. *I'm yours.*

The two words prickled at my heart. I'd enjoyed hearing them earlier, but now they sounded dull and broken, as if she were accepting the inevitable, not vowing herself to me for eternity.

She looked so fragmented and abused, lying there with her legs spread, naked on the blanket of clothes, her eyes unfocused and unseeing.

I hated seeing her like this, hated that I'd *made* her like this.

"It's the bond," I told her softly. "Once it's broken, you'll understand." We'd be free of this complicated web, able to feel normal again.

She said nothing, her expression void of emotion save that single tear frozen to her cheek. Like a distorted macabre doll. Forever damaged.

No. She'd come back from it. She had to.

I bundled her up in the clothes and lifted her in my arms. The least I could do was carry her back to the house. I left our shoes—I'd grab them later—and phased through the forest to the back door. Much faster than walking. If it bothered Raelyn, she didn't show it, her eyes having fallen closed as if asleep.

She remained in the same state as I entered our bedroom, her breathing slow as I laid her on the bed. "Do you need anything?" I asked softly. "Water? Food?"

Raelyn curled into a ball. No response.

The silent treatment almost had me entering her mind, but I refrained. She deserved peace after the hell I'd accidentally introduced her to.

Ugh, but I couldn't leave her like this.

How had this become so complicated? She was meant as a diversion, a passing entertainment in my very long existence. Yet, she'd come to mean so much more.

I brushed a damp strand of hair from her face, her blank gaze on the glass windows.

We would stay here a few more days and relax before I'd tackle the task of finding someone to fix this for us. It couldn't be Mikael. I didn't trust myself not to kill him in the process. No, I needed a stronger vampire, someone who could defend himself.

My hand curled into a fist. *Or I could keep her.*

No.

That wasn't an option. She was a risk—a weakness—I couldn't afford. And there were too many who would happily hold her against me. Society labeled the ceremony as taboo, but it was really a product of envy. *Erositas* were rare, and none of the royals had one. Well, except Cam, but he killed his before the Goddess took him into custody.

I rolled my neck, exhaustion hitting me hard in the gut.

This shouldn't be so difficult.

Raelyn blinked, her soulless eyes unfocused. She needed rest. We could discuss more in the evening. I removed the scattered clothes I'd used to bundle her and guided her beneath the covers. She didn't fight me, but she didn't help either, her limbs heavy.

"Raelyn," I whispered, agonized. "I'm sorry." I didn't know what I was apologizing for exactly. The unexpected bond, accidentally letting her into my mind, taking her virginity so roughly on the ground, all of the above.

I shook my head.

"Just get some sleep," I told her, not that she seemed to be listening.

I slid into the sheets beside her, yearning to hold her but knowing she needed her space.

Maybe she'd be more herself in the evening.

* * *

Raelyn wasn't more herself in the evening.

Or the next day.

She barely moved from the bed. Zelda had to bring her food, something that only happened because I demanded it. And even then, Raelyn only ate a few bites before lying down again. When I tried to talk to her, she ignored me.

At first, it concerned me.

Now, I was irritated.

I missed my fighter, which only pissed me off more. Fucking her should have killed this obsession, but all I craved was more. All because of this damn bond.

Every vampire I considered for the task of helping me break the connection was immediately vetoed. Either I liked the male too much to risk his life or I hated him too much to let him near something so precious.

"Fuck," I growled, dragging my fingers through my hair. I couldn't even focus on the work I needed to sort through. Messages from constituents, all requesting one thing or another. Some wanted money. Some desired more land. Others expressed needs for promotion.

And then I had the pile of letters of intent to go through for Tremayne's position.

This was why royals had sovereigns. I usually didn't mind all the tasks, preferring the way they passed the time, but I couldn't stop thinking about a certain redhead in my bedroom.

A knock at my door had hope sprouting in my chest, only to be squashed as Angelica appeared.

"My Prince," she greeted, bowing slightly.

Right. I'd summoned her. "I have a task for you."

She entered with her hands at her sides, expression curious. "Yes, My Prince?"

"I need you to accompany Raelyn outside. Try to get her moving around a bit." The two seemed to get on all right in Kylan City. Maybe Raelyn would confide in her, or enjoy the female company.

"O-of course," Angelica replied, her expression conveying doubt.

"She's feeling unwell, but she really likes the snow." My lips twitched at the memory of her awe over the windows that first day, her little trip out onto the balcony. "Make sure she dresses warm, please."

Angelica nodded, her brow slightly wrinkled. "I will."

"And try to get her to eat something more than broccoli and unseasoned chicken." I really wanted to introduce her to chocolate, but the moment hadn't arrived yet. "Oh, and maybe a movie after. Something with humor." I gave her a few titles I knew were in the old movie collection.

"Uh, yes, I'll figure that out," she said slowly. Right, being so new to immortality, she wouldn't be familiar with the old entertainment systems. The only programs on television now were those sanctioned by Lilith and the few lycan-made films.

"Mikael can give you a tutorial." He was awake, but only barely recovered, and apparently not speaking to me either. When I saw him earlier this evening, he'd scowled at me and went back to his room. It seemed all the humans in the house hated me right now. Even Zelda had given me a touch of attitude in the kitchen.

"Okay." Angelica's bemused expression would have been comical if it wasn't so accurate. "Anything else, Your Highness?"

"Yes. Guard her," I demanded with more force than necessary.

She swallowed. "I understand."

"Good. That's all."

"Thank you, My Prince." She bowed, excusing herself.

I blew out a breath, uncertain if this would work, but hopeful. If it didn't, I'd have to enter Raelyn's conscious to search for a solution. When I'd told her I wanted her mind, I hadn't meant like this. I wanted her trust, which I clearly botched. And if I pushed through the thin barriers between us to read her, I'd cause even more damage.

My lips flattened. Why was that even a consideration? I never cared what others thought. If she didn't trust me, I'd make her. That's how I operated. And if she refused, I'd work around it.

Yet, I couldn't bridge the gap between us.

It was as if my soul refused, terrified of hurting her more.

"This fucking bond is going to kill me," I growled. I'd only finalized it to be the first to taste her, knowing full well I'd have to share her.

And now I couldn't fathom the idea of letting another touch her.

I stood.

All right.

Time to take my own advice and get the hell out of here. Beat something up. Wrestle with the wolves. Anything to stop thinking about my predicament with Raelyn.

It was driving me insane.

Or, perhaps, I'd reached that stage in my immortality long ago.

I stripped out of my jacket and dress shirt.

A run.

Yes.

That's what I needed.

And a good fucking.

With Raelyn.

I snorted. Like that was going to happen again anytime soon. I was all for seducing a woman, but that task felt impossible now.

Get it together, I told myself.

Over five thousand years old and a human of twenty-two years had me tied up in knots. Ridiculous.

Maybe I really am going mad.

Chapter Twenty-Five

RAE

The snow on the balcony was thicker tonight. I'd watched it grow the last two evenings, the mountains in the distance my only solace.

I felt dead to the world.

Numbed.

Foolish for falling into a vampiric trap.

I kept waiting for the inevitable, a male of Kylan's choosing to arrive to *fix* our problem. The bond he never wanted to create.

His mind remained closed off, not that I wanted to venture inside that cruelty again. I'd seen enough for my lifetime.

He only fucked me so he could be first, his goal to rid himself of me as soon as possible and pass me off to someone else.

I hated him.

Hated myself.

Hated this life.

But worst of all, I hated how I couldn't motivate myself to do something about it. I felt lost, alone, hopeless. Like a black swirl had consumed me and refused to let go.

Silas would be so disappointed. Willow, too.

How are you? I wondered, my heart stuttering. *Where are you?*

Was Silas still alive?

Was Willow worse off than me?

I shivered, knowing the truth. Of course she was worse off. Kylan would share me, but he owned me exclusively. Willow...

A sob caught in my throat, a dark part of me preferring her fate to mine. Sex, I could handle. But Kylan played with more than my body.

My eyes narrowed, fury bubbling to the surface, followed by a wave of silence.

What could I do? Yell at him? That would only impress him. He wanted to destroy me. He did. The end.

I pressed my palms to my face, a groan slipping through my lips. The same thoughts and impressions kept spinning through my head, pushing me deeper into a place I hated.

A dark abyss with inky claws shredding my soul piece by piece.

My future.

My fate.

My new world.

But I didn't want to exist here. I wanted to live, to breathe, to see the sky, to fly. *And go where?* I almost laughed. The snarky tone sounded too much like Kylan.

I hate you, I growled at him.

A scream built in my chest, demanding release, but the one I wanted to yell at wasn't here. And he would only laugh.

Oh, but just for two seconds to shock him with my fury might be worth the mockery.

I sat up.

Where are you? I demanded.

Nothing.

The wall between our minds locked tight from the other side.

Of course he wanted to keep me out. He was probably working on a list of people for me to fuck.

I flopped backward, my eyes narrowed up at the ceiling. *Asshole.*

He used me. Which was the whole point, wasn't it? But just for a moment, I hoped…

I rolled to my side, refusing to continue that train of thought. It was dangerous. It hurt. It only led to agony.

"Raelyn?" a feminine voice called, followed by a knock.

My eyes fell closed automatically, my desire to be left alone forever overriding the need to acknowledge the vampire. Why bother with decorum anymore? I'd prefer death to this entrapment.

I flinched at the dark notion. It wasn't entirely true. There were reasons to stay alive. I just had to find them.

"Raelyn?" Angelica was next to the bed now. "I know you're awake. I'm supposed to take you outside."

I started to laugh, but it came out as a choked, deranged sound. The urge to bark hit me hard, causing more of that weird noise to spill from my lips.

Outside.

Like a dog.

I fucking hate you, Kylan, I said to him.

Still no reply.

Because of course not. The prick couldn't even acknowledge this bond he'd forced on me. He just wanted to rip it away now that he'd fucked me. No more fun for him. Just a broken toy to eventually kill. After he gave me to all his friends.

That was my purpose, after all, right?

I snorted half-heartedly, a tear prickling my eye.

Goddess, I was tired of crying. Of wallowing in my pain. Of lying in this bed that reeked of Kylan.

Maybe I should go outside. Find an icicle sharp enough to drill into Kylan's skull and pay him a visit.

Oh, I liked that idea.

I'd have to find him, but maybe Angelica knew where he was hiding.

Or I could bring the ice stake back here and wait for him. It would stay cold on the balcony.

Yes.

A sound plan.

Murder by ice.

How touching considering our last interlude in the snow.

I giggled at the hysterical idea, knowing it would never work. Kylan had driven me to madness. Seemed fitting given he owned my mind now.

Angelica cleared her throat. "I don't know what happened between you and Kylan, but he was very specific about accompanying you outside."

"I bet he was," I grumbled.

"I suggest we both obey him," she added, her tone laced with warning. "I have no intention of being on the receiving end of his disappointment."

Part of me wanted to tell her to go away. She could send Kylan in here to punish me, for all I cared. The saner, more practical side of me knew he would discipline not just me for the behavior but Angelica too. And she didn't deserve that. She'd been almost nice to me before; even now she stood by patiently, waiting for my compliance. Most vampires would have reacted violently by now.

I swallowed. "Give me twenty minutes, please." I needed to shower. Find clothes. Try to brush my hair. General things.

"Only if you promise to dress warm," she replied. "Because he also required that."

"Yeah, he pretends to care," I grumbled, sliding out

from between the sheets, naked. Might as well get used to walking around without clothes on amongst vampires. Kylan likely had a parade of them coming my way soon.

Less than twenty minutes later, I had my wet hair pulled up in a bun on top of my head, a sweater and jeans on, and boots covering my feet. Angelica handed me a hat and scarf, which I begrudgingly added, and I followed her downstairs.

Zelda passed us along the way, her surprise at seeing us together evident. She immediately dropped her gaze and continued without a word.

Angelica's lips twitched as she shook her head. "You asked me what it's like the other day. Well, the whole submissive thing is really hard to get used to. I was a human less than a decade ago. It puts me on the outside of humanity while marking me as inferior to all the others. I'm in this in-between zone where no one will talk to me unless they need something."

"Like taking me outside," I said, walking through the door she held open.

"Exactly." She followed me onto the back patio, the snow deep and untouched. "They make you think life will be so much grander, and maybe it will be eventually, but that's not been my experience yet." She kicked some snow. "The only reason I'm not living on the street is because Kylan offered me decent employment. Most royals delegate position assignments for new vampires to the sovereigns or regents."

I followed her into the yard, considering that. "So… did he make you?" No one ever spoke about the task of turning another into an immortal, the conversation essentially forbidden among humans. But I'd already given up all pretenses of decorum with Angelica. Seemed ridiculous to abide by them now.

Her dark eyes flashed, meeting my gaze, but her lips twitched. "You're far braver than I am," she murmured. "I see why he likes you."

My brow furrowed. "Who?"

"You know who."

"Kylan?" I laughed outright. "Yeah, no, he's made it quite clear how he feels about me. And *like* is not the word I'd use to describe that feeling." Lust, maybe. Obsession as well. Like? No.

"Well, he's different with you than with anyone else I've seen," she said softly. "Not that I've spent much time around him. And no, he didn't turn me. Kylan has never turned anyone."

My lips parted. "Ever?"

"Never," she repeated. "Turning a human creates a link between maker and progeny, something Kylan would never allow. He's a loner, relying only on himself and never anyone else. It's what makes him a formidable leader. His loyalties only go so deep. Betray him, and pay the price. That's what everyone says about him, anyway."

Her comment about him never allowing a link to another had me almost tripping over myself.

But he's linked to me.

At least temporarily.

Was that why he felt so strongly about severing the connection between us? Because he couldn't afford to let me be so close to him?

It provided a fresh perspective.

What had he said the other night? That none of this was his intention and it just sort of happened?

I frowned. Did he mean that?

I assumed he'd planned it with all those comments about wanting to possess me entirely. But what if it'd been on accident?

"Yeah, so, life as a vampire, not as glamorous as you'd think," she mumbled, her focus shifting to the night sky. "There's no how-to guide, and my maker isn't exactly a great mentor. So I've learned to rely on my instincts to survive."

"You seem to be doing well so far."

She shrugged. "Yeah. I was worried Kylan might kill me last week for telling him about Tremayne, but I couldn't stop myself even if I tried. The whole—" Something started singing in her pocket. She pulled out the slender device and frowned at the screen. It displayed a long number with no name. "Speaking of makers," she grumbled. "I need to take this."

"Okay." I forced a smile. "I'll just be here."

She nodded, looking grateful. "Thank you," she mouthed before answering the phone. "Vilheim." She walked back toward the manor, leaving me to my musings and the clear night above.

Peaceful.

Beautiful.

Lonely.

Was that why Kylan enjoyed it out here? Why he preferred the secret lake in the woods? *Are you there now?* I whispered, knowing he wouldn't hear me.

I closed my eyes, wallowing in the cool breeze.

I wish you would talk to me, Kylan.

He could at least explain this bond to me and what it meant. Or maybe I didn't want to know since he intended to break it.

"Raelyn?" Mikael's voice floated over me, pulling my lips up in the first smile I'd experienced in what felt like years. He sauntered toward me in a pair of jeans and a sweater, his expression somewhat reserved, but his eyes grinning.

I threw my arms around his neck, more than a little relieved to see him again.

"You're okay," I whispered, tears pricking my eyes. I knew he would be fine, but seeing him brought home the emotions of the last few days. "Goddess, I'm so glad you're okay."

He patted my back and gave me a wry smile. "You missed me?"

"You have no idea. Kylan is a lot of work to handle alone."

He chuckled. "Tell me about it."

I almost accepted his rhetorical statement as an

invitation. I wanted to talk to someone so badly, but instincts held me back. Some sort of warning that Kylan wouldn't approve, and as much as I wanted to ignore it, I couldn't.

So instead I released him with a smile. "I really am glad you're okay. I was worried."

He kissed me on the cheek. "I like you, Rae."

My cheeks heated. "I like you too, Mikael."

"I know." He put his arm around my shoulders, guiding me on a walk through the yard. "That's why this is so hard."

"What do you mean?"

"Life." He sighed, gazing up at the night. "You know Kylan bought me eleven years ago this month? Seems like a lifetime ago. He's given me a lot. I should be grateful, but he's so…"

"Mercurial?" I suggested, recalling the time I called him that to his face.

"Yes, and overindulgent, too." He shook his head, sighing. "He makes you want things that he'll never completely give. He gets you addicted to him. Forces you to love him. But he never loves you back."

His words were nails to my heart. "I know," I whispered.

"He'll destroy you, Rae," he whispered. "I don't want him to wreck you."

I bit my lip. *Too late for that.*

"It's really my only choice," he continued softly. "You understand that, right?"

My brow furrowed. "Only choice?"

"Yes." He turned me to face him, his gaze sad. "What we're doing, it's the only way to protect you."

"I don't…" I swallowed. "What are you saying?"

"That he's sorry," a feminine voice said from the left. Zelda emerged from the tree line, her slender shoulders straight, her head high. I'd never seen her exude such confidence.

Mikael went to her, wrapping his arm around her and kissing her temple. "Yes, exactly that. I'm sorry."

I frowned at him. "For...?" I trailed off, thinking about everything he'd said. About Kylan being addictive, his penchant for manipulating humans into caring for him, Mikael's desire to protect me *from* Kylan.

No.

He couldn't mean—

Zelda twirled a blade between her fingers.

My eyes rounded. "You..." I couldn't finish the statement. But wasn't Mikael with Kylan when the harem died? "But how...?"

"It's complicated," he murmured, taking a step toward me as I took two steps back. "You have to see this as a gift, Rae. He'll only bring you misery. Trust us, we know."

"I'd prefer that over being killed," I snapped, shocked by the ludicrousness of their actions. "Have you both lost your minds?"

He chuckled. "Probably. Kylan has fucked with mine long enough." He sounded so sad, so broken by that. "Please don't fight, Rae. I can make it quick."

My brows shot up. "Quick?" He was completely insane. "Kylan will kill you when he finds out."

"He'll be too busy dealing with other things," Zelda said. "Like the fallout from murdering yet another harem member. It's perfect timing. Right before his big event and after showboating you around the city. Everyone expects to see his precious Raelyn again. But where did she go?" Zelda tapped her chin with the knife. "Oh, that's right. Kylan killed her for sport, just like all the others. And yet, he punished Tremayne for doing the very same thing. Not looking good, is it?"

I gaped at her, seeing beyond her meek chef's presence for the first time. "Who are you?"

Her lips curled. "This is so much bigger than you, Rae. You're just a victim of circumstance and the last nail in Kylan's coffin."

That was not an answer at all, just further proof of her madness.

Mikael pounced, his hand snagging my bicep before I could jump away. His gaze held mine, a note of indecision blinking down at me. "I'm sorry," he whispered, real pain entering his expression. "I really do like you."

I almost laughed, but the glint of Zelda's blade had my brain taking over.

They're going to kill me.

I struggled, yanking myself away from him, only to have Zelda catch me from behind. She locked my arms together in a practiced way, immobilizing me.

Trapped.

My shoulders ached as I tried to shift, to dislodge her from behind, but I couldn't move.

This can't be happening.

My heart pounded in my ears.

Why had I stood here talking to them? I should have run. But shock and confusion had trapped me before them.

"We can't delay any longer," Zelda said, her voice sounding far away despite being right behind me. "Prove yourself, Mikael."

He compressed his lips into a fine line, a glimmer of irritation flashing in his eyes. "Compassion goes a long way, Zelda."

"Not when we're on a timeline. He'll only stall for so long."

He? He who? Kylan? No. That wasn't right.

"Fine." Mikael stepped forward, sending my pulse through the roof.

"Don't do this," I pleaded, trying futilely to escape Zelda's hold. "Please don't do this."

His light eyes radiated grief, but a hint of resolve flickered in his irises. "I'm granting you peace, Rae."

Oh Goddess, he really believes that.

"Mikael..." But there wasn't any hope. I could see it in the way he looked at me. He was going to do this—kill me and frame Kylan. Just like someone else—Zelda?—did with his harem.

Kylan! I shouted to him, needing him to hear me. *Kylan, please!*

But the door between us remained closed.

If he heard me, he didn't acknowledge it.

Kylan... I need you!

"I'm sorry," Mikael said again.

"Do—" My plea ended on a gargle, my neck radiating fire.

A blade.

From Mikael?

"Goodbye, Rae," he whispered, his hand dropping, fresh blood—*my blood*—dripping from his knife.

Time froze, my mind refusing to believe, to accept...

He did it.

He actually did it.

Warm liquid pooled in my throat, flooding my airway. Too fast. Too much.

Kylan, I whimpered. *Help me...*

Nothing.

Zelda and Mikael betrayed you, I told him, needing him to know.

A harsh gurgling sound filled my ears, suffocating my reality.

Kylan...

No reply.

Tears filled my eyes. He'd blocked our connection so thoroughly he couldn't hear me at all.

Because he never cared.

Discarded me.

Our bond.

I should have t-tried h-harder.

I should—

My side screamed in agony, something sharp digging inside of me, blackening my world, splitting it in half.

I—I can't...

Kylan... I can't breathe...

Drowning...

I blinked, my vision fading.
The snow was cold. Heavy.
Such failure. Mine. His.
My soul cried out, reaching through the bond, tugging on the only one who could save me now. *Kylan, please...*
The walls were too dark.
So lonely.
So bleak.
Abandoned.
He's not coming for me.
My heart stuttered.
I'm going to die here...
Alone.

Chapter Twenty-Six

KYLAN

I pushed myself faster and harder over the ground, welcoming the intense exhaustion settling over my limbs. The tingling sensation was one I hadn't felt in a very long time. It consumed me, leaving me shaking as I returned to the house.

My mouth was dry, begging me for hydration—blood.

Fuck. I'd not been this spent in... I frowned. Forever? I only needed to feed once a month to maintain strength, and I indulged almost every day, had overindulged just the other night.

I opened the fridge, searching for a snack as a sense of unease washed over me.

Why am I so tired?

It'd been one hell of a run, but not *that* overbearing. I

exercised often enough, even without needing to.

I rolled my neck, loosening my straining muscles, my energy depleting with each breath. Almost as if my life essence was being sucked out of me.

A spasm rolled through me, forcing me to grab the countertop for support.

What the fuck is that?

I closed my eyes, searching inside myself for a source. It hit me like a freight train.

Raelyn.

She was siphoning my immortality—absorbing it—consuming *me*.

I growled and searched for her mind, wanting to know how the hell that was even possible, and found nothing. No consciousness. Just an empty void.

Nonexistent.

"Raelyn!"

I spun around, searching for a scent, finding it lurking in the air. Sprinting up the stairs, I stopped in our room. Empty.

Her blood was up here. Weak, but present.

I followed the scent to Mikael's room, pausing.

If she chose to break this bond on her own by seeking him out for comfort…

My foot met the door, the wood flying open to slam against the wall. No sign of her or Mikael, but the shower running had me darting into the bathroom.

Zelda shrieked, jumping beyond a very naked and wet Mikael. Concern entered his gaze, flecked with guilt. "Y-your Highness?"

Raelyn's blood lingered here, but not heavily. Had she stopped by Mikael's room today? "Have you seen Raelyn?"

He swallowed and shook his head quickly. "N-no. Why?"

Zelda peeked out from behind him, her blue eyes wide. "I saw her heading outside with Angelica a little while ago, My Prince."

The reminder had me leaving them without a word.

Something was very wrong.

I couldn't sense Raelyn at all, apart from her drawing on my essence. My heart hammered at what that could mean.

I was outside in a blink, her blood much stronger.

Why had I come in through the front? I would have sensed her out here after my run had I gone through the back.

"Raelyn!" I called, phasing to where her scent was the strongest.

Angelica looked up at me from the ground, covered in blood, her dark eyes aghast. "Y-your H-highness... I... I..."

I threw her off of Raelyn, the cry of pain distant to my ears.

"Raelyn," I breathed, falling to my knees beside her. My hands floated above her, my mind not knowing where to start. "Oh, Raelyn..." She was ripped apart, her throat torn open, her chest littered with puncture marks, her icy eyes glassy and sightless.

My throat constricted.

I'd failed her.

She was dead.

How?

Why?

Who?

I raised my eyes to Angelica's quivering form near the tree line, her body bent in a bow I yearned to demolish.

"*You,*" I growled, my instincts screaming at me to shred her alive the way she did Raelyn.

"I-I didn't do it!" she shouted, shaking on the ground. "I was trying to h-heal her," she added in a broken sob, lifting her wrist.

I phased to her, grabbing her arm and noting the fresh bite marks. Raelyn's scent was all over her. I squeezed, her yelp of pain suggesting I'd broken bone, but I didn't care.

"Don't move," I demanded, going back to Raelyn's side

to slice my own wrist and hold it to her mouth.

A ridiculous idea.

She couldn't fucking swallow.

She was fucking dead!

I yelled in fury, agony ripping me apart from the inside.

Broken…

My heart thudded loudly, my fingers closing into fists against her chest, my body breaking over hers.

Dead…

Had she called for me in her final moments?

I'd never know because I closed her off. Blocked her from my mind. The one link that could have—should have—protected her.

Instead of going to her myself, I gave her to Angelica.

I'm a coward.

Unworthy.

I knew she was in danger and I left her alone, too arrogant in my own defenses to consider her at risk here.

She deserved better.

"Raelyn," I whispered, touching my temple to hers. "I'm so sorry."

My harem's massacre had hurt, but this…

I shook, my vision clouding, my mind rebelling, my soul…

My mate.

Sometimes you just know, I'd told her. *I knew you, Raelyn.*

My lungs contracted, my body shaking from fatigue.

Her death is killing me…

Would that be so bad? I wondered. I'd lived for so long, alone, just surviving to do what? Manage an empire? Enjoy the pleasures in life that I'd indulged in several times over already?

Raelyn had been the first exciting thing to enter my life in a very long time.

And she's gone.

No heartbeat.

No breath.

Her still-warm body motionless.

Death hadn't fully taken her yet.

I'd been so close. I should have been able to save her.

I failed.

And it fucking hurt.

Crushing my chest, destroying me from the inside out. The ceremony bound our souls, and hers was screaming—taking me under with her, tugging on my essence, as if trying to claw her way back to the surface.

I lifted, my eyes searching.

No signs of healing.

But she still feels alive.

Her mind was vacant, but there. Her soul still attached to mine.

If she was dead, I wouldn't sense her at all.

I recalled everything I knew about the ceremony, the stories, the expectations—*she's connected to my immortality.*

That's why I was so exhausted.

My essence was healing hers.

I lifted her into my arms, standing. How long would this take? Was there anything I could do to expedite it?

Darius would know.

I started toward the house and paused. Someone here had betrayed me. Likely Angelica, from the scene of evidence, but Raelyn's blood had been fresh in the house…

Something isn't right.

Until I knew the truth, I couldn't trust anyone. Except Judith. I'd seen her while out on my run, patrolling the perimeter herself. Which only confirmed that the culprit was already inside.

I balanced Raelyn against my naked chest with one arm and touched the device in my pocket, alerting my security team. It was a panic alarm of sorts that Judith had installed in my phone. They would be able to ping my whereabouts.

Judith appeared, her face filled with concern, her gun already drawn. Relief smoothed her features at finding me alert, then her brow furrowed at Raelyn's mutilated body.

"Oh…" She pressed a hand to her mouth, her reaction confirming she had nothing to do with this mess. I might have a traitor in my midst, but I could still read my people, and true shock shone in her eyes. "Kylan, My Prince, I—"

"I need you to take Angelica into custody. Withhold blood, but no other punishment until I return."

Judith blinked, finally noticing the crumpled vampire in the snow. I couldn't even look at her. Regardless of whether or not she did this to Raelyn, she'd failed me.

And she would be punished.

"Return?" Judith asked, her voice soft.

"I'll be in touch." I dropped my phone, not wanting to be tracked, and traced to the garage with Raelyn before Judith could argue.

Selecting the keys to my fastest car, I secured Raelyn in the passenger seat and flipped off the GPS locator.

If anyone fucked with me in this state, they'd die. Including the city guards.

I navigated the streets quickly, aware of all the icy patches from nearly two centuries of experience. Raelyn remained broken beside me with no signs of life aside from the tug of her soul against mine. Her limber form confirmed my suspicions as well, her body not quite taking on the final stages of death as her soul hung in limbo.

There had to be a way to expedite her healing, something I wasn't doing.

Heavens, the pain she must have experienced, all while I ignored her…

I flinched and grabbed her hand. "I'll never let you down again," I vowed. *Ever.*

The city lights appeared ahead, polluting the dark sky. I always hated this view, much preferring the solitude of my home, but tonight I craved those buildings and a certain vampire lurking inside.

You better be there, Darius.

I didn't know where else he would go, especially considering our ploy to make it look like I was playing with

Juliet. Their bond was pure, true, created out of love. That much had become increasingly clear throughout dinner the other night in the little ways Darius catered to her. She smiled often, her dark eyes brimming with adoration every time she glanced at him.

Raelyn and I didn't have that. I'd created the connection by accident, then finalized it with the purpose of breaking it, because I couldn't stand the idea of someone touching her before me.

So selfish.

And yet, it was the only thing keeping her alive.

My heart skipped a beat, my breathing quickening. I'd inadvertently saved her life. How could I remove such a bond after this? I... I didn't want her to die. Ever.

The realization had my jaw tightening. How had this woman affixed herself so completely in my life? In my mind? In my heart? From the beginning, I'd been obsessed. An innate familiarity had stopped me before her on Blood Day, then her ice-blue eyes had captivated me. And when she bit me, I had to have her.

I expected the infatuation to die quickly, but it'd only grown into this all-consuming obsession. She was inside me.

And I want her to stay there.

I entered the tunnels, my lights off, my night vision and instincts guiding our way. The guards rarely patrolled down here, very few in the city knowing how to use them. My engineers had constructed a maze on purpose, providing me with the only real road map. Gates closed frequently, blocking paths, but I owned the remote to them all. Just a simple touch of a button and the underground became my playground.

Tonight it was a necessary escape.

I accelerated, the need for answers overwhelming me.

She's alive, I consoled myself. *Barely.*

But not breathing.

My hands tightened on the steering wheel, the exit I desired appearing quickly. The city streets were bustling with vampires, all out for midnight lunch.

Fortunately, most were walking on the sidewalks, not driving.

Minutes later, I was parked and had Raelyn in my arms.

My thumbprint called the elevator, the top floor not arriving fast enough.

She still had no heartbeat.

Come on, Raelyn. Where's my fighter?

Darius stood waiting, the call of the lift clearly having notified him of an imminent arrival. His black slacks and half-buttoned dress shirt suggested he'd readied himself quickly.

"I need you," I said by way of greeting, his gaze immediately falling to the bloodied woman in my arms.

His eyebrows rose. "Jesus Christ."

"There's a name I haven't heard in a while," I muttered, walking by him to lay Raelyn on the couch. "She's not breathing, but I can *feel* her." I met his alarmed gaze. "We completed the ceremony."

"Making her immortal," he inferred, his brow crinkling. "But she's not breathing."

"And has no heartbeat." I ran my fingers through my hair. "Help me. What am I not doing that she needs? I know she's there, but she's not... she's not healing."

Darius blew out a breath, nodding. "Right." He glanced sideways as Juliet entered wearing a pair of jeans and a sweater, her hair mussed, her cheeks red. They'd clearly been enjoying themselves. She walked to his side, her big eyes trained on Raelyn's mutilated form.

"How open is your connection?" he asked, his arm wrapping around his *Erosita*.

"At the moment?" I searched, uncertain. "It's hard to say since I can't hear her at all."

"But you feel her," he murmured. "Can you follow that path, push into her mind?"

"There's nothing there but an empty void." A growl underlined my words, born of frustration. The empty void was because I'd closed her off and not heard her cries.

How many times did you call for me, little lamb?

She must have felt so helpless and alone.

Because I deserted her, forced her away, blocked her mind.

"...deeper," Darius was saying. "When Juliet loses consciousness, I can still sense her. It just takes some navigating through the darkness. Don't look for thoughts so much as emotions."

"You can feel me when I'm unconscious?" Juliet asked softly.

"Yes," he replied without elaborating.

I knelt beside Raelyn, touching my forehead to hers. *All right, little lamb, where are you hiding?*

She didn't reply, not that I expected her to.

I slipped into her mind through our link, the absence of her awareness sending a chill down my spine. "Is it possible that her soul is hanging on, but her body is too damaged to recover?" I asked, fearing that her access to my immortality had trapped her in a place she could never escape from, an eternity in hell.

"The *Erosita* shares immortality with her mate. Could you recover from the wounds she suffered?"

"Yes, undoubtedly." It took a lot to kill a vampire, even more so for one of my age.

"Then she will too, but perhaps slower. I'm more concerned that she's shown no signs of healing yet. Even a freshling would be slowly regenerating by now."

"I know," I whispered, refocusing.

What am I missing?

The ceremony was complete. I felt everything snap into place, her being fusing with mine, our minds becoming one. It had scared the shit out of me, forcing me to build an impenetrable shield between us.

What if that had impacted our union?

No.

I was completely inside her now, her vacant essence

surrounding me.

So alone.

Vapid.

Sad.

I frowned, tugging on that last sensation, following it.

Such pain.

Abandon.

A loss of a will to live.

Deep, deep sorrow.

He left me...

The three words were a breath in my ear, not solid, but clear.

Raelyn's illusions of betrayal pierced my heart, not just from my closing her off but from her innate devastation over what I'd done to her. I could *feel* her suffering, all because of what I'd done to her.

And she was wallowing in that self-destruction instead of fighting.

Because she didn't see a point in trying.

I'd given her no reason to come back to me, no cause to survive. If anything, I'd demolished her hope through my insensitivity.

My Raelyn. I tried to caress her soul, to comfort her being, but it was like stroking a ghost.

So fractured and lost and dejected.

Her psyche was refusing to let her heal.

I don't accept that, little lamb, I whispered to her. *You're coming back to me.*

She didn't react or reply, her spirit floating helplessly with little determination or fight left in her. I'd chased it all away without meaning to, having blamed the bond for my unusual fixation, but it was always her that drew me in. Not her blood, or even her body, but her soul.

You're mine, darling. Time didn't matter. I claimed her the moment I saw her. I just hadn't realized it yet.

I cupped her cheek, my mind still flirting with hers. *You can't hide from me. I'll find you, Raelyn.* Enemies called me relentless for a reason. I didn't give up when I desired something, and right now, I wanted her.

If it was strength she needed, I would give it all to her.

My immortality.

My soul.

My heart.

Take it, I encouraged. *Use me.*

My fingers curled around the back of her neck, resolved to force as much of me as I could into her. She would survive this. She would wake up. She would be mine in every way. Whatever the cost, I'd pay it.

Now, Raelyn, I demanded. *You're going to breathe again if it's the last thing I make you do.*

She was stubborn, but I was persistent.

I needed her, not just to know who did this to her, but because I felt empty without her. We were nowhere near done yet. Perhaps we never would be.

Eternity was a long time, but if I could enjoy it with anyone, it'd be Raelyn. She had the fire I desired, possessed an intelligence I admired, and the passion between us went deeper than all my experiences combined. That was why I marked her, why I gave her my blood. I'd never allowed—or even considered allowing—another consort to be close to me. I guaranteed their mutual satisfaction and nothing more.

I'd given Raelyn my blood because I wanted to. I'd bitten her because the heat of the moment required it. I rarely fed from anyone during the act for my own enjoyment, but I couldn't stop myself from tasting her.

She was my addiction.

My renewed purpose.

A reason to enjoy living again.

Breathe, damn it, I growled. *I need you with me.*

Raelyn was resilient. She would survive this. I refused to consider any other outcome, and I told her as much over and over and over again. She could ignore me all she wanted, but I would force her to heal.

All my energy—my being—flowed into her, my age, experience, everything. I pushed it all through our bond, holding nothing back.

Knowledge.

Power.

History.

My deepest, darkest secrets.

Exposed.

Hers.

Forever.

Because I couldn't break our connection now, not after granting her access to the deepest depths of my soul. She would always maintain an awareness of me unlike any other. And I would never repeat this again.

A dull thud snapped my focus.

Just a flicker of sound.

Followed by another distant thump.

I waited, my breath frozen in my lungs.

Seconds ticked by.

And then a third beat. A fourth. A fifth.

Tears filled my eyes, my forehead pressing into hers.

Raelyn.

The singing of her pulse had never sounded so beautiful. She still had a long road ahead of her, but she would recover. And I'd be waiting for her when she finally opened her eyes again.

Chapter Twenty-Seven

KYLAN

"How is she?" Darius asked after knocking on the door, a coffee mug in his hand.

I stroked Raelyn's hair, her naked body pressed up against mine beneath the covers. "Still healing from the blood loss, but she's regenerating steadily."

He set the coffee on the nightstand beside me. "Good. Her skin looks healthy too."

Yes, her creamy complexion had returned earlier today. I'd bathed her again, removing the last of the blood from her body, leaving her clean and ready for rebirth. "Her thoughts are increasing as well."

"Any indication of who did this to her?"

"Not yet." I frowned and decided to go for honesty. "So far all her thoughts are about how much she hates me."

Which sucked. Having her say it was one thing, hearing the truth behind the statement was entirely another. "I really have been an asshole to her."

Darius chuckled. "Well, I'm sure she'll be forgiving when she realizes you saved her life."

I snorted. "You don't know her like I do. She's going to give me hell." Something I was going to enjoy far more than I should.

Something akin to wonder crossed his features, his mouth opening, then closing.

"Say it," I encouraged.

He shook his head. "It's not important."

"I'm not going to retaliate, Darius. Just say it."

He leaned against the wall, hands in the pockets of his black trousers, legs crossed at the ankles. "She's changed you."

My lips twitched. "This world—Lilith's creation—takes all the fun out of life. Raelyn provided something I haven't experienced in ages. A challenge."

"So you're not a fan of the blood alliance," he surmised.

"I can respect certain aspects of the system, but overall? No, I'm not loving this new world." It was boring and too structured.

"I would have taken you as one of her biggest supporters."

"Who? Lilith?" I scoffed at that. "I hate that bitch. All this Goddess shit is just a glorified power trip."

"But she does have a lot of support."

"Unfortunately, she does. For now."

"For now?" he repeated, raising an eyebrow.

"If there's one thing I've learned in this life, it's that dictators only remain at the top for so long. Lilith is very good at pretending she cares, keeping all her royals and alphas in line by stroking their egos when required, but she'll eventually make a mistake. And not everyone adores her, regardless of the facades in place."

"You think there are those who want to overthrow her?"

"Of course." I ran my fingers through Raelyn's hair, holding his gaze. "They won't show their cards for a long while, as the best plans take time, but I imagine we'll see shifting in the ranks soon." Or perhaps we already had.

I eyed his carefully blank expression, searching for signs of his knowledge on the subject.

He didn't blink.

Didn't move.

Didn't even twitch.

Either Darius was an excellent actor or he truly knew nothing. My money was on the former. An old vampire suddenly taking an interest in politics while mating with a human female he clearly cared for? Those were two very intriguing life changes to take on at once. Almost as if he'd planned it.

But who was I to speculate?

I smiled. "Well, what do I know? I'm just the oldest royal in existence, assuming Cam is really dead."

Still as stoic as ever.

"You'll be a fantastic politician, Darius," I murmured. "I'm excited to see where your career takes you."

He finally grinned. "Thank you, Your Highness." He pushed off the wall, his stride confident, and paused just inside the door. "You could try suggesting scenes to her."

My brow furrowed. "To Raelyn?"

"Yes. Telegraph an image of her outside with Angelica, see if she leads you to the truth of what happened." His green eyes met mine. "She's suffered significant trauma. It's fresh in her mind somewhere. You just have to find it." He left without another word, leaving me to consider his suggestion.

Was the answer lurking behind her hatred for me?

Let's see, little lamb.

I caressed her thoughts, flinching when I came up against a wall of frustration engraved with my name.

All just a game. I meant nothing, just a temporary diversion until his new consorts arrive.

I chuckled. Oh, if that were true, I'd have visited the harem camps by now to see whom I wanted to select. Yet I hadn't even studied their files or monitored the videos sent to me from the instructors.

Because I didn't care.

I only wanted the consort beside me.

Not that she'd ever believe that.

He used me. Bonded me to him so he could master my mind and heart, and like an idiot, I let him. I hoped... No. Stop. It's ridiculous. What's the point? I never meant anything to him.

If this stream of conscious was in real time, I could correct her. Alas, her mind only repeated her most consistent thoughts, ones she'd considered again and again—the most important items in her psyche. All centered around me and how I'd failed her.

I sighed and pushed through the initial wall, curious to see what lay beyond it.

Images of a blonde female and Silas flickered in the distance. I followed the strand to a memory of them laughing, my view from Raelyn's point of view.

"His face," the woman said, her full lips pulling into a grin.

"Like Rae's performance was any better," Silas replied, shaking his head. *"Goddess, I thought they'd all know she was faking it."*

Raelyn's giggle pierced my heart—a sound she'd never made in my presence. "Anything to pass a course."

"Not going to move on to the next level, then?" Silas teased, winking.

"Dear Goddess, no. Sexual arts are not for me."

"Hope you don't end up in the harems, then," the blonde said. *"Or worse, the breeding camps."*

But that's where you went, Raelyn whispered, the memory morphing into a thought. *Fuck, Willow, I hope you're okay. I miss you.*

I pulled back, noting the name. She'd mentioned it once or twice, something about the woman being her friend. Seeing their interaction now from Raelyn's perspective, I believed that.

True friends.

All of them.

And society had ripped them apart.

I picked up my tablet, ignoring the coffee Darius had dropped off, and searched the records for an image of the female. Her breeding camp designation and pale blonde hair made her easy to find.

Still alive.

But the updated image of her made her look like she wished she wasn't.

Yes, that was not a favorable fate, especially for a female.

And what about Silas... I pulled the latest stats from the Immortal Cup. Only four left already, Silas among them. The winner would be declared soon, assuming any of them survived the final round. His sapphire eyes lacked the confidence I'd seen on Blood Day, his muscular stature fatigued, but the tightening of his mouth indicated his resolve.

He was a survivor.

Just like Raelyn.

I flipped back to Willow, zooming in on her bruised face. Her downcast gaze made it difficult to tell if she possessed the strong will of her friends, but something told me she was a formidable human too.

A topic to discuss with Raelyn at some point. After we solved our present issue.

I still wanted to know who tried to kill my consort. No, my *Erosita*.

The term warmed my heart, the realization of just *who* she was to me feeling more right than I could have ever imagined.

I set the tablet aside and slipped back into her head, bypassing the onslaught of repetitive phrases about my horrible character and searching for new threads. The idea Darius had mentioned trickled through the bond, but rather than imagine Angelica outside, Raelyn focused on the sky, a hint of wonder trickling through her.

My lips curled at her happiness.

She really did love the outdoors, the snow, the mountains. Her heart sang with it, radiating a pleasure I wished I alone could give her.

And then her joy sped up, Mikael's face appearing.

I growled, low and deep. Why did *he* make her happier than I did? Because I'd left them alone for a week to train?

Wait…

Relief emanated throughout her being.

"Goddess, I'm so glad you're okay."

"You missed me?"

I frowned at the exchange. When had that occurred? Mikael claimed he hadn't seen her, yet her vision showcased him leading her along the tree line outside. Without Angelica.

Was this a dream or a memory?

They kept walking, confusion seeping into her mind, the image blurring at the edges.

Keep going, I urged, squinting.

Everything kept darkening, as if she didn't want to think about what came next. It went black, then illuminated again, her heart pounding as Zelda appeared.

Betrayal sang through our bond.

Kylan. Help me…

My hands shook, the words not current but spoken in her memories. She'd called for me—just as I thought—and her soul had wept when I didn't reply.

…betrayed you.

A lump formed in my throat. Raelyn had… she'd spent her last seconds trying to warn me of the truth. Not cursing my name, but *warning* me.

"Oh, sweetheart," I whispered, pulling her closer. "But who, darling? Who betrayed me?"

I followed her thread of immense sadness to an image that had my heart stopping.

A vision of Mikael slicing the blade across her throat.

"Goodbye, Rae."

I froze.

Mikael?

No. No, that was impossible

He…

I…

The vision flashed again.

And again.

Repeating through my thoughts, fracturing my grasp on reality.

The swipe of the blade.

Raelyn gurgling.

Mikael's sad voice.

It all culminated inside me, ripping my heart in half. I'd trusted him. Loved him in my own way. My best friend…

This couldn't be right. *Why?* I demanded. *Why would he do this?*

"You have to see this as a gift, Rae. He'll only bring you misery. Trust us, we know." His words in her mind were accompanied with such grief, such suffering. Because of me? Because I hurt him? How? I did everything to take care of him. I protected him. I gave him things few humans ever experienced.

And he'd taken the one thing from me I adored.

The one speck of happiness on my horizon.

All to, what, save her from his own misery?

I was an asshole, but not *that* horrible. There were many out there who were much worse than me, but Mikael had never experienced their brands of "affection" because I'd protected him from it.

I held Raelyn tighter, my heart beating in time with hers. *You don't think I'm that horrible, right?* I asked her softly, hearing all her accusations again in response. *Right, you probably do.*

I sighed, Mikael's betrayal simmering between us, heating my blood.

I'd failed them all.

Her.

Him.

Not on purpose, just by habit.

But that didn't justify Mikael taking Raelyn's life.

My throat constricted, my heart hammering in my chest. How had it come to this? Why?

Mikael was with me during the massacre of the harem. He'd shed real tears, his agony tangible. I'd soothed him in the only way I knew how. But had he known the entire time? Had he been involved? Who helped him?

Trust us, we know, he'd said.

Who was "us"?

Raelyn's mind opened up again, the scene flickering back and forth, revealing bits and pieces. Mikael's light eyes held so much heartache, his regret tangible.

"He makes you want things that he'll never completely give. He gets you addicted to him. Forces you to love him. But he never loves you back."

"I know."

My heart faltered with the words, so fresh, so brutal. Was that what they thought? That I forced them to feel this way while refusing to reciprocate?

"Fuck," I whispered harshly.

The memory continued in jumbled order. Raelyn's shock mingled with my own, her fear heightened as...

"Zelda," I said, my jaw tightening.

I stopped listening, her knife captivating my attention.

She'd been a part of this, her taunts making Raelyn cringe. Mikael looked so resolved.

And that blade slit Raelyn's throat again.

And again.

And again.

"Fuck!" I shut it off, unable to see it anymore.

I couldn't...

This hadn't...

I buried my face in Raelyn's neck, my mind racing with conflicting needs.

Revenge.

Punishment.
Sorrow.
Loyalty.

Raelyn whimpered again in her mind, my name repeating over and over, followed by a deep sadness that I'd left her there to die alone.

Fuck, that hurt worst of all—her anguish.

She thought I didn't care.

That I'd abandoned her to her fate.

"No," I whispered, locking my arms around her. "No."

I wouldn't leave her again. Not now. Not ever.

Mikael…

I cursed against her hair.

He'd have to wait.

Everything had to wait.

Raelyn mattered most.

I'm here, I promised her. *I'm never leaving you again.*

Not even to seek vengeance.

Chapter Twenty-Eight

RAE

Soap. My nose crinkled. *Minty. Masculine.*

Odd. The scent was everywhere. All over me. Inside me. Consuming me. And I was overly hot too, my clammy skin pressed against something equally warm—the source of the heat.

Kylan.

I blinked into the darkness of the room. No snowy mountains, just dark drapes like the ones in his penthouse.

My brow furrowed. Had he moved me while I slept? I blinked again. When had I slept? I couldn't remember, everything was foggy, the last few days a blur.

Kylan took me back to his home. We went for a hike. My heart stuttered, recalling what happened there. The subsequent days of pain. Angelica urging me to go outside.

And—

I flew upward on a gasp, my hand at my throat.

Mikael.

Zelda.

Kylan abandoning me to my fate.

It hit me so hard I couldn't breathe, the pain of my death so sharp and vivid. They just kept stabbing me. Over and over and over, my body dying while my soul held on, feeling everything.

I touched my bare side, my breasts, my stomach.

No marks. No blood. Just smooth, warm skin.

How?

I touched my unmarred throat again, convinced this was a trick somehow. Humans didn't just magically heal.

Am I no longer mortal?

"No, you're mine," Kylan replied, his voice low, cautious, and underlined with a darker emotion.

I spun to face him and winced as my head whirled with it. Both my palms went to my temples, a shudder of pain ricocheting throughout my being. "Ow," I mouthed, my voice failing me.

"Here." He put something between my lips—a straw. "Sip this and swallow."

I almost refused, but I needed the liquid, my throat aching without it. Cool water touched my tongue, soothing the burn inside my mouth and downward. It felt good. Relieving. Calming. My eyes fell closed while I continued to drink, my muscles relaxing until all I wanted was to lie down again.

Kylan set the cup aside and pulled me into his arms, my head finding his shoulder. It felt right—comfortable—and so, so good.

I yawned, my body slowly falling—

"Raelyn," Kylan murmured, jolting me awake.

I'm in his arms.

How had I allowed him to lure me into this position? He abandoned me when I needed him, pushed me away, used me and broke me, and—

"Saved your life," he added softly. "Not that it forgives everything else, but your link to my immortality is why you're alive." He tightened his hold, his lips brushing my temple. "You wanted to give up and I wouldn't let you."

What? The last thing I remembered was screaming for him in my mind and receiving no reply.

"Ouch," he muttered, flinching. "Yeah, I deserve that."

Deserve what? I wondered to myself.

"The memory," he replied. "And the pain associated with it."

My lips curled down in confusion. *What is he...?* My thought trailed off as an image of my mutilated body floated through my mind, trailed by a rush of emotions.

Confusion.

Fury.

Distress.

Not my own, but Kylan's feelings.

Followed by an onslaught of words intertwined with his memories.

Raelyn! Where are you? What's happened?

She's dead...

I'll murder whoever did this, rip them apart, scatter their remains, burn everything.

I failed her.

The link...

She's fighting it.

Because of me.

Fuck, Raelyn, don't do this. Don't you dare let go.

That's it, little lamb. Breathe for me. I'm not leaving you until you're awake. Maybe not even then.

You're stuck with me now, princess.

I need you to tell me who did this to you. Who is behind all this?

That last one had me pulling away from him, his true motives finally shining. "Y-you..." I swallowed, my throat still sore even after the water. But I had to say this. "You only saved me to learn—"

"No." He pressed his finger to my lips, pushing me down onto the bed as he hovered over me. "Look deeper, Raelyn, and you'll know that's not true."

I stared into his near-black eyes, shrouded in thick, dark lashes. He didn't glance away, his gaze open, his mind mine to explore. More words rushed over me, all laced in fury and confusion, hints of lust, murmurs of devotion, regret, sadness, and utter devastation.

Mikael's name was the loudest among them.

And a restrained rage lurking in wait for Zelda.

Kylan had seen my memory when I first woke... *No...* He'd seen it in my nightmares while I was healing.

"You already knew," I breathed.

He nodded. "Yes."

"Yet you stayed here?"

He cupped my face. "I promised not to leave you again, Raelyn. I meant it."

My lips moved but no sound escaped. He stayed with me.

I reached for his thoughts again, needing more explanation. He remained patient, granting me full access to everything. All of him.

The ceremony made me his *Erosita*, like Juliet to Darius. And granted me access to Kylan's immortality.

That's how I survived, and his mental urging that I not give up hope.

His memories overwhelmed me, his anguish when he thought I was dead, his reaction when he realized my soul still flourished, him driving us here, cocooning me in his penthouse for nearly a week while I healed.

Promises.

Decisions.

He never truly wanted to break the bond—it infuriated him to even think about—but he had never meant to instill it either. And now he refused to destroy it. Yet a hint of uncertainty remained, his desire to let me choose, to not force the connection upon me.

"It can only be broken by another vampire fucking you," he said softly, naturally aware of my snooping through his head. Which meant he'd allowed it and was continuing to leave himself open to me.

"I remember that part," I grumbled, recalling his original intentions clearly.

A flurry of possessiveness overwhelmed me, restricting my ability to breathe. It pressed on my chest, agonizing my insides, setting my blood on fire, sending tears to my eyes.

And then it was gone in a blink, leaving me winded and slightly dizzy.

"That's a mere fraction of how I feel when I think about sharing you, Raelyn." He stared down at me, his dark eyes intense. "While my intention may have existed in the beginning, there's a reason I couldn't follow through with it and refuse to do so now."

I gaped at him, shocked by another blast of that covetous energy from his mind to mine. "How are you doing that?" I managed to say, my voice raspy.

"We're mated. I can share everything with you and vice versa, including intense emotions."

"And thoughts."

"Yes, and images." He traced my bottom lip with his thumb, his gaze dropping. "I can see your memories just as you can view mine. Our connection is wide open, making us able to push things to each other as well."

"Which can trigger us to remember certain things." *Like what happened outside.*

"Yes," he whispered. "I pictured you outside. You showed me the rest."

I shivered and caressed my throat again. "It-it was awful."

Kylan rolled to his side, pulling me with him, our heads sharing the same pillow, our gazes locked. He ran his fingers through my hair, brushing it back from my face.

"I should have been there, should have been listening for you. Instead I left you with Angelica and assumed she would protect you." His irritation at that last part hummed through our connection, causing me to frown.

"You blame her."

"Partly, yes. Mostly, I blame myself."

"But you blame her too." I could hear his lethal intentions for her, all because she left me unprotected. "Her maker called. That's why she walked away." I didn't fully understand the link between maker and progeny, but I imagined it made him her superior.

"Vilheim called her," Kylan repeated, a crease marring his forehead. "That's coincidental timing."

His comment triggered a memory. Something about a timeline...

"Not when we're on a timeline. He'll only stall for so long."

Zelda's words played through my head. I hadn't known whom she meant at the time, but what if—

"She meant Vilheim," Kylan finished for me. "He's the reason I employed her. Vilheim recommended Zelda to me." His body tensed around mine, his memories of their conversations flickering through our bond. He didn't hide a single detail, letting me see everything from his point of view. "That was two years ago."

Suggesting she was put in place by Vilheim with the intention of discrediting Kylan. I listened while he reasoned through the plots, considerations, and potential partnerships.

Vilheim isn't experienced enough to inherit the region.
But he could become a sovereign under another's rule.
So which royal promised him power in exchange for overthrowing me?

Names rolled through his mind, motives judged and assigned, until he had a firm list of suspects who could be trying to take over his land. As well as a list of bored royals and alphas who might be having a go at him for pure sport.

"Our dinner party next week should be fun," he murmured, a plan forming and taking hold in his thoughts.

So quick and thorough, and undeniably intelligent.

I stared at him in awe, loving this side of him—the complicated musings of a clever being with thousands of years of experience. His perceived cruelty was the result of insightful plotting. Kylan didn't thrive on pain. He punished others to make a statement, to keep everyone in line. And he bore the weight of the region on his shoulders alone, trusting no one to help him.

He slid his palm beneath my hair, wrapping around the back of my neck.

"I've never let anyone see this much of me, Raelyn." A hint of fear underlined his proclamation.

"You believe confiding in others is a weakness," I whispered, hearing the confirmation in his deliberations.

"Providing others with the opportunity to harm me is an innate fault, yes."

"But it can also make you stronger." I cupped his cheek, holding his gaze. "I only ever survived because I trusted Silas and Willow to have my back. They helped me when I was shortsighted, and I returned the favor. Sometimes having an ally can give you the leverage you need to succeed."

"There's a difference between having an ally and a confidant," he replied. "I have many allies—"

"Whom you don't trust," I interjected. "You didn't even tell Judith we were here." A thought I'd overheard when he was reviewing his revengeful plans for the party. "And she's done everything to earn it." According to everything he'd shown me, anyway. "You push away everyone who could help you, relying solely on yourself to survive. It's a stressful way to live."

"It's more stressful to worry about when someone might betray you," he countered. "People are cruel, Raelyn. I've learned that the only one I can trust in this life is myself."

He showered me in his experiences, showing the way others had harmed him throughout his very long existence. All minor incidents that collectively added up to one sound conclusion—he could only rely on himself.

"Yes, I agree; looking out for yourself guarantees the outcome to always be in your best interest. But that doesn't mean you can't trust others to help you, Kylan. You've let a handful of bad experiences dictate your approach to life." I pressed my palm to his face. "My entire life has been ruled by vampires and lycans, most of whom were cruel. Should I not trust you as a result of their behavior?"

"You don't trust me," he said softly. "I can see your indecision, Raelyn. You worry I'll hurt you."

"Yes, and I imagine I'll feel that way for a long time," I admitted. "But that doesn't mean I won't take a risk and give you a chance to prove me wrong." And I meant it. Even after everything he'd put me through, I still wanted to trust him. Part of it stemmed from my access to his mind, granting me the ability to understand his motives and methods, but a larger part of it was my soul's innate belief in Kylan being my destiny.

I couldn't begin to comprehend it, but I relied on the instinct.

What did I have to lose?

Absolutely nothing.

I was born into this life as a servant, and Kylan gave me the opportunity for more. It was the closest I'd ever be to immortality, to living an actual life.

"Those are not the best reasons to agree to this, little lamb," Kylan said, a touch of sadness in his tone. "But they are practical."

"What other reasons would you give me?" I asked softly, studying his features.

Yes, he'd spent the last week nursing me back to health, but the thing that saved me—our bond—was never planned. And if I understood everything correctly, to remain immortal required my fidelity, not his. What kind of relationship was that? A one-sided one where I benefited from his life energy while being forced to remain faithful for eternity whereas he could do whatever he wanted.

"You want commitment," he murmured, following my

thoughts. He brushed his thumb over my eyebrow, his fingers skimming upward to run through my hair again. "I've never given that to anyone, Raelyn."

I nodded, having seen that in his thoughts as well. "I know."

"I've never bonded in this manner with anyone, either," he added. "I can't tell you what to expect because I don't know." He tilted his head to the side, his dark eyes simmering. "But I know I want you."

"For now."

"Yes, for now." He brushed his lips over mine, the movement slower and more tender than his usual embrace. "I think we both need time to figure this out."

Which he'd given me by extending my mortality. "Yes."

"And first, we need to deal with those trying to discredit me."

"We?" I repeated, my eyebrows lifting.

"Oh, yes." He nipped my lower lip before pulling away. "I have an idea and it very much involves you."

"I'm listening."

His lips curled. "Yes. Yes, you are."

Chapter Twenty-Nine

KYLAN

"Lilith, how lovely of you to join us." I greeted the blonde vampire with a superficial hug after she descended the grand staircase. Her deep-red gown revealed everything, giving her a devilish appearance rather than a holy one. Very, very appropriate.

"Kylan," she murmured, brushing her lips against my cheek. "You know I never miss one of your parties, as rare as they are these days."

"Yes, it has been a while," I murmured, extending my elbow to escort her into the main room. "It's just so much to organize, and I never know who may or may not make an appearance." *And your late arrival means I can finally start the show,* I thought with an internal grin. *Let the countdown begin.*

"Well, from what I hear, most of society planned to

attend."

I smiled. "It's almost as if they're expecting some sort of entertainment."

Her lips twitched deviously. "I believe they are."

Rumor of Raelyn's death had spread, something Jace helped circulate. He also suggested in casual conversation that it might be time for someone to step in temporarily as leader of Kylan Region.

The latter was why nearly all the royals and alphas were in attendance tonight.

Jace's offhanded remarks had grown into speculation as to whether or not he would challenge me tonight.

Exactly what we intended.

All these bored immortals wanted a show.

I'd be giving them one, just not the reveal they expected.

"I'm sure it'll be an enlightening evening, Kylan." Lilith winked as she left me to mingle with the others, her intrigue clear. There was a reason she'd ascended to the highest throne, her age and experience marking her as queen on the chessboard. Strategy was her version of foreplay, and she'd mastered the art long ago.

I both despised and admired her.

You're giving me heart palpitations, Raelyn whispered, making my lips curl.

I picked up a champagne flute from a passing waiter to hide my reaction behind the crystal glass. *Why? Because I'm destroying your perspective on religion, little lamb?*

You're destroying a lot of things.

I sipped the blood-laced liquid, amused. *Good. Remind me to show you a few religious texts at some point. I think you'll find some of the passages familiar but with slightly altered language.*

Her amusement fluttered through me, almost distracting me from the task at hand, but not quite. *You're all right, yes?*

I'm the same as I was when you asked me five minutes ago.

Can you blame me for worrying? Mikael and Zelda were in the same building as her, albeit completely unaware of her presence. The only ones who knew Raelyn was alive were

Judith, Darius, Juliet, and Jace. *Judith is still with you, right?*

Her mental sigh almost had me smiling again. *Yes, Kylan. She better—*

Not go anywhere, she finished for me. *Yes, we know. And I'll tell you if something is wrong, as I've promised a thousand times now.*

My lips twitched at her familiar fire. *Stop being defiant. Stop being mercurial.*

"You appear in good spirits," a familiar voice purred, Robyn drawing her nails up my suit-clad biceps. "What has you grinning like that?"

"A man never reveals his secrets, darling. You know that." I kissed her cheek, causing Raelyn to growl in my head. *Calm down, little lamb. Robyn isn't my type.*

Would you like me kissing another man?

I almost shattered the flute in my hand. *Absolutely not.*

Then stop kissing other women.

It's part of my charade, love.

Her responding snort said how she felt about that.

Your possessiveness is actually quite endearing, Raelyn.

You won't find it endearing later when I bite you again. She sent me a graphic image of exactly what she intended to bite, causing me to laugh out loud.

At this point, love, even that small attention might make me come. It'd been nearly two weeks since I'd last been inside her, mostly because I'd wanted her fully healed and prepared for tonight. And partly as a result of my concern over Raelyn's feelings toward our bond.

"Kylan?" Robyn snapped, pulling my attention back to her.

"I'm sorry, darling. Were you saying something?"

Her blue eyes widened. "What the hell has gotten into you?"

"I've had a very illuminating month," I replied. "And I'm not quite myself anymore."

True concern entered her expression. "Kylan—"

"Actually," I said loudly, deciding to begin the show. "Now that everyone is here, I'd like to say a few words." I set my drink on a nearby table and sauntered toward the middle of the room.

Ready, Raelyn?

Not like I have much choice now, she thought back at me, her mental voice amused. *Just say the word and I'm there.*

My resulting smile caused a few guests to take a step back. They all clearly thought me mad. This was going to be fun.

"Thank you all for joining me in Kylan City this evening. I know it's been a while since I hosted a gathering, and I just thought, with recent events, it might be a grand time to entertain you all." Several vampires chuckled at that, the implication clear. They all gathered here tonight because they expected a diversion, and I'd just confirmed that I intended to give them one.

"As you all have heard, I recently massacred my harem for sport and my latest consort met a similar fate. To be fair, she was a defiant little female from the beginning, as several of you observed, yes?"

Murmurs of agreement sounded throughout the room while Raelyn scoffed in my head. *Thanks for that.*

You're very welcome.

Smart-ass, she growled, entertaining me immensely. I adored that sound. It made me want to force it out of her in the bedroom, specifically in the form of my name.

Stop distracting me, little minx. I have a show to put on.

Then get on with it already.

I cleared my throat to disguise the laugh ready to burst out of me. Raelyn made this almost enjoyable, an emotion I would need, considering the tasks at hand.

"Oh, before I continue, may I introduce tonight's cuisine?" I snapped twice, indicating to Cherise that I was ready for her presentation.

The former reception manager had proven herself quite capable at organizing the dining rooms of K Hotel, so I'd opted to provide her with another opportunity to impress me—this time by catering tonight's event in the ballrooms of the hotel.

Maeve had helped as well with organizing all the guests' rooms and greeting everyone appropriately. The new hotel manager was in for a treat with acquiring them as staff. Another announcement for me to make this evening.

Humans dressed in varying degrees of lingerie filed out of the kitchen, their hands full of trays. It was typical for a host to offer blood. I asked Cherise to improvise by lacing popular hors d'oeuvres with blood, as well as to spice up the entertainment with revealing outfits.

Approval radiated throughout the room as the mortals were admired and fondled. The few lycans in attendance gravitated toward the meatier appetizers, while the vampires focused on the mortal offerings more than on the food options.

If anyone wished to take a human upstairs after the party, I couldn't deny them. Not without raising suspicion. Whether I approved or not, that was the nature of our world.

Zelda appeared in the mix, her expression confused, her eyes searching.

I'd purposely asked Cherise to add the woman to the lineup. She usually hid in the kitchens. Not tonight.

And finally, Mikael. I'd requested something very special for him.

He sauntered out in a tuxedo, flanked by two of my security guards—both items marking him as my equal, not my servant.

It was the first time I'd seen him since the night of Raelyn's murder, and it took considerable effort to force my lips upward in a welcoming smile.

"Ah, my favorite blood virgin," I murmured while silence fell over the room, the shock at my chosen attire for him evident in the way everyone stilled. "I haven't seen him in two weeks," I informed them all. "After what happened to my consort, I was afraid that a similar fate might befall my beloved Mikael and opted to keep him out of my reach for his personal safety."

A faint blush painted his cheeks as he made his way toward me, his lips curling. He'd interpreted my words the way I desired, as a subtle apology for abandoning him for so long. I wanted him to believe I'd meant to keep him safe while having everyone else assume I meant to protect him from my insanity. Dressing him as an equal only further proved my weakening mental state, at least to the casual observer.

He stopped at my side, his posture submissive while still holding an edge of confidence. It physically hurt not to react to his nearness.

He betrayed me. Framed me. Hurt Raelyn.

Yet, the bastard had the audacity to smile as if all was right in the world.

I gave him everything.

And I would leave him with nothing.

I pressed my palm to his lower back, a gesture of support that helped to hide the tension radiating up my arm.

Almost there, I told myself, retribution simmering in my blood.

The final feature of the flesh parade elicited several gasps from the crowd, including one from Lilith herself. She'd appeared unfazed so far, but her lips finally parted as Angelica stumbled forward beneath a layer of silver chains. Her emaciated form shivered, her dark eyes crazed from the lack of blood.

Kylan... Raelyn's discomfort cooled my nerves. While I'd mentioned this part of the plan, she'd not fully grasped what I intended until now.

Trust me, sweetheart, I whispered. *Let me focus.*

Okay, she replied, warming my heart. I expected her to hesitate, but she didn't. Not even a blink.

Thank you. I caressed her mind with mine, an intimate version of a hug.

Angelica stopped before me, her head bowed. The taller of the two security guards who escorted Mikael—Gavin—

stepped forward to give her a shove, forcing her to her knees. She whimpered as she landed, the silver digging into her skin. Unlike lycans, vampires were immune to the precious metal, but the chains were thick and heavy, especially to one in such an emaciated state.

"Hmm, we're missing someone." I glanced around for show, knowing exactly where my weasel was standing. "Oh!" I caught the jackass's gaze and smiled theatrically. "Vilheim, this one belongs to you, yes?"

"Yes, My Prince," he replied, his eyebrows rising.

"Then you should join us." I punctuated the invitation with a grand wave of my hand, fully aware of how insane I appeared to the room. It was that or kill all the guilty parties without proper explanation, and I much preferred this route. Especially as I hoped it would produce the real player behind the scenes.

After much deliberation with Darius and Jace, we decided the culprit had to be someone merely desiring a bit of chaotic fun. Because all those who were eligible to inherit my territory were either uninterested in expansion or too far away to truly reap the rewards of my land. And while I had as many enemies as the next royal, proving me insane yielded very little reward in the long run and would only ensure my retaliation.

Which meant I had it narrowed down to a handful of candidates, and only two of those candidates had deigned to attend this evening.

Robyn and Walter. The old alpha was on his way out the door, old age forcing him to step down. He would enjoy one final row among the higher-ranking members of society, especially if it left him with a legacy to enjoy.

Of course, that didn't mean I discounted Robyn. She was equally as likely, especially considering her penchant for fucking with others.

"Vilheim," I greeted as he stopped beside us, his expression bored. "Now we can begin." I took in the silent crowd, pleased that everyone was more intrigued by me than by the half-naked humans on display throughout the room. Perfect. "How would you all feel about observing a vampire trial?"

"That depends on what you're accusing her of," Lilith replied, her face carefully blank.

"Murder." My single-worded reply inspired several murmurs and exchanged looks of confusion. "Right, maybe I should explain. There are certain rumors spreading of my mental state, of which I won't question, but the assumptions surrounding my harem is something I would like to address. You see, I didn't kill any of them."

The voices grew, several explanations of disbelief and a few chuckles littering the air.

"Oh, come now, Kylan. We all know you have a penchant for blood," Robyn said, her voice filled with humored surprise.

"Undoubtedly," I agreed. "But not reckless murder. I wasn't home when my harem was killed, and Raelyn's murder occurred while I was out for a run. I found Angelica standing over her body covered in my consort's blood. That's why I've kept her locked away and blood-starved for two weeks. Tonight I am putting her on trial for murdering my property."

A chorus of disbelief and outright annoyance answered my claim, several stating they couldn't believe I was mad enough to blame another. Others claiming that punishing a vampire for the murder of a mortal was ludicrous. And many more sighing that I'd officially lost my mind. Clearly.

"Enough." Lilith raised her hand, calming the crowd, her green eyes sharp with knowledge. "All right, Kylan. I'm intrigued. Proceed."

I smiled. She'd just agreed to a trial for not only Angelica's sins but mine as well. If this went the wrong way, she'd use the incident to claim me as mentally unstable. It's what I would do in her position.

"Thank you, Lilith." I inclined my head in mutual understanding and released Mikael to walk around the vampire dressed in chains, hands behind my back. She appeared so broken and fragile that I almost felt bad, then I remembered how she abandoned Raelyn. "You know the murder I'm accusing you of, Angelica. How do you plead?"

"I d-didn't d-do it," she whispered, shaking her head. "I-I d-didn't."

"That's fascinating considering I found you covered in her blood at the scene of the crime. Explain to me what happened."

"I… I was t-talking to V-Vilheim." She paused, shuddering violently. "I-I found her like that. I found her a-after I hung up the phone."

My eyebrows rose in mock surprise, my gaze going to Vilheim. "She's using you as an alibi. Can you believe that?"

He laughed, his execution flawless. "It's ridiculous. Why would I call her?"

"Y-you did!" She lifted her head, a fire in her gaze that bespoke of desperation and fury. "Y-you called me!"

He took a step forward, but I stopped him with a hand on his shoulder. "Shh, let's hear her out," I encouraged. "If anything, it'll amuse me."

He fixed his jacket, backing off, and nodded. "Yes. Fine. But I want the honor of killing her."

"Of course," I replied. "The honor will be all yours." I crouched in front of Angelica, meeting her infuriated gaze. Most would be sobbing in her condition, but she looked ready to commit murder. "What did he say when he called you?"

"He asked me what you had me doing," she growled. "He wanted to know about Rae." Her expression fell on that last word. "I sh-shouldn't have left her. But I d-didn't kill her. I swear it."

Vilheim snorted. "That wasn't even entertaining. Why would I care about a consort?"

I stood and smoothed my tie. "Yes, why indeed?"

Are you ready, Raelyn? I asked while feigning a thoughtful expression.

Yes. Her immediate response was laced with fire. She wanted to avenge Angelica despite barely knowing the woman. I admired that tenacity and sense of loyalty, even if I questioned it. *She's been punished, Kylan.*

Has she? I countered, gazing at the emaciated female. *I gave her a task and she failed.*

But she's not the one who attacked me.

You wouldn't have been attacked if she had done her job, I pointed out.

She sighed in my mind. *She's suffered enough.* A blast of guilt hit me, Raelyn unleashing her inner turmoil at seeing Angelica disciplined over something she felt was uncontrollable. *Please, Kylan.*

My command overrode everything else in this territory, something Angelica should have known before accepting that call. But soothing Raelyn's discomfort meant more to me than making an example out of Angelica.

All right, little lamb. It's time.

"I feel as if we need another witness," I said to the room, glancing around. "Someone who may be able to speak to Angelica's account of what happened." I pulled a device from my pocket and hit a button. "Judith, we're ready for you."

"Of course, My Prince," she replied over the speakerphone, playing her part as requested.

Mikael noticeably stiffened, but Vilheim remained unaffected. I couldn't wait to see his exterior shatter.

Hushes of speculation fluttered through the air, the majority of the guests quiet and intrigued while a few discussed my mental state in whispers. Jace met my gaze from across the room. He gave away nothing in that icy stare, but I knew he approved. This was exactly how he would handle it.

Heels clicked over the tile, causing several to look in the direction of the grand ballroom entrance.

My lips began to curl, ready to welcome my big surprise.

She appeared at the top of the staircase, her auburn

strands piled high on her head to expose the delicate column of her throat. The red gown I'd chosen for her flowed to the floor and cut suggestively to her upper thighs while the opaque fabric clung to every inch of her skin without exposing it.

Gorgeous, I thought, smiling widely now. "May I introduce my *Erosita*, Raelyn."

Chapter Thirty

RAE

Chaotic conversation and whispers of disbelief trailed around me as I descended the stairs, my legs shaking from the effort to remain confident. Judith walked behind me, her presence helping to ground me in the moment.

I could feel their gazes on me.

The hunger.

The shock.

The general lethality lurking in the room.

Lycans and vampires, most of status, all waiting for me to join them as the star witness.

Just breathe, little lamb, Kylan whispered, his mind brushing mine. *I'm waiting for you at the bottom.*

I couldn't see him, my eyes averted in a display of subservience necessitated by my role. Knowing he was there helped me move faster, my heels clacking over the marble stairs, my dress shifting with my movements.

"Hello, little lamb," Kylan greeted, his hand wrapping around the back of my neck to draw me in for a kiss as I reached the bottom. "You look delicious."

"Thank you, My Prince." The words were whispered against his lips, my heart pounding in my ears.

I have you, love, he promised. *Trust me.*

Warmth flooded my thoughts and my blood. *I know.*

He took a step back and extended his arm. "Now, let's see about getting some proper answers."

Some of the heat fled my body as Kylan led me closer to Mikael. Gavin stood behind him, his stance protective as he held Mikael's biceps. Others would think he meant to guard the blood virgin, and perhaps that was even what Kylan told him. But I knew the truth, as did Mikael. His light eyes met mine, horror mingling with sorrow radiating from him.

Because he felt bad about what he did to me?

Or because he pitied his situation?

If he was sorry about what he did to you, there would be at least a spec of relief inside him. I sense none. The last three words were a growl in my head, Kylan's displeasure raising the hairs along my arms. He had expected—hoped—Mikael would show some semblance of care regarding my being alive, but his pulse rang of fear more than anything else. Proving to Kylan that Mikael only ever cared about himself.

Deep sadness crept through our connection, Kylan truly distraught over having failed his blood virgin.

But you didn't, I told him, certain. *You treated Mikael better than anyone else ever had or ever would.*

Yes, however, he always desired more from me. Something I never could give. He opened the line of thought, showing me what he meant.

Mikael taking care of Kylan through small acts such as bringing him evening breakfast, coffee, serving him wine—doing whatever was asked of him even when it clearly hurt.

He never said no.

He always obeyed.

And he never stopped looking at Kylan as if he were the sole purpose for living. His desire evident in every glance, his body bending to whatever will was bestowed upon him, and his heart always there for the taking.

Love, I realized. *He wanted your love.*

"All right, where were we?" he asked out loud instead of replying to me.

Glancing at Mikael's broken features, a confirmation wasn't needed. His sorrow stemmed in knowing he'd failed Kylan, that he would never have him again. That he'd lost the love of his life forever. And everyone would know after today.

"Oh, right, Angelica said she had to take a call and that's why she left Raelyn alone. I'm curious to hear my *Erosita's* side of the tale, since she lived through it after all." He turned me toward him, his fingers tilting my chin up to meet his gaze. "Speak." A hint of mischief followed that word through the bond, his way of trying to lighten our dark situation by reminding me of our first time together.

I narrowed my gaze. *I'm not a dog, Kylan.*

Yes, of that I am very much aware, pet. "Now, Raelyn."

"Angelica and I were outside when her phone rang. She said it was Vilheim, her maker, and she had to take the call. Mikael found me shortly after." I paused to glance sideways at him, his light eyes rimmed with tears. My heart stuttered, uncertainty filling me inside.

What will you do to him?

"What happened next, Raelyn?" Kylan demanded. *I'm sorry, love, but I need you to say it.*

But what will you do to him? I asked, my focus still on Mikael, watching him fracture beside us. He knew what was coming. He knew his fate. I should have been thrilled by the prospect of revenge, but all I felt was immense sadness for our situation. Of the lengths at which he'd gone to keep Kylan to himself, all at the expense of his own life.

I don't know what I'll do yet, Kylan admitted softly. *But I need you to finish the story.*

The unease and expectations of the crowd were closing in on us, their eagerness at what I had to say overwhelming me. I swallowed, shuddering, and closed my eyes, unable to stand the sight of Mikael's tears any longer.

I took a deep breath, steadying myself. "Mikael walked with me for a bit, saying he liked me and apologizing, but I didn't understand why. Then Zelda appeared with a knife, said something about my death being the final nail in your coffin, and told Mikael to prove himself by killing me. So he slit my throat before stabbing me."

I flinched at the memory of the sharp edge piercing my rib cage, my chest, the sensation of drowning in my own blood—

Kylan wrapped his hand around my neck suddenly, squeezing. My eyes flew open to meet his heated gaze, his expression yanking me back into the present faster than a command.

"Sounds like your humans need a lesson in discipline," a female remarked from the crowd.

Kylan's attention slowly shifted toward the woman—Robyn, I realized—and narrowed. "Are you suggesting mortals are intelligent enough to craft a plan like this on their own?"

"Well, I didn't hear mention of a vampire in the mix, so yes."

His lips curled as he released my neck, pulling me to his side to face her. "Fascinating that you mention that. See, from the memory I've pulled from my *Erosita's* head, I can confirm Angelica did in fact receive a call from Vilheim, because the image of the phone number is in Raelyn's head. What's more is the phrase Zelda said about being on a timeline and only stalling for so long."

He snapped his fingers to his left, where Judith appeared with a tear-streaked Zelda in her arms. I'd not even noticed the captive female, but seeing her now had my blood heating for retribution.

My eyes narrowed. *You.*

"I'm going to kill you, Zelda," Kylan said flatly. "The question at this time becomes whether or not I make that a quick death or a long, excruciating one. Care to elaborate on your words to Raelyn?"

She blanched, her focus going over my shoulder with a pleading stare.

Kylan followed her gaze, turning as he went. A dark-haired vampire with ashen features stared back at us, his expression unreadable.

"Oh, right," Kylan said. "Yes, for those unaware, Vilheim used to be Zelda's owner, but he gifted her to me after I expressed gratitude over one of her desserts." He shifted again to face her. "I'm starting to think that wasn't a coincidence, Zelda. I suggest you start talking because he can't help you, and trust me, I'm itching to punish someone for what was done to my property."

The choice of words stung until I felt the purpose behind them. Kylan couldn't risk anyone knowing that I actually meant something to him. He needed to appear strong and infallible, not weakened by emotion.

"I...I..." She began to sob in earnest, her legs giving out beneath her, sending her to the ground.

"Vilheim told her to do it," Mikael said quietly. His heart was in his eyes as he looked only at Kylan. "I figured out that she let him in to destroy the girls, your harem, while we were gone. When—"

"You figured it out?" Kylan repeated.

"Yes. I found a bloody shirt in her room, and when I asked her about it, she broke down and told me what happened. I was going to tell you, but she called Vilheim. And..." Mikael trailed off with a wince, his expression breaking all over again. "H-he said if I helped them discredit you, he would make sure I ended up with you in exile. Rae was my task." His blue-green eyes met mine, apology radiating in them before he refocused on Kylan. "I'm sor—"

"Don't," Kylan growled, pain splintering our bond. He couldn't stand to hear it, not now, not while hiding his emotional frailty. "Is there anything you'd like to say, Vilheim?" He slowly turned to face the shorter male, releasing me in the process. While Kylan's exterior radiated calm, his fury burned between us. He wanted to kill.

"Would you like me to speak for you?" Kylan pressed, his eyebrows rising. "Because if I were to guess, I'd say you wanted to discredit my mental state so someone else would take over my territory and grant you more power. I mean, we both know you're nowhere near the appropriate age to inherit a region yourself, so that leaves having a new ruler as your only option. And that begs the question: which royal did you have in mind?"

"That's a hefty allegation," the Goddess said, moving to stand beside Kylan. "However, I find myself curious as well, Vilheim. And as you know, conspiring against a royal, let alone *your* royal, is punishable by proper death. I'm sure Kylan will want to extend that sentence as long as possible." She raised a blonde brow at him.

"Absolutely," Kylan confirmed.

She nodded. "As I thought. Vilheim, I suggest you speak quickly before Kylan removes your tongue for sport."

The gruesome image formed in my head, compliments of Kylan. His hand caught mine before I could wince, his touch forcing me to remain calm.

"He's insane," Vilheim said. "Surely you see that."

The Goddess's brows rose. "Thirty minutes ago, perhaps I would have considered that, but after everything I've seen tonight? It's quite clear to me that Kylan is very much alive and well." She placed her manicured hand on Kylan's arm and turned to him. "I mean, turning a consort into an *Erosita* just to catch the culprit? That's brilliant."

My blood ran cold at the insinuation. That couldn't—

"It worked marvelously, as you can see," he murmured, prickling my insides.

No. He established the connection by accident, not to

fortify me as bait.

Kylan, tell me that isn't why you did this.

He ignored me, his eyes and focus completely on the Goddess.

She shook her head. "Really, Kylan, sometimes I think you play this game better than I do."

He gave her an indulgent smile. "Oh, come now, darling, you'll always be the queen on the chessboard."

She blushed, her lips curling. "I've forgotten how much fun you can be. I need to visit more often."

"You do," he agreed. "But first, Vilheim?"

My heartbeat was in my ears, rushing through my bloodstream. *Please tell—*

I need to focus, Raelyn, he replied, his mental voice brisk and to the point.

I swallowed. *Of course.*

Once this finished, we could talk. Then he would confirm that he hadn't just forged this bond between us to keep me alive for tonight. He'd opened his mind to me. I would have seen that, right?

Unless he knew how to hide it.

I frowned. Could he conceal details from me? No. He gave me unfettered access to his memories, his being, and I still had the ability to enter, except, it seemed cloudier now, as if he was indeed trying to keep something from me.

The truth of our bonding?

"I have nothing to say." Vilheim appeared unfazed by the threat of the two oldest vampires in existence standing before him.

"Nothing?" Kylan repeated. "Well, that's fascinating because we both know you didn't contrive this plan all on your own. You're not intelligent enough for that, which is why I never promoted you. So that leaves me wondering who put you up to it." He tapped his chin and glanced around the room, searching.

The Goddess eyed him speculatively, as one would an opponent.

Her bright green eyes flicked to mine, causing me to freeze. *Oh...* I wasn't even supposed to be watching. But now I couldn't move, my mind frozen. She tilted her head to the side, curiosity brightening her features. As if she hadn't seen a human in years.

So ancient.
So cold.
So... not a Goddess.

The instinct hit me suddenly, nearly knocking me to the floor. I'd feared this being since my first breath, but now I saw beneath the veneer.

She was just another vampire. Albeit an incredibly old one like Kylan, but nothing ethereal or Goddess-like about her.

"Robyn," Kylan called. "You know how much I adore watching you in action, darling. Would you mind helping me break Vilheim?"

The Goddess—*no, Lilith*—slowly shifted her focus to the crowd.

"Oh, sweetheart, I think you're far more advanced than little old me," the blonde royal replied. "And I much prefer to observe your work."

"Nonsense." He released my hand and held it out to her, his smile so enticing my heart stopped. The male was much too beautiful, and that look only made it worse. "Please. Join us. I insist." His tone held an edge that no one could dare defy, not even me.

Robyn set her drink aside and started through the crowd. "Well, I can't say no to that."

"Excellent. So I was thinking that, rather than removing his tongue, we could bleed him and feed his blood to the humans in the room for fun." Kylan glanced at Lilith. "Such a degrading act should force an old vampire like Vilheim to open up, yes?"

"To waste such precious blood on mortals?" She sounded outright disgusted. "Yes, absolutely. But we'll have to kill the humans afterward, you realize."

"Of course." Kylan waved a hand at that. "I assumed that was the after-party."

Lilith nodded. "Then yes, please, proceed."

Several members of the crowd stepped back as Kylan removed his suit jacket. He handed it to me without a word and began rolling his shirtsleeves. "Have a go, darling. I'll join you in a minute."

Robyn brushed her palms over her dress and stepped toward Vilheim. His gaze noticeably narrowed at her, the first crack in his exterior. She swiped her nails across his jacket, sending the buttons to the floor, and roughly pushed the fabric from his shoulders. He opened his mouth, and she slapped it shut so fast and hard that blood pooled on his lip.

Kylan, I warned.

I see it. But he pretended not to, his gaze on his sleeve.

Vilheim made to speak again, only to be hit even harder, Robyn's nails ripping the skin from his face.

I flinched from the brutality, shocked that a hand could cause that kind of damage. Everyone taking several steps back suddenly made sense, especially as Robyn went full force—on his face.

Lilith placed a hand on Kylan's bicep, her stance tense. She nodded once, some sort of exchange between them.

Vilheim started to fight back, his arms up in front of his face as he struck back at the crazed female.

It was all too fast for my mortal eyes, their movements quick, and words began to pour from the male's mouth in a foreign hiss.

I didn't understand any of it, the scene unfolding at a rate my brain couldn't comprehend.

Air whooshed around me, my head spinning as I collided with something hard. Cement circled me, unforgiving, my lips parting on a scream that was silenced by Kylan's lips. Brief. Enough to ground me, and then I was staring at his back.

What just happened?

My breath stuttered, my heart racing in my chest. I grabbed Kylan's sides, needing my balance, as he growled deep. "Did you just attack my *Erosita*, Robyn?" he demanded.

"What?" She sounded winded, but I couldn't see her. "No, of course not. She clearly moved in my path. You all saw it."

"No, what I saw was you going after another royal's property," Lilith replied, her voice cool. "It also appears as if you are trying to maim Vilheim to a point of incoherence."

"Sh-she iss," the male slurred. "Sh-she s-set me up."

Shocked whispers shattered the silence in the room, sending a chill down my spine. Now what?

I glanced around and found Zelda on the ground in a bow of supplication. Mikael stood beside her, flanked by two of Judith's guards while she stood watch over the quivering Zelda.

Kylan slowly pulled me around to his side, his jacket sprawled out on the ground and smattered in blood. I'd dropped it in the shuffle, not that he seemed all that saddened by it.

"Why, Robyn?" he demanded. "Why orchestrate all this?"

The blonde straightened, her lip bloody, her dress ruined. And she smiled. The look so unnervingly delusional that I questioned whether she'd truly gone mad.

"Oh, come on, Kylan. It wasn't that big of a deal. All I did was tell Vilheim that Jace would inherit your territory and promote him to sovereign—under my suggestion, of course. And really, he did most of the rest. The only thing I had to do was get someone on your plane to send those emails, which was easy after involving your little blood whore." She waved a theatrical hand at Mikael, who flinched as if she'd touched him.

"You attempted to discredit another royal out of boredom?" Lilith asked, her tone incredulous.

"Why not?" Robyn shrugged. "Honestly, it wasn't even

that entertaining."

"Not that entertaining," Kylan replied. "You slaughtered my harem, Robyn, and nearly killed my *Erosita*."

She shrugged. "Humans are replaceable. You know that better than anyone. Don't be angry, love. It was all just for fun, and you figured me out. Easy."

"Don't be angry," he repeated as if tasting the words. "You tried to discredit my sanity, and you want me to be okay with it. Lilith, I think Robyn is the one here suffering from age insanity."

"It would appear that way," she agreed, her tone thoughtful. "I can't let this go unpunished, Robyn."

"Of course." The blonde shrugged. "Do your worst."

Her nonchalance sent a spear of rage through my gut. The woman didn't even care that she'd been caught and didn't fear retribution.

Because royals were rarely ever killed. The last one to face the punishment of death was Cam, for challenging the Goddess herself, and from what Kylan had implied, Cam might actually still be alive.

So no wonder Robyn wasn't afraid.

She knew they wouldn't hurt her permanently.

Lilith clasped her hands. "Robyn, you are hereby excommunicated from all events—including Blood Day—for a decade. That marks you ineligible to purchase or acquire new humans at any point until after your expulsion is complete."

The blonde royal's face went white. "A decade?"

"Hmm, yes, that does seem a bit short." Lilith turned to Kylan. "How long did it take your *Erosita* to recover from her injuries?"

"Seven days," he replied flatly.

"Yes, a much better number. Your term of excommunication will be seven decades, Robyn. Might I suggest you treat your current harem and house staff decently in the interim? It will be a while before you have a chance to replace them, and most will die of old age prior to that point."

Robyn sputtered, her full lips making soundless words of disagreement.

"Would you prefer a longer sentence?" Lilith asked, arching a brow.

"I… No, no, My Queen." Robyn bowed, her legs shaking beneath her. "I… I accept. Of course, I accept."

"Excellent. Then I suggest you leave, as this is a social event and you are no longer welcome here."

Robyn stilled, her body frozen in her curtsy.

"Now," Lilith snapped.

"Yes, of course." Robyn erected her spine, her blue eyes filled with mingling emotions—shock, hurt, fury. She flashed a look at Kylan too fast for me to read and disappeared by phasing out of the room.

"Well, this has been a fascinating evening," Lilith said, turning to Kylan, a bejeweled blade in her hand. "Shall I do the honors or would you like to?"

"Oh, allow me." He held out his palm. "Please."

"He is yours and has harmed your property." She gave him the knife and turned to address the crowd. "Vilheim has been accused of conspiring against his royal. While, yes, Robyn played him, he should have gone to Kylan to report the activity rather than playing along."

She paused as if waiting for questions.

No one uttered a word or a sound.

"Is there anyone here who objects to Vilheim, Vampire of Kylan Region, receiving the required punishment for this crime?"

Silence.

"Hearing no objections, you may proceed, Kylan."

"Thank you." He stepped away from my side to approach Vilheim, who was kneeling on the floor, two unnamed vampires on either side holding him there.

"Asshole," he grumbled.

"Is that your final word?" Kylan asked. "Because I'm not all that impressed."

Vilheim chanted something in a foreign language that had Kylan chuckling and shaking his head. "You were never worthy, Vilheim. And you never will be." He drove the blade into the man's chest quickly and efficiently, a collective hiss following the noise.

Proper death, I realized, shocked.

I'd never seen a vampire die. Didn't even know how they could die. And here Kylan had murdered the male in a room full of his brethren and lycans.

The body disintegrated into ash, littering the floor. Kylan used Mikael's jacket to wipe the razor edge clean before handing the item back to Lilith.

Was she the only one with that weapon?

Was it laced in a special substance or crafted specifically for this purpose?

"Excellent." She hid the weapon somewhere in her dress, the metal disappearing in a blink. "Now, I imagine you'll be handling your human problem, yes?"

"Well, there is one matter that remains unresolved."

She arched a brow. "Oh?"

"Yes. I'm officially one short in my region, a consequence not of my own making but of another royal's. And given the headache all of this has caused with my harem and the false implications against my character, I feel I'm entitled to a new resource."

I didn't quite follow what he meant, but the whispers in the room suggested everyone else did.

"I see," Lilith murmured, her gaze narrowing. "We have rules for a reason, and I'm not sure this incident provides justification to break them, Kylan."

"A life for a life," someone said from the audience. "It does seem justified in this scenario. Vilheim is dead. Kylan requires a new recruit to uphold the balance in his territory. Even numbers and all that."

Lilith glanced in the direction of the speaker. "Are you seconding his request, Jace?"

"I am. I agree that it's only fair given everything he's

been through these last few months." Jace stepped forward with a champagne flute of blood, his hand tucked in his pocket, the picture of nonchalance. "I may not care for the man, but I'm inclined to agree with him on this."

More whispers sounded, the room filling with noise and speculation.

"He's right." The low growl in the voice suggested the words were from a lycan.

"Walter?" Lilith appeared astonished. "You agree as well?"

"I do. It's what I would require if in his shoes."

"Me too," another said.

Several more began to speak up, all agreeing to the terms, and continued until the chatter reached a level Lilith could no longer bear.

"Enough," she said, her command silencing the room.

Kylan stood before her, his expression blank, his mind even blanker. I had no idea what he was thinking because he'd blocked me again. Not entirely, but just enough to keep me from hearing his plans.

I'd been so overwhelmed by my surroundings and the chaos that I hadn't noticed. My heart gave a subtle pang at being pushed away, but I had to believe it was for him to better focus. He'd probably been too inundated with my concerns and confusion to focus.

Yes, that has to be it.

Lilith sighed. "The Immortal Cup is coming to a close, Kylan. I can't give you any of those recruits, as we're already down to two, but given the outcry of support, I could make a concession for next year."

My heart stopped. *Already down to two? Was Silas one of them?*

"Actually, I already have a human in mind," Kylan said smoothly, distracting me from my thoughts.

"You do?" Lilith asked, raising a brow. "Dare I ask which one?"

He smiled. "Yes." He held out a hand for me. "Raelyn."

Chapter Thirty-One

RAE

Kylan's hand wavered before my eyes.

Had he just suggested…?

No.

I'd misunderstood.

There was no way he meant—

"Your *Erosita*?" Lilith asked, sounding even more shocked than I felt. "No, absolutely not."

"Why not?" he countered, dropping his hand to his side. "She was one of the top twelve candidates designated for the Immortal Cup. Her test scores are phenomenal. She's gorgeous, intelligent, and played her part in my game perfectly to catch my betrayers. I cannot imagine a more suitable candidate for immortality."

"She's defiant," Lilith said, glancing at me. "Even now,

she's staring directly at me."

"Because she was born not to be a human but to be a vampire. My vampire."

The murmurs started again, several of them rising in assent, while my heart thudded loudly in my ears.

Kylan, I breathed.

But he remained closed, his attention solely on Lilith.

"Darius," Jace murmured, his focus on the drink in his hand as he swirled the contents. "You became rather familiar with Raelyn over the last week or two, yes?"

The vampire in question smirked. "I did. Kylan failed to remark on her oral abilities in the bedroom, which are a solid ten, for anyone who might be curious."

"So good enough to join our ranks?" Jace asked.

Darius shrugged. "She could use a little refining around the edges, but I imagine Kylan is up to the task. He worked wonders on my Juliet."

All lies. We spent the last week relaxing. Darius's relationship with Juliet was unlike one I'd ever witnessed, his adoration for her obvious. And Kylan hadn't laid a hand on her, too busy plotting for tonight and making sure I was comfortable.

But we never reviewed this part of the plan.

Several around the room voiced their consent, one of them even saying to give Kylan what he wanted because he'd earned it.

Lilith took my measure again, the curl in her lip suggesting she found me lacking.

She would never approve.

And I didn't even know if I wanted her to, not anymore.

Wouldn't becoming a vampire mean giving up my bond to Kylan?

It hit me then, the reason he was doing this.

You're giving me a way out. The gift of immortality without tying me to him forever. *Kylan...*

"She will be my responsibility, and I promise you'll be impressed by the next Blood Day."

She tore her gaze away from me and lifted her eyebrows. "You're proposing to make her yourself?"

"I am."

"Your first progeny," she said, sounding flabbergasted. "I never thought I'd see the day, Kylan, let alone see you waste it on someone so unworthy."

"You forget that I can see inside her mind through the bond. Trust me when I say there is no one worthier of this honor than Raelyn." The veracity of his proclamation sang through our connection, his pride in me shattering the temporary barriers he'd put up before.

He was not only giving me a way out but also providing us with the opportunity to be with each other out of desire, not necessity.

Because I wouldn't rely on him for immortality.

Which meant he'd have to work to keep my interest.

And he wanted to work for it.

How had he kept this from me? Looking in his mind now, I knew this was always part of his plan—to demand compensation for his loss in the form of my eternal life.

I didn't know what to say.

All I could do was gape at him.

"All right," Lilith murmured. "If that is your request, consider it granted."

"Thank you." He inclined his head.

"But I expect to see considerable improvement the next time I see her."

"Of course," he replied. "Disciplining Raelyn is one of my favorite pastimes." His amusement rolled over me, but I was still too shocked to respond or even mentally roll my eyes.

He wants to turn me.

To become my maker.

"Now, there is the small matter of what to do with the rest of you," he said, facing Angelica first. He crouched to remove some of the chains from her naked body. "You are badly in need of some blood."

Her hollow eyes glared up at him. "You knew," she growled.

"I did, but you still failed me, Angelica. I told you to guard Raelyn, and you left her." He ripped more of the chains off of her, his strength showing in each pull as he freed her from the restraints. "When I tell you to do something, it carries weight over everyone else. Do you understand?"

She swallowed, her body shuddering as he removed the last of the metal by snapping the shackles off her ankles with his bare hands. "Y-yes, Your Highness."

"Good. Then consider your punishment complete." He looked up at Mikael, his expression cruel. "Can I offer you a drink, Angelica?"

Mikael's lips parted, his eyes tearing up again. He wore the look of a broken man, a lover abandoned and destroyed.

My heart ached for him.

Even after everything he'd done to me, I couldn't help the catch in my breath.

All he ever wanted was Kylan.

And he'd never have him.

"Kneel," Kylan demanded.

Mikael dropped to the ground, his head falling. He wasn't even going to beg. He just knew.

A pang shot through me, the source of it Kylan. His struggle hurt my heart more, his mind not knowing what to do. To kill him quickly, to extend the pain, to slaughter him for the room… to let him live.

"Give her your wrist." His voice never wavered, but inside, the act was killing him.

You don't have to kill him, I whispered. *Not to avenge me.*

What would I do with him? he asked softly. *Lock him up until he dies?*

Can you give him to someone?

He deserves a worse fate, Raelyn.

I know, but he did it because he loves you.

Mikael whimpered as Angelica pierced his vein, her

ravenous mouth sucking and pulling for the sustenance her young vampire body required to survive. She was half-starved and faced with a blood virgin. His essence was addictive to even the oldest of vampires. Against her, he stood no chance. She'd devour him unless Kylan stopped her, and Mikael knew it.

Kylan stood, ignoring the scene despite his aching heart, and focused on Zelda with a sadistic smile. "Cherise," he called.

"Your Highness," she replied, practically running forward to meet him, hope in her gaze. "You've pleased me greatly with your improvement. We'll discuss promotional opportunities later, but for now, I need you to handle that one for me." He pointed to Zelda. "She's a former chef. Perhaps she can help you create something featuring her blood."

My stomach rolled at the notion. *Kylan...*

She deserves worse. Be thankful I won't be the one killing her.

"Of course, My Prince," Cherise replied, her lips curling. "I'll be happy to handle that for you."

"Thank you. Be sure to drain her completely. I no longer have use for her, and she's unemployable in this region."

"I understand." Cherise bowed and grabbed Zelda by the hair. "Come along, former chef."

He looked at Judith and his security team before finally returning to a fading Mikael. His mind rioted between right and wrong, finishing it and allowing forgiveness.

He really did care about Mikael.

I could see it inside his soul. It wasn't love, but a deep friendship established over a decade.

His mental sigh was heavy and tired. "Enough, Angelica," he said, pulling her away from Mikael. She only fought for a second before realizing who had tugged her away, and she scrambled backward, wiping her bloody mouth. "Judith, please take Mikael to my quarters. I'll finish this on my own time."

"I'll prepare him for you, My Prince." She stepped

forward and lifted him with ease.

Kylan nodded and glanced around the party. "Well, I hope I've provided an eventful evening for you all."

A few chuckles answered him, as well as a shake of the head from Lilith. "Never a dull moment in your company, Kylan."

"It's the only way to live." He smiled at everyone, but inside, his heart was fracturing at the task he had before him, and it hurt me to hear his pain. "Everyone, enjoy yourselves. Eat. Drink. Be merry. And of course, revel in my hospitality. It might be the last party I host for a while." He held up his hands, taking a theatrical bow. "I have a few things to see to, including an *Erosita* to fuck one last time, so I'll leave you all to it."

Lilith raised her glass, as did Jace and Darius.

Kylan took my hand and pulled me past them, his steps slow as he murmured farewells to guests who shifted into our path. When we finally ascended the stairs and entered the elevator, he blew out a long breath and brushed his fingers through his hair.

"Just give me a minute before you say anything," he said, hitting the down button to take us to the reception area.

Rather than reply or point out that I still didn't know what to say, I wrapped my arms around him.

He didn't move at first, his surprise slipping through the bond. Then he returned the hug, his face falling to my neck to bury against my skin.

I'm here, I whispered. *You're not alone.*

He shuddered and tightened his hold. *What was my life before you?*

Boring? I suggested. *Complacent? Easier?*

He chuckled in my mind. *Boring sounds right.* He kissed my pulse and released me as the doors opened. Maeve stood waiting for us in the lobby, handing Kylan his keys. "Excellent. Thank you. I have a final task for you, if you don't mind."

"Of course, My Prince."

"Inform everyone that I've promoted you and Cherise to Tremayne's old position. One of you can maintain K Hotel here, while the other can take over Tremayne Tower, but just be sure to rename it. I'll maintain the property in Lilith City. And feel free to split the other properties appropriately between yourselves."

Her mouth fell open. "B-but, Your Highness—"

"You didn't apply, I know. But I am tired of promoting old vampires to positions of power they bear no respect for. It makes much more sense to hire someone who actually understands and appreciates the business, which clearly you and Cherise do. She just needed a subtle reminder, is all."

Tears filled the woman's eyes, her lips curling into a breathtaking smile. "I don't know what to say."

"Start by saying you won't disappoint me, and we'll go from there."

"I won't disappoint you," she promised, her exhilaration palpable. "Thank you, Your Highness. Thank you."

He nodded, his palm going to my lower back. "Be sure to tell the others for me, including Cherise, and let me know who is going where."

"Of course. Yes." She actually bounced on her heels. "Forgive me, I'm—"

"Excited, I know. Enjoy your evening, Maeve. You've earned this." He pushed me forward, his steps quick as we passed several humans bowing in the reception area.

After situating ourselves in the car, I turned to him. "That was very kind of you."

He pulled out onto the street. "It was practical, Raelyn."

"It was nice," I corrected. "You're not nearly as formidable and cruel as you long for everyone to believe, you know."

He snorted. "Don't let anyone else hear you say that."

"Don't worry." I patted his thigh and relaxed in my seat. "It'll be our little secret."

He glanced at me sideways. "I think we're going to share a lot of those, Raelyn."

Chapter Thirty-Two

KYLAN

"Are you sure this is what you want to do?" Jace asked, his expression unreadable. He'd left the party early with Darius and Juliet and met me at my estate, just as I requested.

I nodded. "Yes, I'm sure." There was no other alternative.

"He doesn't deserve your kindness," Darius said, leaning against the doorway to my office.

"Is it really kind?" I asked as I signed the last of the documents.

He shrugged. "It would be to some."

Perhaps. I picked up the file, eyeing them both. "I can't kill him," I admitted. "As much as I know I should…"

"You care," Jace finished. "Our kind is obsessed with calling it a weakness, but it's not. It's what links us to humanity and keeps us sane."

"I suppose that's one way to look at it," I murmured, handing the file to Jace. "See that he's taken care of properly, please."

My royal counterpart nodded. "Luka will make sure he lives out his days untouched."

"In lycan territory," I said, still confused by his suggested placement.

"Maybe you should visit sometime," Jace murmured cryptically. "You may find something interesting there."

"Why do I feel like I'm being initiated into something?" I asked, wary.

"Because you are," Jace replied, holding out his hand. "You're not alone in your suspicions, Kylan."

I pressed my palm to his. "Regarding?"

"Everything." We shook once, then he released me. "I'll be in touch soon with more details. Until then, I'll handle your blood virgin problem the way you've requested."

"Unharmed," I repeated.

"I've already given you my word. He'll be fine. Just lonely." Jace started toward the door but paused. "Are you really going to turn Raelyn?"

"If that's what she wants, yes."

"Is it what you want?" he asked as he stepped through the threshold. "Be honest with her, Kylan. I hear that's what relationships are founded upon."

Darius snorted. "As if he knows a damn thing about women."

"He seems pretty familiar with them." Jace usually surrounded himself with them, always indulging. Though, the last few trips, he'd been alone. Odd for him.

"Not when it comes to feelings of the heart," Darius replied, following his superior. "Good luck with Raelyn. Follow your instincts. You might find your heart."

He disappeared while I gaped after him.

What horrible advice. My instincts when it came to Raelyn were to lock her in my room and never let anyone see her again.

Which was exactly where I left her—to shower off the evening's affairs and relax.

I hit Send on the email to my constituents, confirming Tremayne's replacements, and closed my tablet.

This was the night that never ends, which would continue if Raelyn took me up on my proposal.

She sat waiting for me on the bed in a towel, her damp hair falling over her exposed skin. Her blue eyes met mine, emotion swirling in their depths. "I heard what you did to Mikael."

I paused in front of her, suddenly concerned that she might not approve. "He couldn't stay here."

"I know."

"And I couldn't kill him." Even if he did deserve it. I just couldn't bring myself to finish it, not after our last eleven years together. He'd loved me, which was his own fault, but also kind of mine. Subjecting him to a life of loneliness seemed punishment enough.

Raelyn's lips curled into a sad smile. "You made the right choice, Kylan. As hard as it was for you, I get it."

"So you're not mad at me?"

She snorted, climbing to her knees to place herself at eye level with me, and grabbed my shoulders. "I can't fault you for showing compassion." She brushed her lips over mine, her willing kiss the best reward. We'd been chastely intimate over the last week due to her healing, the complete opposite of what my body craved, but what hers required.

I traced the seam of her mouth with my tongue, requesting entry, and pushed inside. She accepted the invasion with a moan, her arms sliding around my neck. I palmed her ass, pulling her up against me, needing more.

It'd been a long fucking night.

I needed to lose myself just for a moment, to let the sensations take over, to just enjoy Raelyn. Her hypnotic touch. Her citrusy scent. The caress of her mind against mine. The feel of her bare skin. Her taste.

"Fuck," I whispered, unable to stop myself from taking more of her. I deepened our kiss, taking her the way I craved, mapping every inch of her mouth with my tongue. So fucking addictive. So gorgeous. So *mine*.

I threaded my fingers in her damp strands, holding her to me as if she might disappear. Once I turned her, she could. But I needed her to have that option, to be my equal in every way except age, or this relationship would always be one-sided. I wanted her to choose me.

My heart hammered in my chest.

Just one more time.

As mine.

That's all I needed. Then I could set her free if that's what she decided.

But for tonight, I would have her completely.

"Raelyn," I whispered. "I need—"

"Yes," she replied, already seeing my thoughts. "A thousand times yes, Kylan. Take me. Keep me. *Fuck* me."

I shuddered against her, my cock already hard.

She unbuckled my pants without asking, her touch knowing, her skill impressive. I tossed her towel to the floor, my lips falling to her neck and lower to her gorgeous breasts. Ripe and beautiful with perky little nipples. I sucked one into my mouth, causing her to arch her back on a moan while she unzipped my trousers.

I switched to her other rosy bud, licking and nipping.

"You're perfect, Raelyn," I praised. "Everything about you is just so damn perfect." I meant what I said to Lilith earlier. I couldn't imagine a more qualified candidate for immortality.

She pushed the fabric down my hips and started on my dress shirt. By the third button, her patience was gone and she ripped the rest of them off by tugging on the fabric. I shrugged out of the remains, leaving me shirtless before her.

"Pants. Off." They were stuck around my thighs.

I smirked. "Are you commanding me?"

"Yes, I am."

I chuckled while obeying her. "Lie on the bed, princess. Legs spread. I want to see how wet you are for me."

She groaned, her muscles clenching in response. The sweet aroma of her arousal welcomed me home, my body aching to join with hers.

No one had ever made me feel this way—so complete. As if I could lose myself forever in her arms.

I never wanted it to end.

Never wanted to say goodbye.

My clothing disappeared to the floor as she positioned herself the way I desired, her pussy glistening in wait. I kissed her damp lips, needing to taste her. My tongue dipped inside her, coating my taste buds with her unique flavor.

"Fuck, Raelyn. You have the prettiest cunt." I nibbled her clit and nuzzled the soft red curls on her mound. She'd stopped shaving at my request but continued to keep herself groomed. I kissed her everywhere, worshiping her, cherishing every inch, and memorizing her intimately.

"Kylan," she growled, her fingers in my hair, pulling. "I need more."

"Oh, so do I," I whispered. "So do I."

A night.

A month.

A year.

A decade.

An eternity.

It would never be enough.

I gave up trying to understand it. Stopped trying to fight it. And just embraced it.

Because fuck if I had the energy to continue disputing these feelings. It was never about the bond, but about Raelyn.

It was always her.

That fire.

Her spirit.

Her heart.

I kissed a path up her body, adoring every inch, and

ignoring my cock's urge to flip her over and fuck her from behind.

This had to be different. Special. *Real.*

I wanted to make love to her. Something I'd never done with anyone, had never seen the point of doing, but with Raelyn, she deserved it and so much more. And I wanted to experience that with her. To honor her in a manner unlike any other, to revere her and love her.

"Raelyn," I breathed against her lips, my hips settling between hers. "You've changed me irrevocably." I slid inside her, my dick begging me to take her hard while my heart compelled me to keep it slow.

She pushed up against me, forcing me deeper. "You've destroyed me for anyone else," she whispered. "You've taken every part of me and made it yours."

"Ah, but, Raelyn, I haven't." After all the taunts of doing otherwise, it was never her mind or her heart or her soul that I captured. "It's you who owns me, sweetheart. Every piece of me exists inside you and no one else."

I kissed her softly, rocking into her oh-so slowly, savoring the feel of her, the way her walls clamped down around my shaft, the way she moaned every time I finished a thrust.

"Kylan." Her icy blue eyes glistened, her cheeks flushed. "Will it hurt?"

"Turning?" I asked, my lips tracing hers. "No, sweetheart." It'd been ages since my rebirth, but I showed her the pieces I remembered. The deep sleep, waking to new sensations, the initial thirst.

"Will we lose this connection?" she breathed, her body arched beneath mine as she sought the pleasure she craved.

I kissed her jaw, her neck, nibbling a path to her ear, and told her the truth. "I don't know what will happen." My maker had died shortly after my rebirth. "We'll still be linked, but differently."

"Will I still be yours, Kylan?" she asked softly, her nails digging into my shoulders. "Tell me I'll still be yours."

"A demand?" I teased, nipping her pulse and shoving my cock deep inside her. She moaned in response, her pussy clenching around me. "Mmm, keep doing that and I might accept forever."

"Kylan," she growled, scratching my back, marking me in the most delicious fashion.

"Again."

"Agree to stay with me," she countered, her legs tightening around my waist. "Tell me I'll be yours."

I pushed into her again, hard and fast, and smiled when she gasped my name. "I love that sound." I kissed her as I repeated the action, limbs trembling, her orgasm mounting. It wouldn't take long.

I swiveled my hips in a way I knew she'd enjoy, her responding cry confirming it.

My name left her lips on a curse, her mind rebelling as her body begged for more. She wanted a response almost as badly as she wanted to come.

"You're soaking my cock," I whispered. "Possessing every inch of me with your pretty cunt." I grabbed her hips, angling her upward to go even deeper and drive her wild. Her heels dug into my back, her skin vibrating with need. "Scream my name, Raelyn. I want everyone to hear you claiming me as yours."

The words sent her over the edge, her mouth obeying my command.

With each syllable, repeated over and over again, I felt her ownership over me solidify and grow, consuming me from the inside out.

She might be mine, but I was most definitely hers.

In all ways.

My climax hit, spilling into her with an impact I felt down to my very soul. It almost hurt, so intense, so complete, so fucking amazing. She milked me dry, squeezing out every last drop as I shook above her.

I'd never felt this empty, this replete, and yet full, in my entire life.

Love.

Devotion.

Energy.

Flowing openly, cocooning us in this private moment meant only for mates. My heart belonged to her. My spirit. My mind. I didn't hold anything back, allowing her to feel the full weight of everything I owned and giving it to her for safekeeping.

"Now," she whispered, melting into me. "I want to do it now."

"The turning?"

"Yes. Make me yours. Your equal. Your proper mate. Please, Kylan. It's what I want, what I *need*." Her thoughts confirmed it, her decision made. But not because she desired freedom or a way to escape me.

Raelyn desired immortality to be with me always as my partner.

I couldn't imagine a more deserving female.

She truly wanted this, always had.

And I wanted it for her.

It was the one gift I could give her, the one way to reward her for everything she'd given me.

My Raelyn.

My heart.

My mate.

I kissed a path to her neck, my incisors already aching for one last feed. It wouldn't be the same when she turned; it would be better. Sinking deep, I began to drink, her essence coating my throat as she moaned beneath me, coming again from the impact.

Fuck, it felt good around my cock, still lodged within her.

"Kylan," she chanted, her nails embedded in my skin. "Oh, Kylan."

Keep moaning my name like that and I'll be forced to stop and fuck you again.

She groaned, her mental voice nearly incoherent from

the onslaught of pleasure I was unleashing on her bloodstream.

I continued drinking, monitoring her heart rate, waiting for the right moment.

Her connection to my immortality prolonged it, her soul already pulling on mine while she continued to squirm.

But eventually, it dimmed.

Her screams quieting to moans.

Whimpers.

Raelyn's skin cooled, her heart slowing.

I pulled away to see her partly conscious, her eyes drooping. This was the crucial moment where the soul began to slip away from a mortal, dancing with death.

I bit my wrist, placing it at her mouth, forcing my life essence over her tongue.

She didn't react at first, her sleep-induced mind fogged from understanding what was needed. But her body began to take over, her instincts rushing to the surface as she latched onto the life-reviving liquid, taking her fill.

Seconds turned into minutes, my body nearly hollow. I took my wrist away, Raelyn's cry of disappointment making me chuckle darkly. "You'll have more later, baby. But for now…" I kissed her softly, hating what I had to do next.

This was the part that might hurt a little.

Temporarily.

I covered her mouth completely and pinched her nose.

Some preferred a bullet. Others strangulation. The occasional broken neck.

But I couldn't do any of those things, not with her.

I closed my eyes, my body shaking with the effort of having to suffocate her. To stop her heart completely.

It's okay, she whispered.

It's not, I replied. *But it will be.*

I trust you.

Those three words brought tears to my eyes, because she did. She really did. And I trusted her too. Something I never thought would be possible with another, but it was with her.

She drew her palm over my lower back, a final brush before letting it fall to her side. A tear fell from my eye as she began to convulse, her body fighting despite her mind's acceptance.

Panic began to well within her, the last stage of her death where reason no longer existed.

And then she went still.

Her heartbeat slowing.

Slowing.

Silent.

I gave it a final moment before releasing her, my forehead against hers. "Sweet dreams, Raelyn."

Chapter Thirty-Three

RAE

Darkness engulfed me, leaving me blind. Trapped. Alone.

Was this a dream?

A nightmare?

Reality?

I pushed against the hard surface beneath me, beside me, in front of me. It didn't budge.

Kylan? I could feel him nearby, his thoughts amused. *Kylan, what's going on?*

You can do better than that, princess. Unless you're still a lamb?

His taunt had my lips curling downward. *What are you talking about?*

Shuffling had me looking left, the sound close. Feet crunching over snow. Kylan's steps. His pants stretched as he crouched above, providing me with the perfect image of where to find him, just not how.

What is this?

A coffin. Push it open.

It won't move.

"Because you've barely tried. Give it another go," he encouraged out loud, his voice close.

I placed my palms on the wood above me and gave it a shove. The door creaked open, revealing a sliver of moonlight. Another push opened the casket completely, allowing snow and dirt inside.

I jumped out of it, my bare feet hitting the cold earth with far more ease than I anticipated.

Kylan's eyebrows popped up, his expression one of surprise. "Well, that was impressive for a newbie." He stood, in his arms clothing and shoes. "As much as it pains me to say it, would you like something to wear?"

I spun around, the shifting of a paw alerting me to our audience.

Wolves.

Six of them.

All lounging by the frozen pond, observing us.

"Why am I outside?" I asked, eyeing the glistening ice dangling from the frozen trees. The frosty bite to the wind. And wow, the moon practically glittered.

This was amazing.

I knelt, my fingers raking through the crystallized water on the ground. *Snow*, I marveled, as if seeing it for the first time all over again. *Wow...*

Kylan's amusement warmed my cooling skin, his enjoyment at watching me react to my new senses palpable.

Wait... "I can still hear you," I said, standing again, my feet barely acknowledging the cold. "And feel you."

"Yes," he murmured, moving toward me. "I'm not aware of anyone having that ability between maker and progeny but suspect it's related to our mated souls. I could sense you throughout your rebirth as if it were happening to me."

I tried to recall how I'd felt, my mind hazy. "It's all so... obscure." He bit me. Suffocated me, maybe. His blood in my mouth. I shook my head, the entire experience a blur. "I don't really remember."

"That's typical. You'll find aspects of your mortal life fading as well, as you are officially transcended to your immortal life." He handed me pants that I pulled on and a sweater, then socks and boots. I only dressed out of habit, not really feeling the need despite the cold weather.

"But why am I outside?" I asked again, still confused by that part.

"The final stage of the process is being one with the earth." He pulled a hat over my head and kissed my nose. "I thought you might prefer to wake here, and I already had a nook in the ground anyway."

I raised my brows. "Why?"

He shrugged. "Every vampire has hiding places, Raelyn. Now you can share this one with me because no one knows it exists." He closed the box, the top covered in grass, and brushed snow over the area to blend it with the surrounding landscape.

I recognized the log behind it, my lips parting. "That's where we first…"

"Yes." His lips twitched. "All the more fitting for your resurrection site, in my opinion."

I smiled and shook my head. "You have so many layers, Kylan."

"Do I?" He stalked over to me and grabbed my hips, pulling me against him. "You must be starved, love."

My brow furrowed. "Actually, I don't feel hungry at all."

"Really? Most freshlings wake up starved." He brushed his lips over mine. "Let's head back to the house. Maybe the scent of blood will trigger your appetite."

I scrunched my nose, the image of biting a human not

appealing. But of course, that's how I would feed. I just hadn't really considered the reality of it until now.

"Okay," I replied, another realization settling over me and sending a blast of adrenaline through my blood. "I'll race you."

He chuckled. "Raelyn, you're a baby vampire. Let's take this one step at a time."

My eyebrows rose. "Are you saying I can't keep up?"

"I'm over five thousand years old. I know you can't."

"Then you won't mind racing me." I took a step back, feeling more energized than, well, ever. "Unless you're afraid."

"The only fear I have is of you hurting yourself, princess. You're immortal, not unbreakable. Not yet, anyway."

"I feel pretty durable." Strong, even. And fast. A part of me wanted to sprint just to see what I could do. I'd never felt so alive, so free, so exultant.

"Most vampires wake up weak and starving for blood." He tilted his head, his gaze curious. "I don't sense any hunger in you."

"Because I'm not hungry." At all. I just wanted to run, to feel the elements against my skin, to fly.

"All right, darling. I'll race you, only to see if it inspires your appetite and because I can feel your eagerness." He nipped my bottom lip hard enough to bleed and lapped at the wound. "Still delicious."

I narrowed my gaze. "I can do that back now."

"You can try," he taunted. "Catch me and I'll let you." He released me. "I'll even give you a head start." He gestured to the path. "You know the way."

Pure cocky male gazed at me, his eyebrow arched in challenge.

"Can I bite you wherever I want when I win?"

He smirked, his expression all confidence. "Sure, princess. And when you lose, I'll bite you wherever I want."

I shivered, liking the sound of that. "Okay."

"Go."

I blew him a kiss and started running, my legs carrying me over the snow with ease—unlike the first time I tried this.

You'll have to do a lot better than that. His taunt radiated through me, urging me to push myself harder. *Remember, love. You're not human anymore.*

He opened up his mind, pushing experience and knowledge through our bond. It set my blood on fire, exciting my nerves and my very being.

So much power. Strength. Agility.

And I possessed all of those traits now.

His blood was my blood.

His soul married to mine.

Our hearts beating as one.

I closed my eyes as I moved, my senses taking over, my body shifting and moving down the path on muscle memory alone—*his* muscle memory.

It was exhilarating.

Staggering.

Beautiful.

My hand found the back door mere seconds before Kylan appeared, his expression one of wonder.

"You phased," he breathed, looking me over. "You actually fucking phased."

I stared up at him, confused. "Uh, yeah." I supposed I did. It felt incredible, as if I were flying over the land but without my feet touching the ground. "Let's do it again."

He grabbed my shoulders before I could take off, his eyes holding mine. "Raelyn, only the oldest vampires can phase. It took me almost two thousand years to acquire that ability."

My lips parted. "What?"

"Exactly." He took my measure in full, his thoughts running through a myriad of scenarios at once. I followed them all, taking in every detail without blinking. "Our bond seems to be giving you my level of ability," he summarized out loud. "I've never heard of anything like this, but it's the only conclusion that makes sense."

"No one has ever turned their *Erosita* before?"

"Not that I'm aware of, no." He cupped my cheek. "You're one of a kind, Raelyn."

"Rae," I corrected, smiling. "Now that I'm a vampire, I can choose my name."

His gaze glittered in response, darkness brewing inside him. Possession, adoration, domination, all poured out of him, swathing me in a mental blanket that was all Kylan. "You will forever be my Raelyn, but if you prefer others to call you Rae, that is your choice."

I went onto my toes to press my lips to his. "I'll always be your Raelyn," I agreed. "But to everyone else, I'll be Rae." It felt intimate to grant him sole use of the name—the one he gifted me—while regulating everyone else to the shortened version. "I'm still yours, Kylan. For as long as you'll have me."

"Careful, sweetheart," he whispered against my mouth. "Because I'll keep you forever if you allow me."

"I hope you do." And I meant it. "But only if I get to keep you too."

"Oh, Raelyn, when will you understand?" He pressed me up against the door, his mouth capturing mine in a domineering kiss that took my breath away. "You already own me, love. Always. Forever. Completely."

I shuddered against him, his words searing my being.

"You're inside me, Raelyn. You've been there since the moment I first saw you, that first defiant bite solidifying my fate." Both his hands were on my face, holding me to him, his hips pinning mine against the hard surface behind me. "My soul chose you, my mate, my partner, and my blood married yours. I'll never desire another, not when it'll jeopardize what we share, not when I have you in my bed every night. What would be the point?"

The sincerity in his voice rivaled the words in his mind, the promises he left unsaid, the emotions he reserved only for us. He gifted me immortality to grant me freedom, the ability to choose, because he wanted a partner at his side in life, not a servant. That was his biggest secret of all, the one he would never admit to the world because it wasn't necessary. I knew and that's all that mattered.

Kylan never desired a lamb.

He craved a fighter.

Me.

And he'd do everything in his power to prove himself worthy of my love. Like granting me immortality even while knowing it provided me the tools to escape him.

Not that I ever would.

"You're inside me too," I whispered. "I want this—you—Kylan."

He kissed me, his lips worshiping mine, his tongue a familiar presence in my mouth. I never wanted this to end, and it didn't have to.

We'd battle the new world together.

With me by his side.

As an equal.

His mate.

"For eternity," he vowed.

"Yes." I wrapped my legs around his waist as he lifted me into the air. "Make me yours again, Kylan."

"Oh, Raelyn." He nibbled my lip, his nose touching mine. "Now that's a command I'll accept."

Amusement warmed my chest. "Good. Expect it often."

"Only if you anticipate mine in return." He carried me inside, directly up to our room. "I want these clothes off and you on the bed. Now."

"Still as dominant as ever."

"That part will never change." He nipped my bottom lip. "Now obey before I start disrobing you myself."

"You still owe me a bite," I reminded him, my feet

touching the floor.

"I do. You can bite me when you're naked."

I smiled. "Still making the rules." Not that I would have it any other way.

"Always, little lamb."

"I'm not a lamb anymore."

He tossed off my hat and threaded his fingers through my hair, yanking me to him. "No, sweetheart, you're not. You're my Raelyn."

"Then you're my Kylan."

"'Til death do us part," he teased. "Or so the vows go."

"Which means you're stuck with me for a very long time." I started unbuttoning my pants while he held me before him. "I should warn you: I'm rather defiant."

"Yeah?"

"Yeah." I grabbed his sides, leaving my jeans loose at my waist.

"Prove it."

I lifted to press my mouth to his while holding his gaze. And tugged his bottom lip between my teeth.

Biting down.

Hard.

Claiming him.

My mate.

My royal vampire.

My Kylan.

Epilogue

RAE

One Month Later...

Kylan had a surprise for me, something he kept hidden in his mind behind a carefully crafted wall. He refused to give me any details other than to say all would be revealed at tonight's event.

A month of coaching and I still wasn't prepared for this.

I constantly wanted to drop my gaze.

To hide.

To stand in a corner.

To be invisible.

But on Kylan's arm, none of those actions were an option. He introduced me to everyone as Rae, his new progeny and lover, and they all greeted me with unfettered curiosity in their gazes.

Kylan had declined to take a harem this year, stating he didn't require any new members. That only added to everyone's interest.

A royal with no harem, just a vampire mate.

Very few in his position lived such an existence, the alpha of Majestic Clan being one of them. I'd met Luka and his mate, Mira, earlier this evening. We were at some sort of lycan bonding ceremony. The Clemente Clan Alpha, Walter, was officially stepping down and handing the reins to his son, Edon.

"May I present my progeny, Rae," Kylan said, introducing me to yet another alpha. Niko of the Ernest Clan. Two females flanked him, one I recognized as his mate, the other a female with dark eyes and dark hair that matched his own.

"Lovely to meet you, Rae," Niko murmured, taking my hand and kissing it a little too suggestively.

Isn't that his mate? I asked.

Cora, yes. He's not known for being faithful.

Clearly. I forced a smile while carefully removing my palm from his and threading my arm through Kylan's. "Nice to meet you as well."

"My mate, Cora, and our daughter, Luna," he said gesturing to the female behind him.

Luna has been promised to Edon, Kylan murmured.

She doesn't look very thrilled about that.

An alpha female promised to an alpha male? No. It's a match made in hell, but she has no choice. "I assume you're looking forward to the festivities this evening," Kylan said out loud.

"Yes, very much. The Clementes have agreed to take Luna tonight to help acquaint her with their customs."

Luna flinched with her father's casual words, her lips curling downward even more.

She's a lycan, though. Doesn't she have certain rights?

Oh, sweetheart, there is so much about this world you don't yet know. "When is the actual mating ceremony?" he asked, feigning interest.

"Next full moon." Niko sounded proud. His daughter appeared ready to throw up. Cora grabbed Luna's hand and gave it a squeeze, whether in reprimand or support, I couldn't tell. The mated female wore an unreadable expression.

"Perhaps we'll attend," Kylan murmured. "I'm introducing Rae to all aspects of society. She may find that particular ritual fascinating."

Niko's lips curled, his brown eyes darkening with lust. "Yes, it can be quite arousing."

That sounds like an affair I'd rather skip, I noted dryly.

You may change your mind in about five minutes. "Speaking of arousing, I'm in need of a proper drink. Walter mentioned a feeding room?"

"Yes, in the main quarters, I believe." Niko gestured to the oversized lodge beside us, the one where most of the guests were staying.

The Clemente Clan estate was very different from our home. Still surrounded by trees, but a lot warmer, and all the homes had a woodsy feel rather than the clean, sharp architecture of Kylan City.

"Ah, yes, thank you." Kylan shook Niko's hand. "I'm sure we'll see you again very soon."

I really hope not, I thought while saying, "Nice to meet you all."

Luna gave me a cynical look while her mother merely nodded once, expressionless. Niko, however, appeared very pleased to have met me. A little too pleased.

He kept his hands to himself this time, mostly because Kylan steered me away from his reach, and we murmured our goodbyes.

Yeah, so I don't like him.

No, I imagine you wouldn't, Kylan replied. *I believe he would have chosen you for his harem, if given the chance.*

I gagged in my mind, causing Kylan to chuckle. *I remember a time you felt that way about me.*

No, I always found you attractive, even when I hated you.

He kissed my temple as he opened the door, escorting me inside. "Do you hate me now, Raelyn?"

"Only sometimes."

He chuckled and led me through another entryway. "Well, perhaps this will encourage you to like me more."

I glanced around, seeing nothing. "What will?"

"You'll see." He released me, taking a step back. "I'll be back in a moment. Don't go anywhere."

I frowned as he disappeared, the door closing softly behind him. *What are you doing?*

It's a surprise. Enjoy.

Another perusal of the small bedroom revealed nothing. *Kylan?*

No reply.

The curtains in the corner rustled as someone slid open the glass doors from the outside. This couldn't have been part of Kylan's plan. I started toward the door, hand on the knob to leave when a familiar voice breathed my name.

I spun, meeting a pair of dark blue eyes I never expected to see again. "Silas."

He smiled and bounded toward me with open arms. I jumped on him, hugging him back fiercely, his broad shoulders accepting my vampire strength with ease.

"You're alive," I whispered. Which I already knew. Kylan had told me Silas won the Cup, but seeing him—here—made it so much more real.

He buried his face in my hair, inhaling. "God, you reek of vampire," he chuckled. "And Kylan."

I laughed. "Um, yeah, he sort of—"

"Turned you," he finished for me. "Yes, I've heard—everyone's heard—and I also saw you with him outside, but I couldn't approach."

I pulled away to study his face. "What? Why?"

"Oh, Rae, you really don't know?" He chuckled, releasing me to brush back his sandy hair. "Hierarchy, sweets. You're on the arm of a royal, while I'm just a newbie lycan. They consider me a baby. Talking to an alpha, let alone a royal, yeah, I'm lucky to even be given a job at this party. Clemente Clan has delegated me to security duty."

"You're not allowed to talk to me?" I asked, flabbergasted.

"It's not customary, no," Kylan said as he entered the room.

Silas took a step back, his eyes dropping. "Your Highness."

"Silas," Kylan murmured, his palm sliding to my lower back.

"I apologize for the intrusion. This was all me. Rae did nothing wrong."

Kylan remained silent for a moment while I stared between them, shocked by Silas's submission and words.

When mortals were granted immortality, they acquired rights.

But Silas appeared as nothing more than a human in this moment, not a brand-new lycan.

And I *knew* that Silas wasn't a submissive, could see it in the way his hands curled even now while he deferred to another male.

"You're a good friend to her," Kylan finally said. "Which is how I knew you'd scent her out when I left her alone."

My gift, I realized.

Yes, was his single-word reply. "I don't mind you two keeping in touch. Just be discreet."

Silas lifted his gaze warily, his brow furrowed. "You're giving us permission to socialize?"

"You're Raelyn's friend. I accept that." He brushed his lips against my temple. "That doesn't mean Walter or Edon will, but I've never been very fond of the rules. Just ask my consort." He winked at me and turned to leave. "Five more minutes, love. Then we're needed back outside."

He closed the door behind him, giving us privacy once more.

Silas stared openmouthed after Kylan, making me giggle.

"You look shocked," I teased.

"That's Kylan?" he asked, gesturing. "The formidable, sadistic royal we read about in university?"

"He has quite the reputation, yes, but he's not all bad. Sometimes I like him." I knew he could hear me, and felt his humor in my mind. "But enough about me, what about you? A lycan, huh?"

Silas grimaced. "Yeah, Walter had first pick since he's retiring. His son is actually the one who turned me, much to Edon's chagrin."

"He didn't want to turn you?"

He snorted. "No. I'm his first, and probably his last given the experience. It's all part of the alpha trials. His ascension will conclude at the next full moon."

"I thought tonight was the ascension."

"Oh, no, tonight is just the initial ceremony." He palmed the back of his neck, sighing. "It's going to be a bloody month."

"How so?"

He just shook his head. "A lot of it is clan ritual, secret, and all that."

"But you'll be okay, right?" I pressed.

"Pfft, how long have you known me, Rae?" He nudged my shoulder. "I'm a survivor, same as you."

I smiled, somewhat reassured. "Yeah, we are."

"And Willow too, somewhere," he said softly.

My heart broke a little. "Yeah, she's surviving too." *I hope.*

"Well, I better get back before someone notices I'm missing. But I'm glad you're okay, Rae."

"You too, Silas." I hugged him again—hard—and watched as he disappeared through the sliding doors with a backward wave.

Kylan joined me again, his arms sliding around me from behind. "You want to see him again next month?"

"At the full-moon ceremony?" I guessed.

He nodded against my shoulder.

"Yes."

"I thought so." He kissed my neck. "Shall we return to the party or make an early exit?"

I twisted to face him, my blood heating as I took in his sinful tuxedo. "I'm all for an early exit."

"A woman after my own heart," he murmured, kissing me softly.

"No, I already own it," I reminded him. "It's your cock I want."

"Raelyn," he growled. "What am I going to do with that mouth of yours?"

I gave him my best innocent look. "Punish it?"

"I'll be doing more than that." Another kiss, this one harder. "Always so defiant."

"You love it."

"No, I love you," he whispered.

I smiled. "I love you, too."

The Story Continues with Regally Bitten...

Blood Alliance Series

WHAT'S NEXT

Dear Reader,

Thank you for reading *Royally Bitten*! I hope you enjoyed Kylan and Rae as much as I enjoyed writing them. You'll see more of them throughout the series. Trust me.

Regally Bitten is up next. I'm really looking forward to playing with the lycans and learning more about Silas. Yes, he's the hero. And Luna will be his heroine. But what about Edon? Decisions, decisions… Maybe I'll include him, too. ;)

Thank you again for reading!

Cheers xx
Lexi

Acknowledgments

First and foremost, thank you, Julie Nicholls, for creating such inspiring cover art. Without your designs, the Blood Alliance series would have remained a short story, but you just had to go make those beautiful white wolves and inspire the lycan side of my story. Now I have this giant world to write and it's all your fault. Thank you! <3

Second, to my husband for your endless support, love, and wisdom. Oh, and for understanding/accepting that you can never read this series. Ever.

Allison: Thank you for all the late-night chats, for reading all my words (even the bad ones), and for always keeping me focused on the right path. I appreciate you so, so much!

Bethany: You've mentioned how amazing it is that I keep all these worlds in my head. Well, I think it's amazing how you keep all the CMOS rules in *your* head, because I could never in a million years master the art of punctuation. Case in point, this paragraph. I'd be lost without you.

Delphine & Pam: Your eyes for detail help bolster my confidence in my words/books, and I'm so thankful for your proofreading skills. Thank you!

Louise & Melissa: You two make my world go round. I'll send photos later in thanks/payment for all your services. ;-) I love you both!

Amy, Joy, Louise, Katie, Melissa, & Tracey: Thank you all for beta-reading *Royally Bitten* and helping me finalize the plans for *Regally Bitten*. I'm going to need you all to help me with this threesome. I have a feeling Silas and Edon are going to be a handful. Or, well, two, actually.

Famous Owls: Thank you for being such an important part of my team and for always making me smile. You all rock!

None of this could be possible without my ARC team and Foss's Night Owls. Thank you, thank you, thank you!

And to the readers: Thank you for reading Kylan and Rae's story. You'll see them again, very likely in *Regally Bitten*. ;)

About The Author

USA Today Bestselling Author Lexi C. Foss is a writer lost in the IT world. She lives in Atlanta, Georgia, with her husband and their furry children. When not writing, she's busy crossing items off her travel bucket list. Many of the places she's visited can be seen in her writing, including the mythical world of Hydria, which is based on Hydra in the Greek islands. She's quirky, consumes way too much coffee, and loves to swim. Cheers!

Also By Lexi C. Foss

Blood Alliance Series
Chastely Bitten
Royally Bitten
Regally Bitten

Dark Provenance Series
Daughter of Death
Son of Chaos

Immortal Curse Series
Blood Laws
Forbidden Bonds
Blood Heart
Elder Bonds
Blood Bonds
Angel Bonds
Blood Seeker

Mershano Empire Series
The Prince's Game
The Charmer's Gambit

Printed in Poland
by Amazon Fulfillment
Poland Sp. z o.o., Wrocław